SUPERNOIRTURAL TALES

SUPERNOIRTURAL TALES

IAN ROGERS

Cemetery Dance Publications
Baltimore
❧ 2025 ❧

Cemetery Dance Publications
132B Industry Lane, Unit #7
Forest Hill, MD 21050
www.cemeterydance.com

Trade Paperback Edition

ISBN:
978-1-964780-46-7

Cover Artwork © 2025 by Ben Baldwin
Cover layout and Interior Design © 2025 by Steven Pajak

Praise for Ian Rogers and the Black Lands Series

"With *Sycamore*, Ian Rogers delivers a serpentine narrative involving missing people, mobsters, rogue intelligence agents, and monsters that refuse to stay dead. Private investigator Felix Renn is a masterful creation—arch, world-weary, clever and tenacious. Fans of Jim Butcher and Richard Kadrey will be enthralled with the world of the Black Lands."

— Nick Cutter, author of *The Troop* and *The Queen*

"...a fast-paced entertaining story that gleefully mashes up all things supernatural with his hardboiled PI."

— Paul Tremblay, author of *A Head Full of Ghosts*

"Indomitable PI Felix Renn is back for another case and I'm delighted to follow him once again into the fray. Rogers' writing is pure gold."

— Laird Barron, author of *Not a Speck of Light (Stories)*

"If Carl Kolchak had a grandson, his name would be Felix Renn. Readers who know Renn from his appearances in Ian Rogers' eerie Black Land stories will be glad to see him back in this bullet-quick killshot of a novel, and readers who haven't met Rogers' supernatural detective yet are in for a real treat. Slot this one on your bookshelf while you can grab it—smart money says it's the first of many!"

— Norman Partridge, author of *Dark Harvest*

"No mere pastiche, this is crime noir where the noir is something richly black and thrilling, where demonic madness lingers on the fringes of stories cut from the cloth of Chandler."

— Robert Shearman, winner of the World Fantasy Award

"...there's a lot of shading to Renn—the humour, the regrets, the resourcefulness... the chilly isolation of the human soul is felt throughout... Truly, this is one of the most chilling horror stories I've read in years. Make that, that I've read period."

— Jeffrey Thomas, author of *Punktown*

"...an imaginative and original writer with the skill to fully execute his plots."

— *Publishers Weekly*

For Dad and Jan

One of my wishes is that those dark trees,
So old and firm they scarcely show the breeze,
Were not, as 'twere, the merest mask of gloom,
But stretched away unto the edge of doom.

—Robert Frost, "Into My Own"

Night streets were my territory,
and would be till I rolled in the last gutter.

—Ross Macdonald, *The Drowning Pool*

INTRODUCTION

You wouldn't necessarily classify Ian Rogers' wicked, insidious horror stories as contemporary social commentary. But — with the Sunday papers strewn around my desk and the world going to hell in a handbasket — I'm going to argue that they are. Bear with me, just for a moment. I'm closing in on a point.

Like two paired photons launched at the same time out of some exotic piece of lab apparatus, Ian Rogers and I simultaneously went out into the void and interacted with a whole bunch of other particles in remarkably similar ways. Specifically, we created fictional universes that mirror each other very closely.

We both have protagonists who are named Felix. We both have them ply their trade in the mean streets of an unforgiving city. It's the same sort of trade, too, broadly speaking (even though Ian's Felix Renn calls himself a private detective, where my Felix Castor calls himself an exorcist). We even both have a ghost named Rosie, (although my Rosie was raised from a silk handkerchief by an arcane ritual; Ian's is attached to a very different object, and she turns out to be... well, you'll see.)

The biggest similarity, though, lies in that detective/exorcist juxtaposition. These are narratives that exist in that big, nebulous-but-wonderful über-genre called noir, and they draw on a whole lot of tropes that are very familiar in that context. Compromised heroes who can't catch a break; cynical cops who cut corners to get the job done; hired leg-breakers with limited vocabularies; scarily ruthless gangster types who straddle the boundary between the criminal world and the respectable one, and so on.

But at the same time, and very importantly, both Ian's narratives and mine are supernatural horror stories, set in a world where the supernatural has become an unpleasant but inescapable fact of life.

I confess a great relish for stories like this (which is maybe why I write them) — stories in which ghosts and monsters, far from being liminal and mysterious and problematic, are out where everyone can see them or at least is forced to acknowledge them. Stories where the intersection of the mundane and the mystical worlds has reached a point where the mundane has to give ground and accommodate. Stories where the world has been changed irrevocably by the advent of a spiritual dimension in the heart of everyone's everyday lives, and (to misquote Blake, as my Felix sometimes does) what was once only imagined is now proved.

I like this stuff. It's in my comfort zone.

But within that broad church (noir-tinted supernatural crime fiction), Ian's core device, the Black Lands and their portals, is something very special. You could compare them, if you wanted, to Terry Pratchett's dungeon dimensions, or to Lovecraft's R'lyeh, or to the realms inhabited by Clive Barker's Cenobites. But there are a great many doors that lead to the Black Lands, and more opening all the time. Some of them have their own idiosyncrasies, like Old Frightful, which periodically spews out water from an unknown source, complete with indigenous lifeforms. Others are innocuous on this side, but lead to terrifying, deadly and inexplicable places on the other. The one thing they've got in common: they can't be closed, once opened. And given the largely antisocial nature of the creatures that inhabit the Black Lands, that's a problem rapidly developing into a crisis.

But for Felix Renn — much as he hates to admit it — it's all in a day's work. He doesn't seek out cases with a Black Lands aspect to them, but somehow they seem to find him. And you'll notice as you work your way through these stories that the nature of the threats he faces gets more and more intense. Vampires and werewolves show up right at the outset, but Ian's supernatural bestiary goes far beyond the usual suspects. Poltergeists, demonic children, evil trees, ash angels... they're all on the docket, and they're symptomatic of a world that's undergoing an invasion — unstoppably, and in terrible slow motion. The sense of being besieged and overwhelmed is part of the slow-burn effect of the stories.

It's also, to get back to my first observation, something that links Ian's fictional universe to mine. It seems to me that we're both writing apocalyptic fiction. But in keeping with the nightmare scenarios the human race is currently facing — the collapse of the global financial system, peak oil, climate change — our apocalypses are grain-at-a-time gradual. The end of the world isn't a Roland Emmerich kind of deal, with recognisable landmarks going down like card houses and a lot of indecorous shrieking and fleeing. It's subtle, and it's slow. A headline here. A rumour there. A shadow crossing the hall outside your bedroom. Slow burn.

And when the sky begins to roar
It's like a lion at the door.
And when the door begins to crack
It's like a stick across your back.
And when your back begins to smart
It's like a penknife in your heart.
And when your heart begins to bleed
You're dead, and dead, and dead indeed.

So what you're about to read is a very topical book. It might not look like one, but it's the story of your life. Trust me. You'll feel right at home here. And, of course, that's the scariest thing...

Mike Carey
August 2012
London

TEMPORARY MONSTERS

1

THE WAITER GOT killed before he could drop off the bill.

I happened to be looking toward the back of the restaurant and saw him coming: a tall smooth-faced man in a black vest, carrying a slip of paper on a small plastic tray, winding his way through the maze of tables. Gel didn't have a lot of space, and although it tried to make the most of what it had, there were simply too many tables for so small a room. All through lunch I kept waiting for one of the waiters to trip and deposit someone's order in their lap. It was something to do while I waited for Sandra to stop talking.

Presently she said, "It's just not enough, Felix."

I sipped my coffee and muttered, "It never is."

"You're not even listening to me," she said, using that petulant tone I didn't miss at all.

"I'm listening, Dee. I just don't care."

She fell silent. I didn't need to look at her to know she was pissed. I could feel her eyes burning a hole in the side of my head. Not because of what I'd said, but because of what I'd called her. I plead ignorance on that one. The divorce lawyers never told me I was supposed to relinquish the nickname along with the house key.

Sandra heaved a big sigh. "Would you at least look at me when I'm talking to you? I hate it when you zone out like this."

I turned and looked across the table at her — Sandra Clifton Renn, although she'd probably be dropping the "Renn" in the not-too-distant future. She didn't need it for me or for her work. Not anymore. She was on the downslope of her acting career, and she knew it. Her last sitcom effort, *Not Tested on Animals*, had been cancelled a month ago, after only three episodes aired. The network said it was dumping it because of low ratings. I knew the feeling.

"I'm listening," I told her. "You said it isn't enough. I know. I've heard this bit before."

"You *hear*, Felix, but you don't *listen*."

I took out my wallet as the waiter approached. At the table next to ours, a young guy stared at an untouched tuna melt. He was alone, but that wasn't unusual. Gel was one of the few restaurants in downtown Toronto where you could dine alone and not look like a dateless loser. It was a hangout for actors, both successful and struggling. I thought the kid looked familiar, but I couldn't make the connection. Early twenties, black feathered shoulder-length hair, white Oxford shirt, dark slacks. He had probably done a pilot that never got picked up. He had that kind of look, the one that said, *You might remember who I was, if I ever did anything memorable.*

And then he did.

As the waiter was placing the bill on our table, the kid suddenly leaped out of his chair and looped his arm around the waiter's neck. His other arm encircled the waiter's waist, pulling him back into a tight embrace. The kid pivoted them both around, like a couple performing a clumsy dance manoeuvre, and I saw something that made me drop my wallet and my jaw.

The kid had fangs.

I only saw them for a split second before he sank them into the side of the waiter's panic-taut neck.

A surreal couple of seconds followed. Everyone in the restaurant kept eating and talking as if nothing unusual was happening. Then the waiter reached out with one flailing hand, grabbed onto our tablecloth, and pulled it away like an amateur magician. Everything on the table

— our plates, cutlery, my glass of water, Sandra's glass of white wine — went crashing to the floor.

Then, as if this was his cue, the waiter began to scream.

The other diners started turning around. They looked on silently as the kid whipped his head back in a spray of blood, a chunk of the waiter's neck clenched between his teeth. Then they started screaming, too.

The kid fastened his mouth over the spouting wound and began to drink. The waiter was lying rigidly in the kid's arms, his legs sticking straight out, his hand still clutching the tablecloth.

Most of the diners went running for the door. They didn't have the waiters' skill of manoeuvring around the tables, and a few people tripped, fell, and were trampled by those herding behind them. A few remained seated and continued to watch. Their eyes had the glossy sheen of people in severe shock. Sandra's eyes were the same. She was sitting stock-still in her chair, making a sound somewhere between a scream and a gasp. "Guh. Guh. Guh."

"Yeah, guh," I muttered, and stood up.

The waiter's spastic twitches slowed down, then stopped. The kid unclamped his mouth and licked the film of blood off his lips. He lowered his arms and the waiter dropped limply to the floor. He surveyed the room with the glazed eyes of one who has just enjoyed an exquisite meal.

I reached instinctively for my gun, then remembered I wasn't wearing it. One shouldn't come armed to lunch with one's ex-wife. I think Confucius said that.

I looked around for something I could use as a weapon. The kid was looking around, too, but for something else. He found it and whipped out his arm, grabbing hold of one of the patrons still sitting in stunned surprise. In a flash of movement that was almost too fast to track, his head tilted to the side and darted forward at a deadly, questing angle. The woman's eyes flew open and she began to howl.

It was all happening too fast. In moments of extreme panic things were supposed to move in slow motion. But not now, not here. I felt like I was having one of those nightmares where you're completely powerless to do anything except stand and watch. I looked over my shoulder at the early afternoon sunlight pouring in through the wide front window.

It didn't make any sense. No, it was more than that. It was impossible. The kid should have been dust in the wind. Maybe we didn't know as much about them as we thought we did.

I decided to worry about all that later on. I reached around, picked up my chair, and advanced on the kid.

He didn't take any notice of me. He was hunched over the woman, as if he had swept her off her feet for a kiss, except his mouth was clamped on her neck instead of her lips. His eyes were rolled back in his head like a shark's and his mouth was making horrible slurping sounds. I raised the chair high and brought it down on his arched back. It shattered and the kid went on drinking.

I grabbed the kid's arm. It was rail-thin but felt strong as an iron bar. I tried to pull him off the girl and he flicked me away like a bothersome insect. It was a brusque, offhand gesture, but it sent me flying across the restaurant. I landed next to a table occupied by another lone diner, a grizzled old man dressed in black with a white collar around his neck. I stood up shakily, gripping his shoulder for support.

"Little help, Father?"

The old man shook his head frantically. "I... I'm not a real priest," he stammered. "I just play one on TV."

"Right."

As I resumed my search for a weapon, a heavyset man with a ponytail clipped my shoulder and sent me spinning to the ground. From this new vantage point, I spied the broken leg of my chair. I picked it up, then picked myself up. I touched the pad of my thumb to the splintered tip of the chair leg. It would do.

I moved stealthily behind the kid, but I needn't have bothered. He was as lost in the hunger-bliss with the woman as he had been with the waiter. The lower half of his face was awash in blood. It dripped off his chin in a lurid stream. His eyes had turned a dark, eldritch red. It was like staring through the isinglass portal of a blast furnace.

Being married to an actress for seven years, I found we had unconsciously taken on certain types of movie-cliché behaviour. Sandra, for example, had become a professional door-slammer. At the conclusion of particularly scathing arguments — which became more frequent as our marriage sank progressively deeper into the toilet — she would leave the room in a flourish, punctuating her exit by slamming the door, some door, any door. One time, when we were fighting outside on the patio, she stormed back into the house through the sliding glass door, which was very heavy and near-impossible to slam. So she threw a chair through it instead.

My own movie-cliché habit was the witty final remark. Famous last words, they're sometimes called. Before Sandra would make her inevitable door-slamming exit, I would call after her with some fiery retort such as, "Nice talking to you, sweet pea!" or "I see those anger management classes are helping!" Not exactly David Mamet dialogue, I know, but then I'm a private eye, not a writer.

Standing over the kid with the broken chair leg, I couldn't think of anything clever to say. *Here's your dessert!* came to me later on, but at that moment my mind was as empty as my chequing account. So I just raised my improvised stake and brought it down on a spot between the kid's straining shoulder blades. I drove down with all the strength that fear and adrenaline had given me. The chair leg went into the kid's back with a horrible, meaty punching sound. It came out his chest in an eruption of blood that sprayed the unmoving body of the woman in his arms. The kid immediately dropped her and made frantic, scrabbling attempts at pulling the stake out, but he couldn't reach it. In a panic, he tripped over the prone foot of the dead waiter and went stumbling backward. He landed flat on his back, and the stake exploded out of his chest in a volcanic gush of blood. His arms and legs quivered madly, and for a moment he looked like a giant insect that had been pinned alive to a piece of corkboard. Then his movements stilled and he lay as motionless as his victims.

I went over and stood by Sandra. She rose shakily, leaning on me for support.

"I see you still know how to show a girl a good time," she said in an eerily calm voice. Then she doubled over and heaved up her lunch. I turned away, and a moment later I heard the tock-tock of Sandra's heels as she left the restaurant.

I waited for the door slam, but it never came.

2

I HAD a few minutes before the police would arrive, so I knelt down next to the kid and went through his pockets. I found some change and a lizard-skin wallet. *Expensive,* I thought, *just like the kid's clothes.* Inside the wallet I found five crisp one-hundred-dollar bills and a Screen Actors Guild card with the name Jimmy Logan on it.

So the kid was an actor. It made sense. He did a great impersonation of a vampire. I picked up his wrist to see if he was actually dead and noticed a blue mark on the back of his hand. It looked like a stamp, but it was smeared and I couldn't make it out.

I heard the sirens and the sound of cars pulling up out front. I had to make a choice, and fast. I could have dropped things right there — given the cops their affidavit, signed it, then gone home. I chose to go to work instead.

The kid wasn't a client, but I was curious. I couldn't figure out how he had gotten into the restaurant if he was a vampire. The sunlight should have killed him outright. And while my impromptu stake had immobilized him, couldn't a vampire regenerate if it was removed? If you wanted to kill a vampire completely and totally, you had to take it a couple steps beyond the old stake in the heart. You had to cut off its head and burn it and the body in separate piles. Then you

had to scatter the ashes.

I didn't have time for any of that. As I was standing up the police came bursting in, waving their guns and telling me to get down, get the fuck down. I saw how things must have looked, but didn't bother to say anything in my defence. There had been enough witnesses to the attack that things would get sorted out eventually.

A few minutes later, they had put their guns away and stopped looking at me like I was Charles Starkweather. It didn't take long for them to figure out that I wasn't a mass murderer. I owed it to the guy dressed in the style I thought of as "standard-issue MiB" — black suit, black tie, black sunglasses. He stood in the corner, subtle as an ink-stain on a white shirt. I watched him out of the corner of my eye while I was questioned by a detective named Vincent.

"You're a dick?" he asked.

"That's what my ex-wife tells me."

"I mean, you're a private eye?"

"That's right."

"You got a license?"

I showed it to him.

"You here on business?"

"Sort of. I was having lunch with my ex-wife."

Vincent raised a questioning eyebrow.

"We don't exactly hate each other, but when we get together these days, it feels like business."

He jotted that down like it was important.

"And you saw the suspect before he..." He gestured vaguely.

"Yeah," I said. "He was sitting at the next table."

"Was he with anyone?"

"No."

"Do you think he was waiting for someone?"

"I didn't ask him."

The detective wrote in his notebook.

"What did he have?"

"What?"

"What did he order?"

"Steak."

He gave me a hard look.

"It was a tuna melt, actually."

Once the detective was finished with me, I was steered toward the man in the corner. He said his name was Agent Keel. He didn't show me any identification, but I figured he was with Paranormal Intelligence.

"So you're the hero," he said, taking a cigarette out of an onyx case. He didn't offer me one.

"I think if I was a hero, those two people would still be alive."

Keel shrugged, as if the debate of what made a hero didn't interest him one way or the other.

"You don't see vampires out in the day very often, do you, Mr. Renn?"

"I've never seen a vampire at all. Not in person. Not before today."

"What did you think?" he inquired.

"Excuse me?"

"Seeing your first vampire? I'm curious to hear your thoughts."

"My thoughts? Are you a psychiatrist?"

"No, but I have a side interest in the human response to first contact with supernatural entities."

"What, like a hobby?"

Keel nodded. "I also build ships in bottles."

"Listen, I'm having a pretty shitty day. I need you playing mind games with me like I need —"

"A wooden chair leg in the heart?"

"I was going to say a hole in the head."

Keel tapped his cigarette, allowing the ashes to fall to the floor, then he looked over his shoulder at the dead kid. "You knew right where to get him," he said. "It was a good shot. I know STAR guys who couldn't have done that with a crossbow, much less an improvised stake. You could teach them a thing or two."

"Thank you," I said in a dead voice.

"But you didn't finish the job." He dropped his half-smoked cigarette and stepped on it with an impeccably shined shoe. "Why is that?"

Taking a deep breath, I said, "I reacted out of instinct. I was trying to protect my ex-wife. I wasn't thinking straight. Straight enough to immobilize the kid, I guess, but not enough to... to finish him."

Keel nodded. "Fair enough."

"Can I go now?"

"Do you have any plans to leave the city in the near future?"

"No," I said, "but I'm seriously considering the idea now."

"We may need to call you in for further questioning."

I gave him one of my business cards. He looked at it, then passed me one of his own.

"Try to stay out of trouble," he said.

"All I do is try," I told him.

3

"YO, FELIX!"

One of the police officers was directing me away from the restaurant when I saw a short fat man pushing his way through the crowd of onlookers. He was holding a spiral-ring notebook and a digital camera. I turned around and started walking in the opposite direction. The fat man caught up with me, huffing and puffing and tugging on my sleeve.

"Geez, Felix, that hurts."

He put his hands on his knees and took long, shuddering breaths, like he had run a mile instead of only a few feet.

"I don't have anything to say to you, Parsons."

"Come on, man. Nobody has anything on this yet. You gotta give me something."

Horace Parsons was a reporter for *Hollywood North*, a tabloid sheet that covered celebrity gossip in Toronto. We used each other for information from time to time. I needed him, but I couldn't act like I did. It was part of the dance.

"What's in it for me?" I asked.

"I'll hook you up with Sandra Bullock."

"You don't know Sandra Bullock."

"No, but I had dinner with her assistant last night."

"What did you do, tell her you were a producer? Give her the spiel about how she could be a star herself instead of working for one?"

"Hey, whatever works, baby."

"You get greasier every time I see you, you know that?"

"From one dick to another, I'll take that as a compliment."

"So what do you want to know?" I asked him, feigning impatience.

"Who was it in there that went vamp on everyone?"

"His name was Jimmy Logan. And he didn't 'go vamp.' He *was* a vampire. Near as I can figure, anyway."

Parsons gave me a look like I was pulling his leg. "Jimmy Logan? A vampire?"

"You know who he is?"

"He's one of the up-and-comings. They say that about every young actor, of course, but with this kid they actually meant it. They said he was going to be the next Brad Pitt. Or maybe even the next Bobby De Niro."

"He's not going to be the next anything now. What was he doing in town?"

Parsons didn't seem to hear me. "Jimmy Logan," he muttered. "I can't believe it. People are going to go apeshit."

"What was he doing in Toronto?" I asked again. "Filming something obviously, but what?"

"It was a horror movie. A horror-comedy, actually. *It Sucks.*"

"What?"

"That's the name of the movie — *It Sucks.*"

"The critics will love that."

Parsons put the camera in his pocket and took out a pen. "How do you know he was a vampire?"

"I was having lunch and he was sitting at the next table. He attacked my waiter." I realized then that I never did pay for my meal.

"Yeah, but how did you know he was a vampire?"

"I saw his eyes, his teeth. And he threw me across the room with a swat of his hand."

Parsons began writing furiously. "Talk about life imitating art."

"What does that mean?"

"Jimmy Logan was playing a vampire in *It Sucks.* I've heard of method acting, but..." He trailed off, shaking his head as he continued taking notes.

I suddenly didn't feel well. I started to lean backward; fortunately there was a building there to prop me up. "He was *playing* a vampire?"

"Yeah," Parsons said. "You think he went to the Black Lands to get himself ready for the part?"

I shook my head absently.

"How'd he die?"

"I... I staked him."

"*You* killed Jimmy Logan?" Parsons said incredulously. He took a step back and looked at me in a new light. "That's great!"

I closed my eyes. I could hear the mad scratching of Parsons' pen, the querulous gabble of the crowd gathered in front of Gel, and, beneath it all, the steady pounding of my own heart. It all seemed very loud, closing in around me like smoke. I stumbled away from Parsons, and when he called my name, I started to run.

4

I STOPPED off at the Toronto Public Library on my way home.

All I knew about the Black Lands was what they taught in school. A military rescue team came upon it by accident in 1945. They were looking for Flight 19, a fighter squadron that had disappeared off the coast of Florida in an area now known as the Bermuda Triangle. The world treated the Black Lands in much the same way the U.S. treated Cuba. It was a shunned place, illegal to travel to. But can you imagine trying to impose an embargo on an entire dimension? Especially when other portals were constantly being found; some of them floated in mid-air — like the one that had swallowed Flight 19 — while there were others on the ground, even some underwater. Scientists had even managed to create man-made portals.

I went to one of the reference computers and performed a catalogue search on "Black Lands." I got over 50,000 results. I skipped past everything on the physics of inter-dimensional travel, the various laws and amendments that came after the discovery of the Black Lands, and focused instead on the inhabitants of that dark dimension. That brought me down to 12,000 results. I filtered it further by limiting my search to vampires — 752 results. Still too many. I asked the computer to give me the volumes related specifically to vampire biology and behaviour — 207 results. I figured that was as close as I was going to get, so I wrote down the five most recent publications and went looking for them in the stacks.

I ended up spending the rest of the day and most of the evening in the library learning about vampires. There was a lot of conflicting evidence and wild theories, even after 60 years of study. The only thing that the scientists agreed on was that vampires were very dangerous, and I didn't need a book to tell me that.

One volume suggested that vampires might not be indigenous to the Black Lands. The author put forth the theory that people from our world had travelled over to the Black Lands hundreds of years ago and became vampires as a result of some unknown catalyst — a virus, a mutation or a natural stage of human evolution.

I came upon a scientific paper entitled "The Black Lands and the Vampire Myth" that further enforced this idea. It said that if you subtracted the parts of the vampire legend added by Hollywood — the creature's power to hypnotize its victims, the ability to transform itself into a bat or a wolf or smoke — vampires were not much different from any other earthly carnivore. But there were inconsistencies.

While vampires weren't afraid of crosses, field experiments had shown that they were agitated by the presence of priests and other holy figures. Some scientists believed this reaction was due to a racial memory, hearkening back to the time of their creation, presumably in the Dark Ages — a time when people were routinely being hung and burned at the stake for the crime of witchcraft. It probably taught the vampires the necessity of discretion, and it made me wonder just how many real vamps had been destroyed back then. Not too many, I was willing to bet.

This in turn made me think about Jimmy Logan. He was neither a scapegoat accused of being a vampire, nor was he a true supernatural entity. At least I didn't think he was. He had tossed me across the restaurant like a lawn dart, but sunlight didn't affect him. It didn't make sense. There was a piece missing.

My research confirmed that the only way to kill a vampire was by destroying the heart with a wooden object or by exposure to sunlight. It was no wonder they flourished in the Black Lands, where no sun ever shone.

I never understood why government agencies like the PIA bothered to keep people out of there. It's like punishing the guy who sneaks into the polar bear habitat at the zoo. If he's stupid enough to go in there, then he deserves what he gets.

Did Jimmy Logan go the Black Lands, and if so, why? To prepare for his next role? I didn't know. And by the time I had finished reading, I was too tired to care.

5

I'D ONLY BEEN in my apartment for about three seconds when there was a knock at the door. I reached instinctively for my gun, remembered again that I wasn't wearing it, and opened the door anyway.

It was Sandra. She looked excited. I figured she must have the wrong house, and told her so.

"Oh, let me in, you broomhead."

I stepped aside and watched her zip down the hall. She was carrying a stack of newspapers. From the lurid photos and blaring headlines, I guessed they were tabloids.

"Did you get a paper route?" I asked, following her into the kitchen. "It's really a good thing for you. Gets you out of the house, earns you some extra cash. And think of all the exercise you'll get."

She gave me a light slap and dropped into a chair. She spread the papers out on the table. "Look at these," she said.

I had already seen them on my way home, but I looked anyway. *Hollywood North* had run a special evening edition. In my experience, the only thing that works faster than the media is the trash media.

Though sometimes I can't even tell the difference between the two. It was their business to turn molehills into mountains, and once again they had come through with flying colours. In his "exclusive report," Horace Parsons made the death of Jimmy Logan sound like the crucifixion. A young actor cut down in his prime by a low-rent private investigator, who claimed to have seen Logan transform into a vampire. That word "claimed" disturbed me a great deal. I felt my knees start to tremble, so I sat down.

Sandra reached across the table and squeezed my hand. "God, Felix, you're as white as a ghost."

"Ugh."

"He didn't give you any choice." She squeezed my hand harder. "You know that, don't you?"

I nodded mutely.

"He killed two people."

"I know, Dee." I winced. "Sorry. Habit."

"Forget about that. I came over to apologize to you."

"That's funny. I was going to apologize to you."

She gave me a look. "What do you have to be sorry for?" she said. "Saving my life?"

"It wasn't exactly the lunch I had planned."

"I think everyone who was in that restaurant today feels the same way, Felix."

"I guess so."

I didn't know what to say. I had expected her to be upset, maybe even angry, and seeing that she was neither turned me into a stammering idiot. It was like our first date all over again.

"Well, I'm sorry you had to be there. How about that?"

"Fair enough," she said with a curt nod. A moment later she grinned. "You know what they're calling you? The Fearless Vampire Killer."

"Oh yeah? Polanski would be proud."

"I'm proud of you."

I raised my head and looked into Sandra's eyes.

"I don't want to be married to you," she amended. "But I'm proud of you."

"I'll take it."

6

I DIDN'T FEEL like getting out of bed the following morning, but I forced myself to get up and shower and put on clean clothes. The phone had started ringing almost immediately after Sandra left, and I promptly unplugged it. I kept the TV turned off and stayed away from the windows, too. That was probably overkill, but I thought it best to play it safe. I had done my own fair share of snooping, and I knew it wasn't completely unheard of that some eager-beaver photographer might have my apartment staked out.

I needed a break, and that made me think immediately of a break in the case. But I wasn't on the case. The investigation into the death of Jimmy Logan, Hollywood wunderkind, was being led by the PIA with the Toronto Police taking up the slack. I was just a player in this particular piece, and it wasn't a part I wanted. Unfortunately, the only way I could see of extricating myself was to do the very thing that could get me into more trouble — that could get me dead.

I figured there would be less of a chance of that happening if I was wearing my gun. After putting it on, I peeked out my front door, verified there weren't any reporters sleeping in the hallway, and headed downtown.

To find a film shoot in the city all you had to do was follow the little orange cones until you came to the monstrous trailers that Sandra always called "the movie gypsy caravan." It was a closed set that day, if only because everyone and their dog wanted to see where the late Jimmy Logan had been filming his final movie, or to get a quote from one of his no doubt grief-stricken co-stars.

I made my way around the rubberneckers and reporters until I found a young woman who was wearing a headset and had a plastic card clipped to her shirt, identifying her as CREW. I showed her my own card and told her that I was investigating the death of Jimmy Logan. I tried to sound bored, thinking it would make me stand out from the rest of gawkers.

"Are you with the police?" she asked.

"Nope."

"Then what do you want?"

"Is the director on set today?"

She gave me an appraising look. "Is she expecting you?"

"Nope. Just tell her the Fearless Vampire Killer would like a few minutes of her time."

The young woman looked at me a moment longer, then walked off. A few minutes later she came back and beckoned me with an imperious wave of her hand.

"Follow me, please."

She brought me to an open area hemmed in by trailers. One of them, I noted, had Jimmy Logan's name on it; a lick of police tape had been plastered across the door. Along one side of the clearing, a long table had been set up with coffee, donuts and various pastries. A broad-chested man in a muscle shirt was pouring coffee from a huge gleaming urn.

I was escorted over to a tall, slender woman with wide, green eyes and a strained look on her face that might have been caused by the painfully tight ponytail her white-blonde hair had been pulled back into. She was wearing blue jeans and a T-shirt that said I EAT UNION WORKERS. She scrutinized me with a look that said I had already wasted oodles of her time, and I had better get to my point, and fast.

"Help you with something?" she inquired brusquely. She was holding a cinnamon-coloured cellphone and there was a small black address book open on her canvas director's chair. "I'm kind of busy managing a crisis here."

"I'll try not to add to your stress," I told her. I held out my hand. "Felix Renn."

"Van Toren," she replied. There was a slight huffiness in her tone, as if she was annoyed that I didn't recognize her on sight. "I'm the conductor of this train wreck."

"Van," I said. "Is that short for something?"

"Yeah, my full name."

I grinned patiently and she softened... a little.

"Vanessa," she said. "But no one ever calls me that. Is that one of the questions you wanted to ask me?"

"No. I... uh... I'm the one who..."

"I know who you are," she said, without rancour. "You killed my lead. Do you know how many times we had to go back and forth with his agent to get him on this picture?"

"I don't know. A lot?"

"Not that much, actually. Jimmy Logan is — or was — going to be a hot item, but he wasn't there yet. All actors make demands, even the little ones. It's the way they convince themselves they're in control."

"Did Jimmy Logan make a lot of demands?"

"Not really. But it's all about putting up a good front."

I nodded. Sandra had explained to me the power dance of actors and agents. With all the hair-splitting that goes on, it was a wonder that any movie ever got made.

"He was supposed to be on set yesterday afternoon, and I was pretty fucking pissed off when he didn't show up." She ran her hands over her pulled-back hair and sighed loudly. "Why the hell couldn't he have waited until the wrap party to OD?"

"What do you mean he OD'ed?"

"Well, didn't he?" She gave me a bland stare. "They said he was high as a kite and attacked a bunch of people."

I weighed my next words very carefully. "You heard what happened, right? About... Jimmy?"

"What, that he was a vampire?" Van gave me that annoyed look again. "For God's sake! Jimmy Logan wasn't a vampire. He was *playing* a vampire."

"He was doing a pretty good job in the restaurant."

"It doesn't matter. It's not like it changes anything. I've still got a movie minus one of its lead actors. And my other one..." She cast a contemptuous look at one of the other trailers.

"Eve Sutter," I said, reading the name on the door. "She's in this movie?"

"She's not here for the ambience," Van replied tartly. "Although she might as well be. That's all we have now without Jimmy. An $80 million pile of ambience. The studio's going to freak," she added with a groan.

"Eve Sutter," I said, trying to steer the conversation back on track. "Did she know Jimmy very well?"

"Not that well. I don't think they knew each other before they came to work on this picture. But they seemed to hit it off okay."

"Were they involved romantically?" I asked, hating the way I sounded, like a doctor taking a family history.

"No," Van replied, "but they were sleeping together. She hasn't been out of her trailer since she heard about Jimmy."

"Do you think she'd talk to me?"

Van waved her arm in a gesture that said *be my guest*.

I went over to Eve Sutter's trailer. I had seen her in a handful of movies — horror flicks, mostly, like *Jowls* and *Demon Daze*.

I knocked on her trailer door.

"Go away!" a high, trembling voice cried from inside.

I turned the knob and walked in.

The trailer was dark except for the aura of light coming off the bulbs that ran around the border of a large vanity mirror. Eve Sutter was sitting in front of it, her face buried in her freckled arms, hitching and sobbing. "Get out!" she growled.

I ambled toward her, glancing at the clothes strewn about, almost tripping on a stiletto heel that looked long enough and sharp enough to skewer a wild boar. Moving around it, I stepped on something that crinkled under my foot. I reached down and picked up an empty blister pack, like the kind individual doses of aspirin come in.

"Why won't you leave me alone!" Eve's voice rose stridently. It sounded like a jet turbine engine powering up. "Get OUT!"

She whipped her head around and glared at me. I froze. Eve

Sutter's eyes weren't as recognizable as Angelina Jolie's, but I knew the ones I was looking at didn't belong to her, or to any normal woman.

Her eyes were yellow. And they were glowing. It was as if someone had installed a hurricane lantern in her skull. The light pouring out of her sockets caused the freckles on her face to stand out and cast harsh shadows from her nose and lips. It was a terrifying sight, like a brutally carved jack-o'-lantern wearing a red wig. The effulgence bleeding out of her eyes waxed and waned. It made her hair seem to dance. But as I continued to stare, I saw that her hair was actually moving. It was sprouting out of her skin in silky strands that curled and twined in a crimson wave. It was like watching someone spontaneously combust, except instead of bursting into flames, Eve Sutter was bursting into hair.

She rose from the vanity bench and faced me fully. She was wearing a green bathrobe with her initials embroidered over the left breast. She pulled the robe open with hands that were curving into claws, and I saw that her entire body was covered in a gloss of shiny red fur. She made a low, whining sound from the snout that was sprouting out of her face. Her lacquered lips stretched into a maniacal clown grin, and when she opened her mouth in a wide yawn, I saw rows of sharp white teeth.

Throwing back her shaggy red head, Eve Sutter gave vent to a wailing howl that echoed in my ears.

I tried calling her name, but it was no use. She couldn't hear me and I couldn't retreat. I had come too close. If I turned around or even took a single step backward, she would be on me.

I did the only thing I could, even though I knew it was a fruitless gesture. I took out my gun. I wasn't packing silver loads because I hadn't planned on running into any werewolves that day.

Eve Sutter hunched down on her new, crooked hind legs, scrutinizing me and my little gun. I didn't hesitate; I give myself that much credit. I aimed and fired and struck with all six shots. Eve Sutter went flying backward into the vanity, her body smashing the mirror while one flailing arm raked across the border of light bulbs, throwing us into darkness.

I moved nimbly back to the trailer door. I knew the shots wouldn't make any difference. I could have fired six thousand bullets and it would have had the same effect, which is to say none. I glanced quickly over my shoulder and saw those eerie yellow eyes squinting at me with rage.

I stumbled out of the trailer, down the short flight of stairs, and into the broad-chested man. His Styrofoam cup of coffee was held up between us, and it splashed all over him. He looked down at his stained shirt, then to the smoking gun in my hand, then to the open trailer door. He dropped the crumpled cup and grabbed me roughly by the back of the neck.

"*What did you do?*" He screamed into my face, hot spittle spraying my cheeks. Eve Sutter's bodyguard, I presumed. "*What did you DO?*"

I tried to say something, but he kept bouncing me up and down like a yo-yo. I felt my gun slip out of my fingers.

The broad-chested man dropped me rudely on my feet and yelled over my head.

"*Evie! Are you in there? Are you okay? Answer me!*"

Evie was in there, but she was far from okay. She and okay weren't even in the same time zone.

I looked over my shoulder and saw her shaggy form materialize in the doorway. I felt my neck slip out of the big guy's grip the way the gun had slipped out of my fingers. I stepped discreetly to the side.

Eve Sutter looked like a fireball with fangs. Her auburn fur glowed like burning copper in the sunlight. Her triangular ears twitched as her head barely cleared the top of the doorway. She took a tentative step forward. Then another. Then she leaped high into the air and landed on the broad expanse of her bodyguard's chest.

The big man tried to push her away, but Eve clawed her way around to his back, moving as smoothly as an eel through water. When he reached back to pull her off, there was a crunch, like the sound of someone biting into a lollipop, and the bodyguard began to scream. He pulled back a hand minus a couple of fingers. He stared wide-eyed at the severed digits, and twin jets of blood squirted into his blanched face. He let out a final, quavering shriek, then fell over in a dead faint.

I stared into the furry face of the werewolf formerly known as Eve Sutter. Despite the glowing yellow eyes and the blood that dripped from her muzzle, she was still a thing of beauty. You were almost willing to let yourself be mauled to death by her, just as long as you were allowed to watch it happen.

"What in the *hell* is going on here?"

Eve and I both turned our heads in unison. Van Toren was staring at us with a stern expression. The girl with the headset was standing behind her. She managed to keep her composure for about half a second, then bolted. Van came toward us, waving her hand at Eve.

"I didn't ask for this! Who made this! I'm not paying for this!"

Eve threw back her head and a long, mournful howl issued from her throat.

She leaped at Toren, back legs kicking off the pavement. The director let out an *eep!* and went running into her own trailer, slamming the door behind her. Eve threw her shoulder against the door, howled again, and started tearing strips off the metal with her long black claws.

I stumbled over to the craft service table. The whey-faced server was gawking at the short work Eve Sutter was making of the director's trailer. He jumped when I snapped my fingers in front of his face.

"Is this silver?" I held up a glimmering cake server. It wasn't sharp, but I thought I could make it work.

The server gave me an incredulous look. "Are you kidding?"

I dropped the cake server. Eve howled again. It was different this time, and I thought, *She got inside the trailer.* I turned around and saw something I wasn't expecting.

Eve Sutter lay at the foot of the stairs leading up to the director's trailer. I came over slowly, hesitantly. I picked up my gun on the way, reloaded it, and pointed it at her motionless body. She twitched, and I jumped back, steadying the gun with both hands. But it was only her fur, drawing back into her body, parting like a red sea and leaving her freckled skin bare and exposed... and bloody.

I could see where I had shot her. I took off my coat and draped it over her body, as much to remove the view from my sight as to shield her nakedness. I crouched down and picked up her wrist, feeling for a pulse — I found none.

I heard a creaking sound and looked up at Van Toren peeking out her trailer door. "Is it safe?" she asked timidly.

I glanced back down at Eve Sutter's limp wrist. I turned it over and saw something on the back of her hand — a blue mark. It wasn't as smudged as the one I'd seen on Jimmy Logan's hand. I could make out a picture of a butterfly and a single word written across its wings.

Chrysalis.

7

"MARTY, IT'S FELIX."

"Oh boy."

"What's that mean?"

"I don't know if I should be talking to you."

"Why not?"

"Because you're a suspect in a case I'm working on."

"You know I didn't murder those two, Marty. I killed them, but I didn't murder them."

"Felix, I don't know..."

"What?"

"This is a bad one, man. I don't know if I can help you."

"All I want is the blood test results. Just read them to me and hang up the phone. It'll be like it never happened."

"Felix..."

"Please, Marty. I need to know."

"I don't think you're going to like it."

"Just tell me."

8

Sandra stood in her apartment doorway, arms crossed, frowning at me.

"You're not here to kill me, too, are you? Because with my last sitcom in the crapper, I don't think you'll get much coverage for knocking me off."

"Hardy-har."

She let me in. I dragged my feet to the kitchen and dropped into a chair. Sandra went to take my coat and saw I wasn't wearing one.

"A dead woman is wearing it," I told her, by way of explanation.

"Oh," she said, and went to put on coffee.

"You heard?"

"Yeah." She leaned against the counter and stared at the floor for a long moment. Then she looked at me with a bright expression. "No offence, but if you could have done this four or five years ago, it would have really helped out my career. I lost a couple of choice parts to Eve Sutter."

I smiled wanly.

"I just find it so hard to believe, you know? Jimmy Logan a vampire. Eve Sutter a werewolf. Two of the most successful actors of our generation, and they were both monsters. It's all so odd and freaky."

"That's not entirely accurate," I said. "They weren't *real* monsters."

"What do you mean?"

"I don't know exactly." I made a sound between a sigh and a laugh. "I spoke with a friend in the forensics lab. They ran tests on Logan and Sutter. Blood tests, marrow tests, DNA, the whole works. Logan wasn't a real vampire, and Sutter wasn't a real werewolf. It was easy for them to tell in Logan's case. If he had been a real vamp, he would have jumped up the moment they pulled that chair leg out of his chest."

"What about Sutter?"

"I shot her, but not with silver bullets. I knew it wouldn't have any effect, but I thought it would get her attention. She didn't die until after she transformed back into human form. Werewolves and other shifters, on the other hand, don't change back until after they're dead."

"I don't understand."

"Sutter didn't die until whatever it was that turned her into a werewolf wore off. Then, the moment she changed back, she died. Her body couldn't handle the physical trauma it had endured. A delayed response to getting shot six times."

"That can't be right," Sandra said, but there was a hint of doubt in her voice. "Can it?"

I shrugged again.

"You killed Jimmy Logan with a stake through the heart. That's how you kill a vampire."

"Yeah, but that would kill anyone. The same way a hail of bullets would kill anyone. The way it killed Eve Sutter. The way *I* killed Eve Sutter."

I tried to stand up, but my legs felt like matchsticks. I sat back down heavily. I felt sick to my stomach. I felt sick to my soul. "Logan wasn't a vampire," I told her, "and Sutter wasn't a werewolf. They were temporary monsters, at best. And I killed them."

Sandra licked her lips. I was suddenly overcome with an inexplicable certainty that her response to this was going to be the deciding factor in the final turning point of our relationship. We weren't going to get back together; that ship had sailed. This was about whether or not we would be able to salvage something from all of this, or if we had finally succeeded in becoming strangers to each other.

"Felix, temporary monsters or not, they still killed people. Logan would have killed me if you hadn't stepped in. The details may vary, but to me this is no different than some guy wired on PCP knocking off a liquor store and shooting a few innocent bystanders for kicks."

"Thanks, Dee. I needed that."

"Don't be stupid, Felix. You're not a murderer. I never would have married you if you were. You're difficult, you're moody, and you've got a lone wolf complex, but that doesn't make you a psychopath."

"That might be the sweetest thing anyone's ever said to me."

"Your friend Horace Parsons called me."

"What did he want, an exclusive interview?"

"Yes. Over dinner."

"What did you tell him?"

"What do you think I told him? I told him to piss off."

"What else is the news saying about Logan and Sutter?"

"Not much, except that they were in a relationship."

"They weren't involved," I said, "but they were having sex."

Sandra nodded knowingly.

"They both had a mark on the back of their hand. Like the stamp you get after entering a club."

"What was it?"

"A butterfly, with the word Chrysalis."

"I know that place. It's on King Street, I think. Near Bathurst."

"I'm guessing a place like that has a special VIP lounge for celebrity guests."

"It's called Seventh Heaven. Or it was. I haven't been to Chrysalis in a few years."

"Do you think you could still get in?"

"I'm out of work, Felix. I'm not dead." She winced and touched my arm. "I'm sorry," she said. "It just came out."

"It's okay. But I might need you to come along. If you wouldn't mind."

She considered it for a long time. "Okay. But if you keep me out past midnight, you'll have to put me on the payroll."

"Fair enough."

She got a couple of mugs out of the cabinet and poured the coffee.

"If it turns out I can't get another acting gig, maybe I could work full-time as your Girl Friday."

"Dee, you can be my girl any day of the week."

9

I PARKED around the corner from the club, in an alley between a Thai restaurant and a convenience store. I opened the passenger door and helped Sandra out just as if we had pulled up in front of the Royal York. She looped her arm through mine and we walked around to the main entrance. There was a line-up, but Sandra walked briskly past it. She never waited in lines.

The guy manning the door looked like the monolith in *2001: A Space Odyssey*. He was about seven feet tall, with a flat, impassive face and broad, rectangular shoulders. He was wearing a black T-shirt approximately three sizes too small for him, and the clipboard he was holding looked like a drink coaster in his big paw.

Sandra detached herself from me, put her hand on her hip and stuck her elbow out jauntily. "It's been forever, dahling. How come you never write?"

The big guy looked down at her, and a grin slowly spread across his face. It was like watching a fissure opening in some obdurate stone. "Sandy Clifton. Where you been keeping your fine self?"

"Married life hath crippled me," she said, and slumped against his chest with a girlish swoon.

"That's too bad." He sounded genuinely upset.

"It's okay," Sandra said perkily. "I'm getting a divorce."

"Then come on in."

He stepped aside and Sandra took my arm once more. She drew me into a storm of multi-coloured strobe lights and pulsating sound that I supposed passed for music in some circles. To me it was like the auditory test they give you at the doctor's office, or the sound of a computer having the electronic equivalent of a grand mal seizure — high-pitched whining and electronic beeps and boops that made me much too aware of my own thumping heartbeat.

We moved along the edge of the dance floor, where insubstantial shapes gyrated to the rhythm of the cacophony. We went up a set of steep metal stairs to a landing where another man in a black tee took a single look at us — well, Sandra, actually — before letting us pass.

This was Seventh Heaven. It didn't look much different from the level we just left, except I recognized faces from various movies I had seen. I suddenly realized that I didn't know what I was looking for.

"Why don't you circulate?" I said to Sandra, pulling her close so she could hear me. "I'm going to look around, see if I can find someone who was here the night before last."

"Be careful, Felix. Don't go asking too many questions. This is one of Cris Donovan's clubs."

"Cris Donovan? Donnie Drugs to the Stars? I didn't know he was still around."

"He's more of a drug baron now." Sandra looked over her shoulder — as if anyone could overhear us with the music pounding. "He's gone Joe Hollywood. Only sells his stuff to the film types. He thinks it makes him more respectable. But that doesn't mean he's any less dangerous."

"I'll watch my back," I promised.

"And try not to kill any more actors."

"Hardy-har."

She gave me a little wave, then promptly disappeared into the throng. I made my way back to the entrance. The bouncer eyed me suspiciously.

"I hear you're famous," I told him.

He stared at me silently.

"The word is you were one of the last people to party with the late Jimmy Logan."

The bouncer muttered, "I don't remember," and turned away.

I took out a twenty and put it in front of his face. He made it disappear and turned back around.

"He was here. The night before he killed those people. He was with a couple of ladies."

"Eve Sutter."

"Yeah. She was in that movie, *Backbreaker*."

"Who was the other girl?"

"I dunno. Some broad."

"A friend of Mr. Donovan?"

The bouncer's face darkened. He didn't like my mentioning the owner's name.

"You better watch your step, little man."

I held up my hands to show him we were cool, but I could tell that was all I was going to get. I walked back across the room and found Sandra at the bar. I told her how I had struck out and she bucked me up by saying at least I didn't put a wooden stake through the guy's heart.

I started to reply — something witty, no doubt — but she put her fingers against my lips, shushing me.

"There he is. Cris Donovan."

I turned around and saw a tall, pallid man with close-cropped black hair and prominent ears. He was shaking hands with everyone, squeezing the occasional shoulder, patting the occasional ass. He wore a dark red pinstripe suit and an extremely wide grin. He looked like the guy who did all the meeting and greeting in Hell's cocktail lounge.

"Introduce us."

Sandra gave me an incredulous look. "What?"

"Take me over there on your arm, perform a quick intro, and then scram. Go home. I'll call you in the morning."

She looked like she was going to argue, then she grudgingly took my hand, looped it through her arm, and walked me over to meet Cris Donovan.

He turned to greet us, white teeth gleaming. "Good evening!" he beamed. "Sandra Clifton, it has been an age. An absolute *age!*"

I don't know who was more startled, me or Sandra. She touched her chest in an oh-gosh way and stuttered a reply.

"Oh... oh, yes. I haven't been around in... an age." She blushed furiously and looked at me for support.

I stepped in, proffering my hand. "I'm Felix Renn. Sandra's husband."

Donovan's smile turned into a wide O of surprise. "Husband? I had heard you two split up."

It was my turn to stutter. "It's... we're..."

Sandra came to my rescue. "We're still in negotiations."

The three of us chuckled in that exaggerated way people do at public gatherings, whether the joke is funny or not.

"Oh!" Sandra stood on her tiptoes and waved at someone in the distance — real or imaginary, I didn't know. She gave me a quick peck on the cheek, said "I'll be right back!" and was off. *Good girl*, I thought.

"You've got a pretty nice place here," I told Donovan.

"I'm always changing it. I guess it goes with the name."

"I guess it does. Makes me think of life and death."

Donovan gave me an inquisitive look that said, *Oh, really? Please elucidate.*

"Well, what bigger change is there, right? Alive today, dead tomorrow."

"Very true, Mr. Renn."

"Kind of like what happened to Jimmy Logan and Eve Sutter," I said, cutting straight to the bone. Subtlety has never been my strong point. That's my gift and my curse.

"I thought I recognized you," Donovan said dimly. "The Fearless Vampire Killer. I understand you're a Fearless Werewolf Killer as well."

"I'm branching out," I told him. "I'm thinking about extending my service to include drug dealers. Do you know any?"

Donovan turned the smile back on. It was almost blinding in the murky club. He didn't say anything, which made him smarter than most criminals I've known.

I leaned in close and said, "Do you think it was just a coincidence I happened to be there at both incidents?"

The smile faltered, but only a bit.

"The PIA knows all about your operation, Donnie. They're probably at your house right now, cutting open your mattresses and looking inside your toilet tanks. I bet that's where you still keep your shit, isn't it? You got the expensive suit, the chic club, but old ways die hard, right?"

Donovan regained his *sang-froid*. "I'm sure I don't know what you're talking about."

"The vampires and werewolves are coming home to roost, Donnie."

I slipped past him, giving his shoulder a little squeeze as I walked by.

I left and went back to my car. I drove around front and parked across the street from the club. I waited. Then I waited some more. A little over two hours later, Donovan came out of Chrysalis alone. I had time to reflect that he was the first person of power I had seen who didn't travel with an entourage. Even when he was doing the glad-hand bit in the VIP lounge, he didn't have a couple of hoods hovering over him, waiting for the first sign of trouble to punch a hole through someone's ribcage. Somehow that lack of security made him seem even more threatening.

I was playing on a bluff, and a pretty big one at that. I didn't know what the PIA knew about Donnie, if anything, and it really was a coincidence that I was at the places where Jimmy Logan and Eve Sutter had transformed into monsters. I was just hoping it was enough to rattle Donnie's cage.

Someone came around with his car — a silver Mercedes — and I thought, *He has a driver; he's not completely independent.* Then the man jumped out of the Benz and I saw the red vest and dark pants of his valet uniform.

Donovan slipped into the driver's seat and pulled away from the curb.

I followed.

10

SOME PARTS of the lakeshore are nice. This was one of the other parts.

Dominated entirely by warehouses, this area of the city was currently experiencing an urban renewal, with some of the properties being converted into high-rent lofts, while the rest were left to rust and decay. It was the kind of development I could get behind. Much better than all the condos they were putting up, or the historic brownstones that were being torn down and replaced with garish modern-strosities.

I trailed Donovan at a discreet distance, and when I saw him pull up in front of a dark building, I turned down a side street and cut the engine. I closed the car door gently, then approached the corner and peered around it. Donovan's silver Mercedes sat gleaming in the dark. It was so quiet I could hear the engine ticking. There was no sign of Donovan.

I approached slowly, staying in the shadows. That wasn't difficult; it was all shadows down here. Between two of the warehouses, I could see the lights of McLeary Park, where I used to play baseball as a kid. A few years back, the public works department wanted to plow it under and put up a recycling transfer station. Public outcry had put a stop to that, but I had a feeling that what was going on inside Donovan's lakeshore digs was much worse.

I reached the front door. Faint yellow stencilled letters identified it as 818 Commissioners Street. I debated going around back, the way they always do in the movies, but it wasn't my style. Donovan was here, and I had a feeling he was alone. I had given him the forward approach at his club. I didn't see any reason to deviate now.

The door was locked. I took out my Swiss Army knife — a friend of mine in the RCMP had modified it to include picks and pressure wrenches and other handy gadgets — and played with the lock until I got it open. I slipped inside and closed the door quietly behind me.

The inside of the warehouse was almost completely empty. I made out a few dark shapes at the far side of the cavernous room and made my way over to them.

I stood before two strange machines that looked vaguely like old-fashioned printing presses. A conveyor belt extended out of the back of each one, ending at a pair of large industrial bins, like the kind used to cart trash or laundry.

The bins were filled with square cardboard sheets. I reached in and picked one up. Each sheet had ten black tablets encased in blister packs. They were further divided into two rows of five, with perforations between each for the distribution of single doses. Etched on the tiny tablets was the word VAMP. I picked up a sheet from the other bin. These were brown and had the word — or rather the prefix — WERE stamped on them.

Beyond the bins, standing against the back wall, were a pair of tall metallic contraptions that looked like heavily-armoured phone booths. One was painted black, the other brown. A heavy steel door was set in the middle of each, both of them secured with oversized locking bolts. Masses of wires and rubber tubes connected the chambers to a bank of complicated, expensive-looking electronic equipment in the corner.

"I'm so glad you could come, Felix."

I turned around, expecting to see Donovan pointing a gun at me. The fact that he wasn't bothered me more. He was bouncy and radiant, like a kid showing off his roomful of toys to a new friend.

"We're completely alone here. I wanted us to have a private chat. There's a little matter we need to clear up."

"Nice setup," I said.

"It's just a little experiment, really."

"Is that what you call it? Four people are dead."

Donovan shrugged.

"You gave it to them, didn't you? This... drug, or whatever it is. You gave it to Jimmy Logan and Eve Sutter."

"You can't have a pilot project without test subjects. But I can assure you, Felix, they were both willing volunteers."

"They volunteered to be murdered?"

"Well, no." He grinned. "Not that part."

"You killed them."

"Killed them?" Donovan looked wounded. "I did no such thing. I gave them exactly what they wanted. Logan wanted an edge on his new role. He didn't just want to act like a vampire, he wanted to *be* a vampire. I believe it was you who killed them, Felix."

Donovan's words hit me low. He could see it and took a step forward.

"You did," he whispered. "You killed them."

"If I didn't, somebody else would have. The police or a STAR team."

"Don't feel bad, Felix. You don't have to take all the blame. You're only partly responsible."

"What are you talking about?"

"I offered them the drug, yes, but I didn't make them take it. It was the other one who encouraged them to give it a try. The rest of the blame belongs solely to her." Donovan raised a calming hand. "But you needn't worry. I visited her earlier this evening, before you showed up at my club. I gave her a little something to help absolve her guilt." His grin spread and spread until I thought the top of his head would fall off.

"I have something for you, too, Felix."

He took out a small black device. He held it up so I could see it. There were two red buttons on it. He pressed one of them and there was a loud ratcheting click. I turned and saw the metal doors of the black and brown chambers swinging slowly open.

Inside the black chamber was a thin, pallid man. He was strapped to the back of the enclosure with metal bands that crossed at his chest, arms and legs. Next to him, in the brown chamber, a werewolf with silver-grey fur was confined in the same manner.

Donovan pressed the other button on the remote, and the metal bands snapped open. I didn't know how long those two had spent in their containment chambers, but they didn't look happy. The pallid man — a vampire, no doubt — fell out of his chamber and landed on his hands and knees. He rose slowly and smoothly to his feet. It was like watching a curtain rise. I felt like it was curtains for me, too.

The werewolf leaped out of its chamber and landed on its crooked back legs. It raised its shaggy head and sniffed the air. The side of its mouth pulled back in a preview of glimmering white fangs. It made a low growling sound deep in the back of its throat.

I looked over my shoulder and saw Donovan ambling toward a door that led deeper into the warehouse.

I turned back and reached under my coat for my gun. Then something strange happened.

The werewolf whirled around and attacked the vampire.

In my research I had neglected to read up on the relationships between the various creatures of the Black Lands. I had just assumed they all got along, and that when weaker prey presented itself, they tag-teamed up on it together. Not so, apparently.

The werewolf landed on the vampire's back, in much the same way Eve Sutter had landed on her bodyguard. The creature's weight would have driven an ordinary man to the ground, but the vampire barely moved. When he did, it was so fast it was almost a blur.

The vampire's arms bent up and around in a way that ordinary arms weren't meant to bend. Instead of trying to pull the werewolf off his back, he raked his razor-like fingernails down the length of the werewolf's arms. The werewolf let out a howl of pain that hurt my ears. Its head came down and its jaws snapped around the vamp's throat with a horrible mashing sound. Getting your leg caught in a bear trap probably sounded a lot like that.

The vampire let out a cry of his own, but it didn't last long. The werewolf tore off the vampire's head with a powerful yank and flung it to the floor. It also tore off one of the vamp's arms for good measure, bit a chunk out of it, then tossed it in the opposite direction. When it was done ravaging the bloodsucker it leaned back on its hind legs and howled in triumph.

Fortunately, I had come prepared this time. I took out my .38, opened the cylinder and dumped the bullets into my coat pocket. Then I took out the silver rounds I had picked up earlier. I didn't know if I would need them, but getting attacked by a vampire one day, and a werewolf the next, had taught me that it was better to have them and not need them, than to need them and not have them.

The werewolf advanced on me. I didn't want to kill it, but I didn't have any choice. Logan and Sutter had been temporary monsters. This was the real deal. I raised the pistol with both hands, spread my legs in the classic shooter's stance, and opened fire. All six shots hit the were-wolf in its broad, furry chest. It slumped to the ground, let out a single, bubbling moan, and died.

I didn't feel even a little bit good about it.

11

I COULD PROBABLY HAVE LEFT Donovan's warehouse at that point and still felt a sense of accomplishment. I had no mind toward seeing justice done or carrying out revenge for the deaths of Jimmy Logan and Eve Sutter. I didn't know them, and the vehicle of their destruction was now up on blocks. They had taken the drug of their own volition — Donovan was right about that if nothing else — and drugs do kill. It was that age-old public service announcement. All Donovan had done was put a Halloween mask on it.

Unfortunately, curiosity had me by the low and dangly parts. Call it an occupational hazard.

After loading the regular bullets back into my gun, I went over to the door Donovan had gone through. It led into a hallway that bypassed rows of offices with glass partitions that looked like cages in some Dilbert-esque zoo. At the far end I came to a small room with a door on the far side. Standing next to the door was something that made me stop in my tracks.

It was another containment chamber — a pink one.

There was no machine set up in front of it, no dump-bin filled with blister packs, but that didn't mean it was empty.

I could have, and probably should have, left it for the PIA, but by then the curiosity was pulsing through me in heavy noisome waves. I was sick with it. Is there anything more tempting than an unopened box? Curiosity may have killed the cat, but satisfaction brought him back.

I found the manual release for the locks and popped them open. Then, with my gun hanging by my side, I pulled open the heavy steel door.

A cold breeze wafted over me, chilling me to the marrow. Then it was gone.

The chamber was empty.

I heard a clicking sound and whirled around.

I had been so absorbed by the pink containment chamber that I didn't get a good look at the door. I figured it led out to the back of the warehouse, and that was how Donovan had made his escape. But as I looked closer, I saw it wasn't just an ordinary door. It was one of *those* doors.

It had been left open a crack, and a breeze from the other side was pushing it lightly like a prodding finger. I put my hand on the knob knowing it was a bad idea and pulled it open. I stood on the threshold and gazed out on the Black Lands.

A field of tall grass stretched off endlessly. A moon twice the size as the one that filled our sky covered everything in a silver glow. The grass wavered in a chill breeze like thousands of tapering sword blades. It always looked like this here, I realized. There were no sunny days in the Black Lands. It was paradise for vampires and werewolves alike.

The open door was a taunt. Donovan wanted me to follow him through, but he knew I wouldn't. Travelling to the Black Lands wasn't inherently dangerous, just like swimming in the ocean wasn't inherently dangerous. When you jump into shark-infested waters, the sharks may leave you alone, or they might tear you to pieces; it depended on various factors, none of which I felt like testing at that particular moment.

Put a stake in me. I was done for the night.

12

WELL, almost done.

I went over to the door's power supply — a black box with thick insulated cables running into the doorframe — and emptied my gun into it. The box spewed some sparks, then some smoke.

I made the call to Agent Keel as I walked back to my car. I told him I'd answer all of his questions in the morning, after some sleep, coffee and maybe a heart attack or two.

But first I had a stop to make.

13

THERE WERE no photographers or reporters or manic movie fans to push through at the film set. I checked my watch and saw it was coming on three in the morning.

Van's trailer door was open, so I let myself in and went directly to the note that I knew I'd find. It was pinned to a drafting table covered with storyboard drawings. I didn't bother to read it. I knew what it would say. I'm sorry for this, I regret doing that, please forgive me. By tomorrow it would be reprinted in all of the entertainment news rags.

I saw something on the floor and bent down to pick it up. It was a cardboard sheet similar to the ones I found at Donovan's warehouse, except the tablets in these blister packs were pink, and the word stamped on them was different. One of packs was open, a single pill gone.

I felt a cold breeze slip past me. I dropped the sheet and followed it out.

"Boo."

Notes on *Temporary Monsters*

THE QUESTION I'm most often asked about the Felix Renn/Black Lands stories is if I was planning to make it a series when I first wrote *Temporary Monsters*.

The answer is no... and yes.

When I first came up with the idea that became *Temporary Monsters*, I really had only one thing in mind, and that was to write a story that combined my two favourite genres, horror and detective fiction. This was by no means an original concept. Plenty of other authors had written such stories. I'd even tried it myself a year or so earlier in a short story called "Relaxed Best."

I thought *Temporary Monsters* would be an amusing follow-up to that earlier story, something longer and more in-depth, as well as a fun way to spoof on the film industry in Toronto.

Even though I started writing with the thought that it would be a one-off, I could tell from the onset that *Temporary Monsters* was going to be very different kind of story for me. What started as a simple mash-up of Stephen King and Robert B. Parker (I sometimes describe Felix Renn as a "supernatural Spenser") quickly turned into a jumping-off point for a whole series of stories exploring this dark world where the supernatural exists as a matter of course.

I knew this by the amount of material I had to remove from the original version of *Temporary Monsters*, and the fact that I couldn't bring myself to delete it outright. This material was mostly background on the Black Lands, stuff that wasn't really relevant to the plot, but I could see potential in it for some other stories.

Sometimes the best ideas are the ones you never see coming. The ones that seemed to fall out of thin air. As if out of a portal.

THE ASH ANGELS

1

IT WAS 7 P.M. on Christmas Eve and I was just getting into the holiday spirit — a bottle of Glen Breton single malt whiskey. My reward for successfully seeing off my ex-wife without any bloodshed. It was a Christmas miracle.

Sandra had been working as my assistant for the last six months. She had been an actor in film and television, but the work had fallen off recently. Sandra blamed it on the industry's obsession with younger talent. She was thirty-two. She only took the gig as my Girl Friday because she was desperate. I knew this because she told me on a daily basis.

Sandra had left that afternoon to spend Christmas with her sister's family in Peterborough. My plans were decidedly less festive. Seven days of drinking and TV dinners, culminating with my annual New Year's Eve viewing of that holiday classic, *Blade Runner*. The original version, not the director's cut. My plans were not traditional by any means, but I'd done it for the last couple of years, since Sandra and I split up. It wasn't about getting sad and reflective at a time of year when most people need little excuse to feel miserable. I just preferred to spend the holidays in the same manner I did my drinking: alone.

As I used my Swiss Army knife to crack the seal on the Glen

Breton, I replayed the conversation I'd had with Sandra in my office before she left.

"Try not to burn the place down while I'm gone."

"I haven't smoked in years, Dee."

"I was actually thinking of the Christmas tree incident."

"Oh, right." How could I forget that? The truth was, I needn't ever worry, because I could always count on Sandra to remind me. "I think it was a faulty extension cord."

"It was a faulty something," Sandra muttered loud enough for me to hear. She tilted her head to the side and looked at me steadily. "Seriously, Felix. Are you going to be okay here by yourself?"

"What is this? Holiday concern for the ex? You really shouldn't have, Dee. Especially since I didn't get you anything this year."

Sandra frowned and turned to leave. "See you in the New Year," she called over her shoulder.

I was always finding new and interesting ways of insulting my ex-wife, and the truth was I didn't know why I did it, or why I'd continue to do it. A psychiatrist might have said it was reverse psychology at work. Pushing Sandra away when what I really wanted was the exact opposite. That would also explain my hiring her to work for me.

But in my deepest heart of hearts, I truly, sincerely did not believe I wanted her back. Not in that way. Sandra and I were friends, which was how things had started out for us — how it starts out for most couples — and since we had been married and eventually divorced, it made a strange kind of sense that we had gone back to being friends again. Maybe it was all we were ever meant to be. Maybe I was meant to be alone. Happy thoughts for Christmas Eve, I know, but it truly didn't bother me. Just because I was alone didn't mean I was lonely. It doesn't change on account of the holidays. People who are genuinely sad, genuinely lonely, don't tend to take days off. They're miserable 365 days of the year.

My situation with Sandra was messed up, no matter how you looked at it. So, I decided not to. At least not until after the New Year.

All of this self-analysis wasn't helping me segue into holiday drinking mode. Suddenly imbibing alone didn't seem like a good idea.

It wasn't quite a bad idea, but it was on the border. A potentially unhealthy idea. Everyone had unhealthy habits, but my drinking had always been more of a hobby than a lifestyle.

After bobbing back and forth in my swivel chair for a little while, I came to the conclusion that while drinking straight whisky shots could be viewed as unhealthy, this could be alleviated if I had a mixer. A holiday mixer, in fact. Then I wouldn't be pounding drinks straight from the bottle; I would be indulging in the sort of festive drinking that is permitted, practically encouraged, at everything from office Christmas parties to family get-togethers.

That was how I went out in search of eggnog and almost got myself and several other people killed.

2

I WALKED out of my apartment building and into a slow-motion snowstorm. The flakes were coming down thick and lazy. There was no wind to blow them around; they just landed on the ground and piled up like white Lego bricks. Walking down the side street toward Bloor was like passing through an endless cold fluffy curtain. I kept having to blink snow out of my eyelashes. I caught a few flakes on my tongue, but they tasted like the city and I spat them into the gutter.

My destination was a convenience store that I found particularly convenient when I was too lazy to go the extra distance to the super-market. It wasn't much for serious grocery shopping, but it was cheap and it had all the brands of pseudo-food necessary to stock a fallout shelter in the event of a nuclear apocalypse. The dairy products were sketchy, but I figured the eggnog was a safe bet, being a seasonal treat and all.

As I turned onto Bloor Street, I saw flashing red lights and half a dozen police cruisers angle-parked at the curb. Their headlights shone on a vacant lot that stood out in the row of storefronts like a missing tooth in a wide grin. I wandered over.

Three black vans were parked among the police cruisers. They were unmarked, but I had a pretty good idea where they were from. There wasn't much of a crowd, only five people standing in a tight huddle in front of the line of yellow police tape. They might have been carollers if they hadn't been absolutely silent. A scene like that normally would have drawn more people, but the weather was lousy and it was Christmas Eve. Most people were either snuggled in at home or pulling their hair out at the mall as they struggled to finish their shopping. A smooth-cheeked cop who looked about fourteen years old had been saddled with crowd control. He had his work cut out for him tonight. He stood behind the police tape looking cold, bored and miserable. The other cops were milling around their cruisers, huffing warm air into their hands and stomping their feet like a pack of anxious horses.

I wondered what they were waiting for. Then I looked past the kid cop and saw why his buddies were hanging back.

There were a dozen or so people walking around the lot. Half of them were wearing dark topcoats and suits, with Bluetooth headsets sticking out of their ears, but it was the other half that got my attention. They were wearing bulky, white hazmat suits. They were almost invisible in the falling snow, moving around slowly and carefully like unsteady ghosts. I understood why the cops were keeping their distance. I wondered why the suits weren't doing the same.

As if hearing my thought, one of the suits turned and stared in my direction for a long moment. I was about to turn away when the suit came over and joined the cop standing behind the police tape.

"Well, well," he said, "if it isn't the bad penny of my life."

"I've missed you too, Agent Keel."

Keel shot a quick frown at the group of onlookers, who were now looking on us. He was trying to appear upset that I had mentioned his name in public, but I knew it was just an act. Keel was a federal agent, but he was one of the rare few who didn't act as if his every movement was a matter of national secrecy. We had met a few months back after I staked a vampire in a posh downtown restaurant.

"You know this guy?" the kid cop asked him.

Keel grunted noncommittally. He hesitated a moment, then nodded at me to follow him behind the police tape. It made me feel special and important for a fraction of a second, until I realized he just wanted me out of civilian earshot.

When we were a discreet distance away, he turned to me and said in a low, harsh voice, "What the hell are you doing here?"

"The boys in your office hired me," I said. "I left the private eye racket and started my own Christmas strip-o-gram biz. You want me to drop trou right here, or do you want to go someplace..."

"Hardy-fucking-har, Felix."

Keel grabbed my arm and dragged me further into the lot. I didn't like being so close to those guys in the garbage-bag germ suits. Keel must've seen the look on my face.

"It's just a precaution," he said dismissively. "The area is clear."

"Clear of what?" I regretted asking the question the moment it left my mouth. I held up my hands. "Forget it. I don't want to know."

Keel gave me a strange look. It wasn't one he had ever given me before, which had all been variations of the go-away or what-are-you-doing-here look. This was almost the opposite, one that said he might actually want me around. It didn't quite say he needed me; it was more speculative, like he had an idea for how he could use me. I didn't like it.

"Actually," he said, "as I recall you're good at this kind of thing. Maybe you could give me your thoughts on something."

I sighed heavily. "It's Christmas, man. Can't you leave a guy alone?"

"National security," Keel said, with a small grin. "Your country needs you."

"I need eggnog," I said. "It's a Christmas emergency."

"Christmas?" Keel scoffed. "Bah, humbug."

"Bah, eggnog," I said, and tore out of his grip. "You have yourself a happy Festivus, Agent Keel."

I started to leave and Keel grabbed me by the arm again. "Festivus was yesterday," he said, and started hauling me toward the rest of his team.

The hazmat guys ignored me completely. They were busy waving various electronic gadgets at the ground. The suits — operatives of the

Paranormal Intelligence Agency, I assumed — gave me only slightly more attention. One of them came over and scrutinized me with crossed arms and an expression that said he was less than impressed. I knew that look. Sandra gave it to me all the time.

"Supporting an orphan for the holidays, Agent Keel?"

"This is Felix Renn," Keel said to the other suit. "He's a private dick. I met him on the Donovan case."

The suit's expression didn't change. "Kill any movie stars lately?" he asked.

"That's pretty funny," I said.

"Agent Enfield is the comedian on our team," Keel said.

"I can tell," I said. "Especially with that tie."

Enfield bristled, but Keel stepped between us before it could go any further.

"So, what brings you out here, Mr. Dick?" Enfield inquired.

"Eggnog," I said.

Enfield made a face. "Do you know what's in that stuff?"

"It's better not to ask."

Keel cut in. "I thought Felix might be able to offer another perspective on the... whatever-it-is." He gestured with his head. I made a concentrated effort to avoid turning in that direction. "He's had some experience with the paranormal."

I expected resistance from Enfield, or at least a smarmy comment, but he gave me neither. He simply shrugged and went over to join the rest of the suits.

Keel touched my elbow and led me toward the back of the lot. I kept my head down and my eyes fixed on the ground directly in front of my feet.

"You ever find him?" I asked him. "Donovan?"

"Our jurisdiction doesn't extend to the Black Lands," Keel replied.

"He might have come back."

"If he did, we haven't heard about it."

"I guess the word 'fugitive' takes on a new meaning when the perp escapes to another dimension."

"It doesn't happen as often as you'd think," Keel said. "Unlicensed portals are extremely rare, and it takes a certain type of individual to actually use one."

"The insane type," I said, and Keel nodded.

Cris Donovan certainly fit that bill. I knew him years ago as Donnie Drugs to the Stars. A tall, twitchy weasel of a man who sold his wares exclusively to people in the film industry. Eventually Donovan moved from distribution into manufacturing. A few months ago, he decided to test one of his new designer drugs on a couple of actors. One turned into a vampire, the other a werewolf. The effects were only temporary, but they lasted long enough to result in a few deaths. I knew this because I was there for both "tests." I was the one who ended up icing them both. The press had a field day with it. Depending on which rag you read, I was either a private investigator to the stars who had the misfortune of being at the wrong place at the wrong time, or some kind of half-ass Van Helsing who got off on monster hunting. The fact that I was neither of these things didn't matter. The press had spoken. Some people called me a hero, others a murderer. I didn't want to be called anything. The calls kept coming in, though.

Keel led me over to where a couple of the hazmat guys were milling around. They stepped back deferentially as we came closer. Keel gestured with his chin at the ground. Reluctantly, I looked down.

My first impression was that it was a snow angel. The kind made by falling backwards into a patch of fresh snow and fanning your arms and legs up and down. Except the colour was all wrong. This angel was dark grey, almost black. Like it was made out of ash instead of snow. An ash angel.

I crouched down and reached out to touch it, then hesitated. I looked over at Keel as he got down on his haunches next to me. "It's safe," he said, "but I wouldn't bother. Shit's hard to get off." He showed me his own black-stained fingertips.

"Ash?"

Keel nodded. "Near as we can figure. From what, we don't know yet."

"That's reassuring," I said. "Although I figured it wasn't dangerous. Seeing as how only half of your team are wearing hazmat suits."

"As I said, it's just a precaution," Keel said. "SOP."

"You spooks and your acronyms."

"Spectres."

"What?"

"Spooks are spies," Keel said. "We're spectres."

I shook my head. "I'm so behind on the lingo these days."

"Standard operating procedure."

"What?"

"That's what SOP stands for," Keel said. "Those are Paranormal Intelligence scientists in the spacesuits waving all the expensive hardware around."

"My tax dollars at work."

Keel grunted.

I nodded at the ash angel. "So how did you find out about this thing? Were you and the rest of the gang out carolling and just happened upon it?"

"I got a call on my BlackBerry about an hour ago," Keel said. "A voice I didn't recognize said I would find something interesting out here tonight."

"Was the caller male or female?" I asked.

"Male."

"Did he call you by name?" I felt myself slipping back into work mode. So much for my holiday break.

Keel thought about it for a second. "Yes. He said, 'Hello, Agent Keel' when I answered the call. But as I said, I didn't recognize the voice."

"Did you trace the call?"

"Tried to. We didn't get anything."

"What does that mean?"

"That they were using a scrambler better than we have — which is possible but not likely — or that I never received the call in the first place."

"Sure," I said. "Maybe you imagined the whole thing."

"Yes, except we're here and so is that thing." He gestured at the strange mark on the ground. "There was also a PK spike around the same time the call came in."

"A spike?"

"A brief surge of concentrated psychokinetic energy," said Keel. "We have instruments that monitor the level of PK energy across the city. We keep an eye out for any unusual activity. Most PK spikes turn out to be nothing. The one we detected an hour ago was minor, the kind we normally would have ignored. That is, if the caller hadn't told me to come out to the exact same location."

"He gave you this address?"

"He texted me GPS coordinates."

"That's helpful."

"Yeah," Keel said, "a little too helpful."

"You think it's some sort of trap?"

Keel let out a tired sigh. "If it is, then I don't know to what end. So far all we have is that mark on the ground. It's not as if a crime has been committed here. Vandalism, maybe, but even that's a stretch." He drew himself up and sighed again. "Whatever this is, I'd like to figure it out before I leave."

"Leave?" I said. "You score early retirement?"

"I wish," Keel said. "I'm being transferred. To Boca Sombra."

"How nice for you," I said. "No more Toronto winters."

Keel grunted and looked down at the ash angel.

He wasn't the first spook — *spectre* — to be transferred to Florida. PIA headquarters was located in Boca Sombra, and the agency had a number of field offices across the state. A strong federal presence was important when your citizens lived next door to a dimension filled with dangerous supernatural entities. There were more Black Lands portals in Florida than in any other state in the Union. Fortunately, most of them were located off the coast, in the Bermuda Triangle. It was like the fabric of reality in that part of the Atlantic Ocean had been raked over a cheese grater. The wall separating our world and the Black Lands was full of holes out there. I'd once seen a map of the no-fly zones in that particular region and it looked like a plate of spaghetti.

The costs on fuel and time to navigate around the Triangle were enormous, but the alternative was worse. Plenty of ships and planes had ignored the warnings over the years and paid the price — unexplained disappearances and space-time anomalies were the order of the day. It was rumoured that the Russians had lost a submarine in the Triangle sometime back in the '70s. They never said anything official, but if it was true, then it was one Red October they'd be hunting for a long time. These days, the only people who ventured into the Triangle were suicidal lunatics and Cuban refugees who had the misfortune of drifting past Florida on the Gulf Stream in their ramshackle boats.

"At least you'll get a tan," I offered.

"Forget it," Keel said. "I don't want to talk about it."

"You don't want to go?"

"No, I don't want to go," Keel said, a bit defensively. "You got a problem with that?"

"No, I just wish you could have told me sooner. We could have hung out more. Bonded a bit."

Keel gave me a hard look, and I raised my hands apologetically. "Sorry," I said. "I thought all you PIA guys wanted to work down there. I thought it was your dream gig."

"I said forget it, okay?" Keel's cheeks were suffused with colour, and I didn't think it had anything to do with the cold. "I didn't ask you over here to discuss my moving arrangements."

"Fair enough," I said. "What do you want?"

"Your opinion," he snapped. "Of that." He pointed at the mark on the ground again.

"I've never seen anything like it," I told him. "So anything I say would be guessing."

"At this point, I'll take a guess."

"It looks like a snow angel," I said. "Made out of ash."

"So?"

"So maybe it was made by a person. Maybe it *was* a person."

"SHC?"

"I told you I'm acronym illiterate."

Keel waved at one of the hazmat guys. He came over with a boxy device that looked a bit like a Geiger counter, only more complicated, and expensive. He stood close to me and practically shoved the sensor wand up my nose. I swatted it away.

"Hands off my wand," he said. His voice came out high and tinny through the small speaker in his suit's faceplate.

"Then don't stick it in my face," I shot back.

The hazmat guy turned to Keel. "Who the hell is this?"

"Civilian consultant," Keel answered. "Felix Renn. Felix, this is Dr. Kovac."

"The pleasure is mine," I said. The good doctor didn't offer to shake my hand. Maybe he was worried I was contagious. "Where did you get that suit? I've got a feeling they're going to be the must-have gift this season."

Kovac looked at me like I had just crawled out of the sewer. "What kind of a consultant are you?"

"Fashion, mostly. I also do some interior design."

Kovac shot Keel a perplexed look. Keel sighed. "Let's get back on message here, Felix. The sooner we finish, the sooner you can get your stupid eggnog."

"Eggnog?" Kovac made a face. "Do you know what's in that stuff?"

"It's better not to ask," I said. I pointed at the device in his hands. "Can you tell me what you're scanning for?"

Kovac turned to Keel. Keel gave him a brisk nod.

"Psychokinetic residue," Kovac said. "Traces of an interdimensional transfer."

"I didn't know you had a gadget that could detect that."

Kovac looked like he was going to say something, then remained silent.

"Let me guess," I said. "It's classified."

"Not really," said Keel. "It's not much more than a variation on a spectrometer. Except this one is fine tuned to pick up the unique electromagnetic signature of the Black Lands."

"You can actually tell when someone, or something, crosses over?"

"If the transfer is recent," Kovac said. "The field dissipates very quickly."

"Have you picked up anything here?"

Kovac shrugged. "There are some background traces, but nothing conclusive. Something may have happened here. Then again, it could be nothing."

"I guess paranormal science isn't an exact science."

"You got that right."

"What about SHC?" I asked, tipping a wink at Keel.

Kovac's eyebrows rose. "Spontaneous human combustion? It's possible, I suppose. Cases are extremely rare, and there's usually some part of the body left behind. Here we've got nothing but ash."

Agent Enfield wandered over and said, "That's assuming a supernatural cause. This could have been a simple case of self-immolation."

"Not likely," I said.

"Oh yeah?" Enfield said. "What makes you say that?"

"Look at the mark on the ground. It's a clean pattern. Straight lines radiating out from the centre, with little to no smudging. People who set themselves on fire tend to writhe around. They don't usually lie back and let themselves burn up."

Enfield frowned and walked off.

"Have you ever seen anything like this?" I asked Keel.

"No. We've sent some pictures out on the wire, but I doubt we'll get anything useful back. I've seen plenty of strange shit in my time, but this one's new to me."

Kovac stared dreamily at the mark on the ground. "It's almost as if the victim was flash-fried in a matter of seconds, leaving behind nothing except this... this..."

"Ash angel," Keel said.

"Crispy critter," I said.

"Yes," said Kovac, "except without the critter. We haven't been able to find a single bone fragment or piece of charred flesh, which, if this was a body, is extremely unusual."

"Have you had a chance to do any tests on the ash?" I asked.

"We've bagged some samples to take back to the lab." Kovac let out a frustrated sigh that came out electronic and weird through his suit speaker. "All I can say is that whatever it was, it burned hot and it burned fast."

I turned back to Keel. "What about something in the air? There have been plenty of reports over the years of strange stuff falling out the sky. Fish, frogs, blood."

Keel nodded. "The computer gave us a few dozen reports of ash falls. Nothing in this area and nothing that left behind the sort of pattern we have here."

"Was there anyone around when you and your team showed up?"

"The cops arrived shortly before we did and secured the site. They said it was empty."

"Are there any women on your team?"

Keel frowned. "Two of the scientists are women. Dr. Dunning and Dr. Forrest." He pointed them out to me. "Why?"

I glanced over at the women. They were both wearing hazmat suits. "Nope," I said. "We're looking for another woman."

"What woman?" Keel asked, confused.

I crouched down. Keel and his team had been tromping all over the place, leaving behind a zigzagging trail of blocky footprints in the snow, but there was one unblemished print that stood out among the rest. It was from a woman's heeled shoe, size 7. The print was located right in front of the ash angel.

I stood up. Keel was giving me the same crawled-up-from-the-sewer look that Kovac had given me. I ignored him. I looked at the ground around my feet. Once I knew what to look for, they were easy to spot. The woman had come across the lot in a straight line, stopped at the spot in front of the ash angel, then turned around and gone back again. I followed the shoeprints to where they ended at the sidewalk, raising my head just in time to keep from clotheslining myself on the police tape. Keel trailed a few steps behind me.

From here the woman — I assumed it was a woman, but it could just as well have been a man who enjoyed wearing heels — could have gone in any direction. I decided to stick with what I had and kept walking straight ahead. I stepped out from between two of the parked police cruisers and crossed the street to a large, dark Victorian house.

"Where are you going?" Keel called behind me.

I pointed at the house. "The plot thickens."

"What," Keel yelled back, "the burial plot?"

It was a funeral home.

3

ONE OF THE hazmat guys called Keel over, so I went inside the funeral home by myself.

The fact that the door was open at 8 P.M. on Christmas Eve should have bothered me, but strangely it didn't. This was already turning out to be a surreal night, and I had learned from experience that when things start to take on a Lynchian vibe, it's always better to save your questions and just go with the flow.

As I stood in the dark vestibule, I wondered why it seemed that only the businesses of death and dentistry tended to set up shop in houses. You didn't see it too often in other lines of work. Maybe the forced intimacy of those particular industries required a more subtle environment in order to put people at ease.

I went through another door and stepped into a wide foyer with wine-coloured carpeting and cast-iron light fixtures on the walls. There were rooms to my left and right, stairs rising up in front of me, and a corridor straight ahead that led deeper into the house. There were no lights on anywhere. The only illumination came from the bright carnival pulse of the police flashers and the steady orange glow of the arc-sodium streetlights coming in through the front windows.

I called out, "Hello? Anybody home?", then immediately wished I had kept my mouth shut. There was something inherently creepy about asking that question in what looked like an empty funeral home. Like, what if you got a reply?

I did get one, of a sort. I heard a heavy, hollow thump from the room on my left. I walked slowly through the archway, then stopped. The room was full of coffins. A veritable showroom of coffins. They sat on raised platforms, scattered around the room like oversized dominoes. A few glowed with a low shine. The more expensive models, I assumed. Polished wood or polished metal. Take your pick.

As my eyes adjusted to the darkness, I could make out a dim, vaguely human-shaped silhouette standing in front of one of the coffins at the far end of the room. Unlike the other coffins, this one's lid was closed. That was the sound I had heard. There's no mistaking that thud of finality. I'd heard it in a thousand horror movies. It was the sound of a door closing forever.

"Hi there," I said. "Sorry to disturb you."

The silhouette shifted slightly. I blinked my eyes a few times and the shape resolved itself into a person. A woman. I squinted at her feet, trying to see if she was wearing heels, but it was too dark to tell. I considered asking her, but decided it was probably a bad opening question. Instead, I went with, "Do you work here?"

"Yes," she said. "I'm alone."

That was a weird reply, but I let it slide. It was a weird situation. Woman standing alone in a room full of coffins. In the dark. Maybe I had walked into one of those horror movies.

"My name's Felix," I said. "Felix Renn. What's yours?"

"Gwen." Her voice was a barely audible whisper. "Gwen Ambrose."

"Nice to meet you, Gwen. So, you work here?"

She nodded. "I'm alone. Everyone else is gone. For the holidays," she added.

I looked around at the coffins. Yes, I wanted to say, things look dead around here. But I decided to keep my mouth shut. In my experience, the people who worked in the funereal arts either took their business too seriously or not seriously enough. I wasn't in the mood to find out which kind Gwen was.

"I saw it," she said.

"Pardon?"

"I saw it," she repeated. "Before it… burned up."

"It?"

"He, she." Gwen shrugged. "It doesn't matter."

I hesitated. "*What* doesn't matter?"

"It doesn't matter," she said again.

"Why not?"

"It just doesn't."

"I'm sorry," I said. "I'm a little confused here."

"That doesn't matter, either."

Of course it doesn't, I thought. "Why are you telling me this?"

"It said you'd be coming." Gwen turned and started to lift the coffin lid.

I got a bad feeling in my gut. I don't get premonitions, but sometimes my stomach tells me things. A gastrointestinal sixth sense. It was telling me that something very unpleasant was about to happen.

I moved quickly across the room, darting around the coffins like a quarterback snaking between the other team's offensive line. Gwen had the coffin lid raised and was reaching inside. I got to her just as she was turning back toward me. She had a gun in her hand. I grabbed her wrist and twisted it hard. She let out a short, brittle scream and dropped the gun into my other hand. I stepped back a prudent distance, holding the gun daintily away from me — and from her — and looked at it.

It was a little nickel-plated .38 revolver. I popped the cylinder open. All six chambers were loaded. If I had been one or two steps slower, they might all have been inside me. The thought made me swoon a bit. I reached out with my free hand and gripped the edge of a coffin. That didn't make me feel better at all. I let go and waited for the world to swim back into focus.

"I wasn't going to hurt you," Gwen said in a cracked voice. She was holding her injured wrist and looking at me with wet eyes.

"You always keep a gun in your coffin?" I asked, a bit woozily. "A little something to convince your customers to upgrade to the silk head-pillow and the satin-lined interior?"

"The owner, Mr. Harding, gave it to me," Gwen said. "For protection. I work here alone most nights."

"I just wanted to ask you some questions."

Gwen lowered her head. So did I. She was wearing heels. They didn't look wet, but I could see road salt crusted around the toes.

"It wasn't for you," she said, speaking to the floor. "It was for me."

"What? I don't understand." Then I did. "You were going to shoot yourself?"

Gwen was crying openly now. Tears ran down her cheeks. Her throat hitched.

"You need to leave," she said. "Please go."

I started to protest, but found I wanted to leave. I wanted to get away from this strange, frightened woman standing in a dark room full of coffins. This wasn't like walking into a horror movie, I decided. Horror movies weren't real. This was like walking into a nightmare. Nightmares weren't real either, but they felt real when you were in them. I didn't want to be in this one anymore. I backed out of the room.

"I'm going to hold onto your gun, okay?" I slipped it into my coat pocket. "I'll return it when you're..." I didn't know how to finish that sentence. I was going to say, *when you're feeling more like yourself*, but maybe this was how she always was.

"Take it." She sniffled loudly and wiped her nose on the back of her hand. "You're supposed to."

"Says who?" I asked.

"Who do you think?"

4

KEEL WAS WAITING for me outside on the sidewalk. "Anything?" he asked.

I shook my head. I didn't know why I kept quiet. All of a sudden, it seemed like too much effort to explain. I just wanted to go home.

"It was worth a shot, I guess."

I flinched at the word "shot" and took my hands out of my coat pockets. "Sorry I couldn't be of more help," I muttered.

"It's all right." Keel turned and looked across the street at the vacant lot. His team were still fussing around in the falling snow. It might have looked pretty under different circumstances. Like if I had eggnog and had never left my apartment in the first place.

Keel said, "It's typical. I knew I'd end up leaving an 'unsolved' before I left."

"Don't be so hard on yourself," I told him. "It's just a job."

Keel turned back to me. He wore the same sad, defeated expression I had seen on Gwen Ambrose's face. I didn't want to look at it anymore. I extended my hand toward him. Keel stared at it for a moment, then shook it.

"Good luck in Florida," I said. "Drop me a postcard. Or catch me a marlin. Whatever's easiest."

Keel nodded. "Happy holidays, Felix."

I watched him walk back across the street and join his team. I didn't feel like eggnog anymore. I didn't even feel like the Glen Breton. I almost said, It's a Christmas miracle! but I stopped myself. The joke was getting old and the evening was getting on and I was getting tired.

I headed home and wondered if depression was contagious.

5

"HELLO?"

"Hi, Laurel."

"Felix." My ex-sister-in-law's voice was cool and distant on the other end of the line. It was probably the same tone she used when talking to telemarketers. "To what do I owe the pleasure?"

"Just calling to spread some holiday cheer," I said.

"Are you drunk?"

"Not at the moment."

In a snide voice, Laurel said, "It's a Christmas miracle," and I almost dropped the phone.

My situation with Laurel was more complicated than the fact that I had been married to, and eventually divorced from, her younger sister. I had actually dated Laurel for a short time before Sandra and I hooked up. I was the first to admit it was messed up. But the heart wants what the heart wants. I think if I had used those exact words on Laurel at the time she would have removed my lungs with an ice-cream scoop. Relations between the sisters had been strained over the course of our marriage, but things had gotten a bit better after Sandra and I split up. Being able to commiserate over what a jerk I was probably went a long way toward patching things up.

"May I speak to Sandra?" I asked.

There was a loud clunk as the phone was dropped. A few moments later, Sandra came on the line.

"Felix."

"Dee."

"Nice to see you're still pushing people's buttons, even on Christmas."

"Technically it's not for a few hours yet."

"Tell that to Laurel."

"Did I drive her to drink?"

"No, but she's going crazy with the nutcracker. She doesn't even like chestnuts."

"I bet she wishes I was there."

"Parts of you, I'm sure. So, what do you want?"

"Is it snowing there?"

"Uh, no."

"It is here. Great big flakes. I was out walking around in it. It was pretty. Reminded me of when I was a kid and I used to go sledding down near the old brickworks. I bumped into an old friend tonight. He showed me something. An angel made out of ash. Isn't that something?"

"Felix, what the hell are you babbling about?"

"It was an ash angel, Dee."

Sandra sighed. "Felix..." Her voice trailed off. "Felix, I'm worried about you. All alone in your apartment. I told you it wasn't healthy. Is there someone you can talk to?"

"I'm talking to you."

"Someone who can help you."

"Who says I need help?"

A pause. Then, "Are you drunk?"

"I'm as sober as a judge," I told her.

"So, what you're saying is that you have no excuse for acting like a total nut?"

"Maybe I just miss you."

"Right," Sandra scoffed. "And maybe I'm going to release an album of Lesley Gore cover songs."

"Maybe you should."

"Felix, I really don't want to talk to you like this."

"I'm sorry."

Silence fell on both ends of the line. It stretched out to the point where I could almost feel the miles between us. Then Sandra said, "I don't know what you want me to do."

I wedged the phone between my head and shoulder and held it there. I closed my eyes and pretended Sandra and I were lying in bed together, face to face, like we used to.

"You don't have to do anything," I said. "I just wanted to hear your voice."

"This isn't like you," Sandra said. "I've never heard you sound so... maudlin."

"I just wanted to hear your voice," I said again.

"Felix, if this is some sort of joke, I don't find it funny. I'll kick your ass when I get back, and then you can find yourself a new assistant."

"I love it when you talk dirty to me, Dee."

"I'm hanging up."

"Don't, Dee. Please. It's not a joke. I just really wanted to talk to you. I don't know why." I sighed heavily and started to stammer. "Keel is being transferred. Gwen almost shot herself. It's been such a long, fucked-up night, I just wanted to hear a friendly voice."

"Who's Gwen? What are you talking about, Felix?" Her voice was brimming with frustration. Then she let out a deep breath and said, "I think you need to get some rest. Will you go to bed? Right now?"

"Okay." I shifted and nuzzled against the receiver. "Good night, Dee."

She hung up without another word. The click in my ear was very loud.

I hung up the phone and it rang almost immediately. I steeled myself, picked it up, and said, "I miss you, Dee. I'm sorry, but I have to say it. I miss you. And I think I still love you. I made a mistake. I made a lot of mistakes. I know that. But I also know I can fix things. I want to make it up to you. I want to make it all up to you."

The words were as shocking to me as they undoubtedly were to her. I had never articulated my feelings very well, if at all. Stranger still, up until that moment I didn't know I even wanted Sandra back at all.

Too bad it wasn't her on the phone.

6

KEEL SAID, "I need to see you. Right now."

He sounded frantic, almost scared. I didn't know Keel could sound like that. I thought the parts of him capable of producing such sounds had been surgically removed when he joined the PIA.

"It's late, Keel. I was just about to take off my pants. And once they're off, they don't come back on again until the morning. Sometimes not until the afternoon."

"Felix..." Keel's voice was strangled. "You need to come. Now."

"What for?"

"It wants to see you."

I was popular that night.

It looked like I'd have to keep my pants on a little longer.

7

I MANAGED to get an address out of Keel. It was down in the Port Lands, a mostly abandoned industrial area near the lakeshore. Like most of the eyesores in Toronto, it had been tagged for redevelopment. Beautification of the city. It was a good business to be in. Very profitable. As I turned off Cherry Street onto Commissioners, I thought if I ever got tired of the private eye gig, I could always open my own salon. Beautification by Felix.

The drive gave me a chance to think about my phone call to Sandra. More specifically, how I was going to explain it to her. It wasn't going to be easy. I had trouble explaining it to myself. It was like an out-of-body experience. I could have blamed my behaviour on the holidays, but Sandra knew I wasn't prone to the emotional lows of the season. That didn't leave me with much of an explanation for how I had acted on the phone. Maybe I could blame the trouble in the Middle East. Or the economy. Or global warming.

I saw a silver sedan parked in front of a dark sprawling building at the address Keel had given me. I pulled up behind it and got out of the car. I recognized the building. It was the warehouse where Cris Donovan had set up his experimental drug lab. I had almost died here, and I wasn't eager to go back inside.

I needn't have worried. The front door was padlocked shut. A strip of faded police tape clinging to the door fluttered in the cold wind. After Donovan made his great escape to the Black Lands, Keel and his team had swooped in and taken the place over. They spent the next few months doing all kinds of secret government things with Donovan's equipment. None of it made it into the newspapers, but I'm sure it was all in the name of national security.

I went around to the left side of the building and looked down a dark narrow alley. Another private investigator probably would have kept a flashlight in his glove compartment. Not me. Something to ask for next Christmas, I supposed. The newly fallen snow helped brighten things up a bit. At least, enough for me to see the tracks of someone who had come this way before me.

As I was passing the dark bulk of a dumpster, my left arm clipped something. I froze. It wasn't until I tried to turn around that I realized something had bumped into me. Grabbed me, actually. I swivelled my head slowly around and looked down. A black-gloved hand was clamped around my forearm. My gaze moved along the arm to the shoulder, then up to the livid moonface of Agent Keel.

For a moment I thought I was looking at a ghost, but ghosts didn't typically reach out and grab the living. At least not in any of the movies I had ever seen.

"Felix?" Keel rasped. "Is that you?"

"In the flesh," I said, trying to sound cool and calm. "How about you, Agent Keel? Are you... fleshy?"

I prodded the hand gripping my arm. It felt fleshy. Keel let go and slipped back into the shadow of the dumpster. I reached down, grabbed him by the upper arms, and pulled him to his feet.

"What happened?" I asked, brushing snow off his topcoat. "Did you decide to celebrate your transfer by getting ripped?" I sniffed around his face, but didn't smell any booze, just the same industrial-strength aftershave he always wore. Overpaid Government Employee, by Calvin Klein. "You know you're not supposed to actually crawl during a pub crawl, right?"

"I saw it," Keel said harshly.

"Saw what?"

Keel pointed at something on the ground further down the alley. I took a few steps toward it. Even in the dark I could tell what it was. I had seen one just like it earlier that evening.

An ash angel.

8

KEEL GAVE me his story in fits and starts. Getting information out of someone in a state of shock is delicate work. If you use too little pressure, they may drift away on you. Too much and they can turn into a blubbering wreck. I had to coax Keel along at certain parts when he threatened to vapour-lock on me, and at one point, when it looked like he was going to burst into tears, I slapped him hard across the face.

That seemed to put him back on message, and eventually a narrative began to form.

According to Keel, about an hour earlier he'd received a call on his BlackBerry. He recognized the voice of the caller as the one who had sent him to the location of the first ash angel. The caller chastised Keel for showing up with his PIA entourage in tow. He said he was going to give Keel one more chance and sent him another set of GPS coordinates. He told him to come alone this time. Going against his better judgment (not to mention a number of PIA regulations), Keel did as he was told. He followed the coordinates to the warehouse on Commissioners Street and found it locked, as it should have been. It had been his team, after all, that had put the padlock on the door. He decided to go around the side of the warehouse to check the rear door. He never made it that far. As he was coming down the alley, he saw someone at the far end blocking his way. It looked like a very short man. Maybe a child, Keel said.

But it wasn't a child.

"Do you know why I joined the PIA?" Keel asked me suddenly.

I hesitated. "Because you were tired of buying your suits off the rack?"

"Most people join because they're interested in the paranormal. The supernatural. Monsters. Demons. Shifters."

"And you aren't?"

"Of course I am, but that wasn't why I joined. My interest was in UFOs."

I didn't know what to say. I had never heard Keel so confessional. And UFOs? For a moment I wondered if this wasn't some sort of agency practical joke. Or maybe I was about to be punk'd. I glanced around for a camera crew, but we were the only ones there.

"Did you know the number of UFO sightings has increased drastically since the discovery of the Black Lands?"

"Reports of everything strange have gone up since then. One person sees a cougar in their backyard and suddenly everyone is seeing cougars everywhere. It's mass hysteria."

Keel shook his head. "No, it's true. I saw it for myself tonight."

"Saw what?"

"The thing at the end of the alley. It wasn't a man or a child. It was an alien."

I stared blankly at Keel. "You mean like a Mexican?"

Keel didn't seem to hear me. His eyes were focused on a spot somewhere over my left shoulder. "It was an alien," he said in a low, firm voice. "A real, honest-to-god, extra-fucking-terrestrial. Big bald head, small body, almond-shaped eyes, grey skin. You know, the usual." He uttered a shaky laugh. "The usual."

"You mean like a Spielberg alien?"

"It was more *Close Encounters* than *E.T.*, but yes."

"What did it do?"

"It spoke to me." He tapped his temple. "In my head."

"You sure the whole thing wasn't in your head?"

"I thought that might be the case. Then it beamed back up to its ship. It left behind that mark." He pointed at the ash angel. "That's when I knew it had really happened."

"There was a ship, too?"

Keel nodded.

"So, the ash angels are caused by teleporting grey-skinned aliens." I took a moment to digest this. "I suppose that's as good a reason as any. I was going with spontaneously combusting pixies, but your explanation will probably look better on the official report."

"I know what I saw, Felix."

"So, what did Mr. Grey say to you?"

"It said it knew things about me."

"What kind of things?"

"It knew my name."

"Your name is on your business cards, Keel. That's not exactly classified information."

"It knew that I grew up in a green house in Haddonfield, Illinois."

I frowned. "Okay, that's kind of weird."

"It knew that I'm moving to Florida..." He paused. "...and that I don't want to go."

"It knew about your transfer. Maybe the aliens are on your inter-office mailing list."

"It said I didn't have to go."

"Did Mr. Grey offer to send you somewhere else?" I asked. "Neptune, perhaps?"

"It told me I could shoot myself." Keel lowered his eyes. "And I thought maybe I should do it."

"That's one way to get out of moving to Florida."

He raised his eyes and looked at me. "It said you would come."

"Of course I came. You called me."

"It said you would come," Keel said again.

"What about the UFO?" I asked, changing gears. "Are we talking flying saucer?"

"Black triangle."

"That was my second guess."

"It didn't make a sound. No engine noise at all. I wouldn't even have noticed it, but then the lights came on."

"The lights?"

"I thought they were Christmas lights at first." Keel's gaze drifted upward as he remembered. "But they were up in the sky, and they were moving. One moment the sky was black, the next it looked like the Fourth of July."

"First."

"What?"

"We do our fireworks on the first of July. You're in Canada, remember?"

Keel gave me a quizzical look, like he didn't know what planet he was on, much less the country.

"What happened next?" I prompted him.

"The alien left," Keel said simply. "There was a flash of blue light that blinded me for a moment. When I could see again, the alien was gone, the UFO was gone and that mark was on the ground."

I went over to the ash angel. It looked like someone had set off some sort of firecracker, a fancy one that left behind this weird Rorschach-like stain on the snow. I turned back to Keel.

"You said the alien... beamed up to his spaceship?"

"I don't know," Keel said tiredly. "I don't care."

"Aliens are making illegal visitations to your city and you don't care? That's not the Agent Keel I know."

Keel shook his head. "It said you would make jokes."

"I always make jokes."

"But it said you were really sad inside."

"Was it an alien or a psychiatrist? Because, no offense, you seem to be the sad one here."

"Sad?" Keel snapped. "I'm not sad." He paused. "So what if I am? Everyone feels lousy this time of year."

"I don't." That wasn't entirely true. "I think something happened to you tonight."

"Yeah," Keel said, "I was almost abducted and probed."

"No, I think you were infected with something. And I think it was from exposure to the ash angel."

"Infected with what?"

"I don't know, but it seems to work like SAD."

"SAD?" Keel said. "Separation anxiety disorder?"

"Seasonal affective disorder," I corrected him. "A supernatural version of it, anyway. One that takes a person's sad feelings and intensifies them, turns them into full-blown depression."

"Super SAD," Keel said wanly. "Sounds sexy."

"I know you PIA spooks like your acronyms."

"Spectres," Keel said automatically. He raised his hand and rubbed the side of his head. "I admit I was feeling upset about my transfer, but I wasn't depressed about it. At least..."

"Not until tonight."

"I've never felt this bad in my life," Keel said. "But when I saw that..." He looked toward the end of the alley. "It was like everything good inside me suddenly withered and died. I felt empty, hollowed out. It felt like the only thing that would make it better was if I... killed myself." He lowered his head in shame.

"But you didn't," I said, gripping his shoulder. "That's the important part."

Keel didn't say anything.

"Now we need to fix it."

Keel looked up at me. His eyes were glistening and his mouth was a quivering line. "How?"

"The first thing you should do is make a call and have the rest of your team put into quarantine. Everyone who was working at the ash angel site earlier this evening. Put them on suicide watch or something."

Keel nodded and reached into his coat. He took out his cellphone and put it to his ear.

Except it wasn't a cellphone. It was a gun.

I snapped out my hand and swatted the gun away from Keel's head. It went off with an ear-splitting crack and the muzzle flash momentarily blinded me. I launched myself forward and fell on top of Keel. He made a gasping sound as the air whoofed out of his lungs. I gripped the wrist of his gun hand and choked it like a chicken. He wouldn't let go of the gun. I slammed his hand against the ground, once, twice, then I heard the gun go skittering across the asphalt. Blobs of light shifted across my vision, like I had a lava lamp installed in my head. I couldn't see Keel clearly, but I could hear him sobbing.

I blinked my eyes rapidly. The blobs began to dissipate, and my gaze fell on my watch. It was three minutes past midnight.

"Merry Christmas, Agent Keel." I let go of his wrist and slapped him on the shoulder. "You're alive."

Keel began to cry.

"I hate Florida," he sobbed.

9

I MADE the call to the PIA while Keel pulled himself together. A gruff voice on the other end of the line demanded to know who I was and why I was calling on Keel's phone. I answered his questions and explained the situation. He wanted to speak to Keel so I handed him the phone. Keel talked to him briefly, long enough to confirm my story, then passed the phone back to me. The gruff man told me that he would see that the other members of Keel's team were quarantined. He told me to take care of Keel. Coming from a government operative, the words had an ominous ring to them. Even more so since I was now holding Keel's gun in my hand.

"I'm not telling you to shoot him," the gruff man snapped at me. "Put him in his car and send him home."

I jerked as if someone had goosed me. "How did you know what I was thinking?"

"We know everything," the gruff man said, and the line went dead.

I was about to hand the BlackBerry back to Keel, but then I got an idea. There was something strange about this night, about my bumping into Keel so close to where I lived, and the way we had both ended up back at this place where I had almost died. It couldn't have been a coincidence.

I asked Keel if I could borrow his BlackBerry. Under normal circumstances, he probably would have told me to take a long walk off a short pier, but there was nothing normal about this night.

I asked him to show me how to access the PIA intranet, and one file in particular. Again, Keel complied. I should have asked to borrow some money.

As I walked Keel back to his car, I realized I was still holding his gun.

"I'm going to keep this, okay? Just for tonight." I stuck it in my jacket pocket. Another one for my collection. "You can swing by my place before you leave town and I'll give it back to you."

Keel nodded.

I told him to go home. That was where I wanted to go, but I had a stop to make first.

Keel was in no shape to help me, but there was someone else who knew a thing or two about ashes.

10

THE FRONT DOOR of the funeral home was still open, so I let myself in. I stepped through the vestibule into the foyer. Everything looked the same, which was to say dark, except I had a feeling the house was actually empty now.

I stuck my head into the coffin showroom where I had met Gwen Ambrose earlier and stopped her from putting a bullet in her pretty head. She wasn't in there. All of the coffins were open and empty. If one of them had been closed, I think I would have turned around and walked right out the door.

I checked the room on the other side of the foyer — a sitting room with floral-patterned chairs and couches — but she wasn't in there, either.

I walked down the central hall to the kitchen. Stainless-steel appliances glowed dully in the low light filtering in through the rear windows. I walked across the polished linoleum floor to the back door.

The backyard stretched back 50 or 60 feet to a squat concrete building with a large vent on the roof too big to be called a chimney. A crematorium.

I followed a concrete path that led up to the front door of the building. I raised my hand to knock, then decided not to bother.

I opened the door and a wave of heat slammed into me. I shut my eyes instinctively and took a step backward. I let out a gasping breath and the heat rushed into my mouth and filled my lungs. I hacked out a dry cough and opened my eyes.

I was staring straight ahead at the source of the heat — an industrial-sized furnace that took up almost one entire half of the room. Positioned in front of it was a conveyor belt similar to the one you put your case of empties on at the beer store. This one was used to roll caskets into the cremation chamber. The conveyor belt was on casters so it could be rolled out of way when it wasn't in use. At the present moment, Gwen Ambrose was sitting on it with her legs hanging over the side.

She didn't look up as I stepped inside, leaving the door open to let out some of the heat. The air in the room was stifling. I didn't know how she could stand it, sitting so close to the furnace. She didn't appear to be affected by the heat at all. Her head was turned away from me. She seemed to be watching the flames dance within the circular portal set in the furnace's heavy metal hatch.

"Gwen?"

She turned her head and looked at me. "Felix?"

"Working late?"

"I could ask you the same thing."

"I keep odd hours. It's the nature of the job."

Gwen nodded and turned back to the furnace.

I said, "You weren't thinking of using that conveyor belt like a Slip 'n' Slide, were you?"

"A what?"

"You never had a Slip 'n' Slide as a kid?" I edged closer to her. "It's a long piece of yellow plastic that you attach to a garden hose. It gets all wet and slippery, and you slide on it."

"I never had one of those." She wasn't looking at me as she spoke. She seemed to be hypnotized by the flames.

"You said you were working tonight."

"Yes."

"Did you do any cremations?"

That got her attention. "Yes," she said, turning to face me, "I did."

"Only one?"

"Yes."

"A man?"

"Yes."

"What was his name?"

Gwen picked up the metal clipboard sitting next to her on the conveyor belt. "Neil Howie."

I snorted.

"What is it?" Gwen asked.

I took out Keel's BlackBerry and punched up the file I had asked him to access for me. I showed it to Gwen. "Is this the man you cremated?" I asked. "Is this Neil Howie?"

Gwen looked at the small screen. "Yes, that's him."

I put the BlackBerry back in my pocket. "His real name is Cris Donovan. He was a drug dealer and a murderer. The PIA has been looking for him since he escaped to the Black Lands."

"The Black Lands?" Gwen said, confused. "But... who's Neil Howie?"

"A character in *The Wicker Man*. It's a horror movie about a policeman who travels to a secluded island community in search of a missing girl. It turns out to be a hoax put on by the townspeople who end up sacrificing the guy in the hopes of restoring their crops."

"You recognized the man's name from a movie?" Gwen said sceptically.

"It's a cult classic."

"Why would someone use that name?"

"It's a joke," I said. "A bad one. In the movie the guy is burned alive in a giant wicker statue."

"No, no," Gwen stammered. "The man I cremated was dead. I know that for a fact. He's been dead for some time."

"What do you mean?"

"We received the body a few months ago. We had explicit instructions to wait until tonight to cremate it."

"Christmas Eve," I said. "Did you know some people think this is the saddest night of the year?"

Gwen shrugged. "Everyone feels lousy around the holidays."

"Not everyone," I told her. "But I think that's what Donovan was hoping for."

"Hoping for what?"

I ignored her question. "Who gave you the instructions for cremation?"

"Mr. Harding. I don't know where they came from originally. The deceased's family, I guess. Not that anyone showed up for the service."

"There was a service?"

"A small one, earlier this evening. We put a notice in the papers, like we always do, but no one showed up."

"That's not surprising," I said, "considering he was using a fake name. He didn't want anyone to know he was dead, and he didn't want anyone to know that he was having his body cremated."

"But why?"

"I don't know for certain, but I can make a pretty good guess." I looked over at the furnace. I wondered if Donovan was still in there, his body reduced to smoke, ash and bone fragments. Strangely I was more scared of him now than when he was alive.

"I think it was about revenge," I said. "Against a PIA operative named Keel, and against me."

"Revenge?" Gwen said. "Was he planning to haunt you from beyond the grave?"

"Something like that. I think something happened to Donovan in the Black Lands. Either on purpose or by accident. I think he knew he didn't have long to live and he wanted to ensure that when he died, he'd take us along with him. Me and Keel. The two people who ruined his operation, maybe even his life."

"I still don't understand how he could do that if he was dead."

"Are you familiar with SAD?"

"You mean people getting depressed because of the holidays?"

"More or less. Except this is a much more potent version. Instead of making people depressed, it makes them suicidal. You were ready to shoot yourself earlier this evening, and less than an hour ago the PIA agent I mentioned, Keel, almost did the exact same thing. Whatever this thing is — virus, curse, hex — it was triggered by something, and I think that something was the cremation of Donovan's body. Somehow it set this thing loose. It infected you, you passed it on to me, I infected Keel, and he passed it on to God only knows how many others." I suddenly felt sick to my stomach.

"What about you?" Gwen said. "You don't seem to have been affected."

"I'm not entirely sure about that." I was thinking about my phone call to Sandra "I think it might have something to do with the fact that I wasn't feeling sad when I was exposed."

"What does that mean?"

"Keel was upset about a work transfer. He seemed almost

depressed about it. I think this thing magnified those feelings. When I met you earlier tonight, you said you were alone. You mentioned it more than once. Are you going to tell me you weren't feeling sad before you did the cremation?"

Gwen shrugged. "I guess so. But like I said, everyone feels like that at this time of year."

"I don't," I said, "and I think that's why this thing didn't have the same effect on me. Although it wasn't for a lack of trying."

"So, what am I supposed to do?" Gwen asked. "I'm guessing this isn't the sort of thing I can simply take antibiotics for."

"Honestly, I don't know. Keel's team is being quarantined as we speak. I'm hoping this is a temporary condition, something that will wear off with time. How do you feel right now?"

"Not so good."

"Do you feel like you want to kill yourself?"

"I don't think I would go that far."

"Let me put it to you this way: do you feel as bad as you did when you were about to put that gun to your head?"

Gwen thought about it for a long moment, then she shook her head. "I don't feel like skipping around for joy, but I don't feel like blowing my head off, either."

"That's a start, I guess." I looked at my watch. It was late. So late it was early. And I was beyond tired. "I need to go back to my apartment for a few hours. Are you going to be okay here for the rest of the night?"

Gwen nodded. "I think so."

"Okay," I said. "Then how about turning that thing off and going to bed?"

We both turned and looked at the furnace.

I had an idea.

"Is he still in there?" I asked.

Gwen shrugged. "What's left of him."

I told her what I wanted to do.

11

I WENT HOME. Gwen told me she would call me in the morning, at which point I would contact Keel and explain my plan. Until then, sleep.

I let myself into my apartment. It was dark. I should have left a light on. The streetlights bathed the living room in a subdued glow. Enough for me to see I wasn't alone. Someone was standing at the far side of the room. I couldn't make out any features, but I was pretty sure it wasn't one of Keel's aliens. The silhouette was a little shorter than me, but it was human-shaped. Woman-shaped.

"Hello, Felix," she said.

I recognized the voice. I had lived with it for seven years.

"Hello, Sandra."

"You used to call me Dee."

"I still do," I said. "But you're not my ex-wife."

"We thought it would be easier this way."

"Who's 'we'?" I asked.

"Poor Felix," she replied. "Always asking questions."

"That's why they pay me the big bucks."

"We want to help you."

"Then leave."

"We can't do that," she said with mock surprise. "You'd be all alone."

"I'll live."

I caught a glimpse of movement on her face. A smile?

"Are you sure about that?"

"I'm doing okay so far."

I leaned back against the door, trying to look casual. I stuck my hands in my coat pockets and touched the two guns I had confiscated earlier that evening. My stomach did a backflip. My lungs squeezed tight. My scalp tingled.

"Poor Felix," said the woman who looked like my ex-wife. There was a dark humour in her voice. "Poor, poor Felix."

I took the guns out of my pockets. Gwen's .38 in my left hand, Keel's Glock in my right. I held them close to my chest with the barrels pointed upward, like I was preparing to duel. Spots started to dance in front of my eyes, and I realized I was holding my breath. I let it out in a shaky exhalation.

"Even loners get lonely."

"I'm not lonely," I said. My voice was trembling. I couldn't seem to make it stop. "I'm just... alone."

"You can make it stop, Felix."

She was right. I could make it stop. I could make everything stop. I could make her stop, too, I thought. I could point the guns at her, shoot her. But she wasn't really there. Sandra was in Peterborough. This thing wasn't her. I knew that. I could shoot it, whatever it was, but I didn't think I could hurt it. It wasn't trying to hurt me. It was trying to get me to hurt myself. If I shot it, it might go away, but it would come back. I knew that, too. I didn't know what to do so I did the only thing I could do. I kept talking.

"Making a lot of house calls this evening?" I asked. "I know of at least two others who had an encounter with you tonight."

"I only visit three," she said. "Three is the number."

"What does that mean?"

"Three is the number," she repeated.

"So that means the rest of Agent Keel's team doesn't have anything to worry about?"

"Three is the number," she said again.

"You didn't kill them," I said. "Gwen and Keel. You tried, but they didn't go through with it."

"I didn't want them, Felix. I wanted you."

"I'm afraid I'll have to disappoint you. You might as well go ahead and do your Human Torch routine, because I'm not going to shoot myself."

Even as I spoke the words, my hands were pushing the barrels of both guns up under my jaw. They pressed harder, causing my head to tilt back so I was looking up at the ceiling. "I don't want this," I almost shouted.

"Poor Felix," she said. "You don't know what you want."

I knew one thing. I knew I was getting sick of hearing her call me "poor Felix." My thumbs were on the hammers of both pistols. I cocked them back. The sound was deafening in my dark apartment. I swallowed and my throat clicked. My index fingers snaked around the triggers. I didn't want to do this, but a part of me said that it wasn't just the right thing to do, it was the *only* thing. No way out but the bullet. Two bullets. Straight up through my head. I pictured the top of my skull popping open like the lid of a jack-in-the-box. No one was here to knock the guns out of my hands.

My fingers tensed and I heard the shots. Two sharp raps.

I was still alive.

Someone was knocking on my door. The door I was leaning against. There were two more knocks. I could feel them vibrate up my back.

The silhouette of the thing that looked like my ex-wife tilted its head to the side. "I'll be seeing you, Felix."

I opened my mouth to deliver a witty retort — *Not if I see you first* — but all that came out was a watery groan.

There was a flash of light that momentarily banished all of the shadows in the room.

Flame on.

12

IT WAS Gwen at the door. It took me a little while to open it. My hands didn't want to let go of the guns. I had to concentrate and focus all of my will, but they finally opened and the weapons clattered to the floor. I flexed my hands a few times, then opened the door.

"I'm sorry," Gwen said. "I couldn't wait. It was starting to get bad again."

"I understand," I said, "and thank you."

13

WE TOOK GWEN'S CAR. I called Keel on his BlackBerry. He was awake. He didn't sound so good. He said he had spent the last hour or so looking at the big picture window in his apartment and wondering if he should jump out of it. He was on the 27th floor.

"Hold off on that for now," I told him. "We're coming to get you."

"Where are we going?"

"To put an end to this thing, I hope."

We picked up Keel and I explained my theory about Donovan's body.

"The rest of your team should be fine," I said. "This thing, this virus or whatever the hell it is, it was targeted specifically at us. The only thing I can't figure out is how the person who called you about the first ash angel knew that I would go out tonight, much less bump into you."

"When you showed up at the crime scene, it was like déjà vu," Keel said. "I was thinking of you the moment I saw that mark on the ground. I had this, I don't know, intuition that I should talk to you about it. If you hadn't showed up, I was planning to find you."

I nodded. "So I would have gotten infected anyway. I was always the intended target."

Keel was frowning. "There's one thing that doesn't track. If Donovan is dead — has been dead for months — then who called me tonight? His ghost?"

"That's as good an answer as any," I said.

"It doesn't matter," Gwen cut in. "His plan didn't work. We were the only ones who actually felt suicidal." She looked over at Keel. "This Donovan person, he failed. You didn't try to kill yourself tonight, Felix."

"I may have spoken too soon about that," I said. "Let's just say it was close."

"Close?" Keel said. "Are you sure this thing isn't going to infect anyone else?"

"Three is the number," I said.

"What the hell does that mean?"

"I have absolutely no idea."

Gwen and Keel looked at me strangely, but I didn't elaborate.

"Three is the number."

14

I HAD Gwen drive us down to the Port Lands. Instead of turning onto Commissioners, I had her continue along Cherry Street to where it ended at the beach. We got out of the car and walked across the snow and sand. The beach was deserted, which you'd expect at three o'clock on Christmas morning.

Cherry Beach wasn't particularly attractive, even in the summer. It was surrounded by marshlands and abandoned factories. There were no snack bars or even a boardwalk. None of that mattered tonight. It would serve our purpose.

I led the way to the lifeguard station, going around to the small deck that jutted out over the water. We stood three abreast and looked out across the dark expanse of Lake Ontario. I turned to Gwen and she removed a large Ziploc bag from her jacket pocket.

I didn't know how closely together the three of us needed to be to perform this little exorcism, but I figured there was no point in taking any chances. It wasn't as if we'd get another shot at this later on. You can only scatter a guy's ashes once.

Gwen opened the bag and we each took a turn reaching inside and pulling out a handful of Cris Donovan's cremains. Then, on a three count, we scattered them into the lake. The ashes made a brief stippling on the surface of the water, then they were gone. We all reached in for another handful and repeated the process until the bag was empty.

Gwen started to stuff the Ziploc bag back in her pocket, then tossed it into the lake. She didn't want any souvenirs of this night. Neither did I. The memories would last a lifetime.

As we started back to the car, I said, "I could use a drink."

Gwen and Keel turned and looked at me.

"What do you say? First round of eggnog is on me."

Keel said, "Bah, eggnog."

Gwen said, "Do you know what's in that stuff?"

I said, "It's better not to ask."

Nobody laughed, but I thought I caught a sliver of a smile on both of their faces. It was something. A little something. And it was better than nothing.

Notes on *The Ash Angels*

BY THE TIME I finished writing *Temporary Monsters*, I knew Felix Renn was going to return again. At least one more time, anyway.

My friend and fellow writer Richard Gavin provided the germ of the idea that became *The Ash Angels*. Richard was planning a reading event called A Ghost Story for Christmas and asked if I would be interested in participating. The story didn't have to be Christmas-themed, but that was where my mind immediately went after I agreed to take part.

The image that came to me was of a snow angel... except it was black. Maybe not black, but a dirty grey. Like ash. I saw a person looking down at this strange design in the snow and realized it was a certain Toronto detective.

Since I knew I wanted to write a story set around Christmastime, I started by wondering what Felix was up to in the aftermath of *Temporary Monsters*, which took place in the summer. I knew I wanted to write a much more sombre tale than *Temporary Monsters*, something that would explore the more insidious elements of the Black Lands as well as the inner landscape of my fictional PI.

I'm a big fan of detective fiction, but a lot of the early work featured detectives who were little more than ciphers. Two-dimensional tough guys with no thoughts or feelings or personal histories. You followed them through the story, but you don't really know or care about them because they never share anything about themselves. Some of them, like Dashiell Hammett's Continental Op, didn't even have a name.

I wanted people to know Felix, to see his light side and his dark side. I'm not sure if I succeeded, but I think most people would agree that while *The Ash Angels* works perfectly fine as a pseudo-sequel to *Temporary Monsters*, it's still a very different kind of story.

BLACK-EYED KIDS

1

I SPENT THE night in my car waiting for Mandy Clarke to commit adultery. On the passenger seat next to me was my Canon digital SLR with a telephoto lens and a paper bag containing a maple-glazed donut. I hadn't touched either one all night.

My orders were to follow Mrs. Clarke and take pictures of everyone she met. I was on the second day of the job, and she'd only left her apartment once, to go to the liquor store at the corner. She'd been at home ever since.

Home was a high-rise in uptown Toronto, near Yonge and Eglinton, a trendy singles neighbourhood the locals called Young and Eligible. People had been coming in and out of her building since I'd parked across the street the previous evening. Getting pictures of her boyfriend (assuming she had one), much less shots of her cheating in her apartment (she and her husband were separated), was going to be very difficult. I had mentioned this to my client, but he just told me to follow her and see where she went.

I didn't argue. I'd been paid in advance for a week's worth of surveillance, and it was only day two. Mrs. Clarke still had plenty of time to lead me somewhere interesting.

I took out my notepad and reviewed the previous night's log.

6:35 p.m. — M.C. leaves apartment.

6:40 p.m. — M.C. goes to liquor store.
6:47 p.m. — M.C. leaves liquor store.
6:55 p.m. — M.C. returns home.

Dashiell Hammett would be proud.

It was now half past seven in the morning and the street was waking up around me, with people heading off to work, kids walking to school. The air was filled with the background noise of morning traffic: revving motors, squealing tires, the occasional horn honk.

I was considering my donut when I became aware of another sound. I couldn't tell what it was at first, only that it wasn't part of the usual urban morning symphony.

The moment I realized it was a siren, an ambulance went flying past my car and turned into the semi-circular driveway in front of Mrs. Clarke's building. I started to open my door, then pulled it back as a police car zipped by and pulled in behind the ambulance.

I started to get a bad feeling as I got out of the car and jogged across the street. The lobby door had been propped open, and the cops and EMTs had already gone up in one of the elevators. I took the other one up to the fifth floor.

The doors slid open and my bad feeling got worse.

There was a uniformed police officer standing in front of apartment 505.

Mandy Clarke's apartment.

2

I QUICKLY DEBATED MY OPTIONS, then strode down the hallway.

"Excuse me, officer..."

"I'm sorry, sir," he said, holding up his hand, "I'm afraid you can't go inside."

"I'm a private investigator." I took out my license and showed it to him. "The woman who lives here is a client," I lied. "Is she okay?"

"I..." The cop stammered, and I noticed for the first time that his face was sickly pale. "I can't let you in. You'll have to wait for the detectives."

I almost said *I am a detective*, but I knew what he meant. The police detectives.

The homicide detectives.

3

They arrived twenty minutes later. There were two of them — one in a grey suit, one in a brown suit. They went into the apartment and left me out in the hallway with the pale-faced cop. They came back about fifteen minutes later with another uniformed officer. I noticed the detectives were now wearing latex gloves.

"Tell them to bring the whole crew," one of the detectives said to the uniform. "This one's gonna be a circus." The uniform nodded and trotted down the hallway to the elevator.

The detectives decided to notice me then. The one in the grey suit was named Drake. He was a tall, broad-shouldered man in his late thirties with short black hair, pale blue eyes, and cheeks that were still gleaming from his morning shave. His partner in the brown suit was Robichaud, late fifties, bull-necked, barrel-bodied, with salt-and-pepper hair and matching eyebrows and moustache.

"You're a private dick?" Drake asked.

"Felix Renn," I said. "I was hired to follow Mrs. Clarke. Is she okay?"

"Who hired you?"

I hesitated.

"You got a license?" Drake asked.

I showed it to him. Drake glanced at it, then handed it to Robichaud, who gave it back to me without even looking at it.

"Is she okay?" I asked again.

"Come on." Drake jerked his head for me to follow him inside.

We went down a short hallway to the living room. We walked around a couch that was positioned at an odd angle. I looked down and saw small rectangular indentations in the carpet. The couch had recently been moved from its usual position.

Drake led me down another hallway. He stopped in front of an open doorway and looked at me over his shoulder. "Don't touch anything."

He went in first. I followed him. It was a bedroom. Mandy Clarke's bedroom. I didn't see her at first. Then the detective walked around to the other side of the bed and looked down. I came over and stood next to him, following his gaze.

Mandy Clarke's body lay on the floor.

Well... part of it.

Her body had been bisected in a slanting line from the top of her left hip to just below the ribcage on her right side. The cut was perfect, as if she had been chopped in half by a guillotine. Her upper body lay on its side on a wide blood-soaked patch of carpet. Her arms were extended over her head, her hands twined in the blankets tucked between the mattress and the box spring. She had pulled them most of the way out, as if she'd been holding on for dear life. Her head was turned to the side so that her face tilted up to the ceiling.

"Is she the one you were hired to follow?" Drake asked.

"Her name's Mandy Clarke." I closed my eyes and took a deep breath.

"If you're gonna puke," Drake said, "do it out in the hallway."

I opened my eyes. "I'm not going to puke."

I kneeled down and peered under the bed.

"Where's the rest of the body?"

"That's a good question," Drake said.

I looked over at the room's only window.

The detective read my thoughts. "It didn't go out the window. There's no blood on the sill and the screen doesn't open. It's screwed in tight to the frame."

"Maybe the killer took the rest of the body with him."

We went back out to the living room. Robichaud was searching through a red leather purse sitting on an end table. He took out a matching wallet. He opened it, removed a small plastic card, looked at it, and then passed it to Drake. Drake stared at it for a long moment, then handed it back. "Check it." Robichaud took out a cellphone and turned away from us while he punched in a number.

"Who called the police?" I asked.

"Neighbour in the apartment below," Drake said. "He woke up this morning to find blood dripping from his ceiling. He came up here to check it out, saw the vic's door standing open, went inside and found the body." He paused. "Half a body."

"He didn't see anyone?"

"Nope. He's in shock, but we got that much out of him. We won't get anything else until the shot the EMTs gave him wears off. Even then, I doubt he knows anything useful." He glanced back in the direction of the bedroom. "We'll need forensics to tell us for sure, but it looks to me like she's been lying there for a while."

I let that sink in. I'd been sitting outside her building while this woman was being murdered, her body mutilated. For some reason the image that came to mind was of the donut still uneaten in my car. I felt my gorge rise.

I ran out of the apartment to the hallway. I braced one arm against the wall and leaned over with my eyes closed. My stomach bounced and jounced, but I didn't throw up. I stayed like that for a couple of minutes, bent over at the waist, sucking in deep breaths of air. The hallway smelled of grease and carpet deodorizer. Finally, I opened my eyes and straightened up.

Detective Drake was standing in front of me. "Feel better?"

"Not really," I said.

We went back inside. Robichaud was just finishing his call. He snapped his cellphone closed with one hand and tossed Drake the plastic card he'd taken out of Mandy's wallet.

"Tell me about this job," Drake said to me. "For starters, who hired you?"

"Her husband," I said with a sigh. Client confidentiality didn't matter much now. A woman was dead, and her husband was going to be a suspect no matter what I said to the police. "They were separated. He thought she was cheating and hired me to follow her."

"What did you say her name was?" Drake asked.

I hesitated. "Mandy Clarke."

Drake looked at the card in his hand, then turned it around and showed it to me. It was a driver's license. "This says her name is Tara Baxter."

"And she's not married," Robichaud added.

4

"TELL ME ABOUT THIS 'HUSBAND,'" Drake said.

Robichaud had gone off to search the kitchen. I could hear him opening drawers and cabinets and grunting to himself. I couldn't tell what the grunts meant, if they meant anything.

"He was a walk-in," I said.

Drake raised a questioning eyebrow.

"As opposed to a referral," I clarified. "He showed up at my office yesterday morning. He told me he and his wife had just separated. She'd moved out and gotten an apartment. He suspected she was cheating on him and wanted her followed."

Drake's gaze wandered. "Is it still cheating if they're separated?" I couldn't tell if he was putting the question to me or simply musing aloud to himself.

I shrugged. "I leave that stuff to the lawyers."

"Did she meet with anyone?"

"Not while I was watching her, but I only started the job last night. She went out once around 6:30 p.m. to the liquor store, but she came right back and had been at home ever since."

"Did you see anyone suspicious enter the building?"

"It's hard to say. People were coming and going all night."

Drake gave me a sceptical look. "Kind of hard to spot the lady cheating on her husband if you're sitting in your car across the street."

"I told my client the same thing. He said he just wanted her followed."

Robichaud grunted and waved us into the kitchen.

On the counter there was a half-empty bottle of vodka and a lowball glass. Robichaud was down on one knee next to an open cabinet with a small plastic trashcan inside. He held up a wrinkled, paper liquor store bag and a receipt. Drake leaned down to look at the receipt.

"Time stamp goes along with your story."

"Do I need a story, Detective?"

"Probably not," Drake said. "But I'd like to speak to this husband."

"You think he did this?"

"You don't?"

"No, actually," I said. "You don't typically hire someone to watch your wife if you're planning to kill her in her home."

"Maybe you didn't see him," Drake said. "Maybe he slipped in the back, killed her, then slipped out again. Hiring you could have been his way of setting up an alibi."

"I guess, but that's taking a hell of a risk."

"Some guys'll do anything to get out of paying alimony," Drake said. "You said this guy came in off the street?"

I nodded.

"What information did he give you about his 'wife'?"

"He gave me her name, her address, the type of car she drove and the plate number." I hesitated. "He also gave me a picture."

"Let's see it."

I took it out of my inside jacket pocket and gave it to the detective. It was a three-by-five glossy of a young woman with straight chestnut hair framing a long face that was punctuated by a pair of wide dark eyes. The picture had been taken in the winter. There was snow in the background and the woman was wearing a wool hat and a heavy coat. There was a shy smile on her face, but it didn't touch her eyes. She had an awkward look about her that suggested she was uncomfortable in front of the camera, or maybe just uncomfortable in general. The word "haunted" is thrown around a lot these days — especially in a world where the supernatural is as real as the ground under your feet — but that's how the young woman looked in that picture. Haunted.

Drake flapped the photo in his hand. "This all he gave you?"

I nodded.

"The vic, was she a big drinker?"

"Not that I'm aware of," I said. "I don't really know that much about her. Just that she was supposedly married to my client. And it looks like that wasn't even true."

"Well, we've got a half-empty bottle of vodka sitting on the counter," Drake said. "Which means she either had a hell of a lot to drink last night, or —"

"She had a visitor," I finished.

"Maybe this husband, or whoever he was, stopped by for a drink. Maybe they had an argument. There's only one glass on the counter, but he could've washed his and put it back." Drake shrugged. "Or maybe the lady was a lush. What's your client's name?"

"Barry," I said. "Barry Clarke."

Robichaud snorted and shook his head. Drake gave me a look of amused disbelief. "You're serious?"

"Yeah," I said. "So what?"

Drake cleared his throat. "Let me see if I got this straight. You were hired to follow a girl named Mandy by a guy named Barry."

"Yes."

"Barry Clarke."

"Yes." I didn't see where this was going.

"Are you sure his last name wasn't Manilow?"

I didn't say anything for a moment. Then it clicked, and I could hear the song playing in my head. 'Oh Mandy.' It might have been funny if there wasn't a woman's bisected corpse in the next room.

"So, you think it's a fake name?" I said.

"Well, we know her name isn't Mandy." Drake crossed his arms. "What do you think?"

"Clients don't always give their real names," I said. "Some of them are embarrassed to enlist the services of a private investigator."

"Gee," Robichaud said, "I can't imagine why."

I shot him a look but didn't say anything. I deserved that one.

"Did Mr. Manilow give you any way to get in contact with him?"

Drake asked. "An address? A phone number? A schedule of the cocktail lounges he'll be touring this summer?"

"He gave me his number," I said thinly.

I took out a slip of paper and handed it to Drake. He glanced at it and passed it to Robichaud, who had his cellphone out again. He punched in the number, gave me back the paper, and put the phone to his ear. A moment later he closed it.

"Not in service," he said.

"Of course it isn't," Drake said.

I lowered my head, but I could still feel their eyes burning into me.

5

THEY CUT me loose soon after that, on the proviso that I came by the station tomorrow to give a proper statement.

I took the elevator down to the lobby and went back to my car. I put the key in the ignition and sat there for a moment. I looked at the cars passing on the street. A couple of joggers with iPods strapped to their arms zipped by. An old man in a brown cardigan came by walking a small dog in a matching sweater. A group of kids ran past him, laughing and screaming and swatting each other with their backpacks.

The old man moved out of my field of vision and I noticed a boy and a girl standing on the lawn in front of Mandy Clarke's — correction, Tara Baxter's — building. They looked to be the same age, around eight or nine years old, and were dressed much more formally than the kids who'd just gone running by. The boy wore neatly pressed black trousers and a white button-down shirt, while the girl wore a black dress, almost puritan-looking with its high collar, and a pair of Mary Janes. Probably on their way to some private school.

I stared at them and they stared back at me. Then they crossed the street and came up to my window.

I can't explain what happened next except to say that I got scared. Horribly, inexplicably scared. I began to tremble uncontrollably. My spine felt like a column of ice. My hands opened and closed spasmodically in my lap. I clenched them into fists and squinched my eyes shut. I was breathing fast, and I tried to slow it down by taking longer, deeper breaths.

A finger tapped on my window and I let out a high-pitched yip that startled me in its intensity and unexpectedness.

I turned my head and forced my eyes to open. Looking at the boy and girl standing outside my car was like treading water in the middle of the ocean and seeing a pair of shark fins coming at me. The fear I felt was a physical thing — a stomach-dropping, skin-tightening terror that brought sweat out on my face, the back of my neck and under my arms. A voice in my head told me I was alone, all alone, utterly alone, no one would help me, no one *could* help me, I might as well give up, give it all up. I opened my mouth to cry out, but my voice was gone.

"Please, mister," the girl said, looking in at me imploringly. "We missed our bus. Can you give us a ride?"

I shook my head rapidly.

"Please let us in," the boy said. He reached out and wiggled the door handle. "We don't want to be late for school. Our parents will be so angry with us."

I tried to say *I can't help you*, but all that came out was a choked groan.

"Let us in," the girl said. She leaned in close to the glass, almost pressing her face against it, and I felt my bladder release.

I moaned pathetically and fumbled out with my right hand, swatting the keys dangling from the ignition. I reached up blindly — my eyes were still fixed on the kids who were now pawing at my window like a couple of sad kittens — and turned the key. The engine purred to life.

I put the car in drive and dropped both feet onto the gas pedal. If there'd been a vehicle parked in front of me, I wouldn't have gotten very far. But there wasn't, and the car leapt away from the curb. I gripped the steering wheel and drove as steadily as my fractured nerves would allow. My breathing slowly returned to normal and the voice in my head was gone.

I tried to tell myself that nothing strange had happened, that my reaction to those kids was some sort of delayed shock from seeing Tara Baxter's mutilated body.

It wasn't until I reached my apartment that I realized there was something wrong with the children. I couldn't explain why I didn't notice it at the time, or why it only came back to me when I replayed the memory of the encounter in my mind. It didn't make sense, but then nothing about this morning made any sense.

Those kids who wanted into my car... their eyes were black.

Completely black.

6

I PUT on a pot of very strong coffee and took a long, hot shower. The coffee was ready by the time I got out. Wrapped in a towel, I stood at the kitchen counter and downed a cup, black, then filled it again, added milk and sugar, and sat with it at the table.

I was haunted by the mental image of those kids standing outside my car. Despite the shower it was still enough to make me shiver. I didn't want to think about them, but I had to.

The thought that those black-eyed children might be supernatural entities crossed my mind, but if they were, then they were of a type I'd never heard of before.

I took out the piece of paper with Barry Clarke's phone number on it and tried calling it again. A robot voice told me the number still wasn't in service.

I sat for a moment, thinking, then I dialed Sandra at my office. She didn't pick up. Which meant she was late, or quite possibly wasn't coming in at all. It's hard to get good help these days, and when you hire your ex-wife to be your personal assistant, you have to learn to roll with the punches. Sometimes literally.

I poured myself another cup of coffee and tried to work the problem in my mind.

A man hires me to follow his wife, whom he believes is cheating on him. Nothing strange there. The majority of every private investigator's workload is divorce cases.

But why would a man hire a private dick to follow a woman he wasn't really married to? A woman who ends up getting butchered while the detective you hired is on the job. It didn't *feel* like a set-up, but it still didn't make any sense.

The fact that "Barry" had lied to me about his name — and the name of his "wife" — didn't bother me much. The people I worked for usually lied to me about something. They came to me for help, to find the answers to questions they couldn't figure out for themselves, and this made them feel inadequate. As a result, some of my clients felt that they had to leave out certain facts, or change them entirely, as if there was a balance of truth and lies in the universe that had to be maintained. If I felt it would interfere with the job, I called them on it. Otherwise, I didn't bother. I learned early on that in this business everyone lies.

I sat there and let my coffee get cold as I thought about all the reasons why a man who called himself Barry Clarke might have lied to me. Why he might have killed a woman he claimed was his wife.

I decided I didn't have enough information to come up with a plausible theory. I might never know the truth. If "Barry" was involved in Tara Baxter's murder, he was long gone by now. I'd go down to police headquarters in the morning, give my statement, and that would be that.

I sighed heavily and looked at the digital clock on the stove. Ten-thirty.

I didn't feel like going into the office that day. The sight of Tara Baxter's bisected corpse was part of it. The thought of running into those black-eyed kids again was a bigger part. I made an executive decision to stay home and catch up on my talk shows and soap operas.

I didn't even bother getting dressed. I simply transferred from towel to robe and parked myself in front of the television.

I had a fried-egg sandwich and a glass of milk for lunch. When I was done, I started to put the dirty plate and skillet in the dishwasher.

Then I stopped and decided to wash them myself in the sink. I dried them, put them away, and started to leave the kitchen. Then I came back, opened the dishwasher again, took out everything else, and washed it, too.

I didn't tell myself I was trying to find excuses to stay in my apartment, even though that was exactly what I was doing.

When there was nothing left to wash, I forced myself to go down the small hallway that led to the front door. Right away, I felt the old fear creep up like a pair of cold hands skittering up my back.

I returned to the couch at a quick trot, almost a run, and stared at the television for the rest of the day. When it started getting dark, I turned the volume up louder, then proceeded to turn on all the lights in the apartment.

I had a beer for dinner. That beer led to another one, which led to another. I sipped them, to make them last and so I wouldn't get drunk too quickly. Around ten o'clock, I decided it was time to start the heavy drinking, and poured myself a scotch. I carried it back to the couch and sat down. I raised the glass to my nose to breathe in the oaky scent, took a small sip, and almost spit it out as the intercom on the wall behind me buzzed loudly.

I put the glass down and stood up on trembling legs. I stumbled over to the wall, leaned against it for support, and pressed the intercom's "listen" button.

A burst of static came out of the speaker, followed by a voice full of childish yearning: "Please, mister, let us in!"

If I'd still been holding my glass, I would have dropped it. As it was, I almost dropped myself on the floor. I leaned further into the wall, propping myself up, pressing my finger harder against the button. I couldn't seem to pull it away.

"We're lost, mister. Please let us in. We're lost and scared."

The fear came crashing down upon me like a tidal wave. A wave of blackness swept across my eyes. I tried to speak, but my voice was gone again. I felt the scotch and beer sloshing around in my stomach. I opened my mouth, expecting to throw it up, but all that came out was a sour belch.

I pushed off from the wall and stumbled back to the couch. I picked up the television remote and put it on the channel that showed the feed from the security camera in the lobby; the one designed to show tenants who was buzzing them in their apartments.

I stood motionless as I stared at the black-and-white image of the boy and girl I'd seen earlier that morning at Tara Baxter's building. Now they were in my building, still dressed in their preppy, somewhat old-fashioned clothes, standing next to the intercom system. I didn't know how, but they'd found out where I lived.

As I watched, the girl raised her hand and pressed my buzzer again. Even though I saw it happening in real time, the sound of it going off behind me still made me jump.

On the screen, the boy turned and stared up into the corner where the security camera was mounted. His eyes were black. Dead black.

I couldn't tear myself away from the screen. Who were these kids? *What* were they? Why did they fill me with such inexplicable fear? Were they ghosts? Were they haunting me because I didn't save Tara Baxter from being murdered?

While these questions went flying through my mind, the outer lobby door opened and one of the building's other tenants stepped inside. I recognized her, but didn't know her name. She lived below me on the fourth floor with her young son. I sometimes rode the elevator with them.

Her son wasn't with her today as she crossed the lobby to the inner door. As I watched her, I knew this was a pivotal moment in my life. The deciding factor as to whether or not I was going crazy.

Her head was down as she rummaged in her purse. After a long, agonizing moment, she brought out her keys and raised her head. I waited breathlessly. Then she turned and looked over at the boy and girl. She saw them. I could tell by the way her posture changed, the way her shoulders lowered. I wanted to hug her and thank her, but mostly I wanted to scream at her to stay away from those kids.

Instead, she took a step toward them, leaning forward a bit at the waist the way some adults do when talking to children. The girl turned from the intercom while the boy pulled his gaze away from the security camera. They spoke to her, but I couldn't hear what they said. There was no audio on the video feed.

I didn't have to wait long to figure out what they had said to her. What they had *asked* her.

On the screen, the woman turned back to the inner lobby door. She slipped her key into the lock, turned it, and held the door open. The kids sauntered in. Before he walked out of view, the boy stopped, looked back up at the camera, and grinned.

7

THE KNOCK on my door came a minute later.

I had used that minute to run and get my "home gun," the Glock 26 subcompact that I kept in a shoebox on the top shelf of my bedroom closet. I checked the clip, slammed it home, and chambered a round. Then I went back to the front hallway to wait for my guests.

The knock came again, a light, almost timid sound, as if the person on the other side didn't want to disturb anyone but still wanted their presence to be known.

The fear was still with me, clinging to my shoulders like a giant bat with ice-cold talons, but the paralyzing aspect of it had dissipated. I was still afraid, more afraid than I could ever remember being, but I was able to move and act.

I took a small step forward, praying that the parquet floor beneath me wouldn't creak. It didn't, so I continued inching closer until I was standing in front of the door. Tentatively, I craned my head forward, closed one eye, and peered through the peephole.

I half-expected to see my neighbour from the floor below. *Excuse me,* she'd say, *these children say they live here. Can you open the door and let them in?*

But she wasn't out there. Just the kids. The boy and the girl. Dressed in their monochromatic outfits. With depthless black orbs where their eyes should be.

I could see that clearly now and wondered how I could have missed it the first time. I didn't beat myself up over it. My neighbour didn't notice it at all, apparently. Maybe she would later on. I hoped not, for her sake.

Staring through the peephole, I watched as the boy raised his hand and knocked on the door again.

"Please," the girl said, "let us in. We don't have anywhere else to go!"

I pulled my head back and raised the gun so it was between me and the door.

"Why don't you try going to hell?" I suggested. "How about that?"

There was a long, stretched-out moment of silence, then the sound of tinny, high-pitched

laughter erupted from the other side of the door. There was nothing pleasant in that sound. It was like listening to rats being tortured.

"You're funny!" the girl said. "We like funny people."

"Let us in," the boy said. "Let us in so we can be funny together."

For some reason that creeped me out more than anything else they'd said so far. I heard a rattling sound and immediately thought it was one of the kids turning the doorknob. But it was only the sound of the gun in my trembling hand.

My gaze jerked back to the door — specifically the locks. There was a security chain, a deadbolt and a lock in the doorknob. I stared at them, half-expecting to see an invisible hand disengage them one by one. Then the door would swing open and there'd be nothing between me and the black-eyed children except a gun that probably wouldn't have any effect on them.

Not that it mattered anyway. I didn't even know if I *could* shoot them. They were kids, after all. Or at least they looked like kids. What if they were human? What if they were under the influence of the Black Lands or had been taken over by possessing entities? The law allowed one to defend themselves against supernatural invaders, but it was extremely difficult, almost impossible, to prove possession in a court of law. I could see myself on the stand trying to convince a jury of my peers that the two children I'd plugged in my apartment hallway were actually a couple of otherworldly creatures.

I heard a scratching sound on the other side of the door.

"Open the door!" the girl said in a loud, strident voice. "Let us in!"

I stood my ground and waited.

There was nothing else I could do.

8

I WOKE up in a straight-back chair parked a few feet away from my front door. My gun was in my lap and there was a crick in my neck.

The last thing I remembered about the previous evening was dragging the chair over from the dining area and sitting down to wait out the night. I checked the locks on the front door again, but they didn't appear to have been tampered with. Of course that didn't stop me from going through the entire apartment, looking for black-eyed kids under my bed, in the closets and behind the shower curtain.

My brain felt like a Brillo Pad scraping against the inside of my skull. The aftereffects of too much booze and too much adrenaline. A double hangover.

I took a shower, got dressed, and stood next to the front door, with one hand on the butt of the Glock that was now holstered on my hip.

I looked through the peephole, then removed the locks, took a deep, steadying breath, and stepped out into the hallway.

No black-eyed kids, and no sign that they'd ever been here.

But they were real. I knew it the same way I knew that they were somehow involved with Tara Baxter's murder. I didn't have any proof; I just knew it.

And I knew they'd be back.

9

TORONTO POLICE HEADQUARTERS is located at 40 College Street. It's a postmodern pile of glass blocks and pink granite cubes with an octagonal tower and a dome roof over the elevator lobby.

I signed in at the front desk after showing the receptionist my driver's license, my private investigator's license, and my gun permit. She took my Glock, put it in a metal locker, and gave me a claim ticket like I'd just checked my coat. A bored-looking uniformed officer standing near the metal detector gave me directions to the Homicide division.

I took the elevator up to the fifth floor and strolled into a bullpen that looked like something out of a *Barney Miller* rerun. Detective Drake didn't have an office, just a desk, one of four pushed together in one of the room's back corners.

There was a young woman sitting at one of the desks. Her eyes were puffy and red, and she had a determined, almost severe look on her face. Drake was sitting on the edge of the same desk with his arms crossed. He noticed me across the room and motioned me over.

"Mr. Renn," he said. "Thank you for coming by. You want a cup of coffee?"

I shook my head.

"This is Allison Baxter," Drake said, nodding at the woman. "Tara Baxter's sister."

I knew who she was without the introduction. Allison Baxter looked almost identical to her sister, plus about five years, and minus the haunted stare. She had the same long face and dark eyes, but her chestnut hair was cut shorter than her sister's, the tips curving inward along the edge of her jawline.

"I'm very sorry for your loss, Ms. Baxter."

I shook her hand. Her grip was cold and stiff, like shaking hands with a statue. For some reason that made me think of the Venus de Milo, who didn't have arms, much less a hand to shake, and that in turn made me think of Tara Baxter, who had arms, but was missing the lower half of her body.

I was worried this flurry of nonsensical thoughts might have showed on my face, but if they did, Allison Baxter didn't seem to notice.

"You're a detective, too?" she asked.

"Private," I said. "My name is Felix Renn."

While it was clear that Allison Baxter had been crying, I could tell she was done, at least for now. Her cheeks were blotchy and her voice was a bit watery, but there was a sharpness in her eyes that I didn't usually see on the faces of those left devastated by grief. It was the look of someone who had suffered a terrible loss, but still wanted answers, no matter what they might be or what it took to get them.

"You knew my sister," she said. It wasn't a question.

"Yes," I said. "I was hired to watch her by a man who claimed to be her husband."

"Her husband? But Tara wasn't married. She didn't even have a boyfriend."

"Can you think of anyone who might have wanted to harm her?" I glanced over at Drake, to see if I was stepping on his toes, but if I was, he didn't seem to care.

"No," Allison said. "You said you were hired you to watch her?"

"Yes."

"Detective Drake said she was killed in her apartment."

"That's right."

"So where were you?"

She didn't say it in an accusatory way; she just wanted an answer.

I wish I could have given her one.

10

AFTER GIVING DRAKE MY STATEMENT, along with a description of "Barry Clarke," I went over to my office.

Wonder of wonders, Sandra, my ex-wife and current assistant, was at her desk in the outer office. She was holding a paper cup of coffee in one hand, while using the other to scroll through the latest gossip on TMZ.com.

"What's the good word, Dee?"

"That guy who played Batman is getting up to dickens again."

"I meant is there anything going on in the detective biz?"

"Batman's a detective," she said without missing a beat.

I sighed. "Okay, what's he up to now? More verbal abuse directed at a crew member?"

"Nope, this time he reamed out another actor. Apparently, she kept stepping on his bat cape."

"That's why I stopped wearing mine." I started toward the door to the inner office, then stopped. "Can you pull the file on the walk-in from the other day? The guy who wanted his wife followed?"

Sandra made a derisive sound. "You mean Barry Manilow?"

My jaw dropped. "You knew?"

"What, that a guy named Barry wanted you to keep an eye on a woman named Mandy? Yeah, I figured that one out all by myself." She rolled her eyes at me and turned back to the screen.

"You didn't say anything to me." I tried to keep the exasperation out of my voice, but Sandra had a way of bringing it out in me.

"I thought it was obvious," she said with a shrug. "Besides, most of the people who come in here don't give us their real names. What's the big deal?"

"Mandy was murdered last night, half of her body is currently missing, and the guy who claimed to be her husband might be the one responsible."

Sandra turned her head very slowly and stared at me with a slack expression. The cup of coffee trembled slightly in her hand.

"What is it?" I asked.

"Barry Manilow," she said in a small voice. "He came in about ten minutes ago. He's waiting in your office."

11

I TOOK out my gun and Sandra threw up her hands.

"That's it," she said. "I'm out of here." She picked up her purse and keys and darted around me to the door.

"That's probably a good idea," I said. "Why don't you take the rest of the day off?"

"The day?" She scoffed. "I'm taking the week, Felix. See you next Monday."

After she left, I went over to the inner-office door and stared at the pane of glass with my name on it. The glass was pebbled so I couldn't see anything on the other side. I had never knocked on my office door before, and I wasn't about to start now.

I should have called the cops, but I wanted to hear his side of things first. Call it client privilege, or just plain old curiosity.

I turned the knob with my free hand, nudged it open with my foot, and followed my gun inside.

The man I knew as Barry Clarke was sitting in the client chair in front of my desk. His back was to me, and he craned his head around at the sound of the squeaking door hinges. I looked into the face that I had just described to the police: thin blond hair, smooth cheeks, and soft brown eyes that widened when he saw the gun in my hand.

"Mr. Renn?" He started to rise out of his seat. "Your secretary told me it was okay to wait in here."

I kicked the door closed behind me and moved around Barry to my chair, keeping the gun on him the whole time.

"That secretary is my ex-wife," I said. "You know, the way you said Mandy was your ex-wife."

I sat down, propping the gun butt on the edge of the desk. I gestured for Barry to take a seat. His shoulders slumped and he sat back down.

"I lied to you," Barry said, lowering his head guiltily.

"I already know that," I said. "Skip ahead to the why."

"I was afraid."

"Not good enough. Let's try an easy one: what's your real name?"

"Nathan," he said. "Nathan Brossard."

"May I see some identification?"

He raised his head and gave me a sceptical look. I wagged the gun at him to show him that I was serious. He reached into his back pocket and took out a battered wallet. He opened it and turned it around to show me his driver's license. Nathan L. Brossard, it said, with an address on Keele Street. I nodded.

"You want a DNA test, too?" he asked, a little testily.

"I might, if you keep lying to me."

Nathan Brossard, a.k.a. Barry Clarke, lowered his head again and muttered, "I really was afraid. That's the truth."

The funny thing was, I believed him. I put the gun down on the desk and leaned back in my chair, crossing my arms.

"Tell me a story," I said, "and make sure it includes the reason why a young woman was murdered in her own apartment, why half her body is missing, and what all of this has to do with a couple of spooky black-eyed kids."

Nathan's head jerked up. "You've seen them?"

"Twice so far. Once at Tara Baxter's building, and again at my own. I've got a feeling they aren't collecting for UNICEF."

"They killed her, didn't they?"

It wasn't quite a question, but I could tell from the desperate look in his eyes that he was looking for confirmation.

"Somebody did," I said.

"Oh, Jesus." He clutched his head with both hands. "Oh, Christ."

"Get religious on your own time. Right now, I want answers. Who the hell are you and why did you come to me?"

I could see my words weren't getting through to him. His eyes were glassy and his lips were moving silently like he was talking to himself. I opened my bottom drawer and took out the bottle of Glen Breton I kept there for both medicinal and recreational purposes. I placed two glasses on my desk and poured a medicinal shot for Nathan and a recreational shot for myself. I pushed one glass toward him. Nathan stared at it dumbly. I told him to drink and he picked up the glass and slung it back in a single swallow. He let out a loud gasp before slamming the glass back down. I refilled it and took a sip from my own.

"Feel better?"

"No," he croaked.

"At least you're answering my questions now," I said. "So talk."

Nathan picked up his drink and downed half of it. He gritted his teeth and blew air out between them. I took another small sip and waited.

"We were hunters," Nathan said.

"Who's 'we'?"

"Me, Tara, and four others. They're all dead now."

"What kind of hunters?" I asked, even though I already had a pretty good idea.

"Monsters," Nathan said. "We hunted monsters."

"Any particular kind?"

Nathan shrugged. "Monsters are monsters." The sad look in his eyes was being slowly replaced by a kind of low-burning intensity. "We didn't make exceptions. We hunted them all. We put down every single one we could find."

"Any particular reason?"

He gave me a confused look.

"Was this a hobby?" I said. "Because forming a volleyball team would have been a hell of a lot safer."

"It wasn't a hobby," Nathan said, offended. "This was our *duty*. The Paranormal Intelligence Agency can't seem to handle the job, so we took it upon ourselves."

"Not to defend the PIA, but are you honestly going to tell me that a government agency with twenty thousand employees and field offices across Canada and the U.S. isn't doing enough to protect people from supernatural entities, but you and five of your friends are?"

Nathan frowned. "Maybe not on a grand scale, but we were doing our part."

"I won't argue that. You certainly seem to have gotten someone's attention. Or some*thing's*." I tried not to say that last part in an ominous tone, but it was hard not to.

"Whatever these things are, they've been taking us out one by one. Tara and I were the only ones left when I came to you for help. And now she..." The rest of his words were lost in a choked sob.

"Why me?" I asked, although I was pretty sure I already knew the answer.

"I read about you in the newspapers last year," Nathan said. "You're some sort of supernatural PI."

"I don't seek out that type of work. It just has a habit of finding me."

Nathan raised his hands as if to say, *Well, there you go.* I guess I walked right into that one.

"I didn't know what else to do," he said. "I was desperate."

"Why not go to the PIA?"

"Are you kidding?" Nathan said. "Go and ask for help from the pigs who put us in this situation in the first place?"

"The PIA didn't create the Black Lands."

"No, but they haven't done anything about it. They put up fences around the portals, they run gunboats in the Bermuda Triangle, and for what? Every year more people go missing or are killed outright by supernaturals. When is it going to stop?"

His words had the ring of a practiced speech, and I wasn't about to be pulled into a debate on government interdimensional policy, so I turned the conversation back to the matter at hand.

"Why didn't you tell me the truth when you first came to see me? Why didn't you tell me about these black-eyed kids?" Nathan opened his mouth and I raised a hand, stopping him before he could speak. "And don't insult my intelligence by saying that you didn't think I'd believe you. Not after you just told me the reason you came to me in the first place was because I'm a so-called 'supernatural PI.'"

Nathan looked down at the half-full glass of scotch on the desk in front of him. He started to reach for it, and then pulled his hand back. With his eyes still lowered, he said, "I didn't think you would help me."

"What?" I sat up straighter in my chair. "Why wouldn't I help you?"

Nathan shrugged. "Because I figured you only did this sort of thing for money. You know, like a job." He put emphasis on that last word, like it was dirty. "I gave you all the cash I had to watch Tara. I thought if these things did go after her, you'd protect her. But it didn't make any difference."

I didn't feel good about what had happened to Tara Baxter, but it wasn't until that moment that I felt truly guilty about it. Nathan didn't do it on purpose, but he had found the chink in my armour. Because he was right. I only helped people for money. It was my job. I like to think I would have helped Tara anyway, but it didn't matter now. She was dead either way.

"Were you and Tara close?" I asked.

Nathan sniffled and wiped his eyes. "As close as I was to the others on the team. I guess I loved her a little bit, but it wasn't a romantic sort of thing. We fought together, put our lives in each other's hands." He shrugged. "After the others were killed, I wanted to do everything I could to protect her."

"There were six of you all together?"

Nathan nodded.

"And the other four were murdered as well?"

"Yes."

"Were their bodies mutilated like Tara's?"

"Yes." He paused. "Except for Perry."

"Perry?"

"Perry Brannigan. His body was never found, but I know he's dead. He called me the night it happened. He told me they were at his door."

"The kids."

Nathan nodded. "A boy and a girl. Perry said they'd been coming to his place the past few days, trying to get him to let them in. He said he didn't know how long he'd be able to keep them out. I went to his place that night, but it was already too late. The door was wide open and there was furniture thrown all around."

"Maybe he just left town."

Nathan shook his head grimly. "These kids, or whatever the hell they are, I don't think you can get away from them that easily. They'll track you down wherever you go."

I thought of the black-eyed boy grinning at me in the lobby of my apartment building.

"You really think they're the ones responsible for the deaths of your friends?"

"Don't you?"

"They're just kids," I said, even though I didn't believe my own words.

Nathan shook his head. "That's the last thing they are."

12

"WILL YOU GO TO THE POLICE?" I asked. "And tell them the truth about Tara?"

Nathan shook his head. "They'd never believe me. Even if they did, they couldn't protect me."

"How about the PIA?"

"I told you," he said, exasperated. "They won't..."

"They'll believe you. Especially if I corroborate your story. And they're more equipped to help you than the cops."

"No one can help me," Nathan said dismally. He wrapped his hand around the glass of scotch, started to pick it up, then pushed it away and stood up. "I have to go."

I picked up the gun and pointed it at him, pinning him mid-turn.

"I could take you in myself."

Nathan stared impassively into the muzzle. "I'd be as good as dead," he said listlessly. "You might as well pull the trigger right now."

"That doesn't solve my problem. These black-eyed kids aren't just after you. They're after me now, too."

Nathan's shoulders fell. He covered his face with both hands and sobbed. "I'm sorry. I didn't mean for this to happen. I was just trying to protect my team."

I watched him cry for a while, feeling both silly and ashamed to be pointing a gun at this sad, pathetic young man. I put it down and leaned back in my chair.

"I guess this means we're in this together."

Nathan lowered his hands and looked at me with his red, tear-blotchy face. "You'll help me?"

"I'll do what I can."

"I don't have any more money."

I felt a stab of guilt. "This one's on the house," I said.

Nathan nodded. "Thank you."

"Are you sure you don't want me to talk to the PIA? I've got a couple of contacts there and I'm sure they could arrange for a STAR team to protect you. They specialize in this sort of thing."

Nathan was shaking his head before I even finished speaking. "No way," he said vehemently. "I'm not putting any more lives at risk because of me."

I hesitated, and then said, "Just so you know, I'm going to have to go to the police with this. I'm involved in a murder investigation now, and they want answers. I'll try to leave you out of it, but Allison Baxter has a right to know what really happened to her sister."

Nathan lowered his head and nodded.

"Just be careful what you say," he said. "Tell her too much and the black-eyed kids might come after her, too."

13

I ARRANGED to meet with Nathan later that evening so we could discuss our options — assuming we had any. The fate of his crew didn't exactly fill me with confidence. Neither did the fact that the address he wanted to meet at didn't match the one I'd seen on his driver's license. I told myself it might not mean anything. He could be hiding out somewhere else, trying to avoid the black-eyed kids. Or maybe he was still lying to me.

After he left, I got on the computer and Googled "black-eyed kids."

The only results I got concerned child abuse. It looked like I was going to have to do some old-fashioned sleuthing.

The first thing I did was drive back downtown to police head-quarters.

Detective Drake was still at his desk, frowning at a pair of file folders, one in each hand. He grunted without looking up to acknowledge my presence.

"I thought Robichaud was the grunter."

"Robichaud's cooling his heels. I told him to take a long lunch."

"You cracked the case already?"

"Nope, just trying to decide which one to move onto next."

"Do you get bored easily?"

Drake placed the files carefully on his desk, turned his head very slowly, and stared at me with hard, unblinking eyes.

"What did you just say?"

"I'm sorry," I said. "I'm a wise-ass. My ex-wife says it will be the death of me. And a slow, painful death, at that."

Drake seemed about to comment on that, then he shook his head and said, "Forget it. I'm not pissed at you."

I raised a questioning eyebrow.

Drake leaned back in his swivel chair. "The case is closed," he said. "At least as far as the Toronto Police is concerned. I got my orders direct from the chief. If you have any information pertaining to this case, I'm supposed to refer you to the Paranormal Intelligence Agency." He flashed me a wide, PR smile. "We're all one big, happy, law-enforcing family."

"The PIA took the case from you?"

Drake came forward in his chair and picked up the file folders again. "Yes and no. It looks like this was their case already. We just happened into the middle of it."

"How so?"

"It turns out Tara Baxter is actually the fourth person in the past week to have been killed in their home."

"The other bodies were…"

"Mutilated, yeah."

"How did the PIA get involved?"

Drake slapped the folders down on the desktop. "How the hell should I know? They didn't tell us anything. They never do. If I had to guess, I'd say whoever found the first body decided to contact the PIA instead of the cops. It happens sometimes if they find something strange or scary enough. That's likely what happened here, so the PIA was already on the lookout for similar cases. It was probably only blind luck that we were called when Tara Baxter was murdered. Another couple of hours and the PIA would have swooped in and we wouldn't have known about that one, either."

That explained why I hadn't heard about the other murders on the news. The PIA almost never spoke openly about their cases. Or about anything else, for that matter.

"You don't seem too bitter about it," I said.

"I'm annoyed that they took the case away from me," Drake said. "But to be perfectly honest, it wouldn't surprise me in the slightest if the perp turns out to be something from the Black Lands."

"Are you saying a human isn't capable of that kind of violence?"

Drake frowned at me. "Don't be dumb, Felix. People are capable of anything. If they weren't, I'd be working in a flower shop. The problem I have with this case is that a woman was murdered in a high-rise apartment building, her body mutilated, and no one saw or heard a thing — including the P.I. hired to watch her. There have been plenty of serial killers who mutilated their victims, but in almost every instance they left a mess behind. Cutting up a human body can be done neatly, but only if it's planned out ahead of time."

"Or if you're Dexter," I muttered.

"I can't speak for these other murders, but whoever did Tara Baxter didn't have the time to set up a clean room in her apartment, bisect her without her struggling, and then depart with the lower half of her body. Never mind do all that without any witnesses." He shook his head. "I just don't buy it."

"So, you think it was something supernatural."

Drake spread his hands. "It sounds like a cop out, but I do. This is a brave new world, Felix. We're not just dealing with the human animal anymore. There's a whole bunch of other animals roaming around now. It's a veritable zoo out there. Vampires, werewolves, and a slew of other things we haven't even got names for yet. The PIA is convinced that Tara Baxter and those others were killed by a monster, and I'm inclined to agree." He sighed heavily. "I like a good mystery, but if the PIA wants this case, then I say they can have it. I'll go back to hunting the normal human murderers."

I couldn't think of anything to say to that, so I thanked the detective for his time and turned to leave. When I was halfway across the bullpen, Drake said: "A man's got to know his limitations, Felix."

"Who said that? Buddha?"

Drake shook his head. "Clint Eastwood."

14

I USED to know a PIA agent in the Toronto field office named Keel, but he had been transferred to Florida last Christmas. I'd met a few other agents, as well as a couple of PIA scientists, but I didn't know any of them well enough to ask for a favour.

Unfortunately, I didn't have a lot of options.

I placed a call to the PIA's "supernatural watch" line. It's a toll-free number reserved for tips on paranormal activity, sightings of Black Lands entities, etc. I asked the female operator if she could put me through to Dr. Kovac in the Toronto field office. There was a pause, then she asked for my name. I gave it to her and she put me on hold. She came back a few moments later and said she was transferring my call. There was a click, followed by a single buzzy ring, then a voice that was vaguely familiar.

"Kovac here."

"Felix here," I said. "Felix Renn, Dr. Kovac. Do you remember me?"

There was a short silence, and then Kovac said, "The ash angels. How can I forget? Thanks to you I spent New Year's Eve in Level Five quarantine at the Spire."

"Did you make any resolutions against taking calls from desperate private investigators?"

"Clearly not," Kovac said. "And quarantine wasn't all bad. I was able to catch up on my reading. My wife gave me the new Jonathan Franzen novel for Christmas. Under normal conditions it would have taken me months to finish it. Two days in quarantine and I was done."

"At least something good came out of it."

"For me, sure. But there are some others here who are still howling for your blood for ruining their holiday."

"I didn't think the PIA took holidays."

"It's true, we never sleep. Just like you private dicks." Kovac let out a tired sigh. "As much as I appreciate this exercise in witty repartee, I've got some werewolf blood cultures that aren't going to analyze themselves."

"I know you don't owe me anything, Doctor, but I need your help."

"What sort of help?"

"Of the life and death variety. Four people are already dead, and two more will be in the near future. One of them is me."

"What is it you think I can do?"

"I know the PIA recently took over a homicide investigation. The victim was a woman killed in her apartment. Her body was chopped in half. Can you tell me if you're working on this case?"

Kovac paused. "If I was, you know I wouldn't be able to tell you anything about it."

"What if I had information that could help you?"

"What information could you possibly have, Mr. Renn?" Kovac sounded dubious.

"What if I told you this case had something to do with a couple of kids?"

"Kids?"

"Yeah," I said. "A boy and a girl straight out of *The Village of the Damned*."

"Are you saying these children possess psionic abilities?"

"Not that I'm aware of, but there's definitely something freaky about them. They've got black eyes."

"Black eyes?"

"Yeah," I said, "completely black, and when I—"

Kovac cut me off. "How soon can you get here, Mr. Renn?"

15

THE PIA'S Toronto field office was located on the same block as Toronto Police headquarters. There were also buildings for other police and government agencies — RCMP, CSIS, Revenue Canada. The entire area was like one big shopping mall where the only thing for sale was red tape.

The address Kovac gave me was a modest five-storey building with glass windows that once reflected the slate-grey waters of Lake Ontario, but now showed a mirror image of the condominium that was presently blocking the view.

I passed through the automatic doors into a small reception area. A woman seated behind a metallic-blue countertop smiled at me with polite interest. I told her who I was and who I was here to see, and she gestured to the elevator that waited at the end of a short hallway.

As I stepped inside and the doors whispered shut, I reflected that the receptionist hadn't asked me to sign in or even hand over my gun. I couldn't decide if that was oddly trusting or just plain odd.

My gaze drifted over to the elevator's control panel. It had too many buttons on it for a five-storey building. I looked closer and saw it didn't even have buttons for those five floors. All of the numbers on the panel had an S before them. This elevator only went down, it seemed, and to a maximum of twelve sub-levels.

At the same moment that I realized Kovac hadn't told me what floor he was on, the elevator began to descend. I took this opportunity to examine the control panel further and saw they weren't buttons at all but simply circles of plastic that lit up as the car passed each floor. If there was a way to manually select where you wanted to get off, I couldn't figure it out.

The elevator stopped on sub-level seven. The doors slid open and Dr. Kovac was there waiting for me.

I sort of recognized him, even though the last time I'd seen him he was wearing a hazmat suit. He was a short, stocky man with grey hair receding from a perpetually furrowed brow. Today he was wearing a white lab coat over grey work pants, a light blue shirt and a dark blue tie. Both shirt and tie were dusted with a white powder that might have been chalk.

"Felix Renn." Kovac's hand popped up like the flag on a mailbox.

I stepped out of the elevator and shook it. "Thank you for agreeing to meet with me."

He led me down a long hall, made two turns at branching corridors, then held open a glass door into a wide, spacious laboratory. Every square inch of table space was taken up by scientific equipment that looked both complicated and expensive. I made a mental note to touch nothing.

Kovac parked himself on a stool in front of a workstation that had a small space cleared on it. Sitting in the middle of this bare spot was a cardboard box of powdered donuts. The cellophane was peeled back to reveal one partially denuded row, and I realized where the stains on Kovac's shirt and tie had come from.

Kovac picked up the box and offered it to me. "Try one. They're new."

I plucked a donut out of the tray and popped it into my mouth. It tasted like a gooey ball of sugar with a faint hint of donut. "Mmm," I said.

Kovac nodded approvingly. "We don't even know what they are. We found them in the Black Lands."

I stopped chewing. I would have spit out the entire mess if I didn't see the corners of Kovac's mouth turn up in a wicked little grin.

"PIA humour?" I said in a gloppy voice.

"The popular misconception is that the PIA has no sense of humour. The truth is we do, but once people discover it, they wish we didn't."

"I wonder why," I said, swallowing thickly.

IAN ROGERS

Kovac crossed one leg over the other, folded his hands and propped them on top of his knee. "Now," he said, "I understand you're having a problem with the BEKs."

"BEKs?"

"The black-eyed kids."

"The PIA really likes their acronyms, huh?"

Kovac gave a small shrug. "It's what we do in our spare time. We've got to spend those taxpayers' dollars on something."

"So you've heard of them."

"I have."

"Why haven't I?"

A small frown creased Kovac's face. "The BEKs are not what you'd call a natural phenomenon of the supernatural. If you follow me."

"I don't."

"Let me try to explain it another way. Most people have a basic knowledge of the Black Lands — the stuff they learned in school — and as such they are only familiar with the basic entities: vampires, werecreatures, possessors, what have you. They don't see the bigger picture."

"Which is?"

"The Black Lands are vast. Conspiracy theorists would have you believe the PIA has explored the entire dimension, but that simply isn't true. It's not even close to true!" Kovac threw his head back and let out a rusty laugh. "We've managed to map out a substantial section of the Black Lands, but most of it is largely unexplored. And even though we've catalogued dozens of different species, there are dozens, probably hundreds, more waiting to be discovered. Between those we know about and those we don't are the black-eyed kids. A veritable supernatural anomaly."

"What does that mean?"

"It means we know they exist, but we don't know anything about them."

Kovac must have seen the dispirited look on my face.

"Well, I shouldn't say we don't know *anything*." Before I could perk up, he added, "Just nothing useful."

114

"So, you've encountered them before," I said.

"Yeees," he said reluctantly

"I'll take any advice you can give me."

"Tell me about your encounter first."

So I did.

Kovac leaned forward and listened intently while I recounted my story. He watched me with avid eyes and nodded his head at several points during my narrative. It was hard to tell if he was sympathetic to my plight or merely fascinated by it. When I was finished, I asked him what he made of it.

"I think the most unusual part of your story," Kovac said, "is that you were hired by a man named Barry to keep an eye on a woman named Mandy, and you never figured out they were using false names."

"That fact has been firmly established," I said curtly. "Moving on."

Kovac remained silent for a long time. His face was impassive. I couldn't tell if he was deep in thought or if he had fallen asleep with his eyes open.

Finally, he said, "Have you ever heard of Mothman?"

"He sounds like a superhero who wasn't cool enough to make it into the Justice League."

"Mothman was the name given to an entity sighted in Point Pleasant, West Virginia, in the late 1960s. It was described as a humanoid with hypnotic red eyes and enormous wings. One of the most prominent details of the case was Mothman's ability to instil an intense, paralyzing fear in those who encountered it."

I closed my eyes and saw the black-eyed kids standing outside my car door, tapping on the window.

"Most supernatural entities have that effect on people."

"Agreed," Kovac said. "But this case was different. Mothman gave off fear the way a cracked nuclear reactor gives off radiation. By the time things came to a head in Point Pleasant, hundreds of people had seen Mothman and the town was awash in fear and paranoia."

"Did you work on that case?" I asked.

Kovac shook his head. "It was before my time."

"What does this have to do with the black-eyed kids?"

"The people in Point Pleasant weren't just seeing Mothman. Over a year-long period, all manner of paranormal phenomena were reported. UFOs, poltergeist activity, ball lightning, EVP, premonitions, lost time... and Men in Black."

"Men in Black?"

Kovac spread his hands. "Some of those reports were undoubtedly about us. The PIA sent six agents to Point Pleasant in the fall of 1966. They investigated for two months, but they never saw Mothman. They saw something else, though."

"Black-eyed kids."

"Six agents went to Point Pleasant, Mr. Renn, but only five returned. The one who didn't was a man named Trent Lonigan. I've read his file. In fact, you could say I'm somewhat of an authority on the entire Mothman case." Kovac grinned a bit self-consciously. "I did my thesis on it. That's actually how I ended up getting recruited by the PIA. Anyway, Trent Lonigan was a seasoned operative who had a long, decorated history with the agency that included a number of confirmed kills. Black Lands entities, that is."

"You think there's a connection between his service record and his disappearance?"

"I believe the appearance of the BEKs is unique. I think they only show themselves to certain people and only under very specific conditions."

"What kind of people?" I asked.

"I think you already know."

"Monster killers."

Kovac shook his head. "Monster *hunters*."

"Isn't that the same thing?"

"It would appear the black-eyed kids make a distinction."

"How so?"

"Well..." Kovac grinned in a macabre sort of way. "I think if the BEKs went after every human being who did harm to a Black Lands entity, we'd see them a bit more often than we do."

"Sightings are that rare?"

"Rare enough. Especially compared to some of the other entities we've catalogued over the past sixty years. Black-eyed kids are like the marbled murrelet of the supernatural world."

I blinked at him.

"It's a very rare bird." Kovac's eyes took on shrewd kind of look. "You're a rare bird yourself, Mr. Renn. Not many people have encountered the BEKs, and those who have aren't usually seen ever again."

"I guess I'm just lucky," I said. "Although I've got a feeling that my luck is running out."

Kovac nodded. "The last person to see Agent Lonigan alive was his partner. He said Lonigan was in the company of a small boy — a boy with black eyes. No pupils, no irises, just blackness. The agent saw him only for a second as they drove by in Lonigan's car, but he swears that's what he saw. The car was eventually discovered abandoned near the woods outside of town. Agent Lonigan was never found."

"And the black-eyed kids?"

"We've had a few scattered reports over the years, but they don't amount to much. The Mothman case was the only time the BEKs ever directly interfered with the PIA."

"What happened in Point Pleasant after that?"

Kovac gave a small shrug. "The Silver Bridge collapsed, forty-six people died, and Mothman was never seen there again."

"Do you think the black-eyed kids were responsible?"

"No, actually, I don't."

"Why not?"

"The supernatural isn't always a measurable science. Some of the cases we work, we aren't able to draw any conclusions. The best we can do is make connections. In Point Pleasant, logic seemed to dictate that since the BEKs showed up at the same time and at the same place as Mothman, then the two must be connected. But there's a third factor most people at the agency never consider."

"Agent Lonigan."

"Yes. The PIA's feeling is that Lonigan was collateral damage, nothing more. He was a bit wild, a loose cannon you could say, and the general thinking is that he paid for that with his life. My theory, on the other hand, is that Lonigan's presence in Point Pleasant attracted the BEKs. I would go one further and say the BEKs were possibly even aware of Lonigan for some time before he even went to West Virginia. I think his record of interactions with the supernatural — and especially his elimination of so many Black Lands entities — put him on a kind of BEKs watch list."

"The kids who showed up at my apartment kept asking me to let them in. Like they needed to be invited."

Kovac nodded.

"That made me think of vampires. But the first time I saw these kids was in the morning, in the daylight. So, I'm pretty damn sure they're not vampires."

"You're confusing fact and myth," Kovac said. "Vampires — real vampires — don't require an invitation to enter a dwelling. That sort of thing might work on Christopher Lee in the old Hammer films, but there's nothing stopping a real vampire from breaking down your door and tearing out your throat." He tapped his chin thoughtfully. "It's interesting to hear that the BEKs display such behaviour. I'd never heard that about them before. The BEKs are true unknowns."

"So, there's nothing I can do?"

Kovac shook his head. "I'm sorry, Mr. Renn, I truly am."

"Do you think I could get the case files on the other murder victims? Maybe there's something there that could help me."

"I'll see what I can do."

I stood up and started toward the door.

"Mr. Renn?"

I turned back.

Kovac was holding out the box of donuts. "One for the road?"

16

I STOPPED at a restaurant for an early dinner that I barely touched before heading out to Oakville.

That was where Nathan Brossard wanted to meet. I stopped at my office to Google directions to the address he had given me, and to pick up the extra clip I had for the Glock.

I took the QEW out of the city, got off on Bronte Road, and headed north. I drove past parks and golf courses until I reached Lower Baseline Road. I made a left, then a right, and suddenly I was in the woods.

Tall pine trees flanked both sides of the road, which I soon realized was a driveway. I entered a wide clearing surrounded by a twelve-foot chain-link fence topped with three rows of razor-wire. The gate was open and bobbing slightly on its wheels in the early evening breeze. A large metal sign in the centre of it said PRIVATE PROPERTY — NO TRESPASSING!

I drove in and parked on a wide patch of gravel next to an enormous black pickup truck. I got out and looked around. The sun was somewhere behind the trees, and the clearing was filled with a sombre, artificial twilight. I went over to the pickup. The chrome grille seemed to grin at me in a challenging way. I put my hand on the hood. It was cool.

Beyond the gravel drive was a long, squat cinderblock building that looked more like a bunker than a domicile. As I walked toward the front door, I became aware of a low humming sound, like high-tension power lines.

The door was made of steel and looked like a hatch on a submarine. I knocked on it and heard the echo on the other side, resounding like distant thunder.

I tried the handle. It was unlocked, so I pulled the door open and stepped inside.

I stood in a small foyer with rooms branching off to the left and right, and a long dark hallway straight ahead. There was light coming from the room on the left, so I decided to start there.

I entered a long, low-ceilinged room that looked like a cross between a library and a hunter's trophy room.

The walls were crowded with mounted animal heads: deer and moose, mostly, a couple of wolves, and one snarling cougar. The hardwood floor glowed mellowly in the light of half a dozen reading lamps scattered around the room. The furniture was overstuffed chairs and hulking leather couches that looked as if they were about to burst at their seams like overcooked sausages.

A room for rich old men to sit around in their tweeds and smoke pipes as they bragged about their stocks and lied about their golf game.

I went over to inspect the fieldstone fireplace on the far side of the room, fairly certain that I didn't see a chimney on the roof of the building. I crouched down to examine the logs, and sure enough there was a brown electrical cord trailing out from behind them. I picked up the plug, stuck it in the nearby wall outlet, and the logs gave off a rich red glow.

To the right of the fireplace was an archway that led into a luxurious dining room. There was a long cherrywood table surrounded by a dozen chairs. A breakfront filled with china. A sideboard with a silver coffee service on it. Hunting prints on the walls.

I passed through the dining room to a kitchen with a stainless-steel refrigerator and a six-burner stove. On the far side of the kitchen, a door opened to another hallway that led to the biggest room yet. It was long and wide and there was a heavy steel door at the far end. In the middle of the room, on the left side, a short run of stairs led down to a set of double doors. A sign next to the doors said ABSOLUTELY NO ADMITTANCE WHEN RED LIGHT IS ON!

I went down a few steps and saw a red lightbulb in a mesh cage mounted on the wall next to the sign. It was turned on.

I went back up the stairs to check out the steel door on the far side of the room. I gripped the handle with both hands and pulled. The door swung slowly, ponderously open. I reached a hand inside and pawed around until I found a light switch.

Fluorescent lights fizzled to life, casting their stark illumination on a room full of guns. Rifles and shotguns mostly, lined up on racks with the muzzles pointed at the ceiling. I couldn't help but feel a bit inadequate with my little Glock holstered on my hip. I went over and pulled down a Mossberg 12-gauge shotgun, raised it to my shoulder, and took aim at the far wall where a variety of different handguns hung on a piece of pegboard.

Nathan Brossard and his band of merry monster hunters had quite the set-up here. A clubhouse in the woods, complete with an armoury, a kitchen, a dining room, and a lounge for relaxing after a long day in the killing fields.

I put the shotgun back and returned to the stairs.

I took out my gun and started down.

17

I KNOCKED FIRST. Give me that much credit.

"Nathan?" I called out. "Are you in there? It's Felix!"

With my free hand I turned the latch on one of the doors and pulled it open.

It was dark inside, and the hum that I had mostly forgotten about was much louder. The only light came from the screensavers of the three computers on the counter in front of me. Flocks of Canadian geese flew back and forth in chevron shapes across their screens.

I tried to find a light switch, but no joy. I blinked my eyes until they started to adjust to the darkness.

I was in some sort of control booth. The glass walls had that slightly milky quality that said they were shatterproof. On the right side, another one of those steel hatchlike doors led into a large chamber. It was dark in there, too, except for a pair of ceiling-mounted spotlights that shined their beams on a dais in the centre of the room. I stepped around the computers so I could get a better look through the glass. Standing on the dais was a door.

A Black Door.

I'd seen one before, although that one had been an actual door with a knob to open it. This one was purely functional, nothing more than a wooden frame with a thick, insulated power cable running out of it to a generator in the corner.

Despite that, it was still highly illegal and highly dangerous.

I could see through the doorframe to the wall on the far side of the chamber. But looks could be deceiving. I knew that if I walked through that door, I wouldn't come out on the other side. I'd end up in the Black Lands. The red light outside the control booth was on, and that probably meant the door was currently active.

I returned to the bank of computers and tried to find a way to turn off the door. I'd never been good with technology, and I wasn't having any sudden inspirations as I looked at the buttons, switches and read-outs. The last time I encountered a Black Door, I emptied my gun into its power source. I figured if it worked once, then it would work again, and started toward the steel door leading into the chamber.

Then I saw the note.

It was written on a yellow legal pad that had been left on the end of the counter. It said: *I'm sorry. I'm a coward. Please forgive me.*

I looked up from the note to the Black Door.

That stupid son of a bitch.

Nathan had chickened out and committed suicide in a way he probably thought was poetic justice. He had crossed over to the Black Lands to let himself be torn to pieces by the very creatures he had hunted.

I didn't have time to mourn him, and I wouldn't have even if I did. Nathan had lied to me from the beginning and inadvertently set a pair of supernatural entities on me that were responsible for the death of his entire crew.

With Nathan gone, there was no one left to help me. I was alone.

Then something thumped against the glass of the control booth.

18

I DIDN'T KNOW what was in the chamber, but I knew how it got there.

When Nathan Brossard went on his suicide march into the Black Lands, he left the door open behind him and something had crossed over into our world. I couldn't tell exactly what it was. All I saw was a quick blur of movement as whatever it was struck the glass again.

I thought about taking off and placing an anonymous call to the PIA. They could have a STAR team out here to deal with this thing in less than an hour.

But a lot of horrible things could come through an open Black Door in an hour.

I considered firing a few shots into the control room equipment, but there was no guarantee that would shut down the door. The only sure thing was to disable the generator in the main chamber. But there was no way I was going in there with that thing skulking around in the shadows.

I sat down in front of one of the computers. There had to be a way of turning the door off from here. I put my hand on the mouse and the screensaver disappeared. A pop-up window asked me for a password. I went over to the other two computers and they gave me the same spiel. So much for that.

Something struck the glass directly in front of me. As I watched, it shot forward and hit it again.

The noise didn't bother me too much. I was almost getting used to it. It was in the crack in the glass that worried me.

I pointed my gun at the spot where the thing was busting through. In the shadows on the other side of the glass, I could just make out the generator in the far corner. I'd have to take care of the thing in the chamber before I could shut down the door. If it was a vampire or a werecreature, I was screwed. I didn't bring any wooden stakes or silver bullets, and even if the sun hadn't already set by now, it wouldn't do me much good down here. Even if this was one of the entities that were vulnerable to ordinary firearms, I didn't know if my Glock would be enough to take it out.

Then I remembered the armoury.

The thing struck again, punching a fist-sized hole in the glass. Something thin and black darted inside and wrapped itself around the computer monitor I had just been sitting at. It jerked the monitor back toward the hole, but it was too big to fit through. It pulled and pulled, sending cracks through the rest of the glass. Finally, it let go and the monitor toppled to the floor.

Another pair of those spindly, black appendages slithered into the booth. This time they wrapped themselves around the track lighting on the ceiling. As I watched, they tightened and strained, and the main body of the thing they were attached to was pulled up and through the widening hole in the glass wall.

It looked like a tree, which made sense since that's what it was. A blackwood tree. So named because of its black bark. And because it came from the Black Lands.

In addition to being one of the most prominent forms of life in that dimension, blackwood trees were also one of its top carnivores.

This one was only a sapling, but still dangerous enough. Its branches were thin but clearly capable of punching holes in shatter-proof glass. I didn't want to think about what they could do to the human body — which was to say, *my* body. I knew what it wanted to do. Unlike ordinary trees, a blackwood could pull itself out of the ground and move around on its roots. Within those roots there was a voracious, sucker-like mouth. The blackwood's preferred mode of attack was to immobilize its prey — usually by bashing it unconscious-ness with its branches — and then crawl on top of it, securing its victim to the ground with its roots. After that it was free to feed at its leisure.

Blackwoods were more like spiders than trees, which was what made them so terrifying.

I backed out of the control booth and up the stairs. I ran into the armoury and grabbed the Mossberg I'd been looking at earlier. Below the gun racks were rows of drawers. I searched until I found a box of 12-gauge shotgun shells. I loaded the Mossberg, jammed extra shells into my coat pockets, and went back out into the main room.

The blackwood tree stood at the bottom of the landing. It seemed to be scrutinizing the stairs with whatever sensory organs it possessed. It had probably never seen stairs before. I wondered if it could even climb them.

It seemed to sense my presence. Its branches began to flail like the snakes on a Gorgon's head. It moved forward on its bed of quivering roots and began to slide slowly up the stairs. It overbalanced at one point and one of its branches whipped out and wrapped itself around the railing bolted to the wall. It righted itself and continued ascending toward me.

I crouched at the top of the stairs, socked the butt of shotgun into the hollow of my shoulder, and aimed down at the approaching blackwood. I felt a momentary pang of guilt, the way I might have felt if I had been sighting down on a grizzly bear. I told myself I didn't have a choice. Maybe blackwoods were natural in the Black Lands, but over here they were a catastrophe waiting to happen. If this one got out into the world and seeded...

I racked the pump and fired.

The branch that was wrapped around the railing exploded in a spray of wooden shrapnel and a black, sap-like ichor that painted the walls. The blackwood tree wavered off balance, its roots flailing madly.

When blackwood trees are dormant and rooted to the ground, their bodies are as tough and unyielding as any ordinary tree. But when they're awake, something happens to their physiology, their bodies soften and become more malleable. Branches that were stiff and sturdy before are suddenly as sinuous as the tentacles on an octopus. During this time, blackwoods are at their most vulnerable, but they're also at their most dangerous.

I pumped another round and shot it again. The blackwood's trunk evaporated, and all that remained of the creature fell over backwards to land in a steaming, quivering pile.

Timber.

19

I WAITED until the blackwood had stopped twitching, then I reloaded the shotgun and went down the stairs.

In the control booth, I looked around and finally found a switch that turned on the rest of the lights in the main chamber. I pulled open the steel door and went in with the shotgun raised, ready to fire on anything else that might have stumbled over from the Black Lands.

The room was clear. I went around the dais, giving the Black Door a wide berth, and turned off the generator. Then I raised the shotgun and fired two rounds into the thick black cable that fed power to the door.

I dropped the shotgun on the floor and went back upstairs. I searched the rest of the building, but didn't find anything useful.

Outside, I took out my cellphone to call the PIA, and noticed the black pickup truck. I put my cell away and went over to check it out.

The doors were locked, but that was no problem. A few years back, a friend of mine in the RCMP had seen me using my Swiss Army knife to open a package. He asked to borrow it and gave it back to me a week later. At first I wasn't sure it was the same knife. The white cross logo of the Swiss Army had been replaced with the badge of the RCMP, and while the usual knives and gadgets were still there, a number of new tools had been added. I used one of them to open the door of the pickup.

I climbed behind the wheel and searched under the seats and floor mats. I pulled down the sun visors and checked the side pockets. Nothing. I saved the glove compartment for last. Inside I found an owner's manual that looked like it had never been opened, and a notepad. The masthead at the top said MCCAULEY ENGINEERING, along with a phone number, fax number, e-mail address and website.

I pocketed the notepad and hopped out of the truck. I walked around to the back and took my phone out again. I called a woman I knew at the Department of Motor Vehicles. A few years back her husband and a stewardess flew off to start a new life together in warmer climes. I couldn't stop that from happening, but I was able to track him down and made sure he paid his ex-wife for her troubles. She tried to pay me for mine, but I refused to take any money from her. Occasionally I asked her to run a plate for me, as I did now.

The pickup was registered to a Calvin McCauley, with an address on the Bridle Path. McCauley was the name on the notepad. In private investigator parlance, this was known as a clue.

I flipped through the notepad. All of the pages were blank. There was good money in engineering. Good enough that one could afford to live in Toronto's most affluent neighbourhood. Prince was supposed to have a house on the Bridle Path. I wondered if McCauley knew him.

I thought maybe I should go over and ask him.

20

I CALLED the PIA on my way back to the city. I was planning to make an anonymous call, but the moment I punched in their 1-800 number, I was immediately re-routed and a familiar voice came on the line.

"Felix? Is that you?"

Gotta love that Big Brother.

"Agent Enfield," I said. "So nice to hear your voice."

"Save it, Felix. I've spoken to Kovac."

"Did he offer you a donut?"

"What?"

"I don't have time to talk, Enfield. I'm in the middle of something big. I'll tell you all about it when it's over. If I'm still around."

"What are you talking about?" Enfield said. "Felix, I want you to come into the office. Right *now*."

"Can't do it. I have to make a house call."

"House call? Whose house?"

"That's for me to know and you to find out. Eventually. Later. Maybe."

"If you don't come in right this minute, I'm going to put out a warrant for your arrest. You'll have every cop in the city looking for you."

"I suppose it's good to be wanted. But truthfully, Agent Enfield, I think your efforts are better applied elsewhere. There's a compound in the woods north of Oakville that deserves your special attention."

"You're not going to sidetrack me with any of your —"

"There's a Black Door in the basement."

Enfield was silent. I'd said the magic word.

"Is it… active?" His voice was a tense whisper.

"It was. I put it out of commission with a little shotgun surgery."

"Is the door still intact?"

"It was when I left."

"Where are you going now?"

"I can't tell you that."

Enfield started to argue and I said, "I left you the remains of a blackwood tree. Something for Kovac and the rest of the white coats to poke and prod and write classified scientific papers about."

"You killed a blackwood tree?" Enfield sounded surprised, maybe even a little impressed, but I was probably imagining that part. "Did it get outside?"

"Negative," I said.

Enfield let out a sigh of relief. "Thank Christ for small favours." He cleared his throat and resumed his cool, official tone. "Where is this place?"

I gave him the address and broke the connection on his next question. I figured if I could Google the directions, then so could he.

21

MCCAULEY LIVED in a mansion on a street lined with them. I parked a short distance from his house and climbed out of my car. I felt a bit insecure leaving it there on the street. Like someone was going to come along and ticket it for not being a Mercedes or a Beamer.

Most of the mansions were enclosed by high stone walls with gates at the front entrances. Strangely, most of the gates were wide open. McCauley's was one of them.

I walked up the asphalt drive and knocked on an enormous slab of wood that rich people called a door and everyone else called deforestation.

A few moments later, the door was opened by an old man with

stooped shoulders and large, blocky hands that still looked capable of hard work. He was wearing black trousers, a black suit-jacket and a white Oxford shirt buttoned up to his wattled neck. He bore the stolid, slightly bored expression of one who has never been surprised by anything in life. I gave it my best shot.

"Good evening. My name is Felix Renn. I'm a private investigator."

The old man blinked at me patiently. If he was any calmer, he would've been dead.

"Is Mr. McCauley in?" I inquired.

"Yes." The old man's voice was low and raspy. "Are you expected?"

"No," I said, "but Mr. McCauley will want to talk to me." I gave him one of my business cards. "Tell him I've been out to the Oakville compound."

The old man took the card, holding it away from him like it was a soiled diaper, and went away, closing the door behind him.

I stood on the stoop for five minutes. Then the door opened and the old man was back, bearing the same expression of infinite calm.

"Come with me, please."

I followed him down a hallway the size of a subway tunnel, and around a bend to a set of tall wooden doors, one of which was standing open. He directed me inside, closing the door behind me as I entered.

I was in a room eerily similar to the library-trophy room at the Oakville compound. Except this one had been designed on a grander scale. The ceiling was higher and there was more of everything — more mounted animal heads, more leather furniture, more lamps. And the fireplace here was real.

I heard a creak and looked over to see a tall silver-haired man in a burgundy smoking jacket rising from a chair that looked like an enormous catcher's mitt. It was the same colour as the man's jacket, which was why I hadn't noticed him when I first came in. Rich person's camouflage.

When Nathan Brossard told me he and a bunch of his friends hunted supernatural creatures, I didn't bat an eye. It wasn't a common occurrence, but there were people who did it. After I saw their Oakville digs, I realized this wasn't just some group of kids with a hate-on for supernaturals. They had guns, property and their very own Black Door. That meant they were organized. It also meant they had money. As McCauley approached me with his hand extended, I had a feeling I was about to meet their benefactor.

22

I SHOOK HIS HAND. "Felix Renn. Nice to meet you."

"The pleasure is all mine," he said, and seemed to mean it. "I'm Richard McCauley."

My hand froze in mid-shake. "Richard?"

"That's right." McCauley said, grinning broadly. "My friends call me Rich. My enemies call me *that rich bastard.*"

He chuckled while I smiled politely, momentarily at a loss for words.

"This is a most unexpected visit," McCauley said.

More unexpected by the minute, I thought.

"Won't you please have a seat?" He swept his hand at the forty-seven different pieces of leather furniture in the room. I lowered myself into a wingback chair that made me feel like I was on *Masterpiece Theatre.*

"Can I get you a drink?" He picked up a lowball glass and waggled it at me in case I didn't know what a drink was.

"Whatever you're having," I said, a bit distractedly. I was still trying to get past the curve ball he had unknowingly thrown at me. Maybe I should have been sitting in the catcher's mitt chair.

McCauley went over to the side bar and poured me a drink from a crystal decanter. He freshened his own and brought both glasses over. He handed one to me. "To the end of dark days," he toasted.

We clinked glasses and I took a small sip. Bourbon.

"I knew you and I were kindred spirits." McCauley dropped back into his chair, slinging one of his legs over the arm.

"You seem to have me at a disadvantage, Mr. McCauley."

"Please, call me Rich."

"Thank you." I took another sip of my drink. "I'm just a bit surprised that you know who I am."

"I saw you on the news last summer," McCauley said. His grin turned sly and knowing. "You were involved in an incident — a series of incidents, actually — in which you killed a vampire and a werewolf."

"I'm not really permitted to talk about it. The PIA doesn't like it." I injected what I hoped was the right amount of derision into my voice. "The case is still classified." I didn't know if that was true; I just didn't want to discuss it.

"Of course," McCauley said. "We wouldn't want to anger the feds." He sat up straight and leaned toward me. "But tell me, what did it feel like to kill those monsters?"

"They weren't real monsters," I said. "They were just ordinary people under the influence of an experimental drug."

"A drug that turns people into monsters?" McCauley's eyes widened.

"Fascinating." He shook his head as if to clear it. "Well, monsters are monsters in my book. They should all be put down like the aberrations they are. I know a hunter like yourself must feel the same way."

"I don't really hunt them," I said. "They just seem to... find me."

McCauley nodded. "They're drawn to you. Like moths to flame. Too stupid to know how dangerous it is until it burns them."

"That's one way of looking at it," I said.

"That's what they are," McCauley said. "They're insects." His eyes glazed over as he became lost in his simile. "Interested only in devouring everything in sight and multiplying until there's nothing left in this world but them." His eyes cleared and he gave me a shrewd look. "You're telling me you felt nothing when you killed those monsters?"

I looked down at my glass and manufactured a smug grin.

"Well, I suppose that's not entirely true," I said. "That's just what I told the feds and the press. You can't tell them the truth. They wouldn't understand."

McCauley nodded for me to go on.

"The truth is, it felt great putting down those freaks. Staking that vampire and pumping silver bullets into that werewolf..." I stared off longingly. "It was like correcting some horrible wrong in nature."

"They call them supernatural," McCauley said, "but there's nothing super about them. Unnatural is more like it. Their world doesn't even have a sun!" he added, as if this was the greatest insult of all.

"Speaking of which," I said, "I understand you have a son of your own."

"Yes, Calvin." McCauley smiled fondly. "The boy genius. He would have made his mother proud. I wish I could have taken her to Arrow Road."

"Arrow Road?"

"The Oakville preserve." A tinge of doubt came into McCauley's eyes. "I thought you said you'd been there."

My mind raced. "I haven't, actually. But I've heard of the place. Rumours mostly. I heard you were the man to talk to about it. That's why I came to see you."

McCauley ran a finger thoughtfully along the rim of his glass. "It's a very exclusive club," he said. "With a very secretive clientele. As I'm sure you can appreciate."

"Of course," I said. "The PIA doesn't look too kindly on citizens taking supernatural matters into their own hands."

"Indeed. And yet they've left us with little choice. These godless creatures don't belong in our world. Their coming here was a mistake. It's no coincidence that these portals didn't start showing up until the 1940s." He thumped his index finger on the arm of his chair. "At the exact same time we were lighting off nukes in the South Pacific."

I nodded. I knew where this was going.

"We thought splitting the atom was some great achievement, something to be proud of." McCauley snorted with disgust. "It turns out all we really did was punch a hole between our world and the Black Lands; several holes, in fact, with more showing up every year. And now there's no going back."

It was an interesting theory, but one I'd heard before. There were dozens of conspiracy theories about the origin of the Black Lands. I'd heard other people blame solar flares, global warming, the decline of Christian values and even women's suffrage.

"So, have you killed any monsters yourself?" I said, changing the subject.

"Oh yes," McCauley said. "Many times." His eyes took on a faraway look. "I've tracked and slain so many monsters I consider myself something of an expert on them." He focused back on me. "I have no trophies, unfortunately. What do the treehuggers say? Take only memories, leave only corpses." He chuckled amusedly to himself. "Vampires turn to dust, werewolves revert back to human form. Maybe it's for the best. After all, we don't want to draw any unwanted attention to ourselves."

"I understand the club has its own Black Door."

"Of course." McCauley shrugged his shoulders like it was no big deal. "We have to go to the monsters, Felix. We don't have the luxury of having them come to us." He dropped me a sly wink and slugged back the rest of his drink.

"You offer a very unique service, Mr. McCau... Rich. You must charge a fortune to let people hunt on your preserve."

"It wouldn't be a club if we let just anyone come out to Arrow Road." He cleared his throat and his voice took on a more businesslike tone. "Our membership dues are considerable, but most of it goes toward operational costs. You don't know the amount of work that goes into constructing, powering and maintaining an unlicensed portal."

"I can imagine," I said, and downed the rest of my drink.

"I know why you're here."

I was reaching over to put my glass down on a side table and almost dropped it.

"You do?"

"Unfortunately, I can't offer you a membership to the club, but I'd be more than happy to take you out sometime as my guest."

"That's very generous of you."

"It's the least I could do for a fellow hunter. One who's out there fighting the good fight every day."

"You mentioned your son. The boy genius. Was he the one who constructed the club's Black Door?"

McCauley nodded, a gleam of pride in his eyes. "The boy's a builder, just like his old man. When he was little, instead of playing with his toys, he'd take them apart and put them back together again. Or he'd take a bunch of them apart and use the pieces to make new toys."

"He sounds like a talented young man," I said. "I'd love to meet him."

"You will," McCauley said. "I haven't seen him for a few days, but the next time I do, I'm going to have him set up a hunt. A little safari to the Black Lands, just for you and me, Felix."

"I look forward to it."

23

AFTER I LEFT McCauley's place, I decided to play on a hunch.

I got in my car, drove down the street, turned around, drove back, and parked at the curb with a view of McCauley's front gate. Then I turned off the engine and waited.

I had deliberately asked McCauley about his son. It was a shot in the dark, but it ended up paying off. Calvin McCauley was a member of Nathan Brossard's crew. He was the one who built the Black Door, probably on his father's dime. Nathan told me that Tara was the last living member of his crew, which meant Calvin was dead. If that was true, then the PIA had yet to inform his father. He didn't appear to know anything about it. I felt sorry for McCauley. He was in for a rude awakening when he found out his son had been murdered, and he himself was going to be investigated for the construction of an illegal portal.

But if Calvin McCauley was dead, then how did his pickup truck get to Arrow Road? Was that where he made his final stand against the black-eyed kids? Or did Nathan borrow his dead friend's truck and drive it out there to commit suicide? I supposed it didn't matter. They were both dead now, anyway.

McCauley was my last living connection to this case, and I thought if he had really killed as many monsters as he claimed, then he could be expecting a visit from the black-eyed kids, as well.

I had killed monsters, too, as McCauley pointed out, but it wasn't the same thing. At least I hoped it wasn't. My life depended on it.

The black-eyed kids didn't go after everyone who ever killed a creature from the Black Lands. They seemed to focus on those who actively hunted them. Kovac said the PIA agent who went missing in Point Pleasant had killed several supernatural entities over the course of his career. Perhaps he had been more zealous in his work than his fellow agents. Maybe he even hunted monsters in his spare time. I'd never met the man, but I was willing to bet on it.

An hour passed and I started to get fidgety. At first I was just tapping my fingers on the steering wheel. Then I was turning the dial back and forth on the radio, trying to find a station I liked. Then I was counting the change I kept in the ashtray. I'd been on dozens of stake-outs, but for some reason I couldn't sit still. Looking out the window at McCauley's house, I realized what it was.

The black-eyed kids. The first time I saw them I had been sitting in my car. Now here I was, back in my car, waiting for a finger to tap against the window.

I decided to get out and stretch my legs. As I strolled along the street past McCauley's gate, I glanced at his house.

The front door was wide open.

I stood there motionless and wondered how long it had been like that. I couldn't see the front door from where I had parked my car, so it could have been minutes or almost an hour.

Maybe the elderly house man had left it open. Maybe the door didn't latch properly when he closed it behind me. Or maybe someone inside was just getting ready to leave.

I didn't believe any of these things.

I moved quickly up the drive. I had my gun out and down at my side as I reached the front door. I pushed it the rest of the way open with my free hand. I expected a haunted-house squeal of hinges, but there was only silence, which was somehow worse. *Rich people keep their hinges oiled,* I thought randomly.

I stepped inside, bringing my gun up in a two-handed grip as I went down the wide hall.

"Mr. McCauley?" I called out.

I heard a low, frantic sound in a dark room on my right side. I took one hand off the gun and pawed around on the inside wall for a light switch. I found it and an overhead light popped on to reveal a large, gleaming kitchen. The house man was down on the floor, cowering next to a refrigerator that was as big as a bank vault.

I crouched next to him and put a hand on his shoulder. He shrank away from my touch, hands raised in front of his face as if to ward off a blow. I gripped his arm and gave it a little shake. I realized I didn't know his name.

"Hey, it's me Felix. The detective."

"No, no, no." The old man shook his head vehemently. "Please, no. Please, no."

I gave him another shake, harder this time. "Was it the kids?" I demanded. "Did you let them in?"

The old man lowered his hands and I almost recoiled at the look of stark terror on his face. "They said they needed help." His hands came up again to cover his face, and I felt a pang of relief. "Their eyes! Their eyes!"

A high-pitched scream cut through the house. I felt the skin on my back tighten. I left the old man and ran back into the main hall. There was another scream, this one dragging out into a guttural growl of mingled defiance and pain. I went around the bend and saw one of the doors to McCauley's study standing open. I slowed my pace and tried to peer inside.

I could see a couple of chairs lying on their sides, but no sign of McCauley.

I crept closer with my gun raised, moving along the wall so I had a better angle on the rest of room.

I still couldn't see McCauley — but I saw the black-eyed kids. They stood close together, bent over at some task that I couldn't make out because of all the furniture that cluttered the room. A leather sofa near the kids seemed to move by itself, sliding jerkily to one side and then the other.

I moved closer and saw McCauley. He was lying sprawled on the floor, clutching the sofa like it was a life-preserver. The black-eyed girl gripped one of his legs, the black-eyed boy had the other, and together they were pulling and yanking and trying to get McCauley to let go.

I wondered where the kids were trying to take him. Then I noticed something behind them. I thought it was a window at first, but that didn't make sense. Not unless McCauley had decided to put one right in the middle of his study. As I crossed the threshold into the room, I realized it didn't look like a window at all. It was a shimmering patch of darkness, vaguely rectangular in shape, with rough edges. Like someone had taken a saw and cut a ragged hole in thin air.

I suddenly realized what it was, and at the same time I knew how the black-eyed kids had gotten into Tara Baxter's apartment, and out again, without anyone seeing them.

The black-eyed kids possessed the ability to open portals between dimensions.

That said, I'd never seen a portal like this before. Mostly because portals couldn't be seen. They were invisible. That's what made them so dangerous. This portal was different, but I had no doubt that's what it was. McCauley hunted supernaturals, and now the black-eyed kids were here to give him an all-expenses-paid trip to the Black Lands. One-way.

I didn't know if there was anything I could do to help him. I didn't know if I even wanted to. McCauley had brought this on himself. Nathan Brossard had gotten me involved and now my head was on the chopping block, too. I didn't owe these people anything. Maybe McCauley even deserved to be taken. I didn't know. But as I stood there and watched him struggling for his pathetic life, I realized I couldn't just stand there and let it happen.

I started to raise my gun, then lowered it again. There was no way I could take a shot without possibly hitting McCauley. I holstered up and started across the obstacle course of furniture to reach him.

The black-eyed kids managed to detach McCauley from the sofa and started pulling him across the floor to the portal. The boy stepped through with the leg he was holding, but the girl was having trouble with hers. McCauley had curled it up close to his body, while his flailing arms wrapped themselves around a nearby steamer trunk.

I sidestepped the fallen chairs and leapt over a coffee table that had been flipped onto its back.

The girl saw me coming fast and stopped struggling with McCauley's leg. She stepped around to his side and delivered a wicked kick to his ribs. She kicked him again and again until McCauley let go of the trunk. He let out a mournful groan as the girl picked up his leg again and resumed dragging him through the portal.

I reached McCauley and grabbed onto his outstretched arms. He stared at me with wide, pleading eyes. Tears and sweat ran down his face. "Don't let them take me!" he begged.

The girl gave a powerful yank and I gave one of my own. We were playing tug-o-war for high stakes. The girl stood half-in and half-out of the portal. She pulled again and I pulled back. Neither of us gained any ground. McCauley sobbed. The girl took one of her hands off his leg and pointed a finger at me. She was grinning.

The black-eyed kids may have had rules they had to follow, but that didn't mean they played fair. I had already seen evidence of that. And I was about to see it again.

The girl gripped McCauley's leg with both hands and gave a final, tremendous yank. McCauley went through the portal up to his waist. I tried to pull him back out, but I didn't have the strength or the leverage. A moment later, it didn't matter.

The portal closed.

No thunderclap, no flash of light, it was just gone.

So was McCauley's bottom half.

His top half flopped to the ground, a torrent of blood pouring out of his severed trunk.

McCauley made a low, gibbering sound in the back of his throat. His eyes bulged out of his head. He continued to stare at me for a moment, then he seemed to look beyond me, maybe to some distant place where pain couldn't reach him. Then he was gone.

I pulled myself out of his death grip and stood up. I looked down at the man who had just an hour ago invited me to go monster hunting with him in the Black Lands. I noticed that his robe, neatly severed at the waist, was the same colour as the blood still slowly pumping out of him. It was time to leave.

I stumbled out into the hall and around to the front door. I could still hear the house man mumbling to himself in the kitchen.

There was nothing I could do for him. There was nothing I could do for anyone. Not even myself. Nathan and his crew were dead, and so was the man who had financed their operation.

I ran back to my car and slumped against it, trembling. I closed my eyes and saw the black-eyed girl pulling McCauley through the portal. I saw her point a finger at me and smile.

You're next.

24

THERE WAS a package waiting for me when I got home.

It was the case file from Kovac. I took it into my apartment and secured all the locks on my door. Not that it would do any good. I was starting to understand more about fear and the way the black-eyed kids used it. You couldn't keep them out forever. Eventually you reached a point where it was a mercy to let them in, even as they dragged you kicking and screaming into the Black Lands.

I put on a pot of coffee and spent the rest of the night going through the file, examining crime-scene photos, reading autopsy reports and interview summaries.

The bodies in the photos all looked the same even though the mutilations varied from victim to victim. Once you realized the cause, it was easy to figure out what had happened. The cuts were clean, and the parts of the victims left behind always included their hands — in one instance, only a hand. These were people who had gotten stuck between worlds. People who had fought to stay in this one and lost.

The last section of the file was on the most recent victim, Tara Baxter. I flipped past photos of her mutilated body. She had been lying on her side, arms stretched out. I could picture the black-eyed kids trying to drag her into a portal, and Tara fighting back, clinging to the side of her bed as her legs were pulled through. Then...

I turned to a set of notes taken by the Toronto police during their interview with Tara's sister, Allison. Her home address was listed, and I jotted it down in my notebook.

I collected all the papers and photos and put them back in the file. It didn't look like the PIA had discovered the connection between the victims yet. I didn't see any notes about a monster-hunting group or any mention of black-eyed kids. There was also no file on Perry Brannigan, the member of Nathan's crew who disappeared completely. Nathan was sure Perry was dead, and I supposed it didn't matter much either way. Either he was alive and being hunted by the black-eyed kids, or he'd been dragged completely into the Black Lands. If it was the latter, I prayed for him. The others may have died, but I couldn't help thinking they had gotten off easier.

By the time I finished, the sky was starting to brighten in the window over the kitchen sink.

How many days did I have left? How long until the fear was too great and I simply let the black-eyed kids come and take me away?

Would I fight back and end up like Tara Baxter and Richard McCauley? Or would I go with them willingly to meet my fate in the Black Lands?

I didn't know. I figured I'd decide when the time finally came.

Until then, there was one last person I needed to talk to.

25

ALLISON BAXTER LIVED in a high-rise condominium on the lakeshore. She buzzed me in, and I took the elevator up to the twenty-seventh floor. I went down the carpeted hallway to her door, raised my hand to knock and froze.

The door was open a crack.

I reached out to push it the rest of the way open, but just before my hand touched the door, it was pulled open from the other side, and Allison was standing there.

I almost screamed in fright, but managed to keep it in and put on a smile that probably looked more than a little strained.

"Mr. Renn?" Allison gave me a worried look. "Are you okay?"

"Fine," I said in a tight voice. "And call me Felix."

She nodded, still looking a bit concerned, and gestured for me to enter.

We went into a small living room and sat down on a sectional sofa. I cleared my throat and tried to figure out how to proceed.

"I came to talk to you about Tara."

Allison squared her shoulders like she was bracing herself. "Yes," she said.

"I don't want to upset you, but I've recently discovered that several other people have been murdered in ways similar to your sister." I paused so she could take this in before hitting her with the rest. "It turns out Tara knew these people."

"What people?" Allison said, confused.

I thought back to the case file. "Mose Hartwell. Duncan Price. Calvin McCauley."

Allison's face paled. "They're all dead?"

"Yes." I saw something in her eyes. "Did you know these people?"

Allison nodded. "They were all part of the same group."

"Uh, yes." I was taken aback by her casual tone. "You knew about the group?"

"Of course," she said. "I was a member for five years."

I hesitated. "You… were a monster hunter?"

Allison looked at me strangely. "Monster hunter?" she said. "What are you talking about? It was a support group. For people who'd lost a loved one to a supernatural event."

"You…"

"I was a member. Tara and I both were. Our father was a soldier in the Armed Forces. He went to the Black Lands in Operation Shadow Storm. He died there."

She looked down at her hands, which were folded in her lap. "That's what the government told us, anyway. We never saw him again."

I nodded sympathetically. Hundreds of soldiers had died or gone missing during Operation Shadow Storm, the government's one and only assault against the Black Lands.

"Was there someone named Nathan Brossard in this group?"

"Yes," Allison said. She was starting to get impatient. "What does this have to do with my sister's murder? Did you say they were all dead?"

"Dead or missing and presumed dead," I said distantly. My mind was a thousand miles away, trying to put together pieces of a puzzle I thought I'd already solved.

"My God," Allison muttered. "I can't believe it."

"Why didn't you mention any of this to the police?" I said. "That you and Tara were part of this support group."

She shrugged. "I didn't think it had anything to do with her murder. I didn't know the others were dead until you told me." Her eyes suddenly narrowed in suspicion. "How do you know they're dead? I haven't heard anything about this on the news."

"The PIA is keeping a tight lid on the case. If the Toronto police didn't get that call about your sister, you probably wouldn't even know she was dead."

She digested that for a moment, then said, "You mentioned something about monster hunters. Is that what you think Tara was doing?"

"Yes, I do. Do you know anything about it?"

She shook her head numbly.

"I don't believe you."

She lowered her eyes. "My sister and I weren't very close. I hadn't seen her for months before I found out she..." She trailed off.

"Tell me about this support group."

"I only started going because she asked me to," she said, a bit defensively.

"When was this?"

"Five or six years ago." She looked at me with glistening eyes. "Tara was really into it. She said it was the best thing that'd ever happened to her. She thought it could help me, but it didn't. Those people..." She shook her head, and the movement caused tears to streak down her cheeks. "They were just so *angry*. I was angry too, but I didn't want to be anymore. That's why I went to the group. I thought they'd help me deal with all the rage I was feeling. Help me confront it, get rid of it, I don't know." She choked back a sob and sat up straighter. "It was like they didn't want me to lose my anger. *He* didn't want me to lose my anger."

"He?"

"Nathan. He ran the group. I don't know if he still does." She flushed a bright red. "I guess he doesn't now, if he's dead."

I nodded for her to go on.

"Nathan and the others talked constantly about how the Black Lands had ruined their lives, and all the things they could do to hurt them back." She gave a small shrug. "Maybe that was therapy to them, but it wasn't to me. So, I stopped going."

"And Tara stayed."

Allison nodded.

"Did they ever talk about hunting supernaturals?"

"Maybe." Allison wiped at her eyes. "It was a long time ago. I don't really remember. If they did, I never took it seriously."

I thanked Allison for her time and stood up to leave.

"So, what happens now?" she asked.

"I don't know," I said. "There are still some things I haven't figured out."

"If you do, will you come back and see me?"

"I will," I said. *If I'm still alive.*

As I rode down in the elevator, I realized there was only one way to get the last few answers I needed to close this case and save my life.

I had to do the impossible.

I had to talk to a dead man.

26

I KNOCKED on the door and the dead man answered.

He said, "Felix?" and then my fist connected with his nose and he went stumbling back into his apartment.

I followed him inside, kicking the door shut behind me. Unlike the black-eyed kids, I didn't require an invitation.

The dead man slumped back against the wall, one hand pressed against his nose. A steady stream of blood poured out from between his fingers.

"Surprised to see me, Nathan? Or just surprised to see me alive?"

His eyes were wide and stunned. "I thought you were dead."

"That's funny," I said. "I was going to say the same thing to you."

"How did you find me?"

"You showed me your driver's license," I said. "Remember? The other day in my office when I found out you'd lied to me about your name? Turns out you never stopped lying to me."

Nathan closed his eyes, then opened them again. He pushed away from the wall and went into the kitchen. I followed. He grabbed a dish towel, ran it under cold water, and pressed it gingerly against his nose. "I think you broke it," he said in a thick, nasally voice.

"Yeah, well, you set me up. I guess that makes us even."

"What are you talking about?" He gave me a look of total innocence that didn't quite have the full effect with the bloody towel covering half his face.

"You know what I'm talking about," I said. "You sent those black-eyed kids after me."

"What?" Nathan's voice cracked with indignation. "They're after me, too!"

"I don't believe you."

"Why the hell not?"

"Because you're still alive," I said.

Nathan tried to look hurt and angry, but he couldn't quite pull it off.

"Maybe they were after you at first," I said, "but you made a deal with them somehow. Probably after you started seeing your friends getting picked off one by one. Maybe you tried to reason with them when they were knocking on your door and asking you to invite them in. What did you do, offer them some of that big money you were making with your monster-hunting club?"

Nathan frowned. I couldn't see his mouth behind the bloody towel, but I could tell from the way his eyebrows drew together.

"It wasn't a club," he said, spitting the word out like it was something foul. "We didn't do it for money."

"Save it, Nathan. I've been to see Richard McCauley. He's dead, too, by the way. The black-eyed kids paid him a visit last night. But before they did, he and I had a nice chat about your little endeavour. I know that you and your friends were more interested in turning a profit than protecting people from all the nasties of the Black Lands."

"Go to hell," Nathan said, without conviction. "You don't know anything about me or my team. We may have let Cal's father turn Arrow Road into a hunting club, but we didn't have a choice. He was the one bankrolling us. Do you know how much it costs to build a Black Door?"

"Do you really want to make this about money?"

"Why not?" Nathan sneered. "That's all it was about to McCauley. The rest of us didn't care what he did as long as we still got to hunt. So what if we had to take a few rich assholes with us into the Black Lands?"

"I'm guessing the black-eyed kids weren't interested in money, either. They wanted you, didn't they? You, your team and Richard McCauley, the man who made it all possible. Maybe they couldn't be bought, but you found a way to reason with them, didn't you? You offered them a trade. One monster killer for another. You offered them me."

Nathan stared at me for a long time without speaking. His eyes were small and hard. He took the bloody towel away from his face to reveal a twisted little grin.

"And they agreed."

"You threw me to the wolves."

"I had to!" Nathan shouted suddenly. "What the hell was I supposed to do? Let them drag me to the Black Lands like they did to Perry? Fight back and end up in pieces like Tara and the others?"

"You don't seem to have any problem with them doing that to me."

"They wanted you anyway," Nathan said in a petulant voice. "They know who you are over there. They know what you've done."

"I haven't done anything except what I had to. I never hunted them for sport or for money."

Nathan looked at the bloody towel in his hand and tossed it into the sink. "It wasn't like that for us. Not at first. We came together because of our mutual hatred for the Black Lands. Each of us had lost someone to that fucking place. We started out just like I told you. We organized, we got weapons, and then we started going out at night to hunt."

"Then you realized there aren't very many monsters wandering around on this side. You thought, 'Hey, wouldn't it be easier if we had our own Black Door?' You could go over to the Black Lands whenever you wanted, hunt as many monsters as you liked, and come back. No fuss, no muss. You found out that one of your crew was an engineering genius — Calvin McCauley — and everything just came together."

Nathan shrugged. "It was Cal's idea. He'd been thinking about doing it for years. He hated the Black Lands more than any of us. His mother was an accidental tourist."

I'd heard the term before. It meant someone who had gone through a portal and been transported to the Black Lands. Sometimes they came back, most times they didn't.

"How did he build it? Genius or not, Black Doors aren't easy to come by."

"We found the plans online."

"You expect me to believe that?"

Nathan snorted laughter and blood dribbled out of his nose. "Christ, man, you can find plans to build a nuclear bomb on the internet. It's the ingredients that are hard to come by. But if you've got enough money..." He trailed off with a shrug.

"The PIA is eventually going to figure out that you and the others were all in the same support group. From there it won't take them long to connect you to Arrow Road."

"Let them," Nathan said. "I've got nothing to hide. They may be able to connect me to the others, but there's nothing that links me to Arrow Road. If there was any such evidence, I can assure you it's been destroyed."

"That's why you went out there. What about your faux suicide through the Black Door?"

"That was for you," Nathan said. "I needed to keep you from looking for me."

"It worked. Then I spoke to Allison Baxter, and the way she talked about you, I knew you wouldn't commit suicide, not like that. You think too highly of yourself, and you hate the Black Lands too much to let them be the ones to take you out. It was a nice trick. You may be a coward, Nathan, but you're not a dumb coward."

"If I'm a coward, then why am I the only one still alive?"

"Because you sacrificed your friends to save your own pathetic life!" I shouted. "You covered your own ass when you should have been watching out for theirs. That's why you're still here in your apartment, isn't it? You got around the black-eyed kids, but the PIA is going to show up eventually, and they're going to have questions. It wouldn't look too good if you were hiding out somewhere, would it?"

"Not that I don't have reason to." Nathan smiled with smug confidence. "You don't have to worry, Felix, I'll put on a good show for the feds. All of my dear friends horribly murdered, their bodies mutilated by the very same creatures that brought us together. And you, the hapless private investigator I hired to protect poor Tara. A selfless act for the last of my friends, but it was all for naught. So very tragic."

"I'm not dead yet."

"You can't avoid the inevitable. At this point it's only a matter of time. You may keep the black-eyed kids out tonight, maybe even tomorrow night, and the night after that, but eventually you'll let them in." He tapped the side of his head. "First you let them in here. Then you let them into your home. Then..." He spread his hands, palms out, in a gesture of resignation.

At that moment I gave very serious thought to shooting him. Then I thought of calling the PIA and telling them everything Nathan had done. Neither option offered much satisfaction. In the end I decided to do the only thing I could think of.

Go home and wait for the inevitable to come knocking at my door.

27

I DIDN'T HAVE to wait long. They showed up later that night.

I was back in the chair in front of my apartment door. The locks weren't engaged and I didn't have my gun. I didn't see the point.

There was a low, timid knocking at the door.

I stood up. "It's open."

Nothing happened. I guess that wasn't quite invitation enough for them.

I went over and opened the door. The black-eyed kids were waiting on the other side. They looked up at me with wide, expectant grins.

I turned and made a sweeping gesture.

"Come on in."

28

I WAS BACK in my chair that morning when my second visitor arrived. My door was still unlocked, but I'd left it slightly ajar.

My visitor didn't bother to knock. He just pushed the door open and stepped inside.

"Hello, Nathan. Beautiful morning, isn't it?"

Nathan looked monumentally confused. "You're..."

"Still alive, yes. I'm a bit surprised myself."

Nathan shook his head. "You know you can't..."

"Hold them off forever? Yes, I know. The kids made that abundantly clear when we spoke last night."

"You... spoke to them?

"That's why you're here, isn't it? You knew they'd be coming for me, and you decided to swing by this morning to see if there was anything left behind. Maybe you were curious to see if I fought them or if I had just let them take me. Either way, you'd know you were off the hook. Free to live the rest of your life without being hunted down by the BEKs."

"The what?"

"Never mind," I said. "The funny thing is, you were half-right."

"Half-right about what?" Nathan asked sullenly.

"The black-eyed kids did come last night, and I did let them in. But I didn't fight them. I talked to them instead."

Nathan looked at me like I was insane.

"I didn't know what else to do. You didn't leave me with very many options. I knew I couldn't put them off, and I didn't really want to. I'm just not that kind of guy. I prefer to face my problems head-on. That's where you and I are different. You tried to get away from the kids by swapping me for you. Only it turns out we're not exactly at parity with each other."

"What the hell are you talking about?"

"I let the black-eyed kids into my home, Nathan, because I didn't think I was worth one of you."

"Worth one of me?" He shook his head in confusion. "What does that mean?"

"It was a gamble, but then I didn't have anything left to lose. You may have been right, the black-eyed kids may have wanted me, but that didn't mean they could have me."

Nathan stared at me with slowly dawning horror. "You... traded me back to them?"

I shook my head. "You're missing the point. There never was any trade. You offered them me, they came after me, but when I finally let them in, they found out they couldn't have me." I paused. "If it's any consolation, I think it was just as much a surprise to them as it was to me."

"But you've killed monsters," Nathan said.

"That's true," I said, "but I never hunted them."

"What the fuck difference does that make?"

"It doesn't matter much to me, but it clearly matters to them."

I gestured with my head toward the door. Nathan spun around and saw the black-eyed kids standing on the other side of the threshold.

He said, "No," in a small voice and started shaking his head, like if he denied their existence that would be enough to make them go away.

They didn't.

"Please," he said to them. "We had a deal. You said you'd take him instead of me."

I lowered my head. "That exchange rate's a bitch."

Nathan turned and glared at me. "They can't come in," he said. "I didn't invite them."

"This isn't your place, Nathan. It's mine."

"Please, Felix..." He took a step toward me, and I took one back. "Please, don't invite them in."

"I already did. Last night."

As if on cue, the black-eyed kids stepped across the threshold.

Nathan reached out and grabbed me. We grappled with each other.

I threw him to the floor and he crawled away from me, knocking over my chair.

I backed up against the wall. As the black-eyed kids walked past, the girl stopped and looked up at me. "Be careful," she said.

I slipped out, closing the door on Nathan's trembling cries. There was nothing I could do to save him. He had set this chain of events into motion, and it had to end with him.

If there was one thing I'd learned from my dealings with the Black Lands, it was that you never interfere with the supernatural order of things.

Notes on *Black-Eyed Kids*

As much as I enjoyed writing *Temporary Monsters* and *The Ash Angels*, and still look back on them fondly, I must admit that at the time it was first published, *Black-Eyed Kids* was my favourite of the Felix Renn stories.

I know an author is not supposed to pick favourites — much like a parent is not supposed to pick his favourite kid — but with *Black-Eyed Kids* I felt like I was truly able to capture, not just the character of Felix, but the very essence of the world in which he lives. The fact that I got more feedback on *Black-Eyed Kids* (especially regarding the titular BEKs) than I did on any of the other Felix Renn chapbooks tells me I'm not too biased in this regard.

It may have also had something to do with the fact that, up until then, I had been pitting Felix against fairly well-known monsters, vampires and werewolves and ghosts. *Black-Eyed Kids* allowed me to introduce some of my own creations, and to show that there are all kinds of things in the Black Lands that Felix isn't prepared or equipped to deal with.

Maintaining that sense of foreboding and dread is very important to me when I write these stories. I feel it would be very easy to allow the characters to become too comfortable in a world where they already know monsters exist. It makes me have to work harder in order to write better stories, but it's worth it in the end.

THE BRICK

1

IT WAS ONE of those bleak November mornings where the sky can't quite decide if it's going to rain or snow or do nothing at all. I was tilted back in my chair watching the traffic creep along Yonge Street when someone tapped lightly on my inner-office door.

I knew it wasn't Sandra, my ex-wife and current secretary. She never tapped. She preferred to yell.

I swivelled around and said, "It's open."

The door creeped open an inch, then a few more. A tall woman with ash-blond hair peered in timidly. "Excuse me," she said. "I'm sorry to bother you."

"Please," I said, gesturing to one of my client chairs. "Bother me."

She stood for a moment in the doorway, her mouth pursed in hesitation, then she stepped quickly into the room and dropped into the chair. She let out a deep, shuddering sigh as if entering my office required a great deal of courage. Her small dark eyes darted around the room, looking for cameras, maybe, or snipers. She was wearing a knee-length camelhair jacket over black slacks and a white high-collared blouse.

"There was no one at the desk," she said, glancing over her shoulder at the outer office.

"My secretary gave herself the day off."

"My daughter is missing," the woman blurted. "Her name is Aubrey."

"What's your name?"

"Oh!" She put her hand to her mouth, embarrassed. "I'm sorry. My name is Norma. Norma Wood."

"Pleased to meet you, Ms. Wood. Now tell me about your daughter."

"She's fifteen years old. She has long blonde hair. She's very tall, almost five-nine." She fired out these little factoids in tightly measured bursts, like we were playing a speeded-up version of Twenty Questions. "She's a bit of a tomboy. She doesn't do well in math, but she loves astronomy. She's president of the astronomy club at her high school."

"Which high school is that?"

"Leaside High. She's in grade ten."

A horn honked out on the street, and Norma Wood jumped in her seat. Her shoulders hunched up, then gradually came back down again.

"How long has Aubrey been missing?" I asked.

"Since last night."

"That's not very long, Ms. Wood."

"But she's never been out all night before," she said. "She's only fifteen."

"Does she have a boyfriend?"

"No!" Her tone suggested the idea was abhorrent to her.

"Are you sure?"

"Of course I'm sure. I'm her mother."

I decided not to say anything in response to that. Instead, I asked, "Do you and your daughter have a good relationship?"

She looked confused. "What does that mean?"

"Did you and Aubrey fight about anything recently?"

She regarded me with something like shock, eyes widening, mouth slightly open. "Why would you ask such a thing?"

"It's a fairly harmless question. When a kid runs away from home, it's usually after a blowout with their parents."

Norma Wood sat up straighter in her chair and squared her slender shoulders. "We never fight," she said haughtily. "We've always been very close."

I spread my hands harmlessly. "I have to ask these questions. What about Aubrey's father? Where is he?"

"In the ground," she said.

That was an odd way of putting it, but I didn't say anything. Grief sometimes did strange things to people.

"Are there any family or friends she might have gone to stay with?"

"We don't have much in the way of family. As for her friends..." She shook her head uncertainly. "I don't really know. Aubrey *has* friends, but she never really talks about them. She's a quiet girl, keeps to herself. I was the same way at her age," she added defensively.

"Can you think of anything that happened recently that might have provoked your daughter into running away?"

Norma Wood lowered her eyes. "My mother — Aubrey's grand-mother — died last month." Her voice was barely audible.

"Were she and Aubrey close?"

She shook her head, eyes still lowered.

"Was Aubrey upset by her death?"

She shrugged. "A little."

"Where did she live?"

"Richmond Hill."

"Is it possible Aubrey went to her house?"

She wiped at her eyes, even though they appeared to be dry. "I doubt it. She's never been there before."

I leaned back in my chair. I felt like I was standing on the edge of an emotional minefield. I could tell there were bombs inside Norma Wood, just below the surface, waiting to go off at the slightest touch. Sometimes it was necessary to cause an explosion in order to learn some crucial piece of information. The problem was I didn't know Norma Wood well enough to determine how much damage such an explosion would cause, and how much damage she could take. She had lost her mother and her daughter over a short period of time. I knew she wasn't telling me something, but it might not have had anything to do with Aubrey's disappearance. I decided to leave it for the time being.

"Have you been to the police?"

"I just came from there," she said in exasperation. "I filled out a missing person report, but they didn't seem to take it very seriously. They said young people run away all the time."

"They're right."

"They said if there were no signs of foul play, I should just stay at home in case she calls or decides to come back on her own."

"Nine times out of ten, that's what happens."

She shook her head emphatically. "No. *No.* Aubrey's a good girl. She's never run away before."

"And you're sure she left of her own volition?" I was hesitant to use the word *kidnapped.*

"She wasn't kidnapped," she said, as if reading my thoughts. "I saw her go up to her room last night. I usually stay up late. I have trouble sleeping. When I went to check on her this morning, she wasn't in her room. I searched the whole house, but I couldn't find her."

"Is it possible she just left early for school?"

"I called the school. She never showed up."

"How about her bed? Did it look like she'd slept in it?"

"I couldn't tell. Aubrey never makes her bed. I keep telling her, but she never listens." Her eyes widened as she remembered something else. "Her suitcase was gone. She kept it under her bed, and when I checked for it, it wasn't there. And some of her clothes were missing."

"That would suggest she ran away."

She nodded her head rapidly, as if the fact that we agreed on this gave her some measure of relief.

"I'll need to take a look at her room."

"Yes, of course. I'll be home all evening. You can come by any time." She leaned forward, her eyes wide and beseeching. "That means you'll find her?"

"I'll do my best."

I told her my fee. She agreed and wrote me a cheque for two days' worth of snooping. She also gave me a photograph of her daughter. It was a school portrait of a thin-faced girl who didn't like getting her picture taken. Her eyes, small and dark like her mother's, were crinkled in anticipation of the camera flash. Her smile was small and unsure, almost a wince. Her blonde hair was pulled back in a ponytail from which a few errant strands stuck out like golden cobwebs. You couldn't tell she was tall in the picture, but she had the telltale slouch of a girl uncomfortable with her height.

After Norma Wood left, I swivelled around in my chair and resumed watching the late-morning traffic. Yonge Street was always busy. At one time it was the longest road in the world. I think I read that on a paper placemat in a diner.

The phone rang. I swivelled back around and picked it up.

"Felix, it's Jerry. Are you busy right now?"

"Yes, actually. I just got a new case."

"Can you come over to my office?"

"I just said I —"

"I know," Jerry cut in. "But I really need to see you."

"Jerry, I've told you a hundred times, I'm not interested in buying a haunted townhouse."

"That's not —"

"Or a haunted condo."

"It's not that," Jerry said. "I might have something that will help your case."

"What are you talking about?"

"Come over and I'll tell you."

"Jerry, I can't. I have to —"

He hung up.

2

THERE WERE two framed photographs hanging in Jerry Baldwin's office. The one on the wall behind his desk was an old sepia-tinted blow-up of a small English cottage surrounded by lush trees. The one on the opposite wall showed the fire-ravaged ruins of the same cottage. I'd been to Jerry's office many times before but was still taken aback by the grim before-and-after tableau of the two pictures. I thought it in odd taste considering that Jerry was a real-estate agent.

Jerry was seated at his desk when I came in. His blond hair was so fair, and buzzed so short, that at a distance it appeared as if he was bald. He wore suits that were more expensive than mine, but his ties were uglier. Today he was wearing a brown-and-red-print tie that looked like a dead squirrel.

"Felix!" He gave me his big salesman's grin. "Thanks for stopping by."

I sat down in the chair across from him. "I considered ignoring you, but I knew you'd just keep calling until I came over."

"I promise you, this will be worth your time." Jerry folded his well-manicured hands on the desk blotter. "So, tell me about your new case."

"Missing person. Fifteen-year-old girl."

"Ahh," Jerry said. "A wandering daughter job."

"What?"

"Isn't that what you private dicks call it?"

"Maybe in a Dashiell Hammett novel, about eighty years ago."

Jerry brushed this aside. "Whatevs. Tell me about the girl."

"No offence, Jer, but why do you care?"

"Indulge me."

I hesitated. Normally Jerry was bubbling with enough hyperactive energy to make a can of Red Bull nervous. I'd never seen him so cool and calm. His eyes, usually flashing like silver coins, stared at me with a sharpness that was both strange and a little unsettling.

"It's a pretty standard case," I said. "Girl runs away in the middle of the night, her mother wants me to find her and bring her home."

"You got a picture of her?"

"Yes."

Jerry turned his head away and fluttered his hands at me. "Don't show it to me."

"I wasn't going to."

"Let's see." Jerry leaned back in his swivel chair and steepled his fingers under his chin. "She's tall for her age... she's got blonde hair... small brown eyes..."

"What is this, Jerry?"

He leaned forward and blinked at me. "Am I right?"

I took out the picture of Aubrey Wood and tilted it away so Jerry couldn't see it.

"Lots of girls look like that," I said.

Jerry closed his eyes. "She usually keeps her hair in a ponytail."

"Uh huh."

"She ties it with a piece of blue ribbon. The ribbon has a pattern of stars and moons on it."

I looked more closely at the photograph. It was hard to tell for sure, but the ribbon tied around Aubrey Wood's hair did appear to have stars and moons on it.

"Nice job, Kreskin," I said, flipping the photo onto his desk. "You got any predictions for the future?"

"Yeah," Jerry said, grinning. "The Leafs aren't going to win the Stanley Cup this year."

"That doesn't make you psychic."

"I never claimed to be."

I nodded at the photo. "So you know her."

"Never met her before in my life."

I closed my eyes and pinched the bridge of my nose. "Please don't tell me you're banging her mother."

"Never met her either."

"So what is it, then? A trick?"

"It's not a trick." Jerry thumped his finger on the photograph. "I had a dream about this girl last night."

"She's fifteen, Jerry. Don't gross me out, okay?"

"It's not like that," Jerry said. He opened the bottom drawer of his desk and took out a bottle of Glenfiddich and two glasses. "I'm gonna need a drink to tell this. You want one?"

"No thanks."

Jerry poured himself a shot, picked up the glass, and leaned back in his chair.

"This dream..." He trailed off. "I haven't had one like it since..." He sighed and shook his head in frustration. "It's hard to know where to start."

I was starting to get curious in spite of myself.

"Start at the beginning."

Jerry nodded. "First I need to ask you something."

"What?"

"How much do you know about haunted houses?"

3

"THERE ARE three main types of haunted houses," Jerry explained. "And when I say 'house' I'm talking about any manmade building or structure. You dig?"

I nodded.

"The first type of haunted house is one inhabited by a spirit of the dead. Your garden-variety ghost. The second type is when a supernatural entity happens upon a house and decides to move in. They have no strong ties to the location. They're little more than supernatural squatters. Remove the entity and you remove the problem. The third type is when an entity arrives at the house via a portal located somewhere on or near the property. These guys..." Jerry took a sip of his drink. "... they're a bit more territorial."

"What does this have to do —"

Jerry raised his hand. "Let me finish."

I eased back in my seat and gestured for him to continue.

"Do you know where the most haunted house in the world is located?"

I thought about it for a moment. "Amityville?"

Jerry was taking another sip of his drink and almost spit it out.

"No," he choked. "It definitely isn't Amityville." He cleared his throat. "Have you ever heard of Rosedale Cottage?"

"Can't say I have. Any relation to the Rosedale neighbourhood here in Toronto?"

"No," Jerry said. "Rosedale Cottage was in England."

"*Was?* It isn't anymore?"

"Houses are like people, Felix. Some of them live long, happy lives. Others are not so fortunate."

"And Rosedale Cottage was one of the latter?"

Jerry shifted in his seat. He opened his mouth, then closed it again. Finally, he said, "The thing you need to understand is that most haunted houses are harmless. 'Poltergeist' is a good word because it literally means 'noisy ghost.' Most of the entities that inhabit haunted houses, that's all they are: loud, obnoxious, mischievous. Strange noises at night, electrical disturbances, the occasional apparition. In the more serious cases, there are instances of psychokinesis — objects moving by themselves — or pyrokinesis — fires spontaneously breaking out — but they're quite rare."

He filled his glass again.

"Rosedale Cottage, on the other hand..." He sighed deeply. "Let's just say it makes Shirley Jackson's Hill House look like the Playboy Mansion."

"That bad, huh?"

Jerry gave me a grave look. "Rosedale Cottage has killed people, Felix. Lots of people." He took a swallow of scotch. "No one knows exactly how many, but the figure is estimated to be somewhere between forty or fifty people since the place was built in 1886. The records that exist speak of a number of gruesome murders that took place there. All of the bodies were mutilated, and no suspects were ever named, much less caught. These same records describe a variety of paranormal activity in the cottage. Loud knocking sounds, broken windows, strange markings carved in the ground around the building. What's truly unique about Rosedale Cottage — besides its considerable body count — is that, as a case study, it possesses characteristics of both a poltergeist and a haunting."

"What's the difference?"

"A haunting centres on a location — a house, condo, farm, whatever — while a poltergeist tends to focus on a person. Hauntings can go on for years, but poltergeist activity usually passes after a few months."

"And Rosedale Cottage possessed qualities of both?"

"Yes," Jerry said. "The paranormal activity went on for years, and it focused on both the building and the people who lived in it. And when it focused on the people, it wasn't out to annoy them. It was out to kill them."

"What do you call that type of entity?" I asked. "A hauntergeist? A poulting?"

"I call it a serious fucking situation," Jerry snapped. "Rosedale Cottage didn't discriminate, Felix. It killed adults, children, old people. It slaughtered them all without mercy." He let out a deep breath. "One night in August of 1942, there was a fire, and Rosedale Cottage burned to the ground. The family living there at the time escaped, but they never rebuilt on the property. Considering what they went through, and all the people who had lived and died there, I can't say I blame them."

Jerry leaned back in his chair, eyes fixed on the lowball glass in his hand.

I stared at him for a long while. Then my gaze drifted up to the picture on the wall behind his desk. I nodded at it.

"That's Rosedale Cottage, isn't it."

Jerry continued to stare at his glass. "Yep."

I looked over my shoulder at the picture on the opposite wall. "And that's what it looked like after the fire."

Jerry nodded. "That shot was taken a few years later, sometime in the 1950s. Like I said, the cottage was never rebuilt. Probably for the best." He gave me a crooked smile. "I know more about haunted houses than most people."

"Because you sell them."

"I do," Jerry agreed. "But it's also because I live in one."

I felt my mouth drop open a bit. That couldn't be true. Could it? If

Jerry lived in a haunted house, surely I'd know about it. But as I sat there thinking, I realized that in the two years I'd known him, I'd never been to Jerry's house.

"Don't feel bad," Jerry said. "It's not exactly something I advertise. Even though I *do* advertise that I sell haunted houses." He waved his hand through the air and said, *"Put a little 'super' into your 'natural' life."*

I remembered the slogan. It was emblazoned on park benches all over the city.

"I've always been interested in haunted houses," Jerry said. "Ever since I was a little kid. I first learned about the Black Lands in junior high. It's scary stuff to hear at that age, but that's the world we live in, right? I guess they figure we're gonna find out about it sooner or later, and it's probably better if it's sooner. I mean, they can't exactly tell us that monsters don't exist, right?"

I nodded. The exact amount of information teachers told their students about the Black Lands varied from school to school, but most kids learned at least the basics.

"I remember my parents had to sign a permission form," Jerry went on. "Some people didn't want their kids finding out that the supernatural was real. Or at least they didn't want them to know until they were older. My parents didn't care." He chuckled to himself. "I think they were more concerned about sex-ed than what I might learn about the Black Lands. Hell, most kids weren't even *afraid*. We thought it was cool. Just shows how dumb we were." He shook his head ruefully. "It seemed like everyone in my class had one particular thing about the Black Lands they liked most of all, be it vampires or shifters or blackwood trees. For me it was hauntings. Maybe it was because I grew up in a house where my parents were constantly fighting. If I could deal with that, a few bumps in the night weren't going to bother me." His gaze drifted off. "And they never have. I guess that's why I got into the business of selling haunted houses." He looked past my shoulder at the picture on the far wall. "Nothing like Rosedale Cottage, though. The Paranormal Intelligence Agency keeps the real nasty ones off the market."

"But you'd sell them if you could." I didn't mean to say it, but the words were out of my mouth before I could stop them.

If Jerry was offended, he didn't show it. He merely shrugged and said, "Probably. But I still tell people what they're getting into. I provide full disclosure of all paranormal activity on the premises, including related deaths and accidents. Not that it matters. Most of the people I sell to are rich weirdos who have no intention of living in these places anyway. They buy haunted houses for the same reason other rich folks buy old baseball cards or rare stamps. It's a hobby."

"An expensive one."

Jerry shrugged again and poured himself another drink.

"A few years after I got into the haunted real estate racket, I went on a trip to Europe to see some of the most haunted houses on the planet. The last stop on my tour was Rosedale Cottage. This was back in the mid-nineties; the cottage itself was already long gone, but I didn't care. If you're a haunted house nut like me, Rosedale Cottage is Mecca. A pilgrimage to see the ruins is a must. People come from all over the world to see them."

"Out of respect?"

Jerry tilted his head to the side. "Sort of. I think they go mostly because they want to see something."

I perked up a bit. "Are you saying the ruins are still... active?"

Jerry took out another glass and poured a shot. He pushed it across to me. I started to protest, but Jerry cut me off.

"Trust me," he said, "you're gonna need a drink to hear the rest of this."

4

"THE TERM 'HAUNTED HOUSE' is a bit of a misnomer," Jerry said. "At least when there's a portal involved. As you probably already know, in those instances it isn't the house that's haunted, but rather the space that it happens to occupy. You can tear down the house, but the haunting remains."

"Because portals can't be closed," I said.

Jerry nodded. "Someone went to school."

"Everyone knows that."

"Yes," he said, "but did you ever notice how most people try to ignore it?"

"Our planet is being turned into Swiss cheese, Jer. Portals are popping up all over the place and supernatural creatures are being dumped out. It doesn't surprise me that people are trying to ignore it. Ignorance isn't just bliss, it's a survival mechanism. Frankly, I'm surprised there aren't more suicides."

I suddenly needed the drink. I picked up the glass and downed half of it.

"We're kind of moving past the point," Jerry said.

"There's a point to this?" I said. "I thought you were just showing off."

"Hey," Jerry said, smoothing down his tie. "No one knows more about haunted houses than me. I don't need to brag about it. I'm a well-established authority on the subject. And I can tell you for a fact that even though Rosedale Cottage was destroyed, the presence there remained."

"How do you know that?"

"Take another look at the picture behind you."

I turned around in my seat and looked at the framed blow-up shot. I saw fire-blackened rubble, a few jagged pieces of burnt timber, a crooked finger of stone that may have been a chimney at one time.

"Look closer," Jerry said.

I sighed and leaned forward.

The picture was very old, and the fact that it had been enlarged made it look even older. It was yellowing at the edges and there was a large rectangular speck right in the middle. As I peered at it, I saw the speck had clean flat edges and might actually be something in the shot rather than damage to the print itself. In fact, as I leaned back in my seat and looked at the entire photo, it seemed like the rectangular-shaped speck was the subject of the shot. As if the photographer had meant to take a picture of it.

"You see it?" Jerry asked.

"I see it," I said, still squinting at the photo. "What is it?"

"Proof that whatever haunted Rosedale Cottage was still there after the fire."

"Or that someone threw a brick in the air and snapped a picture."

I heard Jerry snort, followed by a pair of sharp, snapping sounds. I turned back around in my seat and saw a briefcase open on the desk, the top of Jerry's head visible as he rooted around inside. After a few moments, he closed the lid, put the briefcase on the floor, and held up something in a large Ziploc bag.

"Know what this is?" he said.

"A brick?"

Jerry shook his head. "*The* brick."

I craned my head around to look at the picture again, then turned back to face Jerry. "The same one?" I said sceptically.

"Yes."

"How can you be sure?"

The corners of Jerry's mouth turned up in a barely perceptible grin. "It told me."

5

"THE BRICK TOLD YOU." I wasn't sure I'd heard him properly. I almost asked him to repeat himself, but then I realized this was Jerry, and it wasn't the strangest thing he'd ever said to me.

Jerry nodded. The Ziploc bag sat in the middle of his desk. Through the plastic I could see the brick was a sickly yellow colour. The same colour as the picture on the wall behind me. A sepia brick.

"The day I went to Rosedale Cottage, I took a train from London to Ipswich. The cottage is on the outskirts of a village called Westerfield, just a couple of miles north of Ipswich. I walked from the train station and got there by late afternoon, which gave me a couple of hours to explore. I didn't plan to stay for very long. I may be a haunted house aficionado, but I had no desire to be at Rosedale Cottage after dark."

"So what happened?"

Jerry settled back in his chair. "It was a very surreal experience. I expected to find the ruins covered in graffiti, with beer cans and fast food trash strewn all over the ground, but it was completely untouched, as if the fire that destroyed the cottage had taken place only a week ago. It looked almost exactly like the picture on the wall. Several of the haunted houses I visited in Europe were old, abandoned buildings, and nearly every single one of them was vandalized in some way. People know about these places; kids would visit them and sometimes spend the night to show up their friends, prove how brave they are."

"But not at Rosedale Cottage."

Jerry shook his head. "It was like the place was in its own private limbo. There was no sign that anyone had been there since the fire. That was strange enough, but to make it even weirder, I didn't hear a single bird or a cricket the entire time I was there. It was very unnerving, to the point where I was reluctant to venture into the ruins themselves. I walked around the edge of the property, following the old fence line. I must have done that five or six times, trying to build up the courage to go inside. The sun was getting low and I knew I had to either go ahead and do it or head back to the train station."

"So you went in."

"Hell no," Jerry said. "I left. Or I started to. I was headed back to the road that would take me to Westerfield when I became aware of a sound. At first, I thought it was just the birds or the crickets finally chiming in, but it wasn't anything like that. It sounded like someone whispering." He sipped his scotch. "At that point my nerves were already cranked up to eleven, and I can tell you that hearing that nearly scared the shit right out of me. I told myself it was some kids playing a prank, trying to scare me. But I'd been all around the property — several times — and I could see into every part of the ruins, and there was no one there."

"You checked it out?"

Jerry nodded. "I didn't want to, but I felt... I don't know, compelled to find out what was making that noise. It was like an itch you shouldn't scratch, but you can't help yourself, because not scratching it is enough to drive you insane. Whatever it was, it overrode my baser instinct, which was screaming at me to run, run away, run away right now! I went back and forced myself to enter the ruins. I started walking around, trying to listen carefully for the sound, but I was making a bit of a racket stumbling over burnt wood and hunks of stone. I finally stopped and stood there for a moment, and I couldn't hear the whispering anymore. If I'd ever heard it in the first place. I thought my mind must have been conjuring up spooky sounds so that my trip to Rosedale Cottage wouldn't be a total bust. I started to pick my way back out of the ruins when I heard another sound. A different sound."

"What?" I was leaning forward in my seat.

Jerry rapped his knuckles against the edge of his desk. "Knocking," he said. "And I have to tell you, that scared me more than the whispering. I was in the burnt-out ruins of a house, there were no doors left, and I was hearing something that sounded exactly like a hand knocking on wood." He lowered his eyes. "I think I pissed myself a bit. Not that there was anyone around to see it. I was starting to think someone was definitely messing with me. But as I was looking around, I realized the knocking wasn't some phantom sound. It was real and it was coming from somewhere in the ruins. I went over to where the chimney had partially collapsed against one of the exterior walls. I was up to my ankles in old cinders and ashes. I got down on my knees and started digging. I didn't know why, any more than I knew why I had come back when I heard the whispering. I just felt compelled to dig. I came to an old piece of timber — probably the mantel from the fireplace — and started to clear it away. That's where the knocking sound was coming from. I pried the timber out of the ground and something underneath it came flying up at me. It happened so fast I couldn't tell what it was. It struck me square in the face and knocked me out cold. When I woke up it was dark out and I was lying on my back in the ruins. I couldn't remember where I was at first. I started to get up, and felt something heavy resting on my chest. It slid off as I sat up. I thought I'd been mugged, but my wallet was in my jacket pocket and there was still no sign of anyone around. It sounds crazy, but I have to admit when I woke up and saw it was night, my first thought was that I was in the Black Lands. I don't know why I thought that, but I can tell you it scared me more than anything else that day. Even though I knew I hadn't actually crossed over, I couldn't shake that fear. I got up to leave and almost tripped over the thing that had been lying on my chest. I reached down and picked it up."

He nodded at the brick on the desk.

"You took it with you?"

Jerry shrugged. "I told myself at the time that it was just a souvenir. But deep down I knew I was taking it for the same reason I went back to Rosedale Cottage and started digging. Because I felt like I had to." He poured himself another shot. "It was when I got home that things started to get real interesting."

"By interesting you mean…"

"Spooky," Jerry said with a grin. "It started with strange sounds — knocking and whispering like I'd heard at the ruins. Then I started hearing scurrying sounds as if something small and fast was moving across the floors. Sometimes there was a deep rumbling that was strong enough to shake the pictures off the walls. A few times I heard shrieking like nails on a chalkboard. Then objects started disappearing and reappearing around the house. At first, I thought I was just getting senile. So, I began carrying out little experiments. I'd put my wallet or my keys in the bowl in the front hallway, and later in the day I'd find them upstairs in the bathroom sink. It was always small objects, and none of them disappeared completely. They always popped up some-where else in the house." Jerry spread his hands. "It was the brick, of course. That much was clear. The presence that dwelled in Rosedale Cottage had now taken up residence in my house. I don't know if the brick was always the focus of the haunting, or if the entity had simply hitched a ride on it after the fire, but it didn't change the fact that I now had my own haunted house."

"Lucky you."

"Not really. The novelty wore off pretty quick. Bumps in the night and playing hide-and-seek with your wallet may sound like fun, but what do you do when you're lying in bed one night and a tall shadow moves past your doorway?"

"I'd probably get rid of the brick."

"Thought about it," Jerry said. "Especially after the dreams started."

"What kind of dreams?"

"Bad ones. The worst I've ever had. In almost every one of them, I'm lying in bed while this huge creature with black skin and burning red eyes literally tears me to pieces. The really messed up part was that I knew they were dreams and I would try to wake myself up, but I never could. It was like I was trapped inside my own mind, lying there screaming while these huge claws sliced the flesh off my body."

"Jesus, Jerry."

"I know it sounds bad telling it, but try living with it."

"Why the hell didn't you get rid of the brick?"

"I didn't connect the dreams with the haunting. Not at first. By the time I did, things had gotten worse."

"Worse?"

Jerry nodded. His face had paled considerably.

"I started sleepwalking. I know that doesn't sound so bad, and it wasn't the first few times it happened. I'd wake up in the same place every time, downstairs in the basement, with no idea how I got there. Then one time I woke up and I was in the basement with a knife in my hand. A big butcher knife. That's when I started thinking about talking to a shrink. But I didn't. I kept telling myself things would get better, that I would stop sleepwalking, that the dreams would go away as bad dreams usually do. Then, one time when I woke up in the basement, again with the knife, I noticed something on the brick wall. Scratch marks that I'd made with the knife while I was sleepwalking. Sleep-scratching," he said with a dry chuckle.

"Sounds wonderful," I said. "Remind me never to crash at your place."

"Then I figured it out," Jerry said. "I knew what the brick wanted."

"If you say the blood of the innocent, I'm out of here."

"It wanted a new home, Felix. That's why it was making all the noise, moving stuff around, giving me those bad dreams. The brick wasn't happy just being a paperweight in my study. It wanted to be a part of the house." He patted the brick in its Ziploc bag. "So that's what I did. I got a hammer and a chisel and removed one of the bricks from the wall in the basement. That's why I'd been scratching at the wall with a butcher knife while I was sleepwalking. The brick wanted to be inserted into the foundation of the house."

"And after that the paranormal activity stopped?"

"Not at all," Jerry said. "It's just not as random and chaotic as it was before. Now my house has a kind of supernatural feng shui. The presence is still there, but it's calmer now. More at peace."

"Still leaving you with a haunted house," I pointed out. "Which is apparently what you want. Why is that?"

"I'm a bachelor and probably always will be. I like the company." He looked down at his hands folded on his stomach. "Of course, it's more than that. It's hard to explain, but I feel very strongly that if I had simply thrown the brick away, things would have turned out... badly. I've come to believe that there's a place for everything in this world, and everything in its place. On the plus side, the dreams stopped." He raised his eyes and looked at me. "At least until last night."

"This is the dream you were telling me about?"

Jerry nodded. "The paranormal activity in my house started escalating this past week. It's like the build-up before a really bad thunderstorm. There's a kind of psychic charge in the air. I knew something was coming, but I didn't know what. Then last night..." He passed a trembling hand over his face.

"Tell me about the dream," I said.

Jerry took a deep, steadying breath and let it out. "We're in a house," he said. "You and me. There's a girl there, too. The young blonde I described to you. She's afraid and we're trying to calm her down. She keeps darting around the room pointing at the windows, saying something over and over again that sounds like, 'Why?' Like she doesn't know why this is happening to her. *Why? Why? Why?* Then I see it."

"What?"

"Something outside the window. Moving around the house. Something stalking us. I can't tell what it is. Something dark and fast, with red eyes. I'm pretty sure it's the same thing that was torturing me in those other dreams. There's a knocking sound, just like the one I heard years ago at the ruins of Rosedale Cottage. You and I look over at the door, but the girl says, 'It's the phone.' And sure enough, there's an old rotary phone on a side table. The receiver is jiggling and it's making a knocking sound. That doesn't make any sense, I know, but it's a dream. I'm actually thinking that at the time, completely aware that this isn't real, and yet I'm very, very afraid. I look over at you, and you say, 'Go ahead, Jerry.' Behind you, I can see the front door being smashed in by whatever it is outside. I pick up the phone and the girl's hand comes down on mine, stopping me. She says, 'It's not for you.' Then I woke up." Jerry licked his lips. "When I opened my eyes, I was sitting up in bed, holding something to my ear. At first, I thought it was the phone on my nightstand. But it wasn't. It was the brick." He picked up the brick in its Ziploc bag. "I had gone downstairs, taken it out of the wall, and carried it back to bed. All while I was asleep."

He put the brick back on the desk, then slid it toward me.

"There's a place for everything, Felix, and everything in its place. And right now, the brick's place is with you."

"It was just a dream, Jerry. It wasn't real."

"The girl is real," Jerry said, "and she's in real trouble. I could feel her fear. I wanted to help her, but..." He shook his head and pushed the brick further toward me. "It's not for me."

I reached out and pushed the brick back. "I'm flattered, Jerry, really I am. But the last thing I need is a haunted apartment. Besides, I'm pretty sure —"

"It's not for your apartment," Jerry snapped. "It's for your case."

"How is your magic brick going to help me find a missing girl?"

Jerry gritted his teeth. "It's not magic," he said patiently. "It's haunted. And I'm not *giving* it to you, I'm *lending* it to you." He stared at me intently. "I want it back when you're done with it."

"You can keep it. I don't want it."

"You may not want it, but you need it. It's going to help you."

"Why would it help me? You told me Rosedale Cottage killed people. *Lots* of people," I mimicked him.

"Yes," Jerry conceded. "But I firmly believe that's because the brick was in the wrong place at the wrong time."

"That supernatural feng shui sure racks up a hell of a body count."

"There have been plenty of supernatural incidents in my house since I installed the brick in the foundation, but none of them have been violent." He paused. "Well, there was that time my mother came to visit and she couldn't find her insulin. But I'm fairly certain the brick didn't hide it. It's more likely she just misplaced it. She's so scatterbrained these days." He paused again and tapped his finger thoughtfully against his chin. "On the other hand, she did buy me these really hideous drapes for Christmas one year. It's possible the brick was reacting to her poor taste in home décor. But that doesn't make it evil. Misunderstood, maybe, but not evil."

"Call it whatever you want, I'm not taking it with me."

Jerry came out of his chair so fast I thought he was going to leap across his desk and tackle me. Instead, he leaned forward and propped his hands on either side of the Ziploc bag. His eyes were wide and desperate, almost scared.

"Please, Felix. I'm not asking you for much. Just carry it with you. Stick it in your pocket and forget about it."

I stood up and looked from Jerry to the brick. I picked it up. It was heavier than it looked. Was that because it was old, or because it was haunted? Or was I just imagining things? I looked at it more closely. It was worn down at the corners, like a well-used eraser, and there were hunks of dried mortar clinging to it like barnacles. I bounced it in my palm and Jerry's eyes snapped wide open, his hands flailing madly in the air. He looked like he was having a coronary.

"Be careful!" he said in a frightened hush, like I was handling a vial of nitroglycerine, or his first-born child. "She's very fragile and... temperamental."

"She?"

A flush creeped into Jerry's cheeks. "I call her Rosie."

"Rosie?"

"As in Rosedale."

"I got it. I just don't understand why you named your brick."

"I named the *poltergeist*," Jerry clarified, a little testily. "It's easier than yelling, 'Hey, invisible force that keeps hiding my car keys!'"

I stuffed the brick in my jacket pocket. "I just want you to know I'm only doing this to humour you."

"Humour me?" Jerry grinned. "You're gonna be *thanking* me when Rosie helps you find your wayward waif."

"Uh huh." I turned to leave.

"Just... be careful with the brick, okay? Don't lose it, don't drop it, and most important of all... don't taunt it."

"The brick has feelings?"

"Yes," Jerry said. "And near as I can tell, absolutely zero sense of humour." He put his hand on my shoulder and gave me a grim look. "Don't be a prick to the brick, okay?"

"I'll try my best." I started out, then turned back. "By the way, why do you keep it in a Ziploc bag?"

Jerry blinked at me as if the answer was obvious.

"Freshness."

6

BY THE TIME I reached the street outside Jerry's office, the brick was already getting on my nerves. I was wearing a quarter-length jacket with low pockets, and the brick kept banging into my leg as I walked. I took it out and gave very serious thought to heaving it into the nearest trashcan.

Instead, I got in my car and tossed it onto the passenger seat. I put the key in the ignition, then sat there motionless. Finally, I took my hand off the key and picked up the brick again.

It was an ugly old thing, with more than a few cracks running through it. One good drop and it would shatter into a thousand pieces. The crusts of mortar gave it the appearance of icing on a very old, very rancid cake.

"You're not exactly the belle of the ball, are you, Rosie?"

I had no intention of taking the brick anywhere beyond the confines of my car. But it was clearly important to Jerry, and I didn't want to misplace it, so I opened the glove compartment and shoved it inside.

That done, I turned the key in the ignition.

Nothing happened.

I turned it again and heard a knocking sound. I tried a third time and got the same knocking sound. It didn't make any sense. The car had been fine on the drive over. I checked to see if I had left the head-lights on and drained the battery, but I hadn't.

I reached for the key again, but before I even touched it, the knocking sound started up again. As I sat and listened to it, I realized it wasn't coming from under the hood.

It was coming from the glove compartment.

"You've got to be kidding me."

I opened the glove compartment. The brick sat motionless inside. I closed the glove compartment and tried the key again. The knocking sound started up immediately, and continued even after I stopped turning the key.

I opened the glove compartment and stared at the brick. I didn't feel it staring back at me or anything like that, but I did feel something. A crawling sensation on my scalp.

I picked up the brick, expecting it to move in my hand, or be hot to the touch, or something, but it was the same cold, unmoving hunk of concrete I had carried out of Jerry's office.

I hesitated, then put it down on the passenger seat. Then I tried the key again.

The engine roared to life.

I glanced over at the brick. "Happy?"

If it was, it gave no indication.

7

I DROVE to Norma Wood's house in Leaside, an upper-middle class neighbourhood in the borough formerly known as East York. A nice place to raise your kids as long as you could afford the six hundred grand or more it cost to buy a starter home there.

I found a spot on the crowded street and stood on the sidewalk admiring the Wood residence as I did every other place that was beyond my tax bracket. It was a large red-brick Tudor with decorative stone work, a narrow driveway, and a large bay window.

Red brick. *The brick.*

I went back to my car and opened the passenger side door. The brick was on the seat in its Ziploc bag. I thought about leaving it in the car, but I had a vision of coming back and finding a large hole in my windshield and the brick sitting innocently on the hood.

"Sorry, my bad." I stuffed it into my jacket pocket and started toward the house. The Ziploc bag made an annoying crinkling sound with every move I made. I couldn't walk around like that, so I made an executive decision and went back to the car. I took the brick out of the bag, put it back in my pocket, and stuffed the bag in the glove compartment.

Walking up to the house along the cobblestone path, I noticed a piece of plywood covering a broken pane in the bay window. It was an odd sight. Plywood covering a broken window in Leaside was a bit like seeing a piece of duct tape covering a scratch on a Porsche. If you could afford a house here, you could certainly afford to replace a busted window.

I knocked on the door and waited. A minute passed, and I knocked again. I waited another minute before the door creeped open and a narrow slice of Norma Wood's face peered out. I gave her a little wave.

"Hi there. Felix Renn. The private detective you hired to find your missing daughter."

Norma looked confused for a moment, then she nodded and opened the door wider to let me in.

"I'm sorry," she said. "I was sleeping."

I nodded. When she said sleeping, I was pretty sure she meant drinking. At least that's what I inferred from my keen detective sense of smell.

"Have you heard from Aubrey?" I asked.

"No, nothing." Her eyes darted to the living room. To the piece of plywood wedged in the broken window.

"Did you and your daughter fight last night?"

"No!" she insisted. "I told you, we never fight."

"What happened to the window?"

Norma ran her hand through her hair. "I thought you came here to see Aubrey's room. Do you want to see it or not?"

I gestured for her to lead the way.

As I followed her upstairs, I noticed a long crack in the plaster on the wall of the landing between the first and second storeys of the house. I didn't mention it.

Aubrey's room was at the end of the hall. Norma stood in the doorway while I looked around.

"Do you want some coffee?" she asked.

"Sure, that would be great."

"How do you like it?"

"Black is fine."

I didn't really want coffee; I just wanted her out of the room. It's hard to search someone's private space with an audience.

Aubrey's room was small and tidy. There were no clothes on the floor and the bed had been made. I figured her mother must've done it since she said Aubrey never did. A small shelf was crowded with trophies and ribbons for various swimming competitions. There was a framed certificate on the wall stating that Aubrey Wood had passed a course in CPR. There was a desk in the corner and a bulletin board covered with photos. In one of them, Aubrey and a boy who looked about her age stood at the edge of a large indoor swimming pool. She was wearing a bright orange bathing suit, while the boy wore matching orange trunks and a strappy white t-shirt. On the bedroom walls were posters of Arcade Fire, Lady Gaga and Diamond Rings. There was a small bookshelf overflowing with *Harry Potter* and *Twilight* and *The Hunger Games*. There were lots of clothes in her closet. I couldn't tell if anything was missing. At a glance, it didn't look like the bedroom of a girl who had run away from home.

I looked through her dresser for a diary. I flipped through the books on the shelf for hidden notes or letters. I even peeked behind the posters for secret hiding spots. Three strikes.

There was a computer on the desk, but I didn't know very much about them. I could turn one on, sometimes, I could surf the web and check my e-mail, but that was about it. Aubrey might have left a note on it saying exactly where she'd gone, but I probably wouldn't have been able to find it. I wished I'd brought Sandra with me. She knew computers.

I bent down to look under the bed, and the brick in my jacket pocket banged painfully into my knee. I took it out and put it on the desk.

There was nothing under the bed, but when I checked between the mattress and the boxspring, I found a book. Not a diary, but a trade paperback with a black cover and the title *Here Be Dragons* written in red Old English lettering. In the bottom corner was another word: *Iapetus*. The name of the author?

The book seemed to be one of Aubrey's favourites, and not just because she kept it under her mattress. The spine was broken, several of the pages were dog-eared, and a number of sections had been marked with a yellow highlighter.

At the back of the book there was a perforated tab where a page had been removed. Possibly a comment card. *Did you like this book? Tell us about it!*

I caught movement out of the corner of my eye. The brick was sliding across the top of the desk. It leapt off the edge and landed in the wastebasket. I dropped the book and crawled across the floor to the wicker wastebasket, certain that the brick would be in pieces. But it was intact, resting on a cushion of crumpled tissues and balled-up pieces of paper. I took it out and brushed it off. I glanced down and one particular rumpled wad of paper caught my attention. It was cream-coloured, like the tab at the back of the book, and when I picked it up and smoothed it out, I saw it had a perforated edge.

It wasn't a comment card. It was a login and password for a website called Portal Watch. Below the URL was a picture of Gandalf in his wizard hat and a word bubble that said, "Keep it secret; keep it safe!"

I put the brick back in my pocket and bent down to pick up the book I'd dropped. I flipped it open to the first page. There was the title *Here Be Dragons* and beneath it: *A Guide to Black Lands Portals.*

I patted the brick in my pocket.

"Thanks."

8

NORMA WOOD CAME in with two steaming cups of coffee on a plastic tray. "I hope you don't mind instant. It's all I've got."

"It's fine," I said, taking one of the mugs. Norma took the other and set the tray on Aubrey's bed. She sat down next to it and looked around the room as if she'd never been here before.

I leaned against the desk and blew on my coffee. I took a sip and burned my tongue. I put the mug down and said, "Looks like Aubrey is quite the swimmer."

"Oh yes," Norma said, craning her head around to look at the trophies on the shelf above the bed. "I think she was swimming before she was walking. My husband and I started taking her to swim classes when she was just six months old."

I nodded at the bulletin board. "I see she's a lifeguard."

Norma nodded. "She worked at the Leaside Rec Centre this past summer. She put in a lot of hours — she wants to buy a car — but it got to be too much once school started, so she quit."

"Who's the boy in the picture with her?"

"That's Jack Carr. He's one of Aubrey's friends from school. Jack helped Aubrey get the job at the rec centre."

"Do you think he might know where Aubrey is?"

I could tell from the look on her face that the idea had never occurred to her. "I don't know. Maybe."

"I'd like to talk to him. Do you have his address and phone number?"

"Probably. I can check."

"Also..." I picked up *Here Be Dragons* and showed it to her. "Does Aubrey have any special interest in the Black Lands?"

Norma gave a dismissive shrug. "No more than most kids her age."

"Is she interested in the supernatural in general?"

She lowered her eyes and shook her head. "Not that I'm aware of."

"There's nothing wrong with it," I assured her. "Lots of kids are."

"I really can't say," Norma said brusquely.

I took a shot in the dark. "Are you from England?"

She raised her eyes and gave me a confused look. "No."

"Have you ever been there?"

"No." Her hand came up and clutched the front of her shirt. "Oh God, is that where you think Aubrey went?"

"No," I said. "I just... It doesn't matter."

Norma stared at me a moment longer, then her hand dropped back into her lap.

"Do you think you could get me the information on Aubrey's friend? I'd like to try and reach him before it gets too late."

Norma nodded and left the room.

While I waited, I flipped through *Here Be Dragons*. I understood why Norma was reluctant to discuss her daughter's interest in the Black Lands. It wasn't like telling people your kid was on the honour roll. But what I'd said was true: lots of kids were interested in the supernatural. How could they not be? They grow up hearing stories about Santa Claus and the Easter Bunny, only to find out that they're not real. It used to be that kids heard stories about monsters and were told the same thing.

Not anymore. Since the Black Lands were discovered, parents had become very careful about the stories they told their children. Many did everything they could to protect their offspring from the darkness that had seeped into our world. The problem is, kids like scary stories. The fact that the Black Lands was real didn't bother them, much less frighten them. For better or worse, they were fascinated by the place.

When I heard Norma coming back up the stairs, I slipped *Here Be Dragons* into my jacket pocket next to the brick. It was getting crowded in there.

Norma gave me a slip of paper with Jack Carr's address and phone number on it. I thanked her and told her I'd be in touch.

9

I WENT BACK to my office. Sandra was there, which was a surprise. She was on the computer, which wasn't. Most of the time she spent "working" for me she was on the Internet cruising the Hollywood gossip sites. Sometimes I was able to get her to answer the phone. I was still hoping to teach her how to make coffee that didn't have lumps in it.

"I'm surprised to see you here, Dee."

Sandra glared at me over the top of the monitor. She'd never actually told me to stop using the nickname, but I could tell she didn't like it. We'd been divorced for over a year, but some habits are hard to break. I would have felt bad about stirring up old memories, but she didn't like being called Dee even when we were married.

"I'm not working," Sandra told me. "My Internet at home is down and I needed to do some banking."

"People don't do that at banks anymore?"

She gave me a look that tried not to be condescending but failed miserably.

"Take your time," I said. "I'm just here to make a call and look up some info on a book." I took out *Here Be Dragons* and waggled it at her. "Remember books?"

"I have a Kindle."

"Of course you do."

She took the book out of my hand and looked at the cover. "*Here Be Dragons*. What's it about? Dragons?"

"It's a phrase used on old maps to describe dangerous or unexplored areas. The Romans used the variation 'here be lions.'"

"Lions and dragons, oh my."

"It's about Black Lands portals."

"Okay!" Sandra dropped the book like it was a hot coal. "I thought you were trying to stay away from supernatural cases."

"I am. A woman hired me to find her missing daughter. I found the book while I was searching her bedroom. It doesn't necessarily mean there's a supernatural element to this case."

As if on cue, the brick in my jacket pocket thumped against my leg.

Sandra noticed it and said, "Is that a brick in your pocket or are you just happy to see me?"

I took the brick out and put it on her desk.

"That's what I figured." She picked up the brick and looked at it. "Is there a reason why you're carrying this around?"

"Maybe, but I haven't figured it out yet."

"You're weird."

"You know your way around computers, don't you, Dee?"

"I guess so," she said with a shrug. "I'm trying to learn a new trade since my acting career is entering menopause. The last audition Bart sent me on was for the role of MILF #3 in the latest *American Pie* direct-to-DVD crapfest. And the only reason I even know what a MILF is is because I started teaching myself about computers and the Internet."

I picked up the book and flipped to the back. "There was a card attached here." I took it out of my pocket and showed it to her. "It's a login and password for a website called Portal Watch. Can you try to access it for me?"

Sandra took the card, glanced at it, and typed in the URL. A window popped up asking for a login and a password. Sandra used the ones printed on the card, and it took her to a rather austere website that consisted of a black door on a plain white background. An animated eye appeared on the door. It opened and closed and then opened again. The words PORTAL WATCH materialized above the door in tall red letters.

"Try clicking on the door," I said.

Sandra turned and glared at me. "I hate backseat drivers."

"Sorry."

She turned back to the computer and clicked on the door. We were taken to a message board with topics such as CONFIRMED PORTAL SITES, RUMOURED PORTAL SITES, and PORTAL PICS.

"That last one should be interesting," Sandra said. "Portals are invisible, aren't they?"

"It's probably pictures of the things that have come out of portals."

Sandra scrolled down to the bottom of the page. It said there were currently 11 other users online. The site moderator's name was Iape- tus, which was the same name as the one on the cover of the book. He or she was currently offline.

"See this?"

Sandra tapped her finger on the upper right-hand corner of the screen. It said, "You are currently logged in as RosemarysBarbie."

"When you access this site for the first time, you're probably prompted to fill out a profile. You know, so you don't have to use the jumble of letters and numbers that comes with the login card. In this case the user, a woman I'm guessing, has chosen the name Rosemarys- Barbie. But it looks like you still have to use the login name that comes with the card in the book. Probably for security reasons. She was prob- ably instructed to change her password, too, but clearly she didn't do that or else we wouldn't have been able to access the site."

I nodded. Sandra wasn't just good with computers, she was able to dumb down the technospeak so I could understand it. Mostly.

"So, this is a private website," I said. "For people who bought the book."

"So it would appear."

"What can you tell me about RosemarysBarbie?"

Sandra accessed the user profile. The field for FIRST NAME said AUBREY. The field for LAST NAME said YEAH, RIGHT. The field for PHONE NUMBER said 1-800-EAT-ME.

Sandra snickered. "I like this girl."

The rest of the fields on the RosemarysBarbie profile had been left blank.

"Is there anything else you can tell me about her?" I asked.

Sandra clicked around a bit. "Not much," she said. "She's been a member of the site since August of this year, and she last logged in... yesterday at nine-forty-seven p.m."

"Can you browse through a few forums?"

Sandra returned to the main page and clicked on RUMORED PORTAL SITES. There were dozens of threads, including ones titled "There's a Portal in my Backyard," "Disappearing Fish Stocks in Lake Champlain = Underwater Portal" and "Five More Missing Hikers in Yosemite — New Portal???"

She clicked on one called "PIA Confirms New Portal Site." It consisted of a message with a single line: "...*in yo mama's ass!!!*" This was followed by a number of colourful replies from other users.

"Next," I said.

We spent a couple of hours cruising the site and reading posts by a variety of users who seemed to share a few common traits. They were all very paranoid, they were all very bad spellers, and they all had a very serious hate-on for the Paranormal Intelligence Agency, which was often referred to as the Paranormal Intelligence Gestapo, or PIG.

In one post, a user named XPat talked about how the PIA had forced his family and several others to move out of their homes because a portal had been discovered in a nearby farmer's field. This happened in Sandusky, Ohio, and I was fairly certain XPat was telling the truth. The portal was real, anyway. I'd heard about it on the news a few weeks back. A number of neighbourhood pets had gone missing over a short period of time. Then a couple of kids disappeared. The police were called in, then the FBI, and finally the PIA. I couldn't recall if the kids were ever found, or if anything ever crossed over from the

Black Lands, but I remembered hearing that the government had invoked its Portal Proximity Relocation Act, which was just a hoighty-toighty version of eminent domain that the PIA used to keep the public away from portals.

There were a lot of bombastic posts by people who claimed to have been illegally detained by the PIA, as well as some remarks about "ouijaboarding."

"What's 'ouijaboarding?'" Sandra asked.

"You don't want to know," I said.

There was talk that the technology to close Black Lands portals did in fact exist, but the government was keeping it under wraps, as they had no doubt done with cold fusion, artificial intelligence and the AIDS vaccine.

That there was a conspiracy involving the Black Lands was a given. If the members of Portal Watch were sure of anything, it was that. The part that they couldn't seem to agree on was the participants. One user said it was a joint effort between the U.S. and Canadian governments in conjunction with Microsoft. Another said it didn't have anything to do with any country's government, but was in fact the brainchild of the International Monetary Fund. Perhaps not surprisingly, there was more discussion of who was involved in the alleged conspiracy than the purpose of the conspiracy itself. Although, one user named Hello-Wabbit pointed out that the Black Lands was discovered in the mid-1940s, right around the end of World War II. He claimed that Adolf Hitler had known the truth about the Black Lands, specifically that the portals were caused by the Jews, and had been trying to rectify the problem. How exactly the Jews were responsible for the arrival of the portals, HelloWabbit never explained, but he theorized that the best way to close them forever would be to gather up every single Jewish person on the planet and march them into the Black Lands. Several users suggested that HelloWabbit find a portal of his own and do the same thing.

"Nerds," Sandra declared, leaning back in her chair. "Nerds with way too much time on their hands."

"True," I said. "I limit my internet usage to porn."

"Please. You can't even turn on the fucking computer."

I picked up *Here Be Dragons*. "What can you tell me about him?" I pointed at the word "Iapetus" on the bottom of the cover.

Sandra glanced at it, then turned back to the computer. She opened another browser window and typed "Iapetus" into Google. She got over 800,000 results. She clicked on the first one, and it took her to Wikipedia.

"In Greek mythology," Sandra read, "Iapetus was a Titan, the son of Uranus and Gaia, brother of Cronus, and father of Atlas, Prometheus, Epimetheus and Menoetius." She scanned down the page a bit. "Iapetus is also the name of Saturn's third-largest moon." She looked at me. "Is that important?"

"Probably not."

I glanced at the clock on the wall. It was quarter past ten. Too late to pay a visit to Jack Carr. He could wait until morning. I hoped the same could be said for Aubrey Wood.

10

I ASKED Sandra if she wanted to grab a quick bite, but she said she was tired and just wanted to go home. I picked up the brick and the book and put them back in my jacket pocket. Sandra and I said our goodnights and headed off in different directions.

I went to a deli and picked up a couple of sandwiches. I ate one on the way to my apartment in the Annex, and the other while I sat in front of the television. There was nothing good on, so I turned it off and took out *Here Be Dragons*.

The book wasn't as poorly written as the message board posts on Portal Watch, but it had the same angry, paranoid tone. It was divided into sections, one for each continent, and then broken down into chapters for individual countries. The largest section was devoted to North America, which probably said more about the author's nationality than anything else. There were, as far as I knew, no greater number of portals in the United States and Canada than there were in other coun-tries around the world. Some had a few more, some a few less, but they were found all over the planet.

I read a section on Old Frightful, a portal on the outskirts of Kitch-ener that spewed out a flood of brackish water at seemingly random intervals. Unlike the majority of other known portals, Old Frightful wasn't always open. Most of the time it was closed. The PIA figured the portal opened on a body of water in the Black Lands. A large one, they said, because Old Frightful had been dumping water into our world for close to forty years and showed no sign of slowing down.

I'd gone to see Old Frightful on a grade seven field trip. I remem-bered some of the kids had chickened out at the last minute and decided to stay on the bus. I didn't. I went into the facility, which had been constructed around the portal back in the 1970s, and had been somewhat disappointed. I already knew that portals were invisible, but I had expected to see *something*. A three-headed shark, maybe, or some tentacled beastie that shot death beams from its eyes. No such luck. All I saw was a tall glassed-in chamber with a concrete floor that slanted down on all sides to a large grate in the center. That was where they collected the water that came pouring out. Some entities had been recovered, but they weren't on display and the tour guide refused to discuss them. "That's classified," she'd said with a cheery smile, and led us on to the gift shop.

I put down the book and stretched out on the couch, lacing my hands behind my head.

There was no doubt Aubrey Wood was interested in the Black Lands. That in and of itself wasn't so unusual. The unusual part was that she felt the need to keep it a secret, hiding the book under her mattress. Norma Wood had been evasive when I asked about her daughter's interest in the supernatural, but that may not mean anything, either. And even if it did, it might not be connected to Aubrey's disappearance.

I stood up and started down the short hallway to my bedroom. Then I stopped and went to the front closet where I'd hung my jacket. I took the brick out of the pocket and held it up level with my face.

"Any idea where Aubrey Wood might be hiding?"

The brick didn't move.

"Any predictions for this week's lottery numbers?"

Nothing.

I sighed. "I'll put you on my nightstand so you don't have to spend the night in the closet. But no nightmares, okay?"

The brick promised me nothing one way or the other.

11

I WOKE up at six the following morning, neither bright-eyed nor bushy-tailed. I reached over to hit the snooze button on the alarm, and my hand fell on the brick. I considered using it on the alarm clock, then decided sleeping in wasn't going to get Aubrey Wood found any faster.

I got up and shuffled into the bathroom. In the shower, I wondered if Jerry ever bathed with the brick, and shuddered at the disturbing image conjured by that thought.

I got dressed, put the brick back in my jacket pocket, and headed off to Leaside.

Jack Carr lived a few streets over from the Woods. I cruised past his place, then pulled up to the curb a few houses away. Leaside High was close enough that Jack probably walked to school. If he got a ride with his parents, I'd follow them and talk to him after they dropped him off. I didn't like dealing with parents. They usually didn't want their kids talking to a private detective. To them we were only a step or two above child molesters. Probably because both groups were partial to trench coats.

A few minutes before seven, a car pulled out of the driveway at the Carr residence. I ducked down as it drove past, but I was still able to catch a glimpse of a man and a woman inside. Jack's parents, I presumed. A half an hour later, Jack Carr emerged from the house. He closed the front door behind him, locked it, and came walking down the sidewalk toward where I was parked.

I slipped out of the car as he sauntered by.

"Hey, Jack!"

He froze like I was a drill sergeant calling him to attention. His head turned slowly toward me. He was a tall, gangly kid with lively green eyes and a mop of brown hair. A backpack hung off one of his bony shoulders. As he turned toward me, he unslung it and held it close to his middle, like he was thinking about flinging it at me like a medicine ball.

"Do I know you?" he asked in a wary voice.

"My name is Felix Renn. I'm looking for a friend of yours. Aubrey Wood."

"Aubrey?" he said. "What do you want with her?"

"She's missing."

Jack frowned. "Missing?"

"You didn't know?"

"I..." He trailed off, then tried again. "I noticed she wasn't in school yesterday."

"She left home. The night before last. Do you know anything about it?"

Jack looked down at the ground. "No," he said. "I don't."

"You're her boyfriend, right? I'd expect you'd know where she is."

Jack's eyes rose to meet mine. "Her boyfriend? Who told you that?"

I had thrown a random dart and missed the bull's-eye, but not by much. Jack was hiding something, but it wasn't a secret romance with Aubrey Wood. I didn't know if what he was hiding was important. It might not have anything to do with Aubrey's disappearance. Kids his age were suspicious by nature.

"I don't care if you're dating her. I just want to make sure she's okay. Her mother is really worried."

"I'm not dating her," Jack said, "and I didn't know she was missing until you told me."

"But you know something."

"I don't know anything," Jack snapped. "If you want to give

someone the third degree, go find my brother. He's the one dating Aubrey."

The suspicion in his eyes had turned to a dull anger. He flipped his backpack onto his shoulder and crossed his arms truculently.

"Are you interested in her?"

"Fuck you!"

It was answer enough, I supposed, and one I deserved.

"I'm sorry, okay? It just sounds like you care about her. Am I wrong?"

Jack didn't say anything.

"Do you think Aubrey might be with your brother?"

Jack shrugged and looked away. "How the hell should I know?"

"What's your brother's name?"

"Are you a cop?"

"No. I'm a private detective."

Jack perked up at that. "Seriously?"

I showed him my license. "Aubrey's mother hired me to find her."

"If she's with Seth, neither of them said anything about it to me. Not that they would," he muttered under his breath.

"Seth's your brother?"

Jack nodded.

"How old is he?"

"Twenty-one."

I sighed. If Seth Carr turned out to be the one who convinced Aubrey to leave home, he could find himself charged with all kinds of things, including kidnapping and statutory rape.

"How did he and Aubrey meet? At school?"

"No way," Jack said. "Seth's a dropout." He uncrossed his arms and let them fall to his sides. "It's my fault. I didn't introduce them, but I might as well have. I never thought Seth would go for her. I didn't think they'd have anything to talk to each other about."

I didn't want to tell him that a guy will find all kinds of nothing to talk about with a pretty girl. He'd figure it out for himself when he got older.

"When did they meet?"

"This past summer," Jack said. "I used to throw these house parties when my folks were gone, which was most of the time. We've got a cottage up in Huntsville and they went up there almost every weekend."

"You didn't go?"

"Seth and I went when we were younger. I stopped going this year because I got a job."

"Lifeguard."

"Yeah," Jack said. "How did you..."

"Private detective, remember?"

"Right. Anyway, I had the house to myself most weekends, so I thought it would be cool to throw a party. I invited some friends from school, and some friends of friends, and it turned into a weekly thing."

"And Aubrey came?"

"Yeah. I didn't think she would — Aubrey isn't straight-edge or anything, but she's not really the party-girl type." He suddenly looked thoughtful. "But then I didn't expect Seth would come, either, so maybe they were destined to meet."

He didn't sound very happy about it. In fact, he sounded like he wanted to give Destiny a solid kick in the chops.

"You mentioned something earlier," I said. "That you didn't think Aubrey and Seth would have anything to talk about."

"Yeah. I mean, Aubrey is one of the nicest people I know, and my brother... well, he's a goon. I couldn't imagine they'd have anything in common. And I never would have guessed that Seth would..." He broke off, shaking his head.

"That he'd steal her from you?"

Jack looked down and scuffed at the sidewalk with the toe of his sneaker. "She's not mine. She never was. She can go out with whoever she wants." I could tell it tore his guts out to speak those words, but it made me like him.

"This thing they had in common, was it the Black Lands?"

Jack looked at me with something like awe. "You really are a detective, aren't you?"

"Do you know why Aubrey was interested in the Black Lands?"

"She had a paranormal experience," Jack replied. "At least that's what she told my brother. We worked together at the pool all summer and she never mentioned it to me. I figured she just made it up to impress him."

"Why would that impress your brother?"

"Seth's big into the supernatural. He doesn't tell me much about him and Aubrey — and to be honest, I don't want to know — but I know he's interested in her because she's into the Black Lands just like him."

"How long has your brother been into the supernatural?"

Jack thought about it for a moment. "The past two or three years, at least. He never talked about it when we were kids. But then there's six years between us. Seth didn't talk to me about much of anything when he lived at home. I was just the dopey little brother he always got stuck taking care of."

"When did Seth move out?"

"Right after he dropped out of high school. My parents told him if he wasn't in school, then he wasn't going to live under their roof. I guess they didn't think he'd call their bluff, but he did."

"He has a place of his own?"

"Yeah."

"Where is it?"

The suspicion slipped back into Jack's eyes. "Why do you want to know?"

"You know why, Jack. Aubrey might be in trouble. I'm not saying your brother would do anything to harm her, but the sooner I find out where she is, the better."

"He wouldn't hurt her. Seth's a creep, but he's no..."

"I'm not accusing him of anything. But Aubrey is a minor. You know what that means, right, Jack?"

He did.

"You don't want your brother to go to prison, do you?"

Jack tilted his head thoughtfully to the side, as if picturing his brother in a bright orange jumpsuit. Maybe he did want Seth to go to prison, but in the end his concern for Aubrey was greater.

"He lives in the Jungle."

"The Jungle?" I said. "Lawrence Heights?"

Jack nodded. "Seth's a man-eater, and man-eaters live in the jungle." He shook his head. "He actually says stupid shit like that."

"I didn't think anyone called it the Jungle anymore. It's a racist name."

Jack shrugged. "That's my brother for you."

"Where exactly does he live?"

"Twenty-two Amaranth Court, apartment thirty-seven. But he's hardly ever there. If Aubrey's with him, he must know that's the first place people will look for him."

"Is your brother a big guy?"

"Kind of, I guess."

"Bigger than me?"

"About the same size."

"Is he going to give me any trouble?"

"Probably."

I thanked Jack and offered to give him a lift to school. He declined. He gave me his cell number and I gave him my card. I told him to call me if he heard from Aubrey or if he thought of anything that might help me find her. Then I got back in my car and headed off to Lawrence Heights.

I stopped at my office on the way and picked up my gun.

12

NONE of the buildings in Lawrence Heights stood more than four stories high. The nearby Downsview Airport prevented the city planners from putting up anything taller. Most of the buildings were bungalows and low-rise apartments. Twenty-two Amaranth Court was one of the latter. A three-story building painted industrial grey with small balconies, even smaller windows, and a shopping cart with an old, mildewy mattress jammed in it parked next to the lobby door.

I found "S. Carr" in the directory, reached up to press his buzzer, and noticed a scrap of paper taped to the intercom with the word "Broken" written on it. The paper was yellow and curling at the edges, suggesting the intercom had been out of order for some time. I went over to the inner door and tugged on it. It was open.

Apartment 37 was on the third floor. There was no elevator, so I took the stairs. Seth Carr's place was at the end of a long, dark hall. All of the lights were either burned out or busted. I knocked on the door, but there was no answer. I tried the knob and it turned in my hand. I pushed the door open.

It was a bachelor apartment, and the bachelor in this one was dead. Seth Carr lay on his back in the centre of the main room. I figured it was Seth because he looked like a slighter older version of his brother. The resemblance was so uncanny that for a split second I thought I was looking at Jack lying there dead. Seth had the same shaggy brown hair, but his was clotted with dried blood and pieces of grey stuff that was almost certainly brains from his shattered skull. His body was a ragged, bloody mess. His throat had been ripped out and his right arm had been torn from his shoulder. It lay a few feet away on the blood-drenched sheets of the daybed.

I closed the door behind me and stepped carefully toward the body, avoiding the pools of congealing blood. I crouched down and, for the hell of it, felt for a pulse on Seth Carr's neck. His skin was as cold as marble. He was dead, and had been for at least a day.

I took a quick walk through the apartment — it didn't take long; there was only one other room, a bathroom, and an alcove for the small kitchenette — but there was no sign of Aubrey.

Back in the main room I looked around at the meager furnishings. There was a sprung couch, an overstuffed chair with cigarette burns on the arms, a small television sitting on an upturned milk crate, and a TV tray with a laptop on it. There was nothing on the walls but bloodstains and a few cobwebs in the high corners.

I went back to the front door, giving Seth Carr's body a wide berth. I took the brick out of my jacket pocket and put it down on the floor.

"Okay, Rosie, do your stuff."

The brick sat there motionless.

"You're a big help."

I bent down to pick it up and my eye fell on something across the room, under the daybed. I went over and hauled out a hot pink suitcase that I was willing to bet didn't belong to Seth Carr. I popped the clasps and opened it. It was packed full of women's clothing, a small makeup bag, another for toiletries, and a couple pairs of shoes. I also found a piece of ribbon. It was blue with a pattern of yellow moons and stars. The same one Aubrey was wearing in her school picture.

I searched through the makeup bag, but didn't find anything unusual. In the bag of toiletries, I found an envelope folded in half. It was addressed to Aubrey Wood, from an Olivia Wood.

I pocketed the letter and the ribbon, and closed the suitcase. I debated taking it with me. I didn't see anything inside that might have a bearing on Seth Carr's murder. But if the police found out, they'd give me holy hell for removing evidence. I also knew that once they got their hands on it, Norma Wood would probably never see it again. If I returned it to her, it might go some way toward alleviating her concerns. At least until I could bring back the girl herself.

I decided to take it with me. I'd already taken the letter and the ribbon. In for a penny, in for a pound.

I was carrying the suitcase back to the door when I heard a low creaking sound from out in the hallway. I thought it might have just been the building settling, but then I saw the doorknob turning.

I put the suitcase down quietly and reached for my gun. It occurred to me that I might be overreacting. I glanced down and saw the brick lying on the floor where I'd left it. I bent down and picked it up instead.

I stood to one side of the door as it slowly opened. I expected someone to come strolling in, or to hear them scream when they saw the body. Instead, a hand entered the room. It was holding a gun. Cops sometimes walk into places like that, but they usually announce themselves first. I had a gut feeling this wasn't a cop.

With my free hand, I reached out and grabbed the hand around the wrist and pulled. At the same time, I drove my shoulder into the door, slamming it against the arm attached to the hand. I heard a grunt of pain from the other side. It was a man, and a big one, too. The wrist I was holding was as thick as my neck. I felt the door being pushed back. I put all of my weight on it and bashed the man's hand against the jamb. He wouldn't let go of the gun, but he didn't shoot it, either, which I considered a plus.

I turned and put my back to the door. I let go of the man's wrist, and with my other hand, I brought the brick down hard on the gun. It fell to the floor as I heard the man on the other side of the door let out another grunt — this one more pissed off than pained. The hand retracted and the door clicked shut. I leapt out of the way a second before it came flying open again, this time on the end of the man's foot.

I didn't give myself a chance to hesitate and freeze up. I just launched myself at the man in the doorway.

It was like trying to tackle a cinder block wall. He was big and wide and he didn't move an inch when I slammed into his body. I caught a glimpse of a leather jacket and a grey shirt, then I was sliding down to the floor.

The man caught me halfway down, gripping my throat in the hand that had been holding the gun. His knuckles were bloody from where I'd hit him with the brick. I had the impression he was a bit put out by that as he hauled me to my feet and then up into the air. He did so effortlessly, with no sense of strain in his arm. He might have been lifting a bag of groceries. He held me up so we were staring at each other eye to eye.

Despite his massive build, the man's face was curiously thin, almost gaunt, with hollow cheeks and a sharp nose. His small eyes, peering out of from beneath a heavy crag of brow, looked at me like I was something he had pulled off the bottom of his shoe.

"I don't know you," he said in a deep, rumbling voice. It was how an active volcano might sound if it could speak.

I might have cracked something wise, but I couldn't say anything with the man's hand clamped around my throat. I thought he might loosen his grip so I could explain myself, but that didn't seem to be on today's agenda. Instead, he stepped back out into the hallway and slammed me into the wall next to the door. My feet were still a few inches off the floor. I could feel the strength pouring out of my body. With the last bit I had left, I pulled my legs up, planted my feet against the big man's midsection and kicked off.

I'd hoped this would have been enough to break his hold on my throat, but it wasn't. Instead, I drove him back into a door on the other side of the hallway, and he pulled me along for the ride. I remembered the brick in my hand and brought it down on his wrist. It was like hitting the trunk of a tree. I hit him again and again, and finally he let me go. I landed on wobbly legs that threatened to spill me to the floor. The big man, towering over me at around six foot seven or six foot eight inches, didn't let that happen. He grabbed me by my upper arms and slammed me back into the wall. I felt the brick slip out of my hand and fall to the floor. I considered pushing him back with my feet like I did before, but I knew this wasn't a game I could win. My opponent was much stronger, and it was only a matter of time before he split my skull open or simply ploughed my body straight through the wall.

I aimed a well-placed kick at the big man's kneecap. He howled in pain and let me go as his leg folded beneath him. He tried to compensate by shifting weight to his other leg, but I delivered another kick to that kneecap. It was kind of dirty, but then this wasn't a refereed boxing match. No one was going to ring a bell to keep this guy from pounding me into ground chuck.

He stumbled backward, propping his back against the opposite wall. We were almost the same height now. As I reached down to pick up the brick, the door next to the big man opened and an old man peered out with wide, startled eyes.

"Call the police," I told him. "Right now."

The old man slammed the door shut and I heard the sound of several locks engaging.

The big man was starting to straighten up. I hefted the brick and gave him a sidelong shot across the chops. Anyone else would have gone reeling down the hallway, but the big man only stumbled a few steps on his unsteady legs. When he turned slightly away from me, I swung the brick at the small of his back. He let out a thick grunt. I stayed on him. I knew if he got his hands on me again, I was finished. I kicked the back of his leg and it buckled. He fell to one knee and screamed in pain. I planted my foot against his spine and propelled him forward. He was able to get an arm up at the last second and keep his face from smashing into the floor. I came around and kicked his arm out from under him. He landed flat on his chest, tried to push himself up with his hands, and I brought my foot down on his fingers. He growled and reached for my shoe. I skipped back around behind him and straddled him. I slammed the brick into his kidneys and then pressed it against the back of his neck.

"I could do this all day," I said, "but it'll probably start getting messy."

"Police brutality, motherfucker," the big man said in his volcano voice.

"I'm not the police."

"Fuck." He spat blood onto the floor. "You sure tossed my salad. For a little guy."

"I'm not little."

"Everyone's little compared to me."

"The bigger they are..."

"You kneecapped me."

"You pulled a gun on me."

"I had it out," the big man said. "I didn't pull it on you."

"It wouldn't have made much difference if you'd shot me."

He grunted and tried to turn his head to look at me. I pressed the brick harder against his neck.

"Why'd you ice the kid?" he asked.

"I could ask you the same thing."

He shook his head. "That ain't my work. The kid was a pain in the ass, but I wouldn't have done that. Not for free."

"You're a hitman?"

I took the brick away and the big man looked over his shoulder at me. "You're not a cop?"

"No."

"And you really didn't kill the kid?"

I stared at him.

"Hey," he said, "it's no skin off my ass. He was a fucking puppy."

"You knew him?" I said.

He tried to shrug his shoulders, but it was hard with me sitting on him. "You could say that," he said.

"You know his girlfriend, too?"

The big man stared back at the floor. "What girlfriend?"

"Seth had a girl staying with him. If you knew him, you must've known her, too."

"I know a lot of girls."

"You know one named Aubrey Wood?"

"She was his girlfriend?" The big man sounded surprised. "He sure handed her off quick." He chuckled. "The things people will do to get ahead in this world."

"What does that mean?"

The big man shook his head. "Business, man. It's just business."

"Who do you work for?"

"You don't want to know."

"Yes, I do."

"No, you don't," the big man said firmly. "I tell you, then you're a dead man. Cause and effect. You want that?"

"I want to know who took Aubrey Wood."

"I can't tell you. Trust me, pal, I'm doing you a favour."

"Tell me his name."

"Fuck you."

"What's your name?"

"Fuck you."

"Are the two of you related?"

The big man craned his head around to look at me again. "You sure you ain't a cop? You talk like one."

I put the brick against his neck again and he turned his head back around. With my free hand I patted him down. I pulled a thick wallet out of his back pocket. It was packed full of cash, crisp hundreds and fifties. His driver's license said his name was William Donto.

I started to ask him about the money when I heard a sound at the far end of the hallway.

Sitting on a bleeding man's back, holding a brick to his head with one hand, the man's wallet in the other.

Naturally that's when the police would show up.

13

I STILL MIGHT HAVE BEEN able to talk my way out of things if one of the officers hadn't slipped past me and looked inside Seth Carr's apartment. His partner had his service pistol trained on me, and when the first officer shouted, "Lord, fuck a duck" and stumbled out, wide-eyed and whey-faced, I knew I was screwed.

Donto and I sat next to each other in the back of a police cruiser, both of us in handcuffs. Donto stared at the floor between his feet and told me over and over in a monotone that I was dead, so fucking dead, once these cuffs were off and he got his hands on me, I was fucking dog meat. I told him I was getting fucking bored of listening to him talk, so fucking bored, so could he please shut the fuck up.

We went on like that for the better part of an hour before the homicide detectives showed up. I recognized them. Drake and Robichaud. Drake was in his late thirties, tall and broad-shouldered, thick black hair cut close to his head. Robichaud was shorter and rounder, in his late fifties, with salt-and-pepper hair and a matching moustache. Drake was the more loquacious of the pair. Robichaud tended to communicate in monosyllables and a series of grunts that only Drake seemed to understand. I'd crossed paths with them before, but that didn't necessarily put me in their good books. At best, I was in their ambivalent books.

One of the uniformed officers was speaking with Robichaud while Drake strolled over to the cruiser and peered in the window at me. He closed his eyes and shook his head with infinite disappointment. He went over and said something to the uniform. The officer said something back and shrugged. Drake came back to the car, opened the back door, and hauled me out.

"Dismembered corpse in an apartment," Drake said. "We've gotta stop meeting like this, Felix."

"I keep trying to ask you out to dinner, but you never return my calls."

"Still a wiseass, I see."

"If it ain't broke…"

"You're gonna get something broke, you keep running your mouth like that."

"You sound like my ex-wife."

"*Ex*-wife?" he said with mock surprise. "You mean someone actually let you go? A prize like you?"

"Hardy-har, Detective. If we're done with the opening repartee, I'd like to go home now."

"You give a statement yet?"

"This doesn't have anything to do with me. I didn't even know the kid."

"You came to see him."

I held up my cuffed hands. "Do you mind? I speak better when I can gesticulate."

Drake took out a small silver key, removed the handcuffs, and tossed them to the uniformed officer. "Gesticulate, eh?" He crossed his arms. "Tell me what you're doing here, but try to use smaller words. Dumb cops like me don't understand anything with more than three syllables."

Robichaud sauntered over with his hands in his pockets. Drake turned to him and jerked a thumb at me.

"You remember Mr. Felix Renn? Super Dick?"

Robichaud grunted.

"Super Dick?" I said.

"That's what we call you downtown," Drake said. "It's short for supernatural detective."

"It's nice to be popular." I nodded at Robichaud. "Good to see you again, Detective. How's tricks?"

Robichaud stared at me.

"Cut the chit-chat, Felix," Drake said. "I wanna know what happened here."

"I don't know," I said. "I'm looking for a missing girl. I got a line on her boyfriend, came over here to question him, and found him dead in his apartment."

"How does Donto fit into all of this?"

"You know him?" I said. "Who is he?"

"Answer the question, Super Dick."

"I don't know. Like I said, I was hired to find a missing girl."

"And the guy upstairs was her boyfriend?"

"That's what I was told."

"You think she killed him?"

"Doubtful," I said. "Unless she's a werewolf."

Drake stared at me.

"I don't think she's a werewolf."

"You think Donto did it?"

I considered that for a long moment. Finally, I said, "No. He showed up shortly after I arrived. He could've killed the kid and then come back to make an alibi for himself, but I doubt it."

"And why's that?"

"Donto's a gunman, isn't he?"

Drake didn't say anything. Robichaud didn't even grunt.

"I don't know exactly what happened to Seth Carr, but it didn't look like he was shot. It's way too messy for a hit."

"Unless the person who ordered the hit wanted it done that way," Drake said.

"I've got a gut feeling. It wasn't a hit, and I don't think Donto did it."

Drake turned to Robichaud. "You hear that? Super Dick has a gut feeling. I guess that means we can let Donto go and take the rest of the day off, then."

"You should hold him," I said. "Guy like that, I'm sure he's guilty of something."

That earned me a grunt from Robichaud. Then he turned and went into the building.

Drake took out his notebook. "You said the vic's name is Seth Carr?"

"That's right."

"You came here looking for him?"

"For his girlfriend."

"What's her name?"

"Aubrey Wood." I figured it was okay to tell him. Client confidentiality didn't seem to matter since Norma Wood had already filed a missing-person report with the police. They had pretty much ignored her, but I had a feeling they'd put some effort into finding Aubrey now that she was wanted for questioning in a homicide investigation.

Robichaud came back with a crime-scene baggie. Inside was a wallet. I thought it was Donto's at first, but it wasn't. This one was cheap-looking, with a Velcro fastener. Robichaud was wearing latex gloves as he took it out and opened it to show Drake the driver's license behind the plastic window. The name was Seth Carr.

It was Drake's turn to grunt. Robichaud spread open the bill compartment to reveal a thick wad of cash.

"Kid was strapped," Drake said, stating the obvious. "Where'd he get that kind of money?" He directed the question at me.

I shrugged. "Paper route?"

"Payoff," Robichaud said. He didn't speak very often, but when he did, he was usually right.

"How much is there?" Drake asked.

"Two grand even."

"How much was laughing boy over there carrying?" Drake nodded at Donto sitting in the back of the cruiser.

"Same," said Robichaud.

"Think he came by to give the kid the other half?"

Robichaud grunted.

"If it was a double-cross, why didn't he take the kid's money?"

Robichaud flicked his eyes briefly in Donto's direction. "He didn't do this."

"You think it was just bad timing?"

Robichaud grunted.

"Same goes for you, too, I suppose?" Drake said to me.

"Story of my life, really," I said.

Robichaud put the wallet in the baggie and went back into the building.

Drake watched him go, then turned to me with a frown. "You know what your problem is?"

"Too much handsome in one body?"

Drake opened his mouth, then closed it and shook his head tiredly. He waved his hand at me like he was casting out an evil spirit. "Take a hike, Felix. You make my head hurt."

I started away, then suddenly remembered the brick. I'd put it down on the floor in the upstairs hallway before the cops handcuffed me. I asked Drake if I could go back upstairs for a minute.

"It's a crime scene, Felix. You know the rules. What's the matter? You leave your purse up there?"

I walked back to my car. Jerry was going to kill me, but there was nothing I could do about it. At best, I could come back later and hope it would still be there. At worst, a crime-scene tech would end up bagging it as evidence and I'd have to pull some strings and call in some big favours to get it back. *If* I could get it back.

I got behind the wheel and put the key in the ignition. Then I froze and turned my head slowly to the right.

The brick was sitting on the passenger seat.

I stared at it for a long moment. "Sorry about that," I said, and started the car.

14

I STOPPED for a coffee at the Tim Hortons in Lawrence Plaza. As I was digging in my pocket for change, I found the envelope I had taken from Aubrey Wood's suitcase.

I took my cup over to a quiet corner table and removed the letter from the envelope. It was several pages long and written in a smooth Palmer Method hand. It was dated two weeks ago, October 25th.

DEAR AUBREY,

I've been putting off writing this letter for some time, and now I fear it's too late. Or too little too late. I wanted to tell you these things while I was alive, but I kept putting it off. Your mother said it would only cause you harm, and maybe that's true, but that doesn't mean you don't have a right to know. More than a right — you *need* to know. But your mother convinced me to remain silent. Your mother is good at convincing people of things. She's even convinced herself that what happened in the past didn't happen at all. And I suppose I let her. Because she's my daughter and I loved her and wanted to protect her. Unfortunately, I fear I've done the opposite. By remaining silent I've put you both in great danger.

It's hard to know where to begin. I don't know how much your mother told you about me, how much you overheard during the screaming matches on the phone that made up the only contact we've had in the years since you were born. I hate myself for that, for not being in your life, but it was unavoidable. I had my reasons, which I'll try to explain as much as I understand them myself, but the thing you need to remember is this: *I stayed away to protect you.* I didn't want you or your mother to get hurt because of me. I didn't want either of you to be contaminated by my presence. It's the great sadness of my life that I couldn't know you, couldn't love you except from afar, without bringing a great darkness into your life.

But it's all coming to an end now. Soon I will be gone and I hope — I pray — that the darkness will leave with me.

I'm writing this letter to you in case it doesn't.

But I'm jumping ahead. I need to start at the beginning, which for me is a long time ago. Young people are often bored by stories told by their grandparents, but I think this one will keep your interest. I've only told it once before, to your mother, and I don't know how much she believed and how much she thought were the ravings of a senile old woman. I like to think she believed it all, that she cut me out of her life not because she thought I was crazy but because she knew what I told her was true. I could understand that. We protect our families, even if we have to cut off part of them. Like removing a rotten limb to save the rest of the body. It's not about love. It's about survival.

Did your mother tell you I was crazy? Did she say I was dangerous? It's okay if she did. I don't blame her. There are many things about my life that I don't understand, but there's one thing of which I am completely certain: *I'm not crazy.* Of course, crazy people say that all the time, don't they? I guess you'll just have to read my story and decide for yourself. As for dangerous, I guess you could say I am. That's part of the reason I live on this island, away from the people I love, away from everyone. But that's not entirely accurate. It's not me that's dangerous. It's the thing that's been following me since I was eight years old.

It was May of 1942. I was living with my family in England. We had a place in London, one of the few that wasn't destroyed in the Blitz a year before. The war was still on, and London was slowly rebuilding itself. Despite that, my mother was growing tired of city life, and my father was able to get a transfer through his accounting firm to a town called Ipswich. We bought a place north of town. It was called Rosedale Cottage. It was quaint and cozy, very different from the flat in London, but I liked it. The only part I didn't like was switching schools and leaving all my friends behind. Rosedale Cottage was out in the country, and since there weren't a lot of other houses around, there were no kids to play with.

It was summer when we moved, and I spent the first few weeks exploring the area by myself. My parents never seemed to worry about where I went or how long I was gone. My father was getting settled into his new job, and I think my mother was getting settled in a different way. Most days when I left in the morning she'd be sitting in her rocker by the front window with a cup of tea, and more often than not that's where she was when I came back later in the day.

One time I came back from my wanderings and my mother

mentioned in an offhand way that the back door had opened by itself. It had happened around noon, and she thought it was me, coming home for lunch. I told her I'd been in the woods all day, and she nodded. She knew it wasn't me, she said, because when she got up to investigate, the front door suddenly opened as well. She thought it was the wind at first, but then the windows in the living room, two at the front of the house and one at the side, suddenly went up in unison. Doors opening and closing on their own was one thing, but windows rising up by themselves? The strangest part was how utterly calm she was as she told me.

She didn't tell my father about the doors and windows opening by themselves. Nor did she tell him about the things that started disappearing and reappearing around the house. There was a big mixing bowl that was kept on top of a tall cabinet in the kitchen. I couldn't reach it even if I was standing on the counter. One morning I came downstairs and the bowl was sitting on the floor in the middle of the foyer. I could hear the creak of my mother's rocking chair in the living room. I asked her about the bowl. She calmly put down her cup of tea, came over to pick up the bowl, and carried it back to the kitchen without saying a word.

I realize in the telling of this story that my mother might come off as mentally unbalanced, perhaps even a little crazy, and while I agree that she was clearly suffering from some sort of emotional malaise — something that probably prompted her desire to move out of London in the first place — I never thought for a single moment that she was the one who put the bowl on the floor.

The strange activity in the house continued over the following weeks. My mother continued to ignore it in her strangely comatose way, while my father was barely aware of it, spending most of his time, including some weekends, at his office. I was the only one who seemed to have a clear picture of what was going on, as well as the understanding that it wasn't normal. I should have felt scared and alone, but in fact it was quite the opposite. I was happy and exhilarated. I was eight, after all, an age when the world still holds fantastic wonders instead of bitter truths. I was young and naïve, and I couldn't see what was really happening. It all came to a head when I fell down that damn well.

Yes, it's true, kids really do fall down wells. It's not something that happens only in bad movies-of-the-week.

One of my favourite things to do was to go running through the tall grass in the overgrown fields behind our house. I liked not being able to see anything except the green stalks whipping past my face. Leaping high into the air every now and then to get my bearings.

It was during one of these mighty frog-leaps that I came down on the rotted well cover. It might have supported my weight if I'd simply sprinted across it, but I hadn't done that. I had come down on it with all of my weight, which wasn't much, but enough to send me falling thirty or forty feet into the rock-lined darkness below.

It was a miracle I didn't break my neck, or even an arm or a leg. Another miracle came later. If you want to call it that.

Something happened to me down there. I only remember bits and pieces of it. I'm not sure if that's because I hit my head or because the things I saw were too big to fit through the doors of an eight-year-old's mental perception. All I know is that it happened, and that at the time I thought of it as "going Wonderland."

Later on I figured out where I really went, and it wasn't Wonderland. I'm sure you know the place, although I hope with all my heart that you never go there.

The Black Lands.

You want to know what happened to me over there. I understand that. Kids are curious about the Black Lands. Generations of parents told their kids monsters weren't real. Now we have to tell them they are. We can't protect them from the truth, because not telling them only puts them in further danger. It's a strange, dark world we live in now, isn't it? It was a strange, dark world at the bottom of the well, too. I remember thinking there must have been a tunnel branching off somewhere because I could feel a breeze on my face. It smelled like flowers, but not like any I'd ever smelled before. I crawled into the tunnel — or what I thought was a tunnel — and I suppose that's why the image of

Alice and the rabbit-hole came to mind. Of course, the tunnel wasn't a tunnel. It was a portal. And it didn't take me to Wonderland. I found myself in a field, not unlike the one I'd been running through before I fell down the well. Only the grass was twice as tall… and it was silver. Not grey. Silver. Like thousands of thin, tapering blades swaying gently in the breeze. They seemed to glow, which is why it took me a minute to realize it was nighttime. The moon was out, full and huge, and the milky glow it cast was so bright I had to squint my eyes against it. It was like looking at the sun. My first instinct should have been to turn away, but I didn't. I stared at that moon — one so similar to our own and yet so different — until I became aware of a low swishing sound.

It was a sound I recognized immediately. I had made it myself only a short time ago. It was the sound of something moving through the grass. I looked around. There were trees at the far edge of the field. I could see their crowns stretching up to the black sky. They were moving. Not swaying like the silver grass, but actually *moving*. I saw one of the trees spread out its branches in a wide star-like pattern and then bring them back in close to its trunk, like it had just woken up and was stretching.

I like most trees, but I didn't like these ones. They seemed more like creatures masquerading as trees. I knew I was the one who had woken them up and that they would be coming for me. I looked around for the tunnel that had taken me to this place, but there was nothing nearby but those tall blades of silver grass. Behind me I heard a heavy crump, followed by what sounded like thousands of voices whispering to one another. I knew what it was. One of the trees was moving through the grass. Moving toward me.

I looked back up at the moon, that enormous white eye staring down into my small blue ones. It was no help to me, but I couldn't tear my gaze from it. I felt almost hypnotized; a part of me wanted to stay there watching it even as the tree — or the thing that looked like a tree — came closer. It was like if I stared at it long enough, the moon might actually start talking to me. I wondered how it would sound, what it would say. I was aware of the whispering getting louder, and I could see the tree getting closer out of the corner of my eye, but I didn't care. I couldn't stop looking at the moon.

There was only one thing I could do. With my eyes still fixed on the sky, I began to crawl backward the way I had come. I may not have been able to tear my eyes from that ghostly orb, but that didn't mean I couldn't move and watch it at the same time.

Off to the right, I saw a massive black branch thrust aside a curtain of grass and silver stalks went flying outward in a spray of dirt. I caught movement at the base of the tree, and saw a mass of flailing tentacles. They reached for me, and it was only after I crawled through the portal and suddenly found myself back at the bottom of the well that I realized what they were: roots. Roots of the tree-thing that surely would have killed me if I hadn't found my way home.

As I laid in that cold, dank hole, I started screaming. I don't know how long it was until my parents finally heard my cries, but it was night when they lowered a rope and pulled me out. Real night, not the lightless void of that other place. People try to draw comparisons between our world and the Black Lands, but I can tell you with authority and experience that they are nothing alike. That place may seem like a world of perpetual night, but it's really the domain of perpetual nightmares. It may look like our world on the surface — the grass, the trees — but it's all an illusion. A deception. Everything over there is filled with a hideous, predatory hunger. Even the moon. I stared at it the entire time I was over there, and I could feel it staring back at me.

In the weeks that followed my trip to "Wonderland," the strange activity in the house grew in both intensity and frequency. Things continued to disappear from one spot and reappear somewhere else. One day I found half a dozen dead birds lined up on the back stoop, the sort of thing an ambitious cat might have left, if we had one. Another time my father was leaving for work and found a large section of the lawn flattened down in what is referred to these days as a crop circle or devil's circle. At night there was rapping on the front and back doors, and when my father would go to check it out, no one was ever there. Sometimes, I'd be awakened by something tapping at my window. I never looked to see what it was. I always turned over or buried my head under the covers. I was too afraid to look. I thought I might see a long black branch reaching for me on the other side of the glass.

It was during this time that I realized something had happened to me when I fell down the well. My parents had looked me over, even taken me to the doctor to have me properly examined, and there was nothing wrong with me. Not on the outside anyway.

I remembered something one of my teachers had said. She was quoting someone, but I can't remember who it was. She said the eyes are the windows of the soul. That phrase came back to me time and time again that summer. I remembered staring up at that alien moon and thinking, *If the eyes really are windows, what happens when they're open? What happens if you let something inside?*

That's the closest I can come to explaining what happened to me. I had "gone Wonderland" and come back with something. Something I carried inside me. It was like I had new eyes and ears that let me see and hear things differently. I still spent my days in the fields and woods around our house, but I never travelled as far as I used to. I wasn't afraid of the world, but I'd grown wary of it. I'd hear a strong wind blowing through the trees, and it would sound like voices whispering. I'd get closer so I could hear what they were saying, and sometimes I was able to make out a few words. The trees were talking about us. Me and my parents. They said we were going to die. Then the wind would rush faster, and the sound of the leaves thrashing was like laughter. Cruel, twisted laughter.

The nights were the worst. I slept with the curtains drawn so I didn't have to see what was tapping at my window.

The first time I heard the voice, I thought it was my father. I thought he had come into my room and was trying to wake me up. I sat up and looked around, but there was no one there. For once there wasn't even any tapping. It was completely quiet.

When the voice spoke again, I realized it was coming from directly behind me. I almost tumbled out of bed as I twisted around to see who it was. But there was nothing there except the brick wall of the cottage.

I lay back down and closed my eyes. As I was drifting back to sleep, I heard the voice again. I didn't open my eyes this time. I didn't even move. I tried to ignore it as I had learned to ignore the tapping at the window. But the voice would not be ignored. It whispered to me like it was lying right next to me. I could feel it hypnotizing me, the same way the moon in the Black Lands had done.

The voice said it meant no harm. Not to me or my parents. It told me it lived in the cottage, and had been living there for a long time. I asked if it was the one who moved the big bowl on top of the cabinet. Yes, it said. It had moved many things since we had arrived. I asked why, and the voice told me it was trying to make us leave. It said we were going to die if we remained at the cottage. It didn't say it the way the trees had said it, like it was looking forward to it. It sounded regretful, almost sad.

The voice didn't speak to me again that night, but that wasn't the last I heard of it. The following night, as I lay in bed, floating in that place between wakefulness and sleep, it came back. Once again it told me I had to leave, that if I didn't, I would die, my parents would die. That's what happened to the others who had lived here, the voice said. They died because they didn't listen, and they didn't listen because they couldn't hear. But I could hear. And when it told me about Rosedale Cottage, about all the people who had died there, who had been killed there, I listened.

The voice told me the whole story over the next few nights, but I only remember parts of it. Not because it wasn't interesting or important — it was both of those things — but because the voice spoke in such a low whisper that I couldn't always make out what it was saying. Also, since it only spoke to me when I was half-awake, I sometimes found myself drifting off while it was talking.

This is what I remember...

Rosedale Cottage was haunted, and not just by the entity that moved things around during the day and whispered to me at night. There was another presence lurking there, a creature that the voice referred to as "the Whyver." At least that's what it sounded like to me. The voice said the Whyver was vicious and violent and it had staked out this area as its hunting ground. I now believe that this creature was drawn to Rosedale Cottage because of the portal at the bottom of the well located on the property. I don't know very much about Black Lands entities, but I've heard that some of them are drawn to portals like moths to flame. The voice said the Whyver kills anyone who moves into Rosedale Cottage, to protect its territory.

That's why we had to leave. The voice said the Whyver was starting to manifest, and it was only a matter of time before it would be able to take physical form. When that happened, it would slaughter me and my parents without mercy. The Whyver had done it before, the voice said. Many, many times. It tried to warn the others before us, tried to make them leave, but they always stayed. And they always died.

It might sound strange, but I sensed that the voice liked me. Maybe because I was the first one who could hear it. Maybe because I was touched by the Black Lands, the place from which the voice had surely come. Perhaps it sensed a kindred spirit. I don't know. But the voice felt like a friend, and it spoke to me with the care and concern of a friend. The only one I'd made since we'd moved. I remember one of the last things the voice ever told me. It said there was a place for every-thing in this world, and everything in its place. It said my place wasn't in Rosedale Cottage.

I told the voice my parents would never agree to leave. We'd just moved, after all, and my father had just started a new job. The voice told me I'd have to make them leave. No matter what.

I put off thinking about it for a few days. The paranormal activity in the house had abruptly stopped, and I started to believe that maybe it was over. Maybe I had imagined the voice. Maybe we weren't really being hunted by some monster from the Black Lands.

But then I started seeing the shadow. A tall, hulking shadow that passed by the windows. I knew it was the Whyver. Stalking the cottage, waiting for that time when it could slip completely into our world and come for us. When the tapping at my window turned into banging, when I finally forced myself to look and saw the dark shape with the burning red eyes... I knew I had to make a decision.

So, I set a fire. In the kitchen, in the box of kindling next to the wood stove. The house went up fast — much faster than I'd expected — and my parents and I only narrowly escaped. They never suspected me, and there was no investigation. The cause was blamed on an errant spark from a fire that hadn't been put out properly. There wasn't much left of the cottage. The parts that would burn had burned away completely, leaving only piles of ash and smoke-stained bricks.

We moved back to London. Strangely, my mother came out of her funk and returned to normal. I guess she missed the city more than she thought. My father got back on with his old accounting firm, and by the time the new school term started, it was like we'd never left. The summer we spent at Rosedale Cottage might have been a dream — a strange, dark dream — if it was the last time I saw the Whyver. But it wasn't.

Eight years later, when I was sixteen, I went on a class trip to Stonehenge to see the portal lights. I'm not sure if you've heard of them, but they're a fairly well-known phenomena in England. They only come out at night — orbs of blue and white light that materialize over the massive stones. Sometimes they move slowly through the air, but they never leave the circle of stones.

The bus dropped us off in the early evening, and we still had an hour or so before the portal lights were due to appear. I was standing with some friends at the barrier when I saw it. At first, I thought it was someone walking among the stones. I pointed it out to my friends, but it quickly became clear that none of them could see what I was seeing. They thought I was joking with them, trying to scare them by pretending to see ghosts. Except I'd seen this thing before, and I knew it wasn't a ghost. It was the same hulking shadow-shape that had passed by the windows of Rosedale Cottage. I recognized it in a way that I can't fully describe. Maybe it was my new eyes. Maybe that's why my friends couldn't see it. It was the Whyver, and it had found me.

I never did see the portal lights. I spent the rest of the trip on the bus. My friends thought I had chickened out, and I let them believe that. I was afraid, but not of the portal lights. They were harmless. The Whyver wasn't.

It didn't take long to realize the Whyver wasn't through with me.

What had started as a territorial dispute had become something personal. Maybe because it didn't get the chance to kill me and my family. We were the first ones to leave Rosedale Cottage alive, and we'd left in such a way that no one else would ever live there again. Or maybe it was because the Whyver knew I was different. Maybe it sensed the Black Lands in me the same way it sensed the portal at the bottom of the well. I don't know. All I do know is that it has been lurking on the edge of my life ever since.

I grew up and moved away from home. All the way to Canada. But there were portals there, too. There are portals all over the world today, and more cropping up all the time. I did my best to stay away from them. I tried to live a normal life. I got married and had a child, your mother, and although we lived in a place far away from any portals — any *known* portals, that is — I could still feel them around me. It was like living in a prison, except it was a prison of the mind, and the fences were always closing in tighter and tighter. There were times when I could feel a portal close by, and I would catch a glimpse of a tall, hulking shadow with burning red eyes. That's when I knew the Whyver would always be with me, always be waiting for me.

It goes without saying that this affected my family life. My husband and I fought endlessly. He didn't believe me when I told him we were being stalked by a creature from the Black Lands, and who could really blame him? My mental state was deteriorating. It came to a point where I stopped leaving the house. I was afraid to go out. Getting close to a portal was like sending up a flare to the Whyver. I feared for my family, and just like when I was eight years old, I knew I had to make a decision.

You see, your mother didn't have the new eyes and ears that I got from the Black Lands. I remember when she was born how happy I was and how afraid. Afraid that I might have passed this thing on to her. But she didn't have it. I knew she didn't. I could sense it the way I could sense when there was a portal nearby. She was normal. She was safe.

Time went by and the number of portals around the world continued to grow. I'm sure I don't need to tell you that. They talk about it all the time on the news. You might even learn about it in school. I didn't need to be told. I could feel the portals closing in around me, and I knew it was only a matter of time before I started seeing shadows moving past the windows. I couldn't let that happen.

So, I left. I left my husband and my little girl, who wasn't so little anymore. Norma, your mother, was old enough to understand that I was leaving, and old enough to hate me for it. That was okay. I hated myself, too. I still do. The only comfort I take, if that's the right word, is in knowing that staying would have been worse. Staying would have meant the death of us all.

I didn't leave their lives entirely. There were phone calls and letters. Your mother grew up and got married and had a child of her own. You may not know this, but we first met when you were only a few weeks old. Your mother and I had a brief reconciliation. The birth of a child is good for things like that. I held you and rocked you and kissed you twice, once on each sleeping eyelid. I can still remember your sweet smell, your tiny curled hands, your soft breath on my neck.

When I held you, I knew you were like me. Your mother thought my tears were of happiness, but they weren't. They were tears of pain and guilt. I tried to tell her, to warn her, but she wouldn't listen to me, just as her father wouldn't listen all those years before. I tried to tell her that she had to take you away. Away from the portals. I didn't want you to draw the attention of the Whyver. I knew he would be looking for you as he had been looking for me. Blood calls to blood. You and me, Aubrey, we're bound by this thing, this gift, this curse. It ties our destinies together. I know you probably don't believe me, but I promise, if you don't stay away from the Black Lands, you'll find out very fast that what I've told you is true.

It's not right for me to burden you with this knowledge, but I have no choice. I've been having dreams, horrible dreams about you and me and the Whyver. I think it's close. I feel it. Sometimes I sit at my window and look out at the lake and think, *All of this happened because a little girl fell down a well.* Now I fear I've passed the darkness onto you. You'll see it coming with your new eyes, but you won't be able to stop it. But maybe I can. Maybe if I'm gone the Whyver will leave, too. All I can do is pray that the darkness dies with me. If it doesn't, you'll need to protect yourself.

First and foremost, stay away from the Black Lands. Stay away from the portals. If you ever notice any sign of paranormal activity in your house, if you see the shadow outside your window, it means the Whyver has found you. If this happens, you *must* leave.

There are safe places in this world. One of them is my house on Wolfe Island. If things get bad, if you ever need a place to stay — or a place to stay *alive* — go there. It's yours now. I've left the house to you. It will protect you as it as it has protected me. As I always wished I could have protected you.

I never meant for any of this to happen. I love you, Aubrey, and I wish nothing less for you than a life filled with happiness and peace.

All my love, always,
Grandma Olivia

15

MY COFFEE WAS cold by the time I finished reading Olivia Wood's letter. Despite the lack of caffeine in my system, I felt more awake than I had in days. I still had a few dozen questions that needed answers, but at least I'd found the connection between the brick and the Wood family.

Olivia Wood may have died, but the entity that resided in Rosedale Cottage still wanted to help her granddaughter. Maybe it knew Aubrey had the same enhanced perceptions as her grandmother. Maybe it felt it owed a debt to Olivia Wood. I couldn't say for certain. The brick didn't speak to me. I hadn't fallen down a well and "gone Wonderland."

It also explained Jerry's story of paranormal activity at Rosedale Cottage, and the sudden escalation into a series of violent murders.

Not to mention the reason why the brick never harmed Jerry after he installed it in his own house.

There were two entities at Rosedale Cottage. One dwelled within the building itself, while the other stalked the grounds on which it stood. One tried to save the people who lived there, while the other stalked and murdered them. Only now, the cottage was gone and the Whyver had left to hunt abroad.

Regardless of the things I still didn't understand, the answers I still didn't have, my purpose was clear.

I had to find Aubrey before the Whyver did.

16

NORMA WOOD WAS drunk when she opened the door. She had to hang onto the jamb with one hand to keep herself propped up. In the other hand she held a lowball glass of gin. I couldn't smell it from the glass, but I got a heavy waft of it on her breath.

She gestured me inside with a grand sweep of her arm, sloshing gin on the floor. "Plenty more where that came from," she said.

I stepped inside. One of the other panes in the front window was broken, but this one hadn't been covered up with plywood. Norma saw me looking at it and said, "That one was me."

"Who broke the other one? Aubrey?"

Norma slumped back against the wall and sipped her drink. "Maybe."

"I don't think it was."

"Who the fuck cares about broken windows?" she blurted. "I hired you to find my daughter."

I stuck my hands in my pockets. "I haven't found her yet, but I've learned some things about her. And your mother."

Norma started to raise the glass to her mouth, then lowered it. "My mother? She doesn't have anything to do with this."

"I'm afraid she does. And I think you already know that."

"What are you talking about?"

She pushed herself off the wall and stumbled into the living room. She went over to a sideboard, picked up a bottle of Bombay Sapphire and freshened her drink. She waggled the glass at me. "You want one?"

"I want to talk about your mother."

Norma scoffed. "She doesn't have anything to do with Aubrey. She never has."

"She wrote Aubrey a letter before she died."

Her forehead wrinkled in a look of such intense confusion that it was almost a caricature. "What letter?"

"I found it in Aubrey's suitcase," I said, and Norma immediately perked up, forehead smoothing, eyes clearing. I raised a hand to forestall the flood of questions. "I didn't find Aubrey, just the suitcase. It was at her boyfriend's apartment in Lawrence Heights."

Norma frowned. "Boyfriend?"

"Seth Carr. Jack Carr's older brother."

"I don't know him."

"You won't get the chance. He was murdered."

Norma raised her hand to her mouth, realized she was still holding the glass of gin, and took a big swallow. "Was... was Aubrey..."

"She wasn't there. And I have no reason to believe Aubrey has come to any harm. But that doesn't mean she isn't in danger. The sooner you start playing straight with me, the sooner I can find her."

"Play straight? I've told you everything."

"The letter."

"I don't know about any letter," Norma snapped. "Show it to me."

I wasn't going to do that. I didn't have time to wait around for Norma Wood to make her drunken way through the long, sad, dark story of her mother's life. I also had a feeling I might need the letter later on.

"I don't have it," I said. "The police took it for evidence. You can expect a visit from them later." I watched as her head came down and her shoulders slumped, then I hit her with it. "But I read it."

Her head snapped up. "What did it say?"

I gave her the *Coles Notes* version. The move to Rosedale Cottage.

The paranormal activity. The fall down the well. The voice in the night. The shadow at the window. The life spent on the run from the Whyver. At one point, I could see Norma's eyes start to gloss over, and I knew she'd already heard some of this before. By the time I finished, her face had become pale and tight. The story was familiar to her, that much was clear, but she had never believed it. Now she did. Maybe not all of it, but enough to realize the seriousness of the situation.

"I'm not a shrink," I said. "I'm not here to help you sort out your feelings about your mother. I just want to find your daughter, and I can't do that unless you give me the whole story."

Norma didn't say anything for a long time. She took a big drink of gin, then gestured with the glass. "What do you want to know?"

"Is it true? The things your mother said in the letter?"

"How the hell would I know?" Norma said. "I wasn't there." She started to giggle, and the giggles turned into coughing. She put her glass on the sideboard and covered her mouth until it was over. "I'm sorry. I don't usually drink this much." She huffed out a big breath of air and smacked her lips. "I don't feel so good."

"That's fine. But I need you to answer my questions."

Norma nodded mutely. Her throat hitched. "I knew about my mother's past," she said finally. "Her childhood in England. She told me what happened at that cottage, but I never believed her. I thought she was crazy. I asked her once, if this *thing* was really stalking her, then how come I never saw it? She told me it was because she was different. She said I wasn't like her." She looked directly at me, her eyes glistening with tears. "Do you know what it's like to hear your mother say you're not special?"

"She didn't mean it that way."

Norma lowered her head. "I was just a kid. That's how I heard it. When she decided to leave, my father was glad. And so was I. I never believed that she was haunted by some creature from the Black Lands. My father and I were the ones who were haunted. By her."

"You didn't see her again after that?"

Norma shook her head, and the tears started to run down her cheeks. "She'd phone me on birthdays, send presents at Christmas, but that was the only contact we ever had. We could have seen each other, but I never asked and she never offered."

"Then Aubrey was born."

Norma nodded. "I felt bad for not inviting her to the wedding, and when I got pregnant, I knew it was time to try to mend things between us. My father probably wouldn't have approved, but he'd died from a heart attack while I was in university." She wiped at her eyes. "I wanted to reconcile. I wanted Aubrey to know her grandmother. I thought... I thought maybe enough time had passed and my mother..." She trailed off, shaking her head.

"Wasn't crazy anymore?" I offered.

"Yes. I thought maybe it was just a phase she'd gone through or something. Sounds stupid, doesn't it?" She gave me a thin, humourless smile. "I thought things could be different."

"But they weren't?"

"She seemed okay at first. She came here to our house, she held Aubrey. I thought this could be the start of a new beginning. But I guess I was hoping for too much. She hadn't changed at all. You know the first thing she said to my husband and I after she put Aubrey back in her crib? She said we had to move. I remember the look of confusion on Rick's face. He probably thought he'd heard her wrong. But I didn't, and I knew what it meant."

"What did it mean?"

"That she hadn't changed! That she was just as crazy as the day she'd left. She told Rick and I that we had to leave the city. She said there were too many portals in Toronto."

"Did she say why?"

"She said Aubrey had the eyes. Her eyes. She said they were eyes that see, but they were also eyes that could *be* seen." She laughed dryly. "I can't believe I remember that. Just goes to show you how well crazy sticks with you."

"Your mother believed Aubrey would be hunted by the same thing that had been hunting her."

"Yes. She even suggested we move in with her. She has a place on Wolfe Island. I've never been there, but I've pictured it in my mind plenty of times. An old, tumbledown shack full of newspapers and cats. The home of a crazy old woman."

"What happened after that?"

"I sent her away. I told her to leave and never come back. And she never did. She was afraid to come to the city anyway. Afraid to be seen."

"By whom?"

Norma shrugged. "Supernaturals. Ghosts. Demons. I don't know. She was paranoid, delusional."

"Maybe not."

"Just because she wrote it in a letter doesn't make it true."

"Something killed Seth Carr. Something tore him apart. Just like the creature at Rosedale Cottage did to those other people."

"How do you know any of that happened either? My mother might have made it all up."

"I have an independent source."

"Who?"

"An expert on haunted houses. And he says in its day, Rosedale Cottage was the worst. Your mother lived there as a child, and she was able to get out alive. The thing that killed the other people — your mother called it the Whyver — I don't think it liked that very much."

Norma shook her head wearily. "She was crazy."

"Did you and Aubrey fight the night before she left home?"

"I told you, we never fought."

I turned and looked pointedly at the broken windows in the living room.

"I broke that window," Norma said defensively.

"And what about the other one?"

Norma didn't say anything. Instead, she turned and poured herself another drink. She stayed like that, with her back to me, and drank gin for a little while. Then she spun around and said, "We argued. We didn't fight."

"What did you argue about?"

"My mother."

"The letter?"

"I didn't know about the letter. Aubrey never mentioned it." She looked off with a thoughtful expression. "But that must've been why she was so upset. And..."

"And what?"

"There's been some... strange things happening around the house lately."

"Paranormal activity?"

Norma nodded and took steadying sip of gin.

"It started with these loud rumbling sounds. We thought they were trucks driving by on the street, but we'd never heard them before — we've lived in this house for years. So, we started racing to the front windows whenever the rumbling would start, trying to see if it really was a truck going by. We turned it into a game. First person to see a truck wouldn't have to do the dishes for a week. But neither one of us ever saw one. Then we started hearing different sounds. They weren't scary or anything. Just the sort of things that you usually hear in an old house. Creaks, groans, bumps. I came downstairs once in the middle of the night to get a glass of water and found Aubrey standing in the living room. I thought she was sleepwalking, but she turned and looked at me, and I saw she was awake. She asked me if I could hear it. I thought she was talking about the noises we'd been hearing lately, but that wasn't it. Aubrey said she'd been hearing a tapping sound the past few nights. She thought it was someone at her window, but her bedroom is on the second floor. She got up and looked anyway, but no one was there. Then she heard the tapping coming from downstairs. She came down and followed it into the living room. She said she thought she saw something outside the bay window. When I came downstairs, she was trying to figure out what it was. She thought she saw a shadow, but it was too dark to tell for certain. I was leading her back upstairs when I heard it, too."

"The tapping?"

Norma nodded. "Aubrey and I turned back to the window, and it shattered. I thought someone had thrown a rock through it. Then there was a growling sound so loud it actually shook the walls. Aubrey started crying. I held her, but I was scared, too. It was like something was trying to get into the house. I called the police, but when they came, they didn't find anything. Aubrey slept in my bed that night, something she hadn't done since she was little. The following morning, we searched the entire living room, but we couldn't find a rock or a brick or anything else that might have broken the window."

"Were there more incidents like that?"

"One morning, after Aubrey had left for school, I heard a groaning sound from somewhere in the house. It was louder than the usual noises that I'd been dismissing as the house settling. After checking all the downstairs rooms, I went upstairs and found the crack in the wall on the landing. When Aubrey came home from school, she saw it and we started arguing. She must have received my mother's letter by then. She knew what was happening. Or she thought she did."

"You still didn't believe?"

"It may have been years since I'd seen my mother, but I've been living with her madness all my life. Now I was seeing it in my daughter. How was I supposed to react?"

"Aubrey thought something was trying to get into the house."

Norma swallowed the rest of her drink. "Into our house, into our world."

"She knew because your mother told her about Rosedale Cottage."

"She accused me of keeping things from her. About my mother. And it was true, but not in the way she thought. She was convinced I knew what was happening in our house. But I didn't remember everything my mother had told me. I was a child at the time, and the parts I didn't forget, I repressed. That only made Aubrey angrier. She said... she said I made my mother leave, so maybe she should leave, too. I just... I never thought she'd actually do it. But she was so angry."

"When exactly did the paranormal activity start?"

Norma thought about it for a moment, then shook her head. "I'm not sure. A month ago? Six weeks? It's not like we marked it on the calendar or anything."

"And when did your mother die?"

"Two weeks ago. October 26th."

I frowned. The house of cards I'd been building had just collapsed.

I figured the paranormal activity in the Wood house was a sign that the Whyver had moved on to Aubrey, presumably triggered by the death of her grandmother. But the timeframe didn't fit. Olivia Wood was still alive when the strangeness started here.

"I'm sorry to ask, but how did your mother die?"

"She committed suicide," Norma said, lowering her eyes. "She drowned herself in Lake Ontario."

I recalled something Olivia Wood said near the end of her letter: *Maybe if I'm gone the Whyver will leave, too. All I can do is pray that the darkness dies with me.*

She killed herself to save her granddaughter. She thought the Whyver only wanted her, and if she was dead, then it would return to the Black Lands. But it didn't work. The Whyver was after Aubrey now. But why? Was it fixated on her because she had the same psychic scent as her grandmother? It was possible, even likely, but I couldn't help feeling there was more to it than that. Something had triggered the paranormal activity in their house. Something that happened a month to six weeks ago. I asked Norma about it, but she couldn't recall anything.

"I remember when the rumblings started, but I don't recall anything else going on at the time. I went to work, Aubrey went to school. We were just doing the same things we'd always done." She suddenly looked at me with a kind of timid desperation in her eyes. "If all of this is really true, does that mean Aubrey is paramental?"

I bristled at the word. *Paramental* was a derogatory term used to describe someone with psychic abilities. "I can't say for certain," I said, "but to quote the Magic Eight-Ball: all signs point to yes."

She let out a sigh that tapered off into a whimper.

"I asked you before if Aubrey had any interest in the Black Lands. You said she didn't. Was that the truth?"

"Yes!" she said in a loud voice that was almost a whine. "She wanted to enter the Miss Paranormal pageant when she was a kid, but every little girl wants to do that. Kids think the supernatural is fun and exciting. It's not until they grow up that they realize how dangerous it really is."

"Sometimes not even then," I said. "Has Aubrey ever been to your mother's place on Wolfe Island?"

Norma shook her head. "Never. I don't think she even knows where it is."

"She does now."

"Do you think that's where she went?"

"I don't know. It's a long way to go for someone with no car." I looked at my watch. "I'm going to make a few more inquiries here in the city, and if I don't get any leads, then I'll take a drive out to Kingston."

"If this thing, this... creature is really after Aubrey, can you stop it?" Her eyes were wide and hopeful, almost pleading. "Can you kill it?"

I could have lied to her, but I would have been lying to myself, too.

"I don't know."

17

I WENT HOME and called Sandra. I asked her to check the Portal Watch website and see if there were any new messages from Rose-marysBarbie, a.k.a. Aubrey Wood. I put a TV dinner in the microwave while I waited. Sandra came back on the line and said there were no new messages. RosemarysBarbie hadn't logged in since we'd last checked the website.

"Have we reached a dead end in the investigation?" Sandra asked dryly.

I grunted.

"Will you be in the office tomorrow?" she said.

"It depends on how my morning goes. I've got to see a teenage boy in Leaside."

"There are laws against that kind of thing."

"You're so funny, Dee. You should forget the acting career and become a stand-up comedian."

"I hate stand-up comedians. They're right up there with lawyers and mimes. I think they should all be lined up and shot."

"As much as I'd like to continue this stimulating conversation, my dinner beckons."

"What is it tonight, Salisbury steak or meatloaf?"

I hung up on her laughter and took the tray out of the microwave. The gravy on the Salisbury steak had congealed into a brown paste. Yum.

I shoved the tray into the trash and grabbed a beer from the fridge. I plopped down on the couch and stared at the sliding glass door that opened onto the balcony. It was starting to get dark out. I drank my beer and watched the sky change from grey to violet. I suddenly remembered the brick. I retrieved it from my jacket pocket and grabbed another beer from the fridge on my way back to the couch. I put the brick on the coffee table and drank my beer while the sky turned from violet to a deep, dusky purple. I decided it was silly to get up every time I needed a beer, so the next time, I grabbed two and carried them back to the couch. I chugged one down, then sat and nursed the other while the sky went from purple to black. I thought about ordering a pizza, but then I closed my eyes and things went black for me, too.

18

I WOKE up with a bad taste in my mouth and a bad feeling in my gut. The bad taste I took care of with mouthwash. The bad feeling was harder to kill. Olivia Wood's letter had gotten stuck in my mind like a fishhook. It tugged at me while I slept, sinking its barbs in deeper.

I took a shower, put on clean clothes, and returned the brick to its spot in my jacket pocket. It was almost 7:30 a.m. I called Jack Carr on his cell, but it went straight to voice mail. I didn't leave a message. I needed to talk with him, but that might not be possible today. Jack and his parents had probably received the bad news about Seth.

I decided to drive over to Leaside anyway.

There was no car in the driveway at the Carr place. I rang the bell, not expecting anyone to answer, but the door opened and Jack Carr stood there: pale and vacant-eyed. He shuffled wordlessly to the side to let me in.

He led me into a living room crowded with sofas and overstuffed chairs, all of them upholstered in floral designs that hurt my eyes. A large mirror hanging on the far wall reflected the room's general hideousness and made it seem like it was twice as big.

As I was lowering myself into a chair with my back to the mirror, the brick banged against the side of my leg. I let out a low grunt of pain and took it out of my pocket. Jack eyed it with wan interest as he slumped down on a couch across from me.

"Are you going to brain me?"

I put the brick on the coffee table between us. "It's my pet rock."

"What's his name?"

"Her," I said. "Rosie."

"Cute," Jack said. Then: "My brother's dead."

"I know."

He went on like he didn't hear me. "He was killed. Murdered in his apartment."

"I know, Jack. I was there."

That got through. I could tell by the way Jack's eyes went from me to the brick to the front door.

"I didn't kill him. I found him."

Jack looked down guiltily. "I didn't mean... I didn't think you killed him. It was just... you took out that brick and it kind of threw me."

"It throws everyone. Even me."

Jack gave me a puzzled look, but I waved it off. "Where are your parents?" I asked.

"They went to identify the body." He gave a snort of wry amusement. "The cops knew it was Seth, but they need my parents to make it official. That's what it's all about now. Making everything official. My mother was standing over there in the hallway making a list of all the things they need to do, people they need to call. A fucking list! Like she was going grocery shopping."

"Everyone deals with death in different ways," I said lamely.

"My parents aren't dealing with anything," Jack said. "They already dealt with Seth years ago, when he moved out. My father yelled, my mother cried. That's how they should have reacted last night when the cops showed up, but they didn't. They just stood there calmly asking questions like they were taking a survey."

"I'm sorry, Jack."

He shrugged. "It was only a matter of time. I knew it, and Seth probably knew it, too. Living that life, working for those kinds of people."

"You lost me on that last turn."

Jack let out a long sigh and sank deeper into the couch. "He always told me never to talk about it. But I guess it doesn't matter now. It's probably the reason he's dead." He sighed again. "My brother worked as a courier."

"Who did he work for?"

Jack shook his head. "He wouldn't tell me his name. He just called him the Godfather. It was a joke between us. When he lived at home, we'd have marathon sessions where we'd watch all three *Godfather* movies, one right after another. We never talked much then. It was the age difference. Six years is a lot between brothers when you're young. We talked more after he moved out, and I told myself it was because we were getting closer, but I knew that wasn't really it. We weren't any closer than before, but it was like Seth needed to talk to someone about the stuff he was doing for the Godfather, and he knew I was safe. He knew I wouldn't rat him out to my parents or the cops or anybody."

"When did your brother start working for the Godfather?"

"In high school. He hung out with some guys who sold drugs. Nothing major, just weed, 'shrooms, sometimes a little X. They weren't committed. That's what Seth said. He said they used as much as they sold and they did lousy business because of it. When Seth started selling, I think he did it more to show up his friends than out of any real desire to be a drug dealer. He's always been competitive like that. And since he never used drugs, he did much better selling them. He liked the money, and he liked the attention he got from the girls who thought he was a badass, but mostly I think he liked knowing he did it better than the other guys at school. It turned out the girls weren't the only ones who noticed him. I guess he made an impression on the guy who supplied the drugs to Seth and his friends too, because a few months after he started, Seth had a meeting with someone he called 'the corporate recruiter.' Apparently, the guy saw some promise in Seth and promoted him to courier."

"Drug courier?"

"Seth never knew. The stuff he moved was always in sealed boxes or locked briefcases. He said he never opened anything."

"You mentioned that he dropped out of school?"

"Yeah. I guess a courier keeps different hours than a drug dealer. He missed enough classes that the school called my parents. They gave him an ultimatum, and he left. He was making enough money by then to afford his own place. My brother wasn't the type to drop out of high school for no reason. He wasn't stupid. But he didn't see the point in staying if he already had a good job. I was worried about him, but I couldn't argue with that. Not if that's what he wanted to do."

"Did you see him much after he moved out?"

"Not much. I told you about the house parties I had this past summer? Sometimes Seth would show up. He didn't care about hanging out with my friends. I think he came because he missed the place. Of course it didn't hurt that everyone treated him like a fucking celebrity. They knew he had sold drugs at school, and they knew he was into something heavier now, but he never told them anything. Some of them thought he was a loan shark, or some sort of enforcer. Others thought he was a hit man. I was the only one who knew the truth, because I was the only one he talked to. Seth told me he had plans. Big plans. He was going to move up in the organization. 'Climb the corporate ladder,' he said."

"But he never told you who the Godfather is?"

Jack shook his head. "Never."

"When I spoke to you the other day, you told me Seth and Aubrey were both interested in the Black Lands."

Jack didn't say anything.

"You said your brother got interested... when? Two or three years ago?"

"Something like that, yeah."

"Around the time he dropped out of school?"

Jack closed his eyes and hung his head.

"You need to tell me what happened, Jack. Your brother's dead and I'm sorry for that. I truly am. But Aubrey is alive, and I need your help to find her."

Jack raised his head and looked at me. His eyes were brimming with tears. He looked sad and tired, or maybe he was just tired of being sad. I had a feeling he'd been this way for a long time, well before his brother died. I couldn't tell if he was heartbroken for Aubrey or Seth. Probably both. His feelings were likely so confused and intertwined that even he didn't know who he was mourning.

"Seth got interested in the supernatural right after he started working for the Godfather. I never made any kind of connection between the two. Not at first. I just thought Seth was trying to sound, I don't know, mature or something. Making a living at his cool job, living in his own place, climbing the corporate ladder, talking about the kinds of world issues that other adults talk about. I didn't think anything of it until earlier this year. Seth invited me over to his place for movies and pizza. It was fun. Like we were catching up. Then he started talking about the Black Lands. And portals. He asked me what I knew about them, how they worked, like he was quizzing me or something. He told me I should tell him if I ever heard any rumours about any new portals being found. He told me to spread the word to my friends. He said he'd make it worth their while in a big way."

"Did he say why he was so interested?"

"I figured it had something to do with the reward the PIA offers. You know the one I'm talking about?"

I nodded. "Ten grand to anyone that provides information leading to the discovery of a new portal."

"A few months ago, Seth came to one of my parties and got really hammered. He took me aside and started asking me about portals again. I made some joke. I think I asked him if he was planning to move to the Black Lands. He didn't laugh, he just got this serious look in his eyes and said, 'Sometimes I think that's what he wants to do.'"

"He?"

"The Godfather," Jack said. "Seth told me it was his boss who was interested in portals. He said the guy's got a whole library of books on the Black Lands, and he was always recording TV shows and documentaries about it. He'd been out to see Old Frightful dozens of times. Seth said the Godfather was obsessed with finding a portal of his own, and if Seth was the one who found it for him, he'd be on easy street."

"Climbing that corporate ladder."

"Yeah."

"Did he say why the Godfather wanted his own portal?"

"Seth joked about it. He said it would be a great way to hide drugs and guns, dispose of dead bodies, things like that. Imagine if you had your own dimension for all the stuff you didn't want the cops to find?"

I thought it was a pretty clever idea. Clever and dangerous. Maybe the mob already had their own personal portal. It might explain what happened to Jimmy Hoffa. The problem was that portals worked both ways. You could dump stuff into the Black Lands, but supernaturals could also cross over into our world. In the end, it didn't seem like it was worth the trouble.

"I think that was what really got Aubrey interested in him," Jack said. "That he was on the lookout for portals. She said they went out portal-caching together all the time."

"Portal-caching?"

"Portal hunting," Jack clarified. "They'd go out to places that were supposed to be haunted and look around for portals."

"People actually do that?" I said, shocked.

"Sure," Jack said. "I know some guys at school that do it, too."

"They're really that interested in the Black Lands?"

Jack shrugged. "Probably more interested in the reward."

"Do you know anyone who uses the Internet name Iapetus?"

Jack shook his head. "I don't think so."

"I found a book about Black Lands portals in Aubrey's bedroom. Iapetus was the name of the author. It's also the name of the moderator of a private website devoted to portals. I don't suppose your brother ever did any writing?"

"Seth?" Jack said, incredulous. "I don't think he's ever read a book, much less written one."

"Do you recall if anything strange happened to Aubrey about a month ago? Sometime around the end of September or early October?"

Jack thought about it for a moment, then shook his head. "I can't think of anything. Honestly, I didn't see much of Aubrey once she started going out with my brother. She was with him all the time during the summer. She'd skip shifts at the pool so she could see him. I covered for her at first, but after a while she stopped showing up at all, and they fired her. I saw her again when school started — we have a few classes together — but we don't talk much anymore. And now she's gone."

The tears Jack hadn't been able to cry for his brother came now.

"Is it my fault?" he asked me. "Should I have told someone about them?"

"It's not your fault," I said. "But the police are going to have some questions for you about your brother. My advice, Jack, is to tell them the truth. You don't have to protect him anymore."

Jack wiped at his eyes. "I guess not."

"I'm still trying to figure out when exactly Aubrey became interested in the Black Lands."

"Does it matter?"

"I don't know. Maybe not. Did you get the impression she enjoyed going portal-caching?"

"She seemed to be into it. But then, she might have just been saying that because Seth liked it." A thoughtful look came into his eyes. "But after what happened at the Bluffs..." He trailed off for a moment, then nodded with conviction. "Yeah, she was definitely into it."

"The Bluffs? You mean the Scarborough Bluffs?"

Jack nodded. "That was us."

"Us who?"

"My geography class. We were on the news. We got our picture in the papers."

"I must've missed it."

"We were the ones who discovered the new portal." He looked at me like I had three heads. "How could you not have heard about it?"

I bit my lip, trying to remember. I didn't watch the news very often, and I usually only picked up a newspaper to read the comics. I vaguely recalled Sandra mentioning that a new portal had been found in Scarborough a few weeks back, but I hadn't asked her for any details. I was one of those people who had taken a policy of don't-know-don't-want-to-know when it came to the Black Lands. I'd found ignorance was especially blissful when a dark dimension full of supernatural creatures was constantly poking holes in your world.

"I've been out of the loop," I said. "Tell me about this trip."

Jack snorted. "It was so lame. First school trip of the year and they take us to the fucking Bluffs. Why didn't they just take us to McDonald's? At least the bio class got to go to the zoo. We spent the entire morning following Mr. Attinger around while he talked about glaciers, continental drift and the formation of the Bluffs. After lunch we went back the parking lot at the top of the Bluffs to wait for the bus. Me and some other guys were over at the edge rolling rocks down the slope, trying to start an avalanche. Everyone else was just hanging out. Aubrey was with some other girls. They were texting each other on their phones even though they were all standing next to each other. I guess Aubrey got bored with them, because she came over and started throwing rocks with me and the guys. I hadn't spoken to her much since school started, so I figured this was a good chance to catch up. But she pretty much ignored me. I said 'hey,' and she said 'hey' back, then she went off by herself to throw rocks at a different spot. I waited a bit and then wandered over closer to her. I was rolling my rocks down the Bluffs while watching her out of the corner of my eye, and that's when I noticed something strange."

"What?"

"Aubrey's rocks were vanishing. Not all of them, just the ones rolling down a certain spot. It was like they were being swallowed up by something invisible. I called the other guys over and we all started throwing rocks at that spot, watching them disappear in mid-air. We figured out pretty quickly what it meant. Aubrey did, too. I could see it on her face. It was weird. She looked like she was scared and excited at the same time. She didn't freak out the way the other girls did. Bess Clark actually started crying. She refused to wait for the bus. She said she wanted to go home right that minute. So she just left, went running out of the parking lot like her ass was on fire."

"Did you get the impression that Aubrey knew the portal was there?"

Jack considered this for a moment. His eyes sharpened and a frown creased his face. "I never thought about it before, but now that you mention it, she was acting kind of weird that morning. Distant, quiet. But I just figured that was the new Aubrey. I thought her mind was on other things."

"Like your brother."

Jack shrugged indifferently. "All I can say is she was really withdrawn that day. And she seemed to go right to that spot where the portal was found. Some of the guys teased her about it later on, asking if she was paramental."

"How did Aubrey react to that?"

"She threw a rock at them," Jack said with an amused grin. "*That* was more like the old Aubrey. The one I used to know. Then she took out her cellphone and called someone. At first, I thought she was calling the PIA. You know, for the reward. But she was way too happy. Then I figured out she was talking to Seth."

"He'd told her to be on the lookout for portals, too."

Jack nodded.

"Did your brother show up?"

"He might have, but I didn't see him. It turned out someone else — probably Mr. Attinger — called the PIA, and they got there real fast. There must've been five or six black vans, guys in suits, some others in those walking garbage-bag outfits."

"Hazmat?"

"Yeah, like the government dicks in *E.T.* That part always freaked me out, the way they just came walking into the kid's house, none of them saying a word. The PIA guys weren't like that. They were running all over the place and shouting at each other, shouting at us."

"Finding a new portal is a pretty big deal."

"Tell me about it," Jack said with a marked lack of enthusiasm. "They hustled us out of there fast enough. A bunch of guys with submachine guns escorted us onto our bus when it finally showed up. And you want to know the worst part? We didn't even get the reward for discovering the stupid thing. They gave the money to the school!"

"At least you got your picture in the papers," I said.

"Have you seen the picture?" Jack asked.

"No."

"It's a group shot, and we all look like criminals, 'cause no one's smiling. Some PIA suit took the picture while we were waiting for the bus, and I guarantee it wasn't so we could show it to our parents later on. They were getting our faces on file so they could track us down if we caused any trouble later on. The thing you don't see in the picture is the other suit that went around taking down our names, phone numbers and addresses."

"Maybe they wanted to send you a framed copy of the print."

Jack shook his head. "Ten grand, man."

"Did you talk to Aubrey at all after that?"

"No," he said, "but I saw her later on, back at school. I was going to talk to her, but I didn't."

"Why not?"

Jack hesitated. "She was crying."

"Do you know why?"

"No, but I can guess. I think she and Seth had a fight. I think he was angry with her for not calling him sooner. I guess he really wanted that portal."

I nodded. "Someone did."

19

SANDRA WAS WORKING on her computer when I got to the office. She looked up at me and said, "You've got to see this."

"I don't care about anything the Kardashians are doing."

"It's not that."

I went over and saw she was scanning through the online archives of the *Toronto Star*.

"What are you looking for?" I asked.

Sandra ignored me. "The missing girl, does she go to Leaside High?"

"Yes."

"I thought so," she said with a satisfied grin. "I was reading some of her message-board posts and found references to that new portal found in the Bluffs. I told you about it, remember?"

I waited a second too long in replying. "Yes."

Sandra shook her head. "You never listen to me."

"What did you find out?"

"I don't know for certain, but I think the girl you're looking for is one of the kids who discovered the portal."

"She is. I just got through talking to one of her friends who was there as well."

Sandra frowned. "Oh, screw. I thought I was being a good little assistant."

"Assistant? Dee, you're a better private detective than I am. You figured all of this out in a single morning, without talking to anyone. I'm the one still playing catch-up."

I told her about my first conversation with Jack Carr, followed by my trip to Lawrence Heights to find his brother, my discovery of Seth Carr's body and my subsequent tussle with a thug named Donto. I told her about my brief detention by the cops, Olivia Wood's letter to her granddaughter — backtracking to tell her Jerry Baldwin's story about Rosedale Cottage — and my exchange with a very drunk Norma Wood. I finished with my second visit to Jack Carr earlier that morning.

"Portal-caching?" Sandra made a face. "We did some dumb things as kids, but that's... *really* fucking dumb."

"Dumb and dangerous," I agreed. "But I guess that's the allure."

"Do you think that's what happened to her? Do you think she's... in the Black Lands?"

"I don't know. I hope not. Because if she is, then she's almost certainly dead."

"And you can't exactly go there to confirm it, Felix."

"I know. But I'm not through looking for her in our world. Not yet. What do you know about Wolfe Island?"

"You think she went to her grandmother's place?"

"It's a long shot, but I'm running out of options. My bigger concern is that she may no longer be in control of where she's going."

"Is that the polite way of saying she's been kidnapped?"

I sat on the corner of her desk and said nothing.

"Wind farm," Sandra said.

"What?"

"Wolfe Island has one of the largest wind farms in Canada. That's all I know about the place. I think it's near Kingston."

"Is it nice?"

"Sure," she said. "If you like wind farms."

I stuck my hands in my pockets, and the left one bumped against the brick. I took it out and put it down on Sandra's desk.

She stared at it, her eyes widening slightly. "So that's the magic brick?"

"It's not magic, it's haunted. And heavy. And abusive."

Sandra leaned back in her chair and laced her fingers behind her head. "I'm sure you've already thought of this, but have you considered simply asking the brick if it knows where the girl is?"

"I asked. The brick didn't say anything."

"Maybe you didn't ask nice enough."

Sandra picked up the brick and held it close to her chest, stroking it like a kitten.

"Oooh, that's a nice brick," she cooed. "Why don't you tell us where the wittle girl is?"

Her eyes suddenly went wide as the brick started to vibrate in her hands. She held it away from her, like a baby with a soiled diaper, and the brick leaped out of her grasp and slid across the top of her desk.

"That's great!" I said, backing away. "Jerry said not to piss it off."

Sandra jumped out of her chair and ran into my inner office.

"You're leaving me to deal with this on my own?" I shouted after her. "Thanks a lot!"

The brick was darting back and forth across the surface of the desk. It would come close to the edge, then stop and swing back in the other direction. I took a hesitant step forward, then reached out and picked up Sandra's laptop before it was knocked onto the floor.

I was thinking about calling Jerry to see if he knew what to do when Sandra came running back into the room. She had something thin and rectangular tucked under her arm. I started to ask her what she was doing, then she took the Ouija board and slapped it down on the desk. It was a gag gift she had given me two or three Christmases ago. I'd been involved in a couple of high-profile cases involving Black Lands entities, and the press had taken to describing me as a "supernatural detective." I didn't care for the term (although I liked "Super Dick" even less), or the crank calls I still received to this day, but the publicity did end up leading to a few jobs.

"Come here, you little devil," Sandra said as she tried to pick up the brick. She finally managed to grab it and place it on the Ouija board. I took a notepad and pen out of the desk and held them out to Sandra.

She gave me a look of amused disdain. "What do I look like, your secretary?"

I grumbled and flipped the notepad open to a blank page, uncapped the pen with my teeth and waited.

The brick was moving slower now, and with purpose. It slid back and forth across the board, stopping at individual letters, and I jotted them down.

OLIVIA BURNED BRIGHT.

AUBREY BURNS BRIGHTER.

"Something's after her," I said.

The brick started moving again.

THE YVER.

"Yver?" Sandra said. "What's a yver?"

"The Whyver," I said. "It's a creature from the Black Lands." To the brick I said: "Does the Whyver want to kill Aubrey?"

The brick swung over to YES.

"Why?"

The brick spelled out: YVER IN THE DARK.

"I don't understand."

The brick kept moving: YVER WANTS THE LIGHT.

"It wants the light?" I said, confused. "Aubrey's light?"

The brick pointed to YES.

Before I could say anything else, it started moving again. PROTECT THE LIGHT.

"I can't do that unless I can find Aubrey. Where is she?"

The brick said: U R THE DETECTIVE.

Sandra snickered. I frowned.

"*How* do I find her?"

The brick spelled out a single word. A name.

DONTO.

20

"WE RELEASED HIM THIS MORNING," Drake said.

We were in the corner of the homicide squad room where Drake's desk and three others were pushed together. Robichaud had gone for lunch, so I was sitting in his chair. Drake said he'd been gone a couple of hours. Apparently all that grunting really worked up an appetite.

"Why'd you do that?" I asked.

Drake spread his hands. "Nothing to hold him on. We kept him overnight to let him stew, then we threw some questions at him about the money in his wallet and the money in the dead kid's wallet. He lawyered up and that was that." He smiled thinly. "He has a very good lawyer."

"Did he tell you what he was doing there?"

"He said he was just passing by."

"Passing by? The building is on a cul-de-sac. Did he say why he went inside?"

"Concerned citizen," Drake said. "Said he saw some suspicious activity, went to check it out, and found you in the dead kid's apartment."

"What about his gun?"

"Says he found it in the hallway."

"You believe that?"

Drake gave me a look.

"Serial number?"

"Filed off."

"Any witnesses?"

"Just the old guy in the apartment across from the vic's. Said he saw a couple of guys wrassling in the hallway — you and Donto — and called the cops."

"Because I told him to. Did he hear Seth Carr getting murdered?"

"He said he heard some screaming earlier, but he doesn't remember when. It might've been that morning or the night before. He drinks," Drake added with a shrug.

"He heard screaming but he didn't call the cops?"

"He said people are always screaming in the building. He didn't think anything of it. End quote."

"Did you find Donto's prints in Seth Carr's apartment?"

"Oh sure. We had our special crime computer do one of those super speedy database searches you see all the time on *CSI*."

"But you did find prints."

"Sure," Drake said. "All over the place. Some of them might belong to Donto, some to the dozens of other people in and out of the apartment. According to the kid's neighbours, Seth Carr was quite the host. Threw a lot of parties. They complained to the super about the noise, but he never did anything about it."

"Maybe he knew the kid was connected."

I was throwing out a line, but Drake didn't bite, just tilted back in his chair and stared at me blankly.

"You got anything on Donto?"

"He's been busted a few times — aggravated assault, receiving stolen property, a couple of B and E's. No convictions." Drake folded his hands neatly in his lap. "Like I said, he's got a good lawyer."

"And who pays for that lawyer?"

"Who wants to know?"

"I do."

"You gonna tell me why?"

"Come on, Drake. I already know Donto's an organization guy."

"Organization." Drake nodded. "That's a good word. If you'd said mob, I would have kicked your ass right out of here."

"Toronto doesn't have mobs?"

"We have independent criminal organizations."

"Which one does Donto work for?" I asked. "The Planets?"

"Nope."

"The Jets?"

"They're from *West Side Story*," Drake said. "And they're a gang, not a criminal organization."

"Isn't a gang a type of criminal organization?"

"Is that what you came here to talk to me about, Felix?"

"No. I want to know who Donto works for."

"I'm not going to tell you that."

"Why not?"

"Because if I do, the next thing you'll ask is where you can find Donto, and then you'll go looking for him, probably get yourself killed, and then it will become my problem. And frankly I don't need the extra paperwork."

"What if I promise not to get killed?"

"You can't promise that."

"I haven't gotten killed yet."

"Luck."

"Could be some skill, too."

"Not likely. And besides, Donto has something you don't."

"A strong, caveman brow?"

"Friends. Dangerous ones."

"Do any of these friends have names?"

"You're exhausting."

I nodded. "It would be easier to just give me what I want."

Drake sighed and leaned back in his chair. "Donto is an enforcer for Joe Levare."

"Levare," I said. "Never heard of him."

"He is what you would call a crime boss, although not a very big one. He's into drugs, guns, stolen merch, a little prostitution on the side. But his operation is small. That's why he's lasted so long. OCU doesn't put any real heat on him, and the other criminal organizations don't consider him a threat. He's either very smart or just lacking in ambition."

"Donto seems brighter than the average leg-breaker."

"He is," Drake said. "Believe it or not, there's a brain in that thick skull. We've brought him in for questioning on two or three homicides that we're almost positive he's good for, but there's never been any evidence to link him to the crime."

"Evidence. The elusive needle in the haystack."

Drake made a face like he wanted to either throw up or punch me in the head.

"Are we done, Felix?"

"I need to talk to Donto."

"He didn't kill that kid."

"I know."

"You want to clue me in on who did?"

"Not unless you want to hand the case over to the PIA."

"I might do that anyway," Drake grumbled.

"Donto?"

Drake leaned forward and picked up his phone. "It's your ass. If you want to get it kicked, it's none of my business." He talked to someone and wrote down an address on a Post-it note. He peeled it off the pad and held it out to me.

I reached for the piece of paper and Drake pulled it away. "You're going to let me know if you find anything?"

"Oh sure," I said. "Your number's still nine-one-two, right?"

"Fuck off, Felix."

21

DONTO LIVED in Etobicoke in a three-storey house that had been divided into separate apartments. It was a decrepit building with a slumped porch, a cracked driveway, and a sign in the front window that said NO SOLICITORS! It made Seth Carr's building look like Wayne Manor.

A Dodge Charger was parked at the far end of the driveway. It was one of the newer models, a 2010 or 2011, painted midnight blue, with a trunk wing spoiler and expensive rims. It might have belonged to Donto, but I didn't know for certain. A smarter PI would've asked Drake what kind of vehicle Donto drove. Apparently, I wasn't that guy. I tried to be, but most times I came up short. The key is to learn from your mistakes. I like to do one better than that. In the face of a particularly embarrassing blunder, I find it's best to restore balance to the universe by doing something extremely clever. I decided to start right now.

I took out my gun and held it down at my side as I walked up the driveway. The brick in my jacket pocket swung a bit with the movement, but I was starting to learn how to walk so that it didn't bash into my leg.

I reached the back of the house and took a look around. The car was parked in front of a detached wooden garage that looked as decrepit as the house. I could see why the owner of the Charger didn't want to park it inside. A deep sigh could have knocked it down. The backyard was a square of patchy grass with a laundry line crossing it diagonally. There was a smashed picnic table in the far corner, a coffee can full of cigarette butts on the stoop next to the door, and a sign bolted to the wall that said KEEP THIS DOOR CLOSED AT ALL TIMES!

I considered shooting out one of the Charger's tires, but that would make a lot of noise — the wrong kind of noise — and the car might not even belong to Donto. I opted to lean against it instead. When that didn't have the desired effect, I tugged on the door handles. Still no joy. Then I hopped on the hood. That did it.

The alarm was loud and strident. It rose like a jet engine spooling up to full speed, then died down to a low, almost mournful howl before rising again. It hurt my ears. I guess it was supposed to, if I had been a car thief. I went over behind the pile of kindling that used to be a picnic table and waited for Donto. At least, I hoped it would be Donto.

It was. He came out the back door in jeans and a white undershirt. He pointed something at the car and the alarm died in mid-shriek. He started to turn back to the house, hesitated, then came down the steps in his bare feet. He didn't close the door behind him. Naughty. He looked down the driveway to the street, then did a slow circle around the car, checking it from all angles for any signs of damage. On his second pass, I stepped out from behind the busted picnic table and strolled over. He didn't see me until I yelled, "Hey!"

Donto was fast for a big guy. He spun around, one hand darting behind his back for a gun that wasn't there. I knew because I'd looked for it as he'd walked over to his car. But that didn't mean he wasn't dangerous.

"I know you?" He squinted at me, then his eyes widened in recognition. "Yeah, I know you. You're the buster."

"My friends call me Felix."

"I ain't your friend."

"I know, but I thought we could at least be friendly." I pointed my gun at him to show how friendly I could be.

Donto looked at the gun. He didn't seem very impressed. "What do you want?"

"Just some questions answered," I said.

"You're not a cop."

"Private."

"You were looking for the kid. Carr."

"His girlfriend."

Donto shook his head. "She's gone."

"Dead?"

"Just gone. You won't find her."

He took a step toward me. There were about five feet between us. I gestured with my gun.

"Stay where you are, big boy. Distance makes the heart grow fonder."

"All dicks talk like you?"

"Only the clever ones."

The corner of Donto's mouth turned up in a thin-lipped smile. "Let's test that theory," he said, and took another step forward.

"How about we see how high you can get your hands up, instead?"

Donto's smile widened. "You want them up?" he said, and threw his hands into the air. "Or you want them down?" His hands came flying back down, one of them striking my gun. I didn't drop it, but he threw off my aim. The gun fired and there was a loud metallic *spack!*

Donto knew what that sound meant. His face crumpled as he turned around and looked at his car. There was a neat little hole in the passenger door, and the alarm was going off again. His head swivelled slowly back toward me.

"You're fucking dead," he said.

I tried to bring my gun back up, but Donto swatted it aside, and this time I did drop it. I reached down for it in the grass, but Donto grabbed me by the arms and pulled me back up. I stared into his face, the look of congested anger blooming like a poisonous rose, and felt sure he was going to bite my head off like a chocolate Easter bunny. He stood like that for a moment, trembling with rage and, perhaps, trying to figure out what he was going to do with me.

Finally he turned, still gripping me by the upper arms, and threw me across the driveway like a sack of garbage. I struck the brick wall of the house next door and fell to the ground. Nothing felt broken, but everything hurt. My left jacket sleeve was torn off at the shoulder and hung limply on my arm like a shed snakeskin. I expected Donto to be on me, kicking and punching, but he was crouched next to his car. I thought he was checking out the damage done by my errant bullet, but when he straightened up I saw the gun in his hand. My gun. He came over with it held down at his side. It looked tiny in his massive paw. He fetched a quick look at the street, but if anyone had heard the shot, they weren't doing anything about it. I listened for the sound of approaching sirens, but there was nothing but distant traffic noise.

Donto hunkered down in front of me, my gun dangling from his hand.

"You shot my car, so I get to shoot you."

"That doesn't seem like fair recompense," I said.

He raised the gun and pointed it at my face. I wanted to close my eyes, but I couldn't. I felt my heart pounding in my chest. Then I realized it wasn't my heart, and it wasn't in my chest.

The brick exploded out of my jacket pocket like the little fanged critter exploded out of John Hurt in *Alien*. The gun went off and the muzzle flash blinded me momentarily. The bullet struck the wall to the left of my head, and I felt something sharp — a shard of stone or a fragment of the bullet — slice through my ear. I threw myself to the right, rolling across the ground and slapping a hand to the side of my head. I couldn't see the blood for the bright blobs of light moving across my vision, but I could feel it, hot and slick on my fingers.

I would have climbed to my feet and started running if I didn't hear Donto screaming. It was a low, muffled kind of screaming, but still music to my ears. I sat up on my knees and blinked my eyes until I could see again. I touched my ear and winced. It was still there, still mostly intact, but it was bleeding badly. I slipped off my torn jacket sleeve and tied it around my head. I tried to imagine that I looked like Rambo, but I knew what I really looked like: an idiot private eye who had almost gotten executed with his own gun. So much for restoring balance to the universe.

My gun lay in the middle of the driveway. I bent down and picked it up.

Donto was pressed up against the side of the house, with his feet about five feet off the ground. The brick was wedged under his chin, pinning him to the wall. His face was bright red, but for a different reason now. He was making a gurgling, retching sound as he clawed at the brick and kicked his legs up and down.

I stood in front of him, well out of range of his flailing feet, and said, "I want to know everything about Joe Levare and Aubrey Wood."

Donto stared down at me with bulging eyes. "Fuck you," he gasped.

"Tell me and I'll call off my partner."

I'd never played Good Cop, Bad Brick before — and I wasn't entirely sure I *could* call off the brick — but I figured it was worth a shot.

"Fuck... you..." Donto's face was changing from red to purple. It was like watching a really ugly sunset.

"Okay," I said, "you leave me no choice. Rosie, tear his head off."

Donto threw up his hands and yelled, "Wait!" It came out in a gritty, high-pitched whisper. "I'll talk."

I didn't need to say anything to the brick. It simply pulled away from Donto, letting him fall to the ground in a crumpled heap. It floated serenely in the air, while I trained my gun on him.

"Where is Aubrey Wood?" I demanded.

"Levare took her," Donto said, rubbing his throat. "The kid gave her to him."

"Seth Carr? He gave Aubrey to Levare? You mean as a..."

Donto shook his head. "It wasn't like that. The kid was brownnosing. He used to call Levare with tips on portals. He knew Levare wants one bad, and he thought it was a way to get in good with the boss. But the tips always turned out to be nothing. Then a few days ago the kid called and said he knew a girl who was special. He said she could find portals."

"Find them how?"

"He said she sensed them or something. Levare was sceptical, on account of all the snipe hunts the kid had sent him on, but he wanted to see her and sent me to pick her up. The kid didn't want to let her go, but I made him see reason."

"You pointed a gun at him."

Donto shrugged. "He was compensated. I gave him a down

payment — half now, half after we confirmed the girl could do what he said she could do."

"And can she?"

"I don't know. I dropped her off at Levare's and took off." He hesitated. "There was something about her, though…"

"What?"

"It was like there was a cloud hanging over her or something. I had a feeling she was bad luck, and if I spent too much time around her, it would rub off on me. Levare felt it, too, but he was excited by it. He sent me back to the kid's place to pay him the rest of the money."

"He must've been pretty confident she could sense portals."

"There was something about her," Donto repeated. "Maybe she just has the Influence."

Some scientists theorized that the portals emitted some sort of contamination. A kind of supernatural radiation that caused psi abilities, deformities and mutations, and sometimes even death. It was first diagnosed in veterans of Operation Shadow Storm, the U.S. military's one and only offensive against the Black Lands, but since then cases have popped up all over the world. It's rare, and the effects vary from person to person, but it happens often enough for people to be afraid of it. There were many different names for the condition, but most people referred to it simply as the Influence.

"Even if she can't find any portals, Levare'll find a use for her," Donto said.

"I'm guessing you're not referring to the steno pool."

"She was scared."

"Of you?"

He shook his head. "Something else. When I was taking her to Levare, she kept telling me to call the kid. She wanted him to leave his apartment. I figured she was worried Levare was going to send someone to take him out. But it didn't make any sense, her saying that to me, since she knew I worked for Levare. It was like she knew something was going to happen to the kid."

"Where does Levare live?" I asked.

"Go to hell," Donto replied.

249

The brick shot forward and hit Donto square in the face. I heard his nose break. Blood poured out of his nostrils in dual streams. He slapped his hands over his nose and groaned in pain.

"I'm afraid I'm going to need an address."

I leaned down and stuck the barrel of my gun under Donto's jaw, where the brick had wedged itself when it pinned him to the wall. He muttered something, but it was muffled by his hands. I asked him to repeat it. He pulled his hands away long enough to give me the address.

"I'll spare you the trouble of telling me how to get there," I said. "That's what Google Maps is for."

Donto said something else that was muffled by his hands. I didn't think it was directions.

I stood up. The brick was still hovering in mid-air. I reached out to grab it and it suddenly went flying off to the side, straight through the Charger's back window and out the windshield. It hung in the air over the hood, then shot back the way it came, smashing new holes in both windows, before landing in my waiting hand. Donto looked like he was going to cry.

I wished him a good evening and walked back to my car.

22

JOE LEVARE LIVED on an estate in a heavily wooded area north of Pickering. It was quiet and secluded, with a twelve-foot-tall stone wall surrounding the entire property.

It was dark by the time I pulled up to the wrought-iron gate out front. I got out of the car and looked around. There was a video camera on top of one of the stone pillars and a call button on a metal box next to the entrance. The box was on a curved pole so that you didn't have to get out of your car to press it. I didn't need to press it because the gate was open. It gave me an uneasy feeling. Gates like these were never left open. I got back in my car and drove through.

I followed a long, tree-lined lane that split in two to form a circular drive in front of the house. In the centre of the driveway was a large stone fountain. I drove around it and parked at the foot of the steps leading to the front door.

I climbed out of the car and stood for a moment assessing the house. It was a large, multi-winged mansion with thick columns, tall arched windows and a two-storey garage. There were no lights on in any of the windows, and I started to wonder if I'd made the drive all the way out here for nothing.

I took out my gun and moved slowly up the front steps. I put my back against the wall next to the door and reached over to try the handle. It was unlocked. I pushed it open and waited, listening. I didn't hear anything, so I took a deep breath and stepped inside.

The foyer was bigger than my apartment. It had a black marble floor, large oil paintings on the walls and a crystal chandelier that perfectly illuminated the bloodbath that had taken place here.

At first glance, I thought I was looking at the remains of two or three bodies. But as I edged around the severed limbs and puddles of blood, I realized it was only one person, spread around. The human body holds a lot of the red stuff, and the vast majority of this fellow's had been used to paint the walls and floor.

There was a faint smell of cordite in the air. I spotted a gun at the foot of the curved staircase, clutched in the grip of a severed hand.

I caught a flutter of movement in a room off to the right. I went over and stood with my back to the wall next to the archway, just as I had done outside, and pawed around on the inside with my free hand for a light switch. I found it and took a quick peek into the room.

It was a sitting room or a parlour — one of those rooms that seem to exist only in mansions. The movement came from a curtain on the far side of the room. There were two of them on the window, one tied back with a gold cord. The cord from the other lay on the floor and the curtain blew in the low breeze coming through the open window. It had been smashed.

I moved slowly across the room with my gun pointed at the floor. There was broken glass everywhere. Someone, or something, had entered the house here and made a beeline out of the room. I could even see the path it had taken — the flipped-over coffee table, a red-leather couch tipped onto its back. Why the intruder picked this particular window I couldn't say. It wasn't for stealth. A broken window makes a lot of noise.

I returned to the foyer, stepped gingerly around the blood and body parts, and approached the left-side archway. I reached around for a light switch, but couldn't find one. I took a deep breath and went in with my gun raised. I knew I was silhouetted against the light behind me, but I wasn't too concerned. The house was a dead place. I could feel it in my churning stomach and the hackles that rose on my neck.

It turned out I was half-right. The guy I found was half-dead.

I turned on a floor lamp that was, surprisingly, still standing in a room that looked like the aftermath of a tornado. A man in a maroon suit lay face down on the floor next to an overturned easy chair. Moving the chair aside, I saw four slashes across the back from which thick wads of stuffing protruded. As I bent down to examine the man, I saw that his suit wasn't maroon; it was drenched with blood.

I put two fingers to his neck and felt a faint pulse. Gripping his shoulder, I turned him gently over onto his back. His right arm was tucked into his middle, and when he rolled over it came up with a gun clutched in his blood-slicked hand. I pulled the weapon out of his grip and placed it on the floor. The hand flopped down onto his stomach with a gushy plopping sound. The man's fancy dress shirt had been slit open — four slashes just like the chair — and parts of the human body that were never meant to see the light of day were poking out.

The man groaned, raised his head a couple of inches, then let it drop back to the floor. I slipped a hand under his shoulders and propped him up a bit. His face was very white, making the stubble on his cheeks stand out like a dark rash. He had the hollow eyes and pale, waxy complexion that signified massive blood loss. Of course, you didn't need to look at his face to know that. The blood was everywhere.

He raised his hand and clenched my arm in a surprisingly strong grip. He stared at me with eyes that couldn't seem to focus properly.

"Whoyou?" His voice was a liquidy croak.

I said the first thing that came to mind. "Donto sent me."

It wasn't exactly a lie.

The man nodded. "You one of the Myers brothers?"

"Yeah," I said. "I'm Mike."

"I'm Russo," the man said, and smiled weakly. "Or you can call me Mud. That's how I feel." He slapped his free hand against his stomach and groaned in pain. Then he lifted his hand and looked at the blood on it. "Mud ain't supposed to be red." He tried to grin, but it turned into a grimace. "Where the fuck's Donto?"

"The cops are still holding him."

"Fucking idiot. He sent you as backup?"

I nodded.

"We're gonna need a fucking army. This thing... I don't know what it is. It took Denny apart." His grip on my arm tightened. "It took him the fuck *apart*."

"What happened?"

Russo closed his eyes and tilted his head back. "I thought it was a fucking bear. Can you believe that shit? A fucking *bear*!"

"Start at the beginning."

Russo sighed. "It was just getting dark. The power kept going out. We thought it was a storm or something, but there was nothing. No rain, no thunder. Leo and I were playing cards when the security monitors started going wiggy. Lots of static. I thought it was because of the power coming off and on. Then I saw something on one of them. A shadow moving across the grounds. Then the power went out again. It came back on once the emergency generator kicked in, and I saw on one of the monitors that the front gate was open. I figured it happened when the power went out, even though that didn't make any fucking sense. Why would the gate pop open just because the power went out? Some fucking security system. Leo went to check it out... Did you find him?"

I shook my head. If Leo was still alive, I'd eat my gun.

"Denny was walking the house, keeping an eye on things like he was supposed to, so I went back to watching the monitors. I was waiting to see Leo at the front gate, but the power went out again. This time it didn't come back on, and that's when I knew something was up. I was looking for a flashlight when I heard the window break. Soon after that I heard Denny yelling. Then I heard him shooting." He paused. "Then I heard him screaming."

"Did you see it?" I asked. "The thing that attacked him?"

Russo shook his head. "I saw Denny shooting... the flash... I saw something. It was big... big and pissed off. Then it was on him. I couldn't see it but I could hear it. I heard it taking him apart." His face contorted with the memory of those sounds. "I was coming to help him, and I felt something warm and wet on my face. I knew it was blood — Denny's blood — and suddenly I couldn't move. I just stood there staring into the dark until he stopped screaming. I had my gun out, but it felt like it weighed a ton. I couldn't lift it up. I couldn't pull the trigger. I've never been that scared in my entire life. I called out to Denny, but he didn't answer. I knew he wouldn't. I knew that thing had killed him. I don't know what it was, but it wasn't human. I thought it was a fucking bear. I thought it came out of the woods and broke into the house. That's what I was thinking even though I knew it was bullshit. I knew it wasn't a bear."

"What was it?"

"It was a monster," Russo said, and grinned at me. There was blood on his teeth.

"From the Black Lands?"

"Where else? That's where the monsters come from, right?"

I looked down at his stomach. "It did this to you?"

"Only hit me once," Russo said. "Felt like it ripped my guts out." He took another look at his stomach. "I guess it did. I stumbled back here, pulled that chair on top of me." He looked over at the easy chair. "It knocked the chair away, and I knew I was dead. I waited for it to jump on me and tear me to pieces, but it didn't. I don't know where it went. It was dark and I couldn't see shit. But it must've left. And not that long ago, so you better watch your back, pal." He gave me the blood-stained grin again, and I felt a cold quiver of fear race down my spine.

"It didn't want us, anyway," Russo said. "It wanted that girl."

"Aubrey Wood."

"Yeah. Donto brought her by a couple of days ago. Something strange about her. We all could tell right away. She gave off a vibe, you know? She was real scared. Kept looking at the windows, jumping at the smallest sounds. Joe said she was going to help him find a portal. He's crazy for that Black Lands shit. Been looking for a way over there for years." He laughed abruptly, then winced. "Looks like the Black Lands found him first." He suddenly stared into my face with a fierce intensity. "You gotta warn him. You gotta find Joe and tell him this fucking thing is coming for him."

"Where did Joe take the girl?"

"Some place near Kingston. An island. It was the girl's idea. She said there was a portal there."

"She said that?"

Russo nodded. "She told Joe they had to leave right away, so they did. That was this afternoon. The girl was afraid, like I said, but not of us. The thing that killed Denny, I think she knew it was coming after her."

"I think you're right."

"You gotta find Joe and warn him."

Russo reached down and picked up his gun. He gripped it by the barrel and held it out to me. "Take it," he said.

"I have a gun."

Russo gave me a wide, humourless grin.

"Trust me, pal. You're gonna need more than one."

23

I FOUND A PHONE, dialled 911, and left the receiver dangling. I had dressed Russo's wounds as best I could. He might make it, he might not. His chances were probably better than mine. He was out of danger. I was driving toward it.

In retrospect, I probably should have taken his gun.

It took me almost three hours to get to Kingston, and another forty-five minutes to ride the ferry over to Wolfe Island. I didn't see any wind turbines, but it was full dark now and I couldn't see much of anything. I used the time to check my wounded ear. It was no longer bleeding, so I tossed the bloody jacket sleeve I'd been using as a bandage into the water. I took out Olivia Wood's letter and checked the return address: 17 Lighthouse Road.

Once I reached the island, I stopped at the first place I found, a restaurant called The Hungry Wolfe, and asked for directions.

"Wrong island," said the old man behind the cash register. He was the only one in the place, sitting on a stool reading a Louis L'Amour novel.

"Wrong island?" I took out the letter. "But this is Wolfe Island, isn't it?"

"Yep." He leaned over to peer at the letter. "You're looking for someone on Lighthouse Road? They pick up their mail here. No post office on Simcoe Island."

"Simcoe Island. That's where Lighthouse Road is?"

"You're a quick one, ain't ya?" The old man gave me a shrewd grin. "Simcoe's a smaller island, just off Wolfe. You got to take the cable ferry to get there."

"Where is it?"

He gave me directions and I left.

The road I took creeped close to the edge of the water. For a little while I could see the lights of Kingston in the distance, then the view was blocked by another island, which I assumed was Simcoe. I turned off on Taggart Lane and took it right to the end, pulling up in front of a length of chain that hung between two poles. Beyond it I could see a shack where the ferryman (or ferrywoman) probably hung out, and past that, the dark shape of the cable ferry moored at a landing too small to be called a wharf. I got out of my car and went over to investigate. The shack was empty.

I looked back up the road and saw a light on in a small white house set among the trees. I jogged over and knocked on the front door. I waited a bit and then heard the creak of approaching footsteps. The door was opened by a tall, lanky man in bib overalls and a tuque with the Toronto Maple Leafs logo on it. "Help you?"

"I need to get over to Simcoe Island."

"Ferry's shut down for the night, bud."

"It's very important." I said, taking out my wallet. "I'll pay you everything I have on me." I didn't have much. "And I can write you a cheque. Two hundred bucks to take me across right now."

"This is about those other guys, isn't it?" the tall man said, rubbing the back of his neck.

"What other guys?"

"City guys, from the look of 'em. They were wearing suits. There was a girl with them. She didn't look like she wanted to be there. I was thinking maybe I should call the police, just to make sure she's okay."

"She isn't. I'm a private investigator." I showed him my license. "I was hired by the girl's mother to find her."

He looked at my license, then back at me. "Is she in trouble?"

"Yes."

"Then I should call the police..." He started to turn away, but I grabbed his shoulder and spun him back around.

"There's no time. When did you take them across?"

"Two, maybe three hours ago."

"I need you to take me across right now. Then come back here and call the police."

His brow furrowed in a deep frown, then he nodded. "Okay." He grabbed a pair of work gloves off a side table and closed the door behind him.

"What's your name?" I asked as we walked over to the landing.

"Chester."

"I'm Felix."

We shook hands.

"I've never met a private detective before. You got a gun?"

"Yes."

"You think you're gonna need to use it?"

"I hope not."

I got back in my car while Chester unhooked the chain and

dropped the ramp on the ferry. It was big enough for perhaps three cars. I parked in the middle and hoped it was in better shape than it looked. Chester went over to the controls and started the engine. I got out of the car and leaned against the hood. The wind was cold and my jacket was missing a sleeve, so I stuck my hands in my pockets. One of them had a big hole in it. In the other was the brick. I looked across the water at Simcoe Island. I couldn't see a single light anywhere along its length. The only way you could tell there was anything out there was from the silhouette of the trees standing up against the sky.

The ferry wasn't as fast as the big one I'd taken from Kingston, but it didn't have as far to go. I went over to talk to Chester. I had to yell to be heard over the growl of the engine.

"You make this run very often?"

"Not really," he said. "Especially this time of year. There's isn't much on Simcoe except some houses, a few farms, and the lighthouse."

"How many people did you take across with the girl?"

He closed his eyes for a moment, thinking. "There was five of them," he said. "In two cars."

Five. That could be a problem. I'd need to catch them off guard, preferably while they were all together. Keep my gun on them until I could get Aubrey out to my car, then take her back to the ferry and... No, that wouldn't work. Chester needed to take the ferry back to Wolfe Island in order to call the cops and bring them across. And there was also the fact that Aubrey had come here for a reason. The Whyver was after her, and her grandmother had told her the house was a safe place. She was so desperate to get here that she'd told Levare there was a portal on the island. Even if I was able to rescue her from Levare and his crew, I'd still have to deal with the Whyver.

When the ferry pulled into the slip at Simcoe Island, I still hadn't come up with any kind of plan. The best I could hope for was to keep Aubrey alive until the police showed up. I didn't have the slightest clue what I was going to do about the Whyver. I wasn't naïve enough to assume it'd been left behind at Levare's place in Pickering. But I didn't know how it was getting around. For all I knew, it was travelling between dimensions, using portals as shortcuts to hopscotch around our world. It might already be here.

Chester dropped the ramp and I got back into my car. I lowered my window as I rolled past him. "Call the cops the moment you get back." He nodded and returned to the controls the moment I was clear. I watched the ferry's running lights fade away in the rear-view mirror. Soon they were gone entirely and I was alone in the dark.

24

THE DIRT ROAD that led away from the landing went over a slight rise, bent sharply to the left, and became Lighthouse Road. I could see a pinpoint of light pulsing in the distance that I presumed was the lighthouse. I didn't see any other buildings, but my headlights glinted off the occasional mailbox. I slowed down as I passed each one, looking for number seventeen.

When I found it, I pulled off to the side of the road. Next to the mailbox a long gravel drive curved off into the darkness. There was a house somewhere out there, and I didn't need to warn the people inside that I was coming by driving up with my headlights on.

I got out of the car and checked my gun. I own two guns, a .357 Ruger revolver and a Glock 26 subcompact. I had the Ruger with me. It was the one I usually carried. The Glock had more rounds in a clip, but not as much stopping power. Gun experts will tell you that stopping power is a bunch of bullshit, and that the only thing that matters is shot placement. Under normal circumstances I'd be inclined to agree. I wouldn't need stopping power against Joe Levare and his boys. But I had a feeling it would come in handy against the Whyver. Assuming it was bothered by bullets at all.

I patted the brick in my jacket pocket. "Feel free to jump in at any time and help me out, okay?"

Then I started up the driveway.

25

THE HOUSE SEEMED to develop against the blackness of the night like the image on a Polaroid picture. It was not the ramshackle crazy-cat-lady house I'd been expecting. It was tall and narrow, two storeys, painted white with either dark blue or black trim, and appeared to be well-maintained, except for the flower boxes, which hung empty off the ground-floor windowsills. Flagstones wound a curving path from the drive to the porch steps.

The front yard was a roughly thirty-by-thirty square of lawn on which a pair of Lincoln Town Cars were parked. On either side of the yard, tall grass grew wild. That's where I was hiding, crouched down among the brittle stalks. I'd walked along the edge of the drive so that I wouldn't make any noise on the gravel. I didn't know if Levare had a man stationed outside. He probably didn't expect anyone to follow him way the hell out here, but I figured him for a man who didn't take any chances. Of course, he was also looking for his own Black Lands portal, so what the hell did I know?

I didn't see anyone at the front of the house, but I kept to the tall grass and duck-walked around to the back. I didn't see anyone there either. All of the ground-floor lights were on, but the second level was completely dark. The curtains were drawn on all the windows I had passed, but when I came to the far side of the house, I saw a thin column of light at a window where the curtains hadn't been completely shut.

I looked around for man-shaped shadows, then slipped out of the tall grass and crouched beneath the window. I tilted my head from side to side, trying to get an angle on the room without alerting anyone inside to my presence. A dark shape moved past the window and I almost had a heart attack. I froze, wishing I could melt into the side of the house, then the shape moved a bit deeper into the room and I let out a long, shaky breath. I thought someone was looking out the window, but it was just their back. A large back, with broad shoulders and a shaved bullet head. The head turned slightly to reveal a grim, stone-faced profile. I creeped a little closer to the gap in the curtains and peered into the room.

The broad-shouldered guy was blocking most of my view, so I couldn't see much, but I could see enough. I'd found Aubrey, for one thing. She was sitting on a straight-back chair in the middle of the room. A silver-haired man in his fifties — Joe Levare, I presumed — sat in front of her in another chair. Two large men in dark suits stood on the far side of the room with their hands folded in front of them. They might have been mistaken for Secret Service agents, but there was a thuggish look about them that said they'd rather inflict pain than protect anyone from it.

Aubrey sat rigidly in her seat, hands gripping the sides of the chair as if worried she might fall off. Levare was leaning in close to her, elbows on his thighs, fingers steepled beneath his wattled neck. He was speaking to her in what appeared to be a calm voice, but from the expression on her face, she didn't seem to like the words coming out of his mouth. Levare stopped talking, and Aubrey shook her head frantically back and forth. She appeared to be unharmed, which meant Levare hadn't decided to get rough with her. Not yet, anyway. That might change if Aubrey couldn't produce a portal.

I was craning my neck around, trying to get a look at the rest of the room, when I felt something cold and hard press against the back of my head. Chester said he had taken five guys across on the ferry. There were four guys in the house.

I'd just found the fifth.

26

"I WASN'T sure you were going to make it," Levare said. He spoke as though we were at a barbecue or a dinner party. I'd been to both but no one had ever brought guns.

Levare didn't have one, but his friends did. The three guys I'd been watching in the room had taken out large automatics, the kind that'll blow a barn door through you if you're unfortunate enough to be shot with one. The guy who'd caught me eavesdropping had an Ithaca 12-gauge shotgun that he held casually with the barrel pointed upward, resting against his shoulder.

I was sitting on the floor in front of Levare. He had turned his chair away from Aubrey to face me. Seeing him up close, I adjusted my initial assessment and put him in his sixties. He had a lot more lines on his face than I had seen from the window. There were long, deep grooves on his cheeks and bracketing his mouth, and nests of crow's-feet around his pale blue eyes. His face looked like it had been carved from an old piece of wood by someone with more enthusiasm than skill.

"Donto called and said you might be dropping by." He grinned. He had a good grin. It gave off plenty of warmth. But then so did a nuclear explosion. "He also told a funny story about a brick. Is this it?"

Levare held up the brick. His men had taken it, along with my gun, when they patted me down.

"It's my good luck charm," I said.

"It's not doing a very good job."

"I wouldn't say that."

"Donto said this brick almost killed him. He also said it trashed his car." Levare looked around the room at the others. "I think he was more upset about the car." They all laughed.

I looked at the floor and said nothing.

Levare placed the brick under my chin and used it to raise my head. "You'll talk to me, Mr. Renn. You can do it now, or you can do it after I've cut off a few body parts. It makes no difference to me."

"I don't know how the brick works," I said.

"Are you psionic?" Levare's eyes widened for a moment, then narrowed. "No, I don't suppose you are. If you were, you'd have already sent this brick flying through my skull." He bounced it in his palm, and I had a déjà vu of doing the exact same thing in Jerry's office: *Be careful! She's very fragile and... temperamental.*

"You don't want to get that brick angry," I warned him. "You wouldn't like it when it's angry."

"I've heard about you. Felix Renn, PI. You have a reputation for getting mixed up with the Black Lands."

"It's my gift," I droned. "And my curse."

"It *is* a gift," Levare said. "Do you know what I'd give to have a portal of my own?"

"Do you know what you'd lose?"

Levare leaned back in his seat. "You think I don't know the danger of the Black Lands?" He threw his head back and laughed. "Mr. Renn, that's the whole point!"

"I thought you just wanted a place to hide your stolen stereos when the cops showed up."

"Portals have a number of uses," Levare said in an ominous tone. "I've been wanting to diversify for years. Explore other interests on an interdimensional level. There's a whole market over there just waiting to be exploited."

"I don't think they want what you're selling."

"You think we're the only outfit looking to use the Black Lands? Some guys are already doing it."

"You'll die."

Levare grinned. "I'll outlive you."

"Maybe."

"How did you know to come here?"

"Woman's intuition."

Levare said, "Marty," and the guy with the shotgun racked the slide and pressed the muzzle against the side of my neck.

"Let's try that again," Levare said. "How did you get here?"

"I was hired by the girl's mother to find her."

This whole time, Aubrey had been staring quietly at the floor. At the mention of her mother, her head came up and she looked at me with faint hope.

"Do you know what she can do?" Levare asked me.

"I don't care. I just want to take her home."

"How touching." Levare got up and went over to stand behind Aubrey. He gripped the brick like he was going to hit her with it, then he lowered it and put his other hand on her shoulder. "Unfortunately, that isn't going to be possible. The young lady's working for me right now, and I can't let her go in the middle of a job."

"Like the job you gave Seth Carr?" I said.

Levare's grin evaporated. "Donto told me the kid was killed. Is that true?"

I nodded and glanced over at Aubrey. Her eyes glistened, then the tears came streaming down her cheeks. She didn't sob, she didn't wail; she just sat there crying in silence.

Levare came around to her side, curling his arm around her neck as he bent down to console her. "I'm sorry, honey. I didn't want to tell you. I thought it might affect your... ability. I'm really sorry about that. I liked Seth. I liked him a lot. He was a good kid. He worked for me for a long time. He was very loyal."

"Loyal to a fault," I said. "He sold Aubrey to you."

Aubrey's eyes widened. She looked from me to Levare and back again.

Levare said, "You don't know what you're talking about, Mr. Renn." But the cold look he shot me said otherwise. "I'm a businessman, nothing more. Seth was a part of my business, and the dealings we had together are between me and him. Just like my dealings with Aubrey are between her and me. You have no part in this."

"It looks like she doesn't want any part in this, either."

"Aubrey and I have an understanding," Levare said, gripping the back of her neck. "Once she finds me a portal, she's free to go. I'm not greedy." He turned the grin back on. "I only want one."

"Aubrey isn't your golden ticket to the Black Lands. She can't do what you think she can."

"That's a lie!" Levare snapped. "I know she can. I've seen it!" He tightened his grip on the back of Aubrey's neck, causing her to wince. Then he moved back around to his own chair and picked up both of her hands. "Seth said you could find me a portal, just like you did at the Bluffs. I saw it on the news. He said you found it. He said you knew right where to look."

"She doesn't know, Levare. She's just a kid. Please, let her go."

Levare leaped out his chair, knocking it over. "She knows!" he yelled. "She better fucking know!" He pointed the brick at her. "We came here because you said there was a portal here. So, where the fuck is it?"

"I told you, I don't know," Aubrey said.

"You knew at the Bluffs."

"I didn't! I was just throwing rocks. I didn't know what I was doing."

I was starting to think Aubrey might not have been stalling for time when she decided to lead Levare and his crew to this place. It was starting to look extremely likely that there was a portal somewhere nearby. It wasn't her words that convinced me. Or the honesty in her eyes.

It was the shadow I'd just glimpsed going past the window.

27

IT WAS HARD NOT to look. I didn't want to tip off Levare and his crew to the danger outside. But it wasn't easy. I felt my gaze being drawn to the windows, like the needle of a compass swinging north. I was afraid to look, but a part of me needed to see what was out there, even if it was a pair of burning red eyes staring back at me.

The guy behind me, Marty, bumped my shoulder with the barrel of his shotgun and said, "What you want us to do with the dick, boss?"

Levare turned from Aubrey and looked at me. He clicked his tongue like he was trying to decide how to deal with some minor annoyance, like a wrinkled shirt or a flat tire.

"Normally I'd tell you to take him out back and fill him with holes. But we can't do that. If we do end up finding a portal" — he turned and gave Aubrey a threatening look — "we'll be setting up an operation here. That means we can't be pulling any shit that'll draw attention to us, like executing nosy detectives." He started bouncing the brick in his hand again and a smile spread across his face. "I think I've got an idea."

Levare's men waited attentively like trained Dobermans.

"Don, Karl. I want you two to go outside and find some rocks."

"Rocks?" said one of the men.

"Yeah," Levare said. "You know, the things in your fucking head."

The other guy shook his head at his friend. "Dummy."

"Shut up, Karl."

"Both of you shut the fuck up," Levare said. "Go and find some rocks. Big ones. Right now!"

Don, the dummy, shot Karl a black look, and the two of them shuffled out of the room. That left Levare, Marty, and the other thug whose name I didn't know.

Levare was looking at me in a speculative way that I didn't particularly enjoy. It gave me an unpleasant feeling, like bugs crawling on the back of my neck.

"I've had my boys weigh down bodies before," he said, "but never while the guy was still alive. This'll be a first for me. I might have to come out and watch."

"We're not gonna mark him up at all?" Marty said. He sounded so disappointed I thought he might start crying.

Levare tossed the brick on the floor and dusted off his hands. "I guess we could leave him with a few parting gifts."

The words had barely left his mouth when I felt Marty's heavy foot slam into my back and send me sprawling onto the floor. As I was trying to push myself back up, a chocolate-brown loafer came crashing down on my right hand. The blow was off by a few inches and Marty got more fingers than hand, but it still didn't feel like a manicure. I stifled a yelp and retracted my hand, tucking it in close to my body. Marty responded by hoofing me in the stomach. I felt all the air blow out of my lungs. I gasped for more and he hoofed me again. That one was hard enough to knock me over onto my side. I closed my eyes, thinking that maybe if I played dead Marty might leave me alone. No such luck. He delivered a sharp kick to my kidneys with the precision of one who has done this many times before. I heard Aubrey sobbing loudly. She was probably thinking about Seth, but I pretended it was because of what was being done to me.

"Don't break anything," Levare said. "We need to make sure he's unmarked when the body washes up." He snorted. "*If* it washes up."

I rolled onto my knees and sat up. A fist came flying and clipped me on the jaw. I felt a tooth break and a vibrating numbness shot up the side of my face. I slumped over onto my hands, grimacing in pain.

Marty said, "You wanna give him a shot, Jack?" and I heard the other guy say, "Pass."

I rolled onto my back and stared at the ceiling. "Jack, huh?"

I heard the guy scoff. "You don't know me, pal."

I looked over at him. He was the broad-shouldered, bullet-headed thug I'd been peering around at the window.

"I know," I said. "I was just thinking now I know all of your names. That's going to make things easier when I get out of here and the cops have me looking at mug shots. Names to go with the faces. They love that. Helps them out immensely."

There was a long moment of silence, then they all started laughing. It was the loud, raucous and slightly pitying laughter reserved for the infinitely deluded. The idea that I would be walking out of there alive was apparently quite amusing to them. Frankly, I thought it would be a small miracle if any of us left this place alive.

Levare rubbed his chin thoughtfully. "We'll need to tie him up so he doesn't try to dump the rocks." He looked over at Marty. "I don't suppose we brought any rope."

Marty shook his head.

"Oh well," Levare said. "I guess you'll just have to break his arms."

Marty grinned and took an eager step forward.

Levare held up his hand. "Outside."

28

MARTY MARCHED me through the back door, prodding me in my sore kidneys with the muzzle of his shotgun. It was very dark. There were no streetlights, no moon, not even any stars. I was looking all around, trying to spot a shadow moving in a way a shadow shouldn't, but I could barely see two feet in front of my face.

"Don! Karl!" Marty shouted. "Where you at?"

"Down here!" one of them yelled back, somewhere off in the distance.

Marty poked me again with the shotgun and we headed off toward the water. I couldn't see it, but I could hear it. The rhythmic lapping of the waves grew louder as we climbed a slight rise and went down the other side. I could sort of make out the water: it was a dark moving blur against the slightly lighter, unmoving blur of the shore.

As we got closer, I spotted Don, the dumb thug, bent over at the waist, squinting at the ground as he wandered aimlessly around. "Rocks," he muttered. "Where am I supposed to find fucking rocks?"

Karl was sitting on the edge of a wooden dock that extended out into the water. He held a pile of rocks in the crook of one arm. "There's rocks everywhere," he said.

"This is the great outdoors."

"Great outdoors," Don grumbled. "Real fucking great."

"Quit yer bitching," Marty said. "It's too fucking cold. Let's get this shit done so we can go home."

"There's a boat." Karl gestured with his chin at a rowboat tied up to the dock. "We can take him out and dump him."

"I ain't getting in no fucking boat," Marty said. "Not in my job description."

"What are we supposed to do," Karl said, "drown the guy in three feet of water? We gotta take him out in the boat."

"You do it. Take Sling Blade with you. I'll watch from shore. If you get in trouble, I'll call the Coast Guard."

Don's face twisted into an expression of simian anger. "The fuck you call me?"

Karl came over and patted his shoulder. "Take it easy, pal. He didn't mean nothing. Why don't you go up the shore a bit and see if you can find some rocks there?"

Don gave Marty a final fuck-you look and wandered off. When he was out of earshot, Karl turned to Marty and said, "Why do you do that? You know he isn't that bright."

Marty shook his head. "If brains were dynamite, he wouldn't have enough to blow his nose."

"He can't help the way he is."

"He's your brother. If you want to make excuses for him, that's your business. If he fucks things up here, then it's all of our business."

"He won't fuck things up. What are we doing, gathering up rocks? What could go wrong?"

Normally I would have jumped on a line like that, but it turned out I didn't have to.

In the distance, Don yelled, "Oh shit!" followed by a splash.

Marty sighed. "The fucking dolt. He fell in."

Then Don started screaming.

29

KARL DROPPED his rocks and whipped out his gun. "Donnie!" he screamed. "Donnie, what's wrong?"

Don went on screaming.

Karl turned and shot me a hard look. "You bring a fucking friend? Is that it? You got a partner out there?"

I shook my head. "I'm a loner."

He looked down the shore. I followed his gaze but couldn't see anything except a small light blur moving around in the distance. It could have been Don. It could have been anything. Or nothing.

Karl took a deep breath and marched off with his gun out in front of him. He kept calling Don's name, and Don kept right on screaming.

Marty and I watched him go. I thought about making a run for it, but considering Marty's stance on kicking people when they were down, I was fairly certain he wouldn't have any qualms about shooting me in the back.

We stood and waited for something to happen. Don's screams

tapered off. We couldn't see Karl anymore. But we heard him when he started screaming, too. To his credit, he managed to fire off a shot, which was more than could be said for his brother. Then his screams abruptly stopped.

The silence stretched.

"And then there were two," I said.

"Shut up," Marty snapped. Then, in a louder voice, he called out: "Karl! Don! What are you assholes doing out there?"

There was no reply except the low, hypnotic whisper of the waves.

"Maybe we should go back to the house," I suggested.

Marty turned and looked at me. "It's true, isn't it? You've got somebody out there." He pointed the shotgun at me. "Tell them to come out or I'm gonna cut you in half."

Before I could reply, a low chittering sound cut through the air.

Marty and I turned in unison toward the water.

"What the fuck was —" Marty started, then something came shooting out of the lake like a long black torpedo. It crashed into Marty and knocked him to the ground. Miraculously, he managed to hold onto his shotgun. In a flash, he rolled onto his side and fired a shot into the dark shape that towered over him. It was a perfect hit, but it didn't seem to have any effect on his attacker.

The Whyver was real and it was here. Straight out of Olivia Wood's letter. It was just as she described it. Tall, maybe seven feet, with a triangular head and shoulders so massive that it had a perpetual hunch. Its arms were long and muscular. Its hands were large, with sharp, barb-like protrusions on the knuckles, and long fingers that ended in jagged claws. Its matte-black skin blended so perfectly with the night it was nearly impossible to see. Not that I wanted to.

Marty pumped another load into the Ithaca, but before he could pull the trigger, the Whyver knocked the shotgun out of his hands. The movement was so fast I almost missed it. One moment Marty was holding the shotgun, the next his hands were empty. He reached behind his back, probably for a backup piece, but he wasn't fast enough, and the Whyver drove one its claw-tipped hands into his stomach. It came out Marty's back with a piece of his spine clutched in its blood-smeared fingers. Marty's eyes went wide with shock. His mouth dropped open and a stream of blood poured out, painting his chin. The Whyver jammed its other hand into Marty's open mouth, the barbs on its knuckles shredding his cheeks like they were made of tissue paper. It dug around inside him for a moment, then yanked its hand back and ripped off most of Marty's face.

I had a sudden vision of a magician pulling away a tablecloth while leaving the place settings undisturbed. Except when the tablecloth was pulled away, underneath was a naked human skull.

I bent over and threw up on the sandy shore.

When I was finished, I looked up and saw that the Whyver had dragged Marty down to the ground. It was crouched over him and tearing into his midsection with both hands, flinging bloody hunks of meat over its shoulder like it was rooting through a suitcase for something to wear.

I wanted to run, but I couldn't. I was frozen to the spot. I didn't know if it was the horror of what I was seeing or if it was like gawking at a car wreck.

There was something shark-like about the Whyver, both in its ferocity and in its silence. It didn't scream or growl or make any sound at all as it ripped Marty apart. It was impossible to tell if it took any pleasure in the act, but it went about it in a way that was different from one animal attacking another out of hunger or territoriality.

When I was finally able to start backing away, I didn't have to tell my legs to move; they were doing so already out of a sense of self-preservation.

Right before I turned to run, the Whyver's head swivelled around and pinned me in place. Staring into its face, I could see the long slit of its lipless mouth running from one side of its triangular head to the other. One corner of it rose in a sneer that revealed row after row of small needle teeth.

Its eyes were red, like Olivia Wood had said in her letter, and I realized when she had described them as "burning," she wasn't just being colourful. The Whyver's eyes really did look like they were on fire. Like they were not so much set in the creature's face as they were burned into it. I thought I could even hear those eyes sizzling in their sockets.

In that moment, as we stood there staring at each other, I knew the Whyver was either going to turn its attentions back to Marty (what was left of him) or it was going to come after me. And if it came after me, then that was it. Game over.

I waited. After what might have been ten seconds or ten minutes — fear had skewered my sense of time — the Whyver finally lowered its head and went back to work on Marty.

I ran.

30

I DIDN'T HEAR the Whyver coming after me, but that didn't mean it wasn't. It could've been hot on my heels and I wouldn't have known until it was right on top of me, digging into my flesh with those long, black claws.

I could see Olivia Wood's house in the distance, impossibly far away. It hadn't seemed like I'd walked this far when Marty led me out with the shotgun to my back. The ground-floor lights were my beacon. I ran toward them but they didn't seem to get any closer. My lungs were starting to burn and my breath came out in ragged white puffs.

Why wasn't the Whyver chasing me? Maybe it was still busy with Marty. Maybe it didn't consider me a threat. Seth Carr hadn't been a threat, either, but the Whyver had still killed him. Was it because Seth had been Aubrey adjacent? Did he have her scent on him? Maybe it was because I hadn't engaged the Whyver as Levare's men had done. Maybe maybe maybe.

It didn't matter. I could ruminate on it all night and still not come up with the answer. The motivations of Black Lands entities were completely alien. Some killed for food, some for pleasure, and I wasn't particularly inclined to go back and ask the Whyver to take a survey.

Approaching the back stoop, I expected to see Levare and his remaining goon waiting for me with their guns drawn. But no one was there. The sounds from the shore must not have carried as far as the house.

I had only seconds to formulate a plan, and I was in no condition mentally to come up with anything complex. There was firewood stacked against the side of the house. I picked up a piece that felt good in my hand and creeped slowly up the steps.

The back door opened on a spring-hinge. It was well-oiled and didn't make a sound. Stepping inside, I pushed the door wide open and let it slap loudly closed. Then I slipped behind the inner door and waited. I didn't have to wait long.

The remaining goon, Jack, came running with his gun raised. He went straight to the screen door and pushed it open. I emerged from my hiding place with the block of wood raised in both hands, and brought it down on the back of his head. Jack made a low grunt and slumped bonelessly onto the back steps. I dragged him inside, checked his pulse to make sure I hadn't killed him, and then went back out to retrieve his gun from where it had fallen on the ground.

I didn't see any red eyes in the night, but I knew they were out there, somewhere, and I knew they'd be coming.

31

THE GUN WAS a Colt .45 automatic. Jack the goon had an extra clip on him, and I took that, too. I clicked off the safety and started down the central hallway.

I came around the corner into the living room. Aubrey was still sitting in her chair. Levare stood next to her. A board creaked under my foot, and he turned and saw me. I pointed the gun at him.

"It's over, Levare."

He either didn't hear me or he didn't care. Maybe he just wasn't used to someone pointing a gun at him for a change. He came marching toward me, one hand reaching into his suit jacket, probably not for a pen, and probably not to ask me for an autograph. I didn't want to shoot him, but he wasn't giving me much choice.

I spotted movement out of the corner of my eye. The brick was sliding across the hardwood floor. It came to a stop right in front of Levare as his foot came swinging forward. He stumbled and went down on one knee. His hand was still inside his suit jacket, throwing off his balance. He swore loudly.

I went over and put my foot on his back, pushing him the rest of the way down to the floor. He landed hard on his shoulder. "We don't have time for this," I said. "We're in trouble."

Levare turned his head to the side and glared at me. "You don't know what trouble is," he said. "But you're gonna find out. Where are my men?"

"Dead." I looked over at Aubrey. She had a frightened, knowing look on her face. "A very large, very pissed-off creature called the Whyver has been tracking Aubrey, and now it's found her."

"Bullshit," Levare said. "Supernaturals can't cross water."

I took my foot off his back. "Maybe you should go out there and tell it that."

Aubrey suddenly let out a scream and pointed. I turned in time to see a dark shape move past one of the living room windows. Levare crawled out into the foyer just as something heavy slammed into the front door from the other side.

"Marty, is that you?" he shouted.

It wasn't Marty. I could have told him that, but there was no point. He'd see for himself soon enough.

The second blow to the door sent one of the brass hinges flying down the hallway. It wouldn't hold much longer. I wondered why the Whyver was bothering with the door at all, when it could've just come in through one of the windows, as it had done at Levare's place. Curious as I was, I didn't plan to stick around to ask it.

I went over to Aubrey and gripped her shoulder. "We have to go," I said. "Right now."

"What's the point?" she asked, looking up at me with wet, red-rimmed eyes. "If it can find me here, then it can find me anywhere."

I tried to pull her up out of the chair, but she slumped limply against me. "Just go," she said. "Leave me."

"Can't do it, kid." I swung her around and pushed her against the wall. She started to slide, then straightened her legs and propped herself up. "Come on. I've got a car out front. And the police are coming."

Aubrey closed her eyes and shook her head. I stuck the gun in my waistband, grabbed her by the upper arms and gave her a hard shake. Her eyes jerked open. I leaned toward her, so close our noses almost touched.

"We may die tonight, but not with our eyes closed. You don't want to fight for your life? Fine. I'll fight for both of us. But you're going to run. Do you hear me?"

I pulled her away from the wall and pushed her toward the hallway. She didn't run, she staggered, but it was better than nothing. The Whyver hit the door again, and this time the sound wasn't a thump, but a splintering crack. I glanced over and saw the wooden frame was collapsing inward. I took the gun out of my waistband as I stepped past Levare, but he didn't even notice me. He was staring at the door.

"You wanted the Black Lands," I told him. "You got it."

32

THE DOOR GAVE the moment Aubrey and I reached the kitchen. I stood transfixed for a moment, watching as the two halves of it flew to either side like curtains to reveal the blackness outside. Then the blackness came in, ducking its strange triangular head to make it through the doorway. Levare stared up at the Whyver with bulging eyes, his mouth hanging open as if the muscles there had gone slack.

The Whyver didn't seem to notice him at all. It had eyes only for me and Aubrey. As it came stalking down the hallway toward us, it flicked its hand to the side in an absent, swatting motion, and Levare's head went flying through the open doorway and out into the night.

The crime boss's body slumped onto its side, blood gouting from the severed stump of his neck.

I glanced at the back door (Jack the goon was still lying unconscious on the floor in front of it). There was no way Aubrey and I would make it outside, around the house, and down the long driveway to my car. Not if I had to keep pushing and prodding her along.

Aubrey whimpered as the Whyver closed the distance between us. I grabbed her shoulder and turned her toward the back stairs, leading up to the second floor. I had to swat her on the can to get her moving. She was crying, but I didn't hold it against her. I wanted to cry, too.

Instead, I turned back to the Whyver, stood in the classic target shooter's stance, and emptied my gun into it.

The shots did damage. That much I can say. I saw the impact as they struck its massive chest. I saw its flesh split open and a dark ichor that I presumed was blood spray out. But for all that, the bullets didn't seem to have any effect. The Whyver didn't scream out in pain or fury, and it didn't slow down. It took the shots, accepted them, and kept coming.

Aubrey reached the top of the stairs and stared down at me. She looked completely lost. I went up after her, swinging the door closed behind me. The Whyver slammed into it a moment later. It didn't seem to understand doorknobs, or maybe it just didn't have the patience for them. Either way, it bought us a few more seconds.

I got to the top and looked around. We were at the end of a hallway with doors on both sides. At the other end I could see the landing and the front stairs leading down to the foyer. Again, I debated leaving the house and trying to make a run for my car. And again, I didn't like the odds of betting my life against a foot race with the Whyver.

I tried to tell myself things would be okay once the police arrived. But there was no guarantee they would show up and, even if they did, what chance did some local cops have against the Whyver? Having seen the creature in action, I doubted if even the PIA could stand against it.

I dragged Aubrey roughly down the hallway. I stopped at the last door and threw it open. It was a bedroom — a guest bedroom from the unused look of it. There was a single bed, a dresser and a small wooden writing desk.

I shoved Aubrey inside and handed her the gun. "Take it," I said. "It's easy to use. Point it at the big, red-eyed monster and pull the trigger until it goes away."

"Where are you going?" she asked me in a small voice.

"I'm going to try to slow it down." I started to pull the door shut, then stopped and said: "Barricade the door."

One door closed, while another came crashing open. The sound rose up out of the stairwell like a portent. I backed out onto the landing and spied a Shaker chair against the wall. I picked it up and held it in front of me like a lion tamer about to enter the cage.

I heard the Whyver coming up the stairs. It wasn't the steady thump and creak of footfalls on old wooden risers. It was a series of sharp, splintering cracks as the Whyver drove its feet into each step.

I saw what I first thought was its shadow reach the top, then the head turned, red eyes glaring, and I realized it was the Whyver itself. It filled the narrow hallway, heavy arms brushing the walls on either side, its head hunched down between its powerful shoulders. I could see the wounds in its chest where my shots had struck, but they didn't appear to be bleeding anymore. I wished I had Marty's shotgun. It may not have done any more damage than the Colt, but it had to be better than attacking the beast with an antique chair.

The Whyver came striding down the hallway. It used its hands to pull itself along the walls, shredding the dusty-rose wallpaper and leaving long gouges in the plaster. Its wide, lipless mouth opened to reveal those rows of needle teeth, and yet it still made no sound. No growls, no hisses, no "My, my, don't you look delicious!"

I backed toward the top of the stairs and peered over the railing at Levare's headless body lying in the foyer below. It was still pumping blood onto the floor. There was a lot of blood in the human body. It seemed I always became aware of that fact when it looked like some of mine was about to be spilled.

I went down a couple of steps with the chair raised between me and the Whyver. It reached the end of the hallway and stood there staring at me. Then it turned its head slowly to the door of the room where I'd stashed Aubrey. It knew. It smelled her or sensed her presence somehow. I backed down another step.

"Come on, you ugly fuck!" I brandished my chair at it. "You don't want a scrawny thing like her! Come and get me!"

The Whyver looked at me for a moment, decided I wasn't worth its time, and turned its attention back to the door. I banged the chair on the bannister, but the creature would not be distracted. It placed both of its long-fingered hands on the door. I could see the thick muscles straining in its broad back. It wasn't going to bash this one down. It was simply going to push its way through.

I made a decision. I didn't know if it was a good one, but at this point I figured it didn't matter.

I went back up the stairs, dashed across the landing, and brought the chair down on the Whyver's back. It shattered to pieces, as I knew it would, and the Whyver decided to pay attention to me again.

I skipped backwards, but not fast enough. The Whyver's reach was long and quick. It swatted me off the landing as neatly as it had swatted Levare's head from his shoulders. Fortunately, I was still in possession of my head as I went flying over the railing, and while I heard a loud popping sound when I struck the floor, the horrible burst of pain I felt in my left shoulder told me I was still alive.

I didn't need an X-ray and a smarmy doctor to tell me the shoulder was dislocated. I only had to roll onto it to realize that for myself. It was like rolling onto hot coals, except when I rolled back the coals were still there, sending burning signals of pain through my upper back and torso and all the way down my arm. I blinked away tears and immediately spotted something near the headless body of Joe Levare.

It was the brick. It was still on the floor in the living room, in the spot where it had tripped Levare. As I watched, it began to tremble. Then it began to shake. It was like there was an earthquake, but nothing else was moving.

Some inner voice or instinct spoke up at that moment, and although it sent another bolt of pain racing through my shoulder, I flipped quickly onto my other side, away from the brick.

I didn't see it come flying at me, but I felt it when it hit my arm.

There was another blast of pain, the worst one yet, and then... nothing. I wiggled my arm tentatively. It no longer felt like someone had surgically implanted a grenade in my shoulder and pulled the pin. The pain was still there, but it had settled into a dull ache.

I sat up and looked down at the brick, which was once again lying motionless on the floor.

"Thanks."

I tried standing up. My chest was sore in a couple of places, but I didn't have any broken ribs. I could still walk and I wasn't coughing up blood. That meant I was still on the clock. We never sleep.

I picked up the brick and started up the stairs.

I reached the top and saw the Whyver leaning all of its considerable weight against the door. It began to split down the middle with a sharp cracking sound, just as the front door had. The Whyver gripped both pieces and flung them aside. Aubrey had made a barricade like I told her to, and it took the Whyver an extra few moments to push away the dresser and the writing desk. Then it was inside.

There were two reasons I didn't go leaping right back into the fray. One, I'd done that already and gotten my shoulder dislocated for the effort. The second reason came a moment later when I heard Aubrey unload with the Colt. None of the shots burst through the walls, so I assumed they all went into the Whyver. For all the good they'd do.

I waited until she'd fired off the entire clip, and when there was no chance I'd get accidentally shot, I came running.

33

THE WHYVER DIDN'T WASTE any time. It had been hunting the Wood women for over fifty years, and now, with its final target in its sights, it would not be denied.

Standing in the doorway, I saw Aubrey cowering in the far corner of the room between the bed and the wall.

The Whyver reached out and flipped the bed out of its way. The frame smashed against the wall, but the mattress bounced back and struck the Whyver. The Whyver turned on it in a rage, flinging both of its arms upward and slashing its claws along its length. The air was suddenly filled with stuffing. The Whyver gripped the mattress by the sides and tossed it over its shoulder. I pressed myself flat against the wall and narrowly avoided getting struck by it.

The Whyver made the low chittering sound it had made down on the shore. I didn't know what it meant, if it meant anything, but I knew I had to do something fast or else Aubrey was dead. I gripped the brick tightly in my right hand. My left hand felt numb and distant, the shoulder still pulsing with the dull pain of having been popped out and then popped back in again. I didn't know what good I could do against the Whyver, but maybe all that mattered was that I tried.

No, that wasn't good enough. There was no consolation in merely trying. Aubrey would still be dead.

But what was I supposed to do? Throw the brick at it? Sure, and maybe I'd get the Whyver's attention. Then what? Put up my dukes and go toe to toe with it? Fat chance.

I wasn't aware that I was moving further into the room until a piece of mattress stuffing landed on my shoulder. I raised my hand to brush it away and found myself staring at the brick. Aubrey screamed. The Whyver chittered. It was time to act.

So, I acted.

34

I WOULDN'T HAVE BEEN able to leap onto the Whyver's back if it hadn't bent down to reach for Aubrey. I switched the brick from my right hand to the left, took three quick steps forward, and launched myself.

Landing on the Whyver's back was like landing on a warm, slightly moist gym mat. Except a gym mat doesn't try to buck you off. And the

Whyver was trying. It leapt up and threw its shoulders back like a bronco, which should have been enough to splatter me across the ceiling, but I managed to anchor myself by looping my right arm around the thick trunk of the Whyver's neck. I gripped the brick in my left hand and prayed that I didn't drop it. With every bump and jump, I kept expecting to see my fingers snap open and the brick go sailing away.

When the Whyver realized it couldn't get rid of me by jumping up and down, it decided to change tactics. It swung me around to the right, then spun to the side and slammed into the wall. The pain in my shoulder turned back up to eleven, and I almost let go of the Whyver's neck. Then it swung me back around the other way and I felt myself collide not with the other wall but the window.

Glass and timber exploded outward into the night. I went along with it as the Whyver stumbled to the side. We both would have gone tumbling to the ground if it hadn't thrown up its hands at the last moment and latched onto the top of the broken window frame. The cold air struck me like a slap to the face. I tightened my grip on the Whyver's neck as it hauled itself back inside.

Aubrey had crawled over to another corner of the room and sat between the wall and the sliding door of the closet. She wasn't cowering anymore; she was just sitting there with her arms wrapped around her drawn-up knees, like she was listening to a campfire story. She should have made a run for it. I was turning my head to yell at her when I caught movement from above.

I twisted my body to the side just in time to avoid one of the Whyver's hands as it reached over its shoulder, trying to pick me off its back like a leech that had latched onto its skin. As I was recoiling away from its questing claws, I realized I was still holding the brick in my other hand. And I figured, *why not?*

As the Whyver's hand probed closer, I pulled back and brought the brick down with all the force I could muster. It shouldn't have been much. My shoulder had been dislocated and popped back into its socket only a few minutes earlier, and at the present moment it still felt like someone was banking a small, hungry fire in there. The fact that I had managed to hold onto the brick at all was a small miracle. The idea that I'd be able to do any damage with it was a sad joke.

While these thoughts were running through my mind, something else ran through my arm.

Power.

I felt it surge through my shoulder like a bolt of lightning. The image that came to mind was of the strength tester at the carnival. The mallet striking the padded base and the chaser flying up the tower's length to ding the bell.

Only when the brick struck the Whyver's hand, there was no ringing sound.

The Whyver howled in pain.

I couldn't blame him. The blow from the brick didn't so much crush the Whyver's hand as explode it. Hunks of dark flesh and black blood went flying. I closed my eyes and felt it spatter my face in a warm, chunky rain. I gritted my teeth against the revulsion twisting in my stomach and pulled back for another swing.

At the same moment, the Whyver spun around, and I felt myself tumbling over and losing my grip on its neck. I landed on the floor, sprawled on my back, my arm and shoulder still numb, but now with power instead of pain. I expected the Whyver to fall on me then and rip me to shreds. But when I opened my eyes, I saw something that dulled my rage, if only for a moment.

The Whyver was cradling its shattered hand and making a low mewling sound. As I watched, its head came down and it licked the wound with a long black tongue. I almost felt sorry for it in the way you feel sorry for an animal that is only doing what comes naturally to it. Then I reminded myself that I wasn't dealing with something natural. The Whyver was supernatural. That didn't make it evil, just like rabies didn't make a dog evil, but it didn't make it any less danger-ous, either.

While still lying on my back, I raised my hand and brought the brick down on the Whyver's foot. There was another pulse of power in my arm, intensifying down its length to my hand, which felt like it was clutching a supernova. I briefly saw the Whyver's foot intact — long and sleek with three clawed toes — before it disappeared in a grisly detonation of flesh and bone and blood.

The Whyver forgot about its hand and lifted its leg. The look of pain on its demonic face was mingled with another expression that I was willing to bet was completely new to the creature: confusion. It had never known pain before and didn't know how to deal with it.

In that moment of hesitation, I swept my foot around and kicked its other leg. It was like kicking a 300-year-old redwood, but it did the trick. The Whyver teetered to the side, brought down its ruined foot to balance itself, cried out in agony, pulled it back up again, and toppled over.

I didn't so much climb to my feet as I was pulled up by the brick. The muscles in my arm thrummed like high-tension wires, and I knew that while the power was here I could pulverize flesh and smash bone, but it would be gone soon enough, and my body would suffer from the exertions of this day. To put it mildly, I was going to be sore in the morning.

I couldn't take credit for my next series of actions. I was merely along for the ride.

The Whyver lay on its back, wounded hand and wounded leg drawn close to its body, rolling back and forth in pain. As I stood over it, the Whyver became aware of my presence and lashed out at me with its intact foot. Before those claws could split my belly open, the brick came flying across to meet them. The impact was incredible. The brick's first two blows had been against unmoving objects. This was a collision between two fast-moving objects.

The brick met the Whyver's remaining foot and tore it off at the ankle. It went flying across the room and shattered against the far wall like a rotten watermelon, splattering gore in a grisly Rorschach display.

Dripping black blood and gobbets of flesh, the brick drew me inexorably forward. I stepped around the Whyver's flailing legs to stand over its upper body. It looked up at me with those burning red eyes, wincing in pain and the anticipation of more to come. It raised one hand and the ruined mess of the other in a defensive gesture. The brick yanked my arm up high over my head, almost pulling me off my feet, and then it came rocketing down with preternatural speed and force.

The Whyver's head exploded like a glass vase thrown on a marble floor. I threw my free arm across my face to protect myself against the shower of flesh, blood and bone shards. One of the Whyver's broken needle teeth drew a burning line across my cheek. It was the only cut the creature gave me that day.

I stumbled away from the Whyver's motionless body. The brick was like a weight tied to my hand. The power was gone. It didn't ebb away; it just left, like someone had turned off a switch.

I looked at Aubrey. She was staring at me with an expectant look on her face. It was over, she must've been able to see that, but it was like she needed verbal confirmation from me. I opened my mouth, but nothing came out. My fingers opened, too, and the brick fell to the floor with a clunk.

I joined it a moment later.

35

"I DON'T HOLD it against you," Jerry said. He downed the rest of his beer, belched, and fired the empty Coors can into the recycling box. He plucked a fresh can from the cooler sitting between us and popped it open. It was his fifth beer of the evening. I was still on my first.

We were sitting on the back deck of Jerry's house. A few weeks had passed since the incident on Simcoe Island. That was what the press were calling it, except in their stories they always capitalized "Incident" to give it that extra sensationalistic sizzle. I was doing my best to ignore their constant calls. I wasn't interested in giving any interviews. I had closed my office for the time being and told Sandra to take some vacation time. Reporters had staked out my apartment building, so I spent as much time as I could away from home. When Jerry called and invited me over, I eagerly accepted.

"Drink up," he said. "Once the beer's gone, we've got rye."

I grunted.

Jerry turned and gave me a long, considering look. "You really feel bad," he said. "I told you not to worry about it. I kind of like how it looks now. It's got like... battle scars or something."

He turned to the plastic patio table next to him and picked up the brick. I'd tried to wash away the stains of the Whyver's blood, but they wouldn't come off. It was no longer a sepia brick. It was now a black brick.

"It's not that," I said, and trailed off.

I didn't want to talk about it. At least, I didn't think I did. I'd spent days answering questions for the police and the PIA. I was sick to death of talking about the Whyver and the Wood family. And yet a part of me still needed to vent. It was different somehow, sitting there in the December chill on Jerry's back porch. The questions I'd answered for the feds had been little more than a debriefing. It was for their benefit. Talking to Jerry... this was for me.

"So, she came through for you, eh? Just like I told you she would." He turned and toasted his can of beer against the brick. "Cheers, darling."

"Better late than never," I said, and instantly regretted it.

Jerry cocked an eyebrow at me. "Meaning?"

"Meaning why didn't the brick help anyone else who lived at Rosedale Cottage." I glanced over at it. "Maybe it's only fitting that it has blood on it."

Jerry frowned. "You know why it didn't help. It was the girl's grandmother. She went to the Black Lands and it changed her. The brick... Rosie... she must have sensed a kindred spirit."

"A lot of people were killed in that cottage, Jer. You said so yourself."

Jerry slumped down in his seat. "Maybe she tried to warn them, but Olivia was the only one who could hear."

"Maybe," I said, and sipped my beer.

"It saved *your* life," Jerry pointed out. "And the girl's."

I nodded. "And I returned the favour."

"What?"

"You're lucky you got that thing back," I said, nodding at the brick.

"That *thing*?" Jerry said with mock offense. "You'd think after she saved your life you'd at least give her the respect of calling her by her proper name."

"Rosie came through," I agreed. "But she'd be in a PIA lab right now if I hadn't put her in the trunk of my car before the cops showed up. I found a rock in the yard on my way back to the house, and I dunked it in the Whyver's blood so they'd think I'd used it to kill the thing. The PIA is still a bit miffed on that one, but they didn't have any choice but to believe me."

"It worked on Goliath," Jerry said.

"And Aubrey backed me up," I added. "She's grateful to me... and to Rosie." I hesitated, then said, "It spoke to her. In the room. That's why she didn't leave. I was hanging off the Whyver's back and she stuck around. At the time I thought she was just in shock, but she told me later that the brick told her to stay. It told her to watch."

"Why?"

"I think it wanted her to see that the Whyver was dead. So she'd know it wouldn't be coming for her anymore."

Jerry grinned. "Good thing you were able to deliver on that one, huh?"

I nodded and took another sip of my beer. "Good thing."

"You're upset about the girl."

I turned and looked at Jerry. I was always surprised by the way he could be cruising along on one level of discussion — usually about women and the myriad ways of picking them up in bars — and then suddenly downshift into a seriousness that was startling in both its depth and honesty. I often wondered if anyone else in Jerry's life saw this side of him.

"I figured that's what it was," he went on. "That's why I asked you to come over."

"I don't need a pep talk, Jer, and I sure as hell don't need to get drunk. It's not going to make me feel better. It's not going to change anything."

"True," Jerry conceded.

"Aubrey's still out there. On the island, living in her grandmother's house. It's her place now, but that's not why she's staying there. She's there because she's afraid to leave."

"I've always wanted a place outside the city," Jerry said longingly.

"She's got her mother bringing her groceries every week, and half a dozen PIA agents staked out in town waiting to see if anything else from the Black Lands is going to drop by for a visit."

"Do you think that will happen?"

"*No*," I snapped. "But how am I supposed to convince her of that? Especially after her grandmother spent her entire life being stalked by the Whyver. Moving away from her family, from her daughter and her granddaughter, all in order to protect them." I shook my head. "Aubrey's just doing what comes naturally to her."

"At least she's alive."

"Living in fear is no life." I sighed. "And who knows, maybe I'm wrong."

"About what?" Jerry asked.

"About Aubrey. The brick said Olivia Wood burned bright, but that Aubrey burns brighter. Maybe she will end up drawing the attention of other creatures from the Black Lands."

"And maybe tomorrow you'll cross the street and get hit by a bus."

"It's not the same thing."

Jerry waved a hand in the air. "What do you see out there?"

"Your backyard?"

"Specifically."

"Your overgrown backyard?"

Jerry gave me a look.

I leaned forward in my seat. "Pink flamingos?" There were five of them — the plastic ones that stick into the ground on metal rods — standing in a huddle next to a small work shed.

"Those aren't mine," Jerry said. "I didn't buy them. They just showed up one day after I put Rosie in the foundation of my house. Sometimes I'll walk past one of the back windows and they've moved to a different spot in the yard."

"Rosie moves them?"

Jerry nodded. "Remember what I told you about supernatural feng shui?"

"Vaguely."

Jerry scoffed and tossed back the rest of his beer. He threw the empty can over his shoulder and still managed to get it in the recycling box. He grabbed the brick and stood up. "Come on, let's go."

"Where?"

"Inside."

He opened the back door and beckoned me. "Today, Felix. Let's go."

I put down my beer and followed him into the house. He led me downstairs to the cellar and over to the far wall. I could see the rectangular slot in the foundation where the brick belonged.

Jerry turned to face me. "You did what needed to be done," he said, pointing the brick at me. "You found the girl, you saved her life, and you got her out of harm's way."

"For now."

"*Now* is all that matters. Later is for later."

"That's very profound, Jerry, but it doesn't change the fact that Aubrey is stuck in a house on an island."

"Maybe that's where she needs to be for now."

"Yeah?" I said. "And what about later?"

"Later is for later."

Jerry held the brick up for me to see, then turned and slid it into the slot in the wall. It stood out, a black brick among all those red ones. But in a strange way, it fit.

"A place for everything," Jerry said.

"And everything in its place," I finished.

Notes on *The Brick*

THE IDEA for *The Brick* came from my own musings on haunted houses and what really makes a place haunted. Is it the building itself, the space it happens to occupy, or is it something else entirely?

I was further inspired by articles I had read on Borley Rectory, at one time declared to be the most haunted house in England. I found a grainy black-and-white photo that showed the remains of Borley Rectory (after a mysterious fire burned it to the ground) and a single brick floating in mid-air. The photo was meant to serve as proof that even though the building had been destroyed, the presence that dwelled there still remained.

I became fixated on that brick and started to wonder what would happen if someone put it in the foundation of another building. Would the haunting carry over? This spurned another thought: who the hell would do such a thing?

Enter Jerry Baldwin. The short, balding, womanizing real-estate agent who only represents haunted properties. Author of several Time-Life books on the Black Lands, he's also Felix's friend and sometimes lawyer.

Jerry had been bouncing around in my head for some time. I liked the idea of a man who sold haunted houses for a living, not just for its inherent entertainment value, but because it went toward one of my goals with the Black Lands series, which was to show how ordinary people have learned to live in a world where the supernatural exists. Jerry also provides some much needed comic relief and works as a kind of foil for Felix, much to his chagrin. I wouldn't be surprised if you saw some standalone Jerry Baldwin stories in the future. Maybe even a novel.

As the longest Felix Renn story published to date, I'm very happy to see *The Brick* in this collection. It provides the perfect bridge between the early Felix stories and the novel series.

MY BODY

IT WAS SUNDAY night and I was driving toward the bright lights of Toronto. I had the gas pedal pressed to the floor and the radio cranked to an oldies station out of Barrie. I also had the dome light on. It made driving a little difficult, and I got a few disapproving honks from some of the other drivers on the road, but I needed it. I had seen enough darkness in Sycamore to last me a lifetime. Once I got home, I planned to turn on every light in my apartment and sit in the middle of the living room floor, as far away from the shadows as I could get.

The Platters came on, singing that heavenly shades of night were falling, and I switched off the radio. I turned off the dome light, too, and that's when I saw her.

She was standing at the side of the road. I thought she was a deer at first, the way the headlights reflected off her eyes. Then I saw her dress. I expected her to dart out in front of me, but she just stood there. A little girl about seven or eight years old.

I pulled over to the side of the road and stepped out of the car. The girl came running up to me, and I could see why her eyes had reflected so brightly in my headlights. She was crying.

"No one would stop," she said, wiping at her cheeks with the back of her hand.

She was wearing a coat with a fur-lined collar over her dress. The dress had some sort of pattern on it, but I couldn't make it out in the dark. I must have stared at her too long, because she pulled her coat close against her body. A red leaf was stuck in her wavy brown hair. She brushed at it absently, but it stayed put.

"What are you doing out here?" I asked. "Are you lost?"

I experienced a brief moment of unreality, standing at the side of a highway in the middle of nowhere with a little girl who should have been at home in bed. It was a school night.

"I don't know where I am," she said dismally.

"Are you cold?" I took a step toward her, and she took a step back. "I'm not going to hurt you, kid. Where are your parents?"

"I don't know." She looked around like she expected them to come wandering out of the woods at any moment.

"What's your name?"

She hesitated, then said: "Millie."

"Millie?"

"It's short for Millicent." She spoke in a challenging tone, as if daring me to make fun of it.

"It's nice to meet you, Millie. My name is Felix." I held out my hand. Millie looked at it distrustfully. "It's okay, I'm not going to hurt you." She still wouldn't take my hand, not that I blamed her. "Do you live around here?"

"No," she said. "I live in Toronto."

"Where in Toronto?"

She frowned.

"You're not supposed to tell strangers where you live, right?"

She nodded.

"That's okay. I just want to help you get home. Did you drive up here with your parents? Maybe your brother and sister?"

"I don't have a sister," Millie said.

"Do you have a brother?"

She nodded. "Mom drove Pete to hockey. Dad took me to the mall for dinner. He hates to cook. And he's not very good at it," she confided in a low whisper.

I smiled.

"He went to the food court to buy us french fries. He said Mom would kill us if she knew, but I said I wouldn't tell."

"Where's your father now?"

Millie shook her head. "He told me to come with him, but I didn't want to. I wanted to stay and watch the kittens."

"The kittens?"

"In the window," Millie said. "At the pet store. I always visit the kittens when we go to the mall. They remember me," she added defiantly, as if I might not believe her.

"I'm sure they do. Which mall did you go to, Millie?"

She shrugged. "The mall. The same one we always go to."

"Do you know where you are right now?"

Millie shook her head. Her lower lip trembled and her eyes blurred with tears.

She was scared, and I didn't want to scare her more by telling her she was, at present, about eighty kilometres away from home.

I went over to the edge of the road where the land sloped down to a drainage ditch and, beyond that, to the woods. There were no streetlights on this stretch of the highway, and the darkness within the trees was total. I took a step down the slope, mostly to see if I could do it without flinching. This new aversion to the dark was looking dangerously like it could turn into a full-blown phobia, and quite frankly I was too old for a nightlight in my bedroom. I took another step.

"Don't," Millie blurted. She came toward me, then remembered that she was afraid of me, and moved back. "The man who looks like Daddy is out there."

I thought I had misheard her. "Your daddy is out there?"

"He's not my daddy," Millie snapped at me. "He *looks* like Daddy. That's why I went with him. He said he knew where Daddy was."

"What did he look like?"

"Like my daddy," she said. "I told you."

"Was he short or tall?"

"He was tall, I guess."

"What kind of hair did he have? Was it long or short? Or was he bald?"

"He's almost bald, like my daddy, but he has some hair. It was brushed across the bald part."

"Do you remember what he was wearing?"

Millie thought about it for a moment. "A grey coat," she said. "It was long, and it had a belt."

"A trench coat?"

Millie shrugged to show she didn't know what that was. "He had a bag. A big one like the kind Pete uses to carry his hockey stuff."

"What did he say to you?"

"He said he knew where Daddy was. So I went with him. He said Daddy was looking for me, and he was getting angry because he couldn't find me. But I didn't go anywhere. I was watching the kittens the whole time."

"Where did the man take you, Millie?"

"Outside to the parking lot. I got scared and started to cry. The man told me to stop, but I couldn't. He started shaking me, but that only made me cry more. Then he hit me with something. He hit me right on the head. It hurt so much." She brushed at the leaf in her hair again, but still couldn't dislodge it.

"What happened after that?" I asked.

"I don't know. It was dark. I tried to move, but it was too tight."

"Too tight?"

Millie nodded. "I couldn't move my arms or legs. I heard a buzzing sound and then I saw the man looking down at me. I was in the bag. He had put me in the hockey bag. I kicked and screamed, but he wouldn't let me out. He tried to push me down, but I managed to get out. I didn't know where to go. I wasn't in the parking lot anymore. All I could see was trees. I ran and ran until I came here. I waited for someone to stop but no one did."

I nodded. Millie was lucky. I didn't want to tell her how lucky. She was unlucky too, in that she had an idiot for a father, one who thought it was perfectly fine to leave a young girl alone in a mall while he went off to buy french fries. But that wasn't Millie's fault. At that moment, I wasn't sure who I wanted to get my hands on more, Millie's dad or the man who had abducted her.

Her abductor must have been close by. He wouldn't stick around for long if he had any kind of survival instinct. Millie had gotten away from him, and he must have known she would eventually find an adult who in turn would contact the police.

I looked off toward the woods again. It was a clear night and the stars were out. A quarter moon brooded over them like a fretful mother. I could see about five feet into the trees, but no further. I didn't want to go in there. There could be anything in those woods. I hated myself a bit for thinking that. There was cautious and there was cowardly, and I was starting to get the two confused. If I couldn't sort them out soon, I'd have to hang up my spurs and quit the private eye racket.

I turned back to Millie. "All right, kid, let's go. I'll drive you to the nearest police station, and then we'll figure out how to get a hold of your parents."

Millie shook her head firmly back and forth. "No way. I'm not supposed to take rides with strangers."

I almost said, *You didn't seem to have a problem wandering off in the mall with one.* Instead I said, "I told you who I am, Millie. I'm Felix, remember?"

"You're still a stranger," Millie said. As if to emphasize this, she took another step backward. I was a real smooth talker with the ladies. At any age.

I put my hands on my hips and looked up at the moon. The dome light of the night sky. I didn't have a lot of options here. Stuck between a car and a dark place. Millie wouldn't let me drive her to the police, and I couldn't leave her at the side of the road while I went to get them myself. I took out my cellphone and wasn't surprised to see there was no signal out here in the willywags.

I went over to my car and opened the trunk. I dug around in my luggage until I found my gun in its clamshell holster. Millie watched raptly as I clipped it onto my belt at the small of my back and covered it with my jacket.

"Are you a policeman?" she asked.

I should have lied and said yes. Maybe it would have gotten her into the car. Curse my honest soul.

"No," I said. "I'm a private investigator."

"What's that?"

"Someone who investigates things privately."

Millie made a face.

"I do some of the things a policeman does, but I don't work for the police."

She pondered this for a moment. "Like Batman?"

"Sort of. Except I don't wear a cape."

"And your car's not as nice as the Batmobile."

"Thanks, kid."

"Pete likes Batman. He has all the movies on DVD. I like Spider-Man better, because sometimes he makes jokes."

"Yeah, Batman is more the serious type."

"Do you have a badge?"

"No, but I have a license."

She looked disappointed.

"Are you going to arrest the man who took me?"

I wasn't sure what I was going to do. I was in a strange and difficult position, and that was really saying something for me. When I worked a case, I usually tried to avoid police involvement. Now I was in a position where I would have danced naked in the middle of the highway to get their attention.

"I'm going to take a look in the woods," I said. "And you're going to stay here."

"Can't I come with you?" Millie said, and huddled deeper into her coat. "It's scary out here."

"Better to be scared than in danger." I didn't know if I believed that myself. Not when I looked toward those woods.

I went around to the other side of the car and opened the passenger door. "I know you don't want to get in the car, but I'll leave it open just in case you change your mind, or if you get cold. Okay?"

Millie nodded mutely.

"I'll be back as soon as I can."

I went down the slope, jumped over the drainage ditch, and started toward the woods. Just before I stepped into the trees, I got an idea and called back to Millie. "If you need me, honk the car horn, okay?"

She nodded and I turned back and stepped into the inevitable darkness.

A HARSH WIND picked up as I moved through the dense woods. The trees seemed to move all around me, keeping pace with me as I walked, sometimes leaping in front of me to block my path. They were everywhere. It was like being in a funhouse hall of mirrors except with trees. I felt disoriented, bordering on panic. I made myself keep walking because I knew if I stopped, I wouldn't be able to start again. Someone would find me the following morning curled in a ball on the ground, rocking slowly from side to side. If they found me at all.

Millie was waiting for me back at the car. I wanted to go to her, but I couldn't. I didn't have any kids of my own, and I didn't plan on having any in the foreseeable future, but a sense of responsibility had descended upon me just the same. It happened the moment I pulled off the road. Millie wasn't my child, but she was someone's child. Her problems were now my problems. Her fears were my fears.

I quickened my pace, and when the wind blew through the trees again, I forced myself to turn and look at them straight on, pinning them, and my fear, in place. The branches seemed to wave at me mockingly. I kept moving.

I held my hands out in front of me so I wouldn't run into anything. It was so dark I could barely see them at the end of my arms. I began to breathe faster. I was starting to feel disconnected from my body. I told myself it was my body. Mine. I lived in it. I hadn't left it. It was still mine. I was here. In these dark woods. In my body.

Dry leaves crackling under my shoes sounded like brittle laughter. The wind hooted and whispered.

I tried to focus on another sound, one that I was just now becoming aware of, an almost musical babbling. A river. Distant, but not too far away. I tuned my ears to it like a radio dial fixing on a frequency, and followed it. I didn't know if the river was where I wanted to go, but it was something to focus on, something to push out the sound of the wind and the woods.

I came out of the trees and into a clearing. No river, but there was a tumbledown cabin with dark windows and a brick chimney. A pickup truck was parked under a sagging carport, next to a towering pile of firewood.

As I walked toward the cabin, I looked around for the road that led to this place, but I couldn't find it. But then I couldn't see much of anything.

I stood on the front stoop, raised my hand to knock, then stopped. I decided I wasn't ready to alert anyone to my presence just yet.

I went over to the carport and put my hand on the hood of the pickup. It was warm. I went around to the back of the cabin. I detected another sound mixed in with the cheerful babbling of the river. A splashing sound.

I went down a grassy slope to a screen of trees. Through them I could see the river. I could also see a man crouched on the bank with his back to me. He was scooping handfuls of water and splashing them on his face and chest. He was wearing a long coat that might have been grey, but it was too dark to tell.

I took a step forward, started to say, "Excuse me," and tripped on something buried in the leaves. I tried to pull my foot back, but whatever I had snagged it on wasn't letting go. I brought my other foot forward and it got caught up, too. I lost my balance and started to fall forward. I got a hand out in front of me and landed on the ground propped on one side like a man doing a crooked push-up. I twisted around and brushed at the leaves. A coil of rusty barbed wire was wrapped around my left foot. I was lucky the wire had snagged my shoe instead of my skin. I tried to pull my foot free, but the barbed wire came with it, along with a couple of hunks of rotten wood from an old fence post. Working slowly and carefully I was able to get unhooked without cutting myself. No tetanus shots for me.

By the time I finally regained my feet, the man at the river bank had stood up and turned around to face me. He didn't say anything, and I didn't blame him. It was not my best entrance. I was just glad there were no women around.

"Good evening," I said, brushing myself off. "How you doing?"

"Good evening," the man said in an odd, reflective tone that sounded eerily like my own. I couldn't tell if he was mimicking me or mocking me. Possibly both.

The man was tall, about six two, and the trench coat he was wearing made him look even taller. He was rail-thin, with unusually large hands, and pale blond hair that was thinning on top.

"Good evening," he said again, and took a step toward me. "Good evening. Good evening."

Something was wrong with him, and not just because he was washing his hands in a river in the middle of the woods, in the middle of the night. I could see stains on his coat and on the clothes he wore underneath. I couldn't tell exactly what they were, but I had a hunch it wasn't Smuckers raspberry jam.

He took another step toward me, smiling. "Good evening."

I went for my gun, but not fast enough. I had let Mr. Good Evening get too close. He was about five feet away when he lunged at me with his hands outstretched like claws. I sidestepped him and skipped back into the trees, reaching around to draw my gun from its holster. At the same time, I felt a tug on my foot. An annoyingly familiar tug. I had enough time to think, *The fence, the fucking fence*, and then I was falling over again. I put my hand out as I had done before, except I was holding a gun this time and it went flying out of my grip. It landed in the brush with a low rustling sound. I got up on my hands and knees and looked around for it, but I couldn't see anything in the dark. I could search for three hours and never find it. I didn't have three hours.

Mr. Good Evening was on me then, driving his knee into my back and pushing me flat on the ground. One of my arms was wedged beneath me, while the other flailed uselessly in the leaves. He pressed down harder on my spine, then gripped my head in both of his massive hands. I felt his fingers probing my face like a bowler looking for the holes in his ball.

I jackknifed my body up and down, but couldn't get him off me. I kicked back with one of my legs, but hit only air. I tried the other and struck something. Mr. Good Evening let out a grunt and climbed off my back. He stumbled away and I found myself being pulled along with him. I twisted around onto my back and saw the leg I had kicked him with was the one snarled in barbed wire. When I kicked him, the barbed wire had become embedded in the seat of his pants.

He took another straining step forward. Those barbs were really sunk in deep. I sat up, planted my hands on the ground as firmly as I could, and jerked my foot back. The barbs tore loose and Mr. Good Evening howled in pain.

The howl dissolved into a low growl as Mr. Good Evening turned and came at me again. He was flexing his hands so tightly I could hear his knuckles pop. I lay there on the ground, turned slightly to the side, propped on one elbow, and when he leaned over me I came around with a right cross that connected solidly with his temple. Mr. Good Evening exited stage left.

I turned my attention to the barbed wire wrapped around my foot. I couldn't see well enough to remove the wire itself, not without cutting my hands to ribbons in the process, so I tried using the pieces of wooden fencing to uncoil the wire from my foot. By the time I managed to free myself, Mr. Good Evening had recovered his *joie de vivre* and came shambling toward me, listing a bit from the shot I had given him. He crouched over me and reached for my throat. I let him.

I was still holding the two pieces of wood with the length of barbed wire strung between them. The moment Mr. Good Evening gripped my throat and started to squeeze, I pistoned my arms forward and looped the barbed wire around his neck. He jerked back instinctively, taking his hands off me to pull the wire away. Big mistake.

I couldn't see the blood at first, but I felt it. Hot wet droplets landed on my face, first in a slow patter, then a drizzle. Mr. Good Evening rose up slightly from his crouch. Not much, but enough for me to get a foot between us, plant it firmly in his stomach, and kick him off me. He landed on the ground and lay there, clutching at his throat with both hands and making a choking, gurgling sound. He managed to pull himself up into a sitting position, and in the faint light of the quarter moon I saw he was done.

I had gotten his jugular. Blood was spilling out between his fingers in an alarming flood. I thought of the small boy with his finger in the dyke. There hadn't been much hope for him either.

Mr. Good Evening tried to stand up. He got his feet under him, then dropped to one knee. He tried again and went down on both knees. He slumped forward until he had to take one hand off his throat to prop himself up. It seemed as if an invisible weight was pressing down on his back, driving him down until he lay flat on the ground.

I got up and went over to him. I counted off three minutes in my mind, and when he still hadn't moved, I reached down and pressed two fingers against his neck. I felt the warm wetness of his blood, but no pulse.

I went over to the riverbank to wash my hands, and that was when I saw the duffel bag. The zipper was pulled down. I reached in and spread it open. There wasn't enough moonlight to show me everything, but I could see enough.

The white dress stained with maroon blotches that I had thought were some sort of pattern. The thin holes in the material where the knife had gone in. For a moment I thought there was a small animal in there with her, but it was only the fur-lined collar of her jacket. Her head was nestled against it. There was a red leaf in her hair.

I turned my head to the right and Millie was standing there.

"So, this is your body," I said to her.

"Yes," she said. "That's my body."

I reached down and plucked the leaf out of the dead girl's hair. I turned back to Millie, but she was gone. I held the leaf on the palm of my hand until a gust of wind picked it up and dropped it in the river. I watched the current take it away, then I stood up and went to look for my gun.

Notes on "My Body"

"MY BODY" is the first Felix Renn short story I ever wrote. Until that point, Felix had appeared only in a couple of novellas (*Temporary Monsters* and *The Ash Angels*), and my hope was to introduce Felix to different audiences while at the same time write enough stories to make a collection. If you're reading this note, then I guess it finally happened.

The story behind "My Body" is a simple one. I'm a big fan of urban folklore and I wanted to explore what ghost stories would be like in a world where ghosts actually existed. The tale of the phantom hitch-hiker is fairly well known, and I knew that some of the people who read "My Body" would be able to figure out the ending before they reached it. But I didn't care. The thing I always found more interesting about this story is when did Felix figure it out?

Two other things. First, I must admit to taking a certain pleasure whenever someone asks me to sign a copy of the book that includes this story. It's not too often I get to write *I hope you enjoy "My Body"* or *Thanks for checking out "My Body."*

Secondly, it's worth mentioning that while "My Body" functions as a fun little ghost story, I actually wrote it as a kind of half-ass epilogue to the first Felix Renn novel, *Sycamore* (which hadn't been written at the time). I admit to a certain sadistic thrill in putting Felix through a little extra danger after his traumatic experience in that small northern town. The darkness is never far from Felix. It's a lesson he is forced to learn again and again.

Including this story, which follows immediately after the events of *Sycamore*, and the four novellas that take place before it, makes *Super-NOIRtural Tales* both a prequel and a sequel to the novel. My friend Neal Carlin called it the *Twin Peaks: Fire Walk With Me* of the Black Lands series. Very high praise for a big-time *Peaks* freak like me. So thank you, Neal!

THE HISTORY OF
THE BLACK LANDS

The Black Lands is the name given to a supernatural world discovered in the mid-20th century. Despite over seventy years of study, scientists have only been able to agree on three main facts about this strange and mysterious place:

- It exists in another dimension that lies next to our own.
- It can be accessed via portals located all over the planet.
- It's home to a variety of dangerous supernatural entities.

Even though the world is aware of its existence, the general public has very little knowledge of the Black Lands. Most of the data collected comes from expeditions carried out by government agencies, and the vast majority of their findings remain classified. Some people believe the government has learned next to nothing from these excursions, while others believe they have made discoveries so horrific that the release of this information would cause worldwide panic.

The following is a short history of the discovery of the Black Lands and the ways in which it has changed our world.

The Disappearance of Flight 19

On December 5, 1945, five U.S. Navy bombers, designated Flight 19, departed Fort Lauderdale to complete a combat training exercise off the coast of Florida. After successfully carrying out their bombing run, the aircraft set course to return to base. They never made it.

In his final transmission, the flight leader reported failure of the compasses in all five planes. Contact was lost with Flight 19 shortly thereafter. A search and rescue effort consisting of several dozen planes and boats was launched. After two planes and one ship, USS *Minotaur*, disappeared, the search was called off.

Due to overwhelming public pressure, as well as a lawsuit filed against the U.S. Navy by the families of the missing pilots, a congressional committee was formed to look into the disappearance of Flight 19. Witnesses were called to testify, among them a navy scientist who revealed the existence of film footage, taken from one of the rescue boats, showing USS *Minotaur* seemingly disappearing into thin air.

The scientist further reported that it was his belief, as well as the belief of his colleagues, that the ship — and Flight 19 — had inadvertently passed through an invisible portal and travelled to another dimension. When asked to explain how he had reached this conclusion, the scientist replied that he and a team of investigators had been there. He referred to this dimension as **The Black Lands.**

Further testimony was conducted in closed sessions. Details of the navy's expedition into the portal were omitted from the committee's final report. Flight 19, USS *Minotaur*, and the two missing rescue planes were simply said to have been lost in the Black Lands. The fate of their crews was listed as "unknown."

Tests with pilotless drone ships confirmed that the number of portals in the area where these disappearances took place was increasing. Some scientists put their number in the hundreds. Due to the danger of other planes and ships disappearing into the Black Lands, a large section of the North Atlantic Ocean was declared a no-fly, no-shipping zone.

This area eventually came to be known as **The Bermuda Triangle**.

Project Black Book

In the years following the discovery of the Black Lands, the level of paranormal activity around the world increased dramatically. Despite the best efforts of the world's various emergency organizations, as well police and armed forces, it soon became clear that no government agency or military body was equipped to deal with these types of incidents.

In the United States, the government continued to deny the public access to information on the Black Lands. Attempts to obtain classified documents through the Freedom of Information Act resulted in the release of material that was so heavily censored that it was virtually unreadable.

Activist groups organized a series of protests across the entire country. They claimed that the pilots of Flight 19 were not the first victims of the Black Lands. They pointed to other unexplained disappearances throughout history, such as the crew of the *Mary Celeste*, the lost colony of Roanoke, and the Native American tribe of Anasazi who were said to have vanished overnight.

Finally, in 1952, the governments of the United States and Canada revealed the existence of Project Black Book, a comprehensive seven-year study of the Black Lands portals located across North America. They concluded that this dimension and the entities that reside there represented a clear and present danger to the security of both countries and the safety of their people.

The study recommended the formation of a special intelligence service to investigate paranormal phenomena and develop defensive strategies against Black Lands entities. The result was the creation of a joint U.S.—Canada government organization called the **Paranormal Intelligence Agency (PIA)**.

Operation Shadow Storm

After several years of study and investigation, the U.S. government decided it was time to create a permanent base of operations in the Black Lands.

Going against the warnings of the PIA, the U.S. military organized a large offensive composed entirely of ground forces called **Operation Shadow Storm**. The purpose of the operation was to transport personnel and equipment into the Black Lands and set up a beachhead from which further military missions and scientific expeditions could be carried out.

There had been rumours of military operations into the Black Lands in the past, but this was the first one to be carried out in the public eye. The media was given detailed information about the operation, which was to be launched from a large portal located in Wyoming, and reporters from several news stations were embedded with military units so they could report directly from the front.

On August 25, 1978, Operation Shadow Storm began.

Two days later, it was over.

Details of the operation remain largely classified, but one thing is known for certain: It failed.

Despite the military's best efforts to suppress information, reports were leaked by anonymous army personnel and the few embedded reporters who managed to survive the conflict. They reported that the military convoy was attacked almost immediately upon entering the Black Lands. They described a variety of nightmarish creatures, some of them displaying supernatural traits similar to vampires and werewolves, living in a landscape of seemingly endless fields and woodland under a sunless sky.

The actual number of casualties of Operation Shadow Storm is a matter of dispute. It is known that several hundred soldiers were killed, thousands more were injured, and some listed as missing in action (presumably lost in the Black Lands).

Following the operation, the families of many of the dead soldiers filed lawsuits against the U.S. government for refusing to release the bodies of their loved ones. The government's only comment on the matter was that the bodies remain in federal custody due to reasons of national security. Rumours that the soldiers' bodies were contaminated in some manner by their exposure to the Black Lands have never been substantiated.

The Influence

In the years after the failure of Operation Shadow Storm, veterans of the conflict began to report unusual medical conditions. Some of these symptoms were physical, in the form of tumours and growths, while others were psychological, in the form of phobias, psychoses, and even psychical phenomenon.

Although these abnormalities were believed to have been caused by the subject's exposure to the Black Lands, this has never been definitively proven. This is due to the inconsistency of symptoms among those afflicted, as well as the fact that many other soldiers involved in the operation never experienced any medical problems whatsoever.

Health officials dubbed this condition **Black Lands Syndrome**. Others described it as a paranormal version of radiation sickness. It has been theorized that the differing symptoms is due to various factors including the subject's medical history and the length of exposure to the Black Lands. Rumours that some soldiers were so badly affected by BLS that they ended up transforming into supernatural creatures has never been substantiated.

Black Lands Syndrome has also been reported by people who live in close proximity to portals. Since these people were not involved in Operation Shadow Storm, their condition has been treated as a completely different ailment. In medical circles, it is referred to simply as the **Influence**.

Neighbours

Over seventy years have passed since the discovery of the Black Lands, and our world is still learning to live with its mysterious, and sometimes dangerous, neighbour.

As more and more portals show up every year, some scientists believe this escalation is building toward some cataclysmic event. A dimensional collision, some say, that could result in one world cancelling out the other, or both worlds being completely destroyed.

With the discovery of new portals, the number of missing persons around the world has increased dramatically. While the majority of these disappearances are accidental, it is known that some people, driven by curiosity or insanity, are purposely seeking out the Black Lands. The few who manage to return sometimes come back changed by the Influence. Those who don't come back at all have been dubbed "accidental tourists."

The world of the twenty-first century is a dark and dangerous place. Electrified fences cordon off the dozens of known portals across North America. Coast Guard gunships patrol the Florida waters along the borders of the Bermuda Triangle. The PIA continues to investigate paranormal activity, while the U.S. and Canadian governments continue to restrict information about the Black Lands. The general public continues to live in the dark.

Some people want answers. Some want the Black Lands and the creatures that live there to go away. Most people are simply trying to find a way to live in this new dark reality. A world where paranormal has become the norm.

Acknowledgments

If you're reading this edition of *SuperNOIRtural Tales*, then you probably think it's the second book in the Black Lands series, but in truth, it was actually the first.

SuperNOIRtural Tales was originally published way back in 2012 as a way of collecting the first three Felix Renn chapbooks, along with a new, longer novella (*The Brick*), and a short story that, oddly, takes place after the first Felix Renn novel, which hadn't been written yet at the time. As I stated in the notes for "My Body," that makes this collection both a prequel and a sequel to *Sycamore*. In the overall series, I think of it as Book 0. (The real Book 2 is coming, I promise. I don't want to say too much about it yet, but think: *Miss Congeniality* meets *Evil Dead 2: Dead By Dawn*.)

I haven't changed anything in the stories between the 2012 edition and this one, but the text is a bit cleaner (thank you, Lisa!), and I had to update some of the story notes. Nothing heavy.

The only thing that's really changed over the past decade or so are the number of people I want to thank. The support for the Black Lands series has been strong since the very beginning, and has only grown since the publication of *Sycamore*. Maybe it's because I hit on something particularly good with these stories, maybe it's because the timing was right. It's hard to say exactly, but what I know for certain is that I couldn't have done it without some very important people.

First of all, thanks to Mike Carey for the extremely kind introduction. There were so many reasons why you were the right person to write it, and I'm proud and honoured to have you be a part of this book.

Thanks to Dan Franklin and Richard Chizmar of Cemetery Dance for giving this book and the Black Lands series a home. Thanks to Lisa Lebel for her letter-perfect copy-edit (see what I did there?), and Ben Baldwin for his always amazing cover art.

Thanks to my agent Jack Gernert and my manager Peter Katz for being champions of my work and helping me to drag as many people as possible into the Black Lands.

I also want to give a shout-out to Monica S. Kuebler for publishing the original edition of this book, and to Justin Erickson for his artwork that lives on for those folks lucky enough to have acquired a copy of that super rare tome.

I'd also like to thank the following people for their support: Laird Barron, Tim Bedwell, Denny Borges, Andrew Burns, Peter Darbyshire, Jason Darrick, Ellen Datlow, Craig Davidson, Jean-Paul Fallavollita, Gef Fox, Richard Gavin, Orrin Grey, Lauren Hughes, Alexus Johnson, Sandra Kasturi, Nicholas Kaufmann, Michael Kelly, Gregory Lamberson, John Langan, Andrew Leonard, David Longhorn, Sean Lynch, Colum McKnight, Jim Mcleod, Gary McMahon, Silvia Moreno-Garcia, Tony Myles, Derek Newman-Stille, Norman Partridge, Mary Rajotte, Michael Rasmussen, Shawn Rasmussen, Michael Rowe, Brett Savory, Jason Shayer, Steve Sharpe, Robert Shearman, Jessa Sobczuk, Simon Strantzas, Jeffrey Thomas, and Paul Tremblay.

Finally, I'd like to thank my wife Kathryn for her endless love and support, and for encouraging me to explore the Black Lands. I'm not sure if she likes the stories or if she just wants me to get mauled by some supernatural creature. Either way I plan to keep going back for a long time to come.

About the Author

IAN ROGERS is the author of the award-winning collection, *Every House Is Haunted*. His novelette, "The House on Ashley Avenue," was a finalist for the Shirley Jackson Award and is currently being adapted into a feature film produced by Sam Raimi. His debut novel, *Family*, originally published by Earthling Publications, will be republished by Gallery Books in Fall 2026. Ian is also the author of *Sycamore*, *The Underwood*, *Grey*, and *Fitted Sheet*. Ian lives with his wife and two cats in Peterborough, Ontario. For more information, visit ianrogers.ca.

To learn more about Felix Renn and the Black Lands, visit theblacklands.com.

www.ingramcontent.com/pod-product-compliance
Lightning Source LLC
Chambersburg PA
CBHW030640020726
47493CB00006B/1804